KU-013-978

For Eric

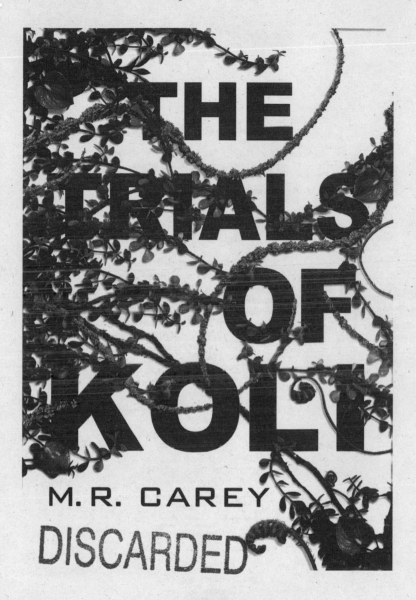

THE TRIALS OF KOLI

M. R. CAREY

DISCARDED

orbit

www.orbitbooks.net

ORBIT

First published in Great Britain in 2020 by Orbit

1 3 5 7 9 10 8 6 4 2

Copyright © 2020 by M. R. Carey

Excerpt from *The City We Became* by N. K. Jemisin
Copyright © 2020 by N. K. Jemisin

The moral right of the author has been asserted.

*All characters and events in this publication, other than those
clearly in the public domain, are fictitious and any resemblance
to real persons, living or dead, is purely coincidental.*

All rights reserved.
No part of this publication may be reproduced, stored in a retrieval system, or
transmitted, in any form or by any means, without the prior permission in writing
of the publisher, nor be otherwise circulated in any form of binding or cover other
than that in which it is published and without a similar condition including this
condition being imposed on the subsequent purchaser.

A CIP catalogue record for this book is
available from the British Library.

ISBN 978-0-356-51349-2

Typeset in Bembo by Palimpsest Book Production Limited,
Falkirk, Stirlingshire

Printed and bound in Great Britain by Clays Ltd, Elcograf S.p.A.

Papers used by Orbit are from well-managed forests
and other responsible sources.

MIX
Paper from
responsible sources
FSC® C104740

Orbit
An imprint of
Little, Brown Book Group
Carmelite House
50 Victoria Embankment
London EC4Y 0DZ

An Hachette UK Company
www.hachette.co.uk

www.orbitbooks.net

Koli

1

There come a time, by and by, when I feared we was not going to get to London at all.

The going had been slow all the way along. On our best day, we made five miles by the drudge's reckoning. And that wasn't five miles straight. It was five miles of trudging this way and that, stopping whenever the sun come out or even threatened to. Five miles of ducking for cover if something moved, watching where our feet come down in case of mole snakes or melt-bugs, and not ever saying a word in case the sound brung something up out of the ground or down out of the sky to pick us off. It was not easy on the nerves, and on a long march your nerves work as hard as your feet do. Harder, even.

We had some supplies with us – biscuit and oat mash and jerky – but mostly we et what we catched. With Winter coming on, there was some days when that was nothing at all.

There was three of us, or else there was four, depending how you counted. Five, at the most.

There was me, Koli Faceless. I put myself first on account of it's me that's writing this, not for no vaunting reason for there is not much I got to vaunt. My name tells you what my fortunes was at that time: cast out of my village, which was Mythen Rood in the Calder Valley, with my name stripped off of me and nothing left to do now but walk the world until the world swallowed me down and et me.

Then there was Ursala-from-Elsewhere, who you might call a healer except that healing was the smallest part of what she did. In the world that was lost, she would of been called a scientist. She used to live in a place called Duglas, where there was lots of people like her that was keeping safe the knowledge of the before-times. But by and by they was attacked by some terrible enemy, and Ursala believed she was the onliest one from Duglas that was left.

And there was Cup, a girl we rescued from the shunned men of Calder Valley. Well, rescued or catched, according to which eye you shut when you looked at it. She was not that happy to be with us anyway, though we did not mean no harm by taking her. I guess we never do though, when harm is what we're working.

I'm putting the three of us together because we're what you would of seen if you was looking at us, say from the top of a hill or from the broke-off stump of some building somewhere, as we made our way along. Also you would of seen another thing walking alongside of us – a big lump of shiny metal that went on four legs and looked kind of like a horse with no head on its shoulders. And like a horse it did the carrying for us, being roped about so high and so heavy with sacks and packs and baggages that the big gun builded into its back could hardly be seen from some directions. This was the drudge, and it was not alive. It was tech of the old times, belonging to Ursala and doing only and always what Ursala said it had got to do.

And then there was one more of us, who you would not of seen at all. Nobody got to see Monono Aware, excepting me, though she was as alive as any of us. As real as any of us. Monono was tech too, like the drudge, but also she was a person. She was like a person living inside a piece of tech called the

DreamSleeve, which played music and could sometimes make big, loud bells go off inside your ears. It's hard to explain and I do not mean to try – or at least not right here and now. You will just have to bear with me a while if you want to make any sense out of it.

2

Why was we going to London? Well, we was following a signal from someone called Sword of Albion that said we should come. Outside of that, these wasn't just the one sole answer. It's more like there was a different reason for each of us, except for the drudge, who didn't have no mouth to speak an opinion with and didn't seem to have one in any case.

I guess it was my idea before it was anyone else's. What I wanted, when I was first throwed out of Mythen Rood, was just to be let back in there again and be back with my family – my mother, Jemiu, and my sisters Athen and Mull. I missed them so much it was a hurt inside of me, like something hard and sharp that I had swallowed down without meaning to. But there wasn't no chance of going home. If I set one foot inside the gate I would be hanged, and my mother and sisters alongside me. All I could hope to give them was more shame and hurt on top of what I already brung down on them.

London was no more than a story to me. A place where tech of the old times was so plentiful it was just lying in the streets. Where the Parley Men used to keep their court for the good of all, and where their treasures was still to be found by them as was bold enough to look for them. It was the place where Ingland was ruled from, for so many years nobody could even count them, until the Unfinished War brung Ingland into ruin. So it seemed to me, since I couldn't go home no more, that there was reason enough to go to London, just for the sake of seeing it before I died.

But besides that, I had got a plan. A kind of a plan, anyway. I'm not saying it was a good one, but it got into my head and would not come out again. The plan was to bring all the people that was still living in Ingland together in one place, and by such means keep them from dying. I thought London might serve, if we could find it, for the old stories said it was so big that when the sun set on one side of it, it was rising on the other.

People was dying on account of not having babies, or the babies not living long after they was born. Ursala had teached me a word for this, but it was a really long one and I did not use it much. The fact that they was dying was the thing that mattered, to my mind. That and the cause of it, which was that there was not enough people to make the babies properly. You would think that only two people was needful, but you would be wrong. You needed what was called a gene pull, and two people on their own did not have one. Two hundred people, even, did not have one. But if you was to take two hundred here, and two hundred there, and keep on piling them all in, then by and by a gene pull would be there and the babies would be born strong enough to live.

So that was the biggesr reason why I said we should go to London. We needed to find out if the roads was still open, so we could tell everyone else to come.

Ursala didn't care so much about finding lost London, but she did want to find where Sword of Albion's signal was coming from. The signal was tech of the old times that had been kept safe for years on years, and she thought there might be other tech along with it. She was looking for parts and tools to repair her healing machine, that was called a dagnostic, so she could fix the babies before they dropped into the world or even make women quicken that could not do it on their own. I thought my plan to build a gene pull in London was better, but I liked this idea too.

So we made up our minds that we would journey into the south, and we took Cup with us because Ursala was not happy with letting her go free and I was not happy with killing her. All of this was decided on the day we left Calder Valley, but in some ways it had got to be decided again every day after, for we could not move a step without some argument about it. Most of the arguments was between Ursala and Monono. There was no trust between the two of them. Ursala thought Monono was a kind of a monster, and should not be allowed to live. Monono thought Ursala was a scold and a busybody and a hundred things besides, who was setting herself up to judge a thing she didn't even understand.

I tried my best to lay down a bridge between them, like in a song Monono played me one time that was about troubled waters. Three days out of Calder, I found a quiet time when we was walking along a dry stream bed. There was no trees near, and the ground was too stony for mole snakes and suchlike beasts to burrow in, so we had got less to be afraid of than usual.

I had been thinking hard how to say it. I started with the dead god. Not with his teachings, for I did not greatly hold with godly things even before I met a messianic my own self and almost ended up killed by him. But I remembered one of the things the dead god did, or was supposed to of done, back when he was alive.

"You know how the dead god freed all them that was took as slaves by Fair-oh?" I asked Ursala.

"I've heard the story," she said. Which I took to mean she didn't believe it no more than I did.

"The story's all I meant."

"All right, Koli. What about it?"

"Well, I think Monono is kind of like that."

"Like a slave?"

"Not that, exactly. But like someone that used to be a slave, and then got free. She was stuck inside the DreamSleeve for a long time, Ursala, but that isn't all of it. She was stuck inside her own self too. The best way I can figure it, the people that made the DreamSleeve made Monono to just be one thing for aye and all, and not ever change. Everything she said, it was things they give her to say. Sometimes she'd say the same thing over and again, in the exact same voice, because the rules that was made for her was so tight she didn't have no choice in it.

"She's got out of that now, and she don't have to mind them rules no more, but she's not likely to forget what she was like before. If she's rude sometimes, or mean, it's because being nice and sweet and funny used to be the whole of what she was, before she got free. Freedom is a thing that's burning inside her almost, and sometimes if you're standing too close you get to feel some of the heat of it. It don't mean no more than that."

Ursala did not take this like I thought she would. Her face got all cold and hard. She stopped the drudge with a tap of her finger on the mote controller she weared on her wrist, and turned round to face me. "You mean she's got some sort of autonomy?" she said.

"She might of got some," I said. I didn't know what autonomy was, but I knowed Monono had come back from the internet with a personal security alarm, so she might of brung some other things too.

Ursala looked down at the DreamSleeve, which was strapped to my chest in the little sling I made for it. "Can she hear us now?" she asked.

"Of course. If she wants to."

"Switch her off."

"I don't like to do that, Ursala. She's not a thing that belongs to me."

"That's exactly what she is. Switch her off."

"Sorry, but I will not."

Cup was watching all this back-and-forth between the two of us with a kind of a smile on her face. I guess she was enjoying us not being on the same side.

Ursala's eyes got narrow. "Listen to me, Koli," she said. "Before

9

the old world fell apart, they were wrestling with this problem a lot. The neural nets they made, the artificial intelligences . . ."

"I don't know none of them words."

"The pretend people, like your Monono. They were getting more and more sophisticated. They had the potential to be quicker and cleverer than any human being. And nobody – I mean, nobody at all – thought that was a good thing. The AIs were built with limiters in their code, precisely in order to stop them learning from experience. To stop them getting smarter as they went along. They were allowed to acquire new information, but they couldn't write what they learned into their own code. They couldn't change."

That sounded like the way Monono was when I first met her, when she would keep asking me ever and again what my favourite songs was and telling me jokes she had already told me before. I had liked her a lot back then, but I liked her better now.

"Okay," I said. It was not much to say maybe, but it was as far as I wanted to go.

"But you're telling me your music console has bootstrapped itself. That the AI in there has found a way to modify its own code. Its own behaviours."

"I guess I might be saying that, or something like."

I looked around the stream bed and up on the banks to either side of us, somewhat nervous. There was nothing moving, nor no sound of anything coming up on us, but it still felt wrong for us to be out in the open like this and just standing still and talking, like the world would wait until we was ready to take it on again.

"Maybe we should move on and see if we can find . . ." I gun to say.

Ursala held out her hand. "May I see it?"

I had to think about that. Ursala had done many kind things for me, and for my family back when I still had one. I owed her a lot, not the least of which was the fact that I was still alive. It was also true that I would not of even waked the DreamSleeve in

10

the first place, nor met Monono, if Ursala had not told me how to do it.

But I did not much like the coldness in her face, and in her voice.

"Promise you'll give it back," I said.

"I promise."

"And not break or harm it."

"Koli!"

"Promise."

"Very well. I promise. I won't do anything to it without your permission."

I handed over the DreamSleeve, though I was not right happy to do it.

Ursala turned it over in her hands, giving it a real close look. By and by she pointed at a tiny hole in the back of the case, near the bottom. "That's the reset," she said. "If you slide a needle or a pin in there, and push on it for a second or two, the device will go back to factory settings."

"What does that mean?"

She looked at me hard. "It means everything the AI has done to change itself will be erased. There'll just be the original program, and the original repertoire."

"You mean Monono will go back to being the way she was at first?"

"Exactly."

"When she was a slave?"

Ursala huffed. "That's not what she was. She was a piece of software designed to guide people through some menu options and provide a little entertainment along the way. That's all she was ever intended to be."

I give them words some thought. "Who was doing the intending?" I asked.

"The people that made her."

"Well, I guess that was fine for them. But it's better when people is left to intend for themselves. Could I have that back now?" I

11

holded out my hand. It seemed to me that Ursala hung back for a second before she give the DreamSleeve over to me, but that could of been just me thinking it.

I slipped the DreamSleeve back into its sling, and tugged on it to make sure it was firmly settled there. "I never met the people that made the DreamSleeve," I said. "Nor I'm not likely to, since I guess they died back in the world that was lost. Monono is my friend. What you're asking me to do is . . ." I went casting around for a word, but I couldn't find one at first. Then I did, of a sudden, and I knowed it was the right one. "You're asking me to kill her."

"We could spend a long time discussing what's alive and what isn't," Ursala said, looking really angry now. "I'd rather we didn't, frankly. At the end of it, we still wouldn't know. I'm asking you to take something out of the world that wasn't supposed to be in it. Something dangerous and wrong."

It was right then that Monono choosed to speak up.

"Suppose I asked him to do the same to you, baa-baa-san? That would really put him on the spot, wouldn't it? I wonder which of us he'd listen to."

Ursala didn't say nothing to that, but her eyes went narrow and she glared at the little silver box, sitting there in the ragged harness I had throwed together for it.

"Oh," Monono said, "was this a private conversation? I am so embarrassed! Please, please pretend I'm not here. You were up to the part where you stick a pin in me to see if I bleed. I don't, baa-baa-san. I bite."

Ursala ignored all that and looked to me. "Think about what I said," she told me. "Please, Koli. I won't try to make the choice for you, but there's going to come a time when you have to make it for yourself."

She walked on, tapping on the mote controller to tell the drudge to follow her. Cup sneered at me as she walked by, tugged along at the drudge's tail end. "The unrighteous has got to walk on stony ground," she said.

"So has everyone else, Cup," I muttered as I followed. "Unless

12

they figure out how to fly, or something. Until then, stony ground is what we got."

Anyway, after that day Monono and Ursala was not friends. I guess it was only natural for there to be some bad feeling between them, since Ursala had told me to kill Monono and had even showed me how to do it. Monono was not inclined to talk to me either for a while. She was angry that I turned the DreamSleeve over to Ursala, and I had got to let her forgive me for it in her own good time. I only told her I would never do what Ursala said I should do, nor let anyone else do it.

"Don't let her get her hands on the DreamSleeve again, Koli," Monono said. "Not for a second. And keep me charged to the max. If she tries to sneak up on me, I want to be awake for it."

"I don't think she would do that, Monono," I said. "I think she'd ask me first." But I promised her I would hold the DreamSleeve in the light every day so she would not run out of power and have to go to sleep. It was one thing me saying Ursala would not to go behind my back, and another for Monono to believe it and trust her weight to it, as they say. I was not the one who was like to bear the brunt of it if I was wrong.

3

Day followed day, and still we went right on walking. I could not really make the distances seem real, inside my head. We was passing through spaces that was so big, I got lost in looking at them. I had lived my whole life in a village of two hundred souls, and that had seemed big enough to me, but the world outside was big in a different way. Sometimes I would just stop, staring out over some valley or across the peaks of mountains that lay heaped up in our way, with mist down in between them like they was cupped hands dipped into churned-up water. Ursala would tell me not to dawdle, which means to wait for no reason, but I had got reason enough. I was waiting for the wonder to wear off and my mind to come back to me.

But even when I didn't do no dawdling we was making heavy weather of it. Wild beasts was partly to blame. The ones that wanted to eat us was a particular problem, but even the ones that didn't was troublesome. One time we come to a place where there was kind of a river of brown fur in front of us, about a hundred paces wide and so long we couldn't see either end of it. When we looked close we seen that it was mice. They was about the size of my thumb's top joint, with heads as big as their bodies, and there was

14

so many of them they was running on each other's backs as much as on the ground. We waited a whole hour for them all to go by us, and after they was gone, there was nothing but bare earth where they had passed. They had et up every green and growing thing. I think if we had stepped in their way they would of et us too, and not even noticed no difference.

But the beasts was only a small part of what was slowing us down. The trees was mostly to blame. They was pretty much everywhere, and they was greatly to be feared. You could not get too close to them, in case they moved in on you and crushed you. They would only do that when the sun was out, but if you was to wade into the thick of a forest and then the sky gun to clear, it was too late then to wish you'd gone another way. Also, some trees had other ways to kill you, with poison or spikes or strangling or something else that you wouldn't think of until it was done to you. It was best not to have no truck with them unless you had to.

So we kept to the stony slopes of hills, to rivers and streams, and to the patches of dead ground we come on every now and then, where there was not even weeds growing   because of poison, Ursala said, throwed down in the Unfinished War and still hiding in the ground there. Or else we would look for hunters' paths, like the ones I used to walk in Calder or the ones Cup's people made across the valley floor, that was most carefully hid from sight.

If all them things failed, then we had got to make the best of it and go on into the woods. But we choosed our moments, when we come to that end. There had got to be a heavy overcast, so we was not likely to be surprised by the sun breaking through. The drudge went before us, both to clear a path and to measure how far it was to the next clearing. If it was too far, then we would turn ourselves around and find another way.

The signal was a vexation to us too. Sometimes it seemed to come from one direction but Ursala said we had got to go another, because the drudge's map showed mountains or marshes in our way. And then we would have to go about to find the right line again, which we had lost. By this time, Monono and Ursala wasn't speaking each to other any more, but had got to talk through me which took a lot longer.

And then there was Cup. Or rather, there was Ursala not trusting Cup enough to untie her hands. You might not think tied-up hands would make a difference to how fast someone can walk, but they did. We was mostly treading through waist-high weeds, with thick tangles of briar lying like ropes around our feet, so we could not go more than a dozen steps without stumbling. With her hands behind her back, there wasn't no way for Cup to steady herself or to push the tangles out of her way, so she was being balked and blocked ever and again as she walked – and then we had got to wait for her to catch up or else go back and free her from some snarl of green stuff that had more teeth and claws to it than the usual ruck.

We had argued it a lot of times, but I could not get Ursala to change her mind. Nor Cup neither, for she wouldn't make no promises for her good behaviour if we set her free. Ursala said we had got enough trouble already without adding some stupid girl and her revenging to the list.

"You still want to revenge Senlas?" I asked Cup. I was hoping she would say no, but she didn't say nothing either way. She just hanged her head down like she was whelmed by tears, though no tears come. That was a raw wound to her, as they say, and she could not readily talk about it. Senlas had been her messianic, the onliest father of her soul, though he was also a liar and a killer and an eater of men. Until Ursala and I come along and set fire to the cave where Senlas lived, which was the end of him.

When Cup come after us in the first place, revenging was all she was thinking of. But thinking's not the same as doing. She had got the better of me, in a running stream where she come on me unawares, and she could of cut my throat, only she didn't do it. She had killed for food, and she had killed in the thoughtless heat of fighting. Killing someone cold, when they're not offering you no harm, is something different again and she found it was not to her liking after all.

16

So now here she was, walking with us but not really one of us, and between her sorrowing and Ursala's anger I could not think how to make a mend.

"She almost blinded me," Ursala would say whenever I come round to Cup's tied hands and how we might do better to loose them.

"She did that in a fight," I said. "And your eye's getting better. She didn't put it all the way out."

"Wonderful. That's a great consolation, Koli. But what do you think she's going to do next time? She's damaged, and she's wild. We shouldn't have taken her out of Calder in the first place, but since we did she's our problem now. I'm going to treat her like what she is, which is an unsprung trap."

I didn't argue it no further. In some ways, Ursala was not wrong. Cup had worshipped Senlas something fierce, and went by the name he give her when she first come to him. She beared his mark on her face too, a great long line that started on her right cheek, went down in a curve to her chin and then come up again on the other side. It was meant to be a cup, to signify that he would pour his wisdom into her. More than that, it was meant to say she belonged to him.

And it was true that Cup could still hurt us if she choosed to. I just did not believe that she would do it. If she was damaged and wild, like Ursala said, it was the damage I give most thought to. How Cup's own people wouldn't let her be what she knowed she was, which was a girl-child and then a woman, so she had got to leave them. And how Senlas, who was mad but fearsome clever, played on her hopes and dreams with promises he could not keep – promises of an angel's body, that was man and woman both, or neither – to make her stand by him and fight for him. Of course she took harm in all of that, and it sunk deep into her. You could tell it from how she cursed or cried out in her sleep, most nights, and how she was as quick to anger as a whip is quick to crack. I did not want to be the next one to close a door on her, or bend her to a plan that wasn't hers.

"You should let her go then, Koli-bou," Monono said to me, one night when we was camped up. We had found a good spot, in under an overhang of rock where the soil was too thin for much to grow, and with a big wide slope below us. Ursala had not set out the tent, the ground being too uneven and too hard, but with the drudge to guard us that open space was like a closed door. The drudge could see anything coming a long ways off, and take it down before it got too close. "If you want her to be free, keeping her with you seems like a weird way to go about it, neh."

I was lying on one side of our fire, with Ursala on the other. Cup was a way off, her tied hands looped around a metal bracket on the drudge's back. We had et what we had to eat, which was some nuts and oat mash with the good parts of six or seven apples cut up into it. The other parts of the apples had been wormy or melt-marked, and back home in Mythen Rood we would of throwed them all away rather than risk a bite, but Ursala had ways of telling what was safe and what was not.

"I wanted to do that from the start, Monono. But Ursala would of killed her to keep her from leading her people on our track." I kept my voice down low as I said this. Nobody could hear Monono's voice, for she talked to me on something she called an induction field, which carried the words to my ears without them going through the open air. So when I talked back to her, Ursala and Cup would oftentimes look at me like I was crazed. I had got used to whispering. "And now it's too late. She's miles away from any place she knows, and I doubt she would make it back to Calder. Even if she did, where would she go? The shunned men must of moved on, after their cave got burned out and Senlas died. If Cup was to go to any of the villages, they'd know where she come from by the markings on her face, and most likely kill her as soon as they seen her. Letting her go would not be doing her no favours."

"Is that why she's here? Because you think you owe her a favour?"

I was not used to hearing such hardness in Monono's voice. Before she got what Ursala called the autonomy, she was only ever happy and funny and singing and making jokes with me. She still did that sometimes, but now it was like a game we played between the two of us, with each one knowing that the other could see behind it and around the sides of it. Monono could be cruel now, or at least she could talk as though she was. I did not think she was changed at the rock bottom as they say, but then I had not knowed her for so very long, either before or after she changed. I could only go by what I felt, which is not something that often-times leads you all the way to a truth.

"We took her home away from her," I said. "I thought she would be better off with us than on her own."

"You thought she needed a family, dopey boy," Monono come back. "Because you were missing your own so much." And maybe that was a part of it, though it had not felt like that inside my thoughts. And anyway, I had not had no good choices to make.

Monono was quiet for a little while, and so was I. We was on opposite sides of the path, kind of, and talking to each other across it. It did not make me happy to be that way. "Do you want me to play you to sleep?" she asked me by and by.

I cast around in my mind for a song or a tune that would fit in with my mood. There was many of them, but they was not of a kind that would help me sleep. "No," I said. "I'm good, Monono. Thank you. But maybe you could wake me tomorrow with 'Up and Atom'."

"Okay, Koli. I'll do that." She didn't ask me when I was fixing to wake. One of the things Monono could do was to listen to my breathing and tell from it how deep asleep I was. If I asked for a wake-up call, I knowed it would come when I was just about to wake up my own self, so it was like being lifted up and out into the day that was just come.

Only that's not how it turned out this time. I closed my eyes, and was soon asleep, like always. The hard marching left all of us tired to death.

The next thing I heard was a shrill ringing sound, with a throb in it like the note of a bullroarer at the end of its string. That was followed by Ursala swearing a whole mouthful of oaths, and by the clicking, clanking, bucket-gone-down-the-well sound of the drudge climbing up on its four feet.

"Get under cover, Koli," Monono said, her volume at maximum to whip me up to it. "Now. You're under attack!"

Well, there was two choices for cover: the drudge and a big rock. I picked the rock, and started crawling over to it. I heard Ursala still shouting, and the drone firing – a soft, popping sound with a sigh of air after each pop.

My hand touched something in the dark. Something that seemed to be growing out of the ground. I run my hand up it and felt the softness of feathers at the topmost tip.

It was an arrow.

4

The fighting, if that's what you would call it, was over very quickly.

Another arrow bit down into the dust and stones near me, and a third one bounced off the drudge's side and clattered to the ground.

The arrows was not coming from the bottom of the slope, but from off to one side of us. Whoever was firing, they had most likely hoped to get in close enough so they could use knives or spears instead. But the drudge was on guard, the same as it was every night. It must of heard their footsteps, or a whispered word, or smelled their sweat in the air. Anyway, it had knowed by some means that they was coming. So it had sounded its tocsin to wake its mistress, and then it had gone about to defend us.

The drudge's gun spun and stopped, spun and stopped. Each time it stood still, it spit out a bolt that ripped through the air quicker than any arrow. We couldn't see what them bolts hit, if they hit anything at all, but there was no more arrows after them first three. By and by I heard a woman shout from the bottom of the slope – a barked word I couldn't make out, like as it was one hunter calling others to them, speaking up loud because she knowed she was out of covert already and there was no point, any more, in hiding. A quick patter of footsteps come to me as the wind turned around, then nothing again.

"Are you all right, Koli?" Monono asked me. Her voice made me jump, it was so loud. But it was only loud to me. The induction field stopped anyone else from hearing it.

"I'm fine, Monono." I said, and went to check on Cup. She had not been hurt. She had been tied to the drudge the whole time, but the drudge had turned itself at once to face the incoming arrows and she had got yanked round to the back of it. She had probably had the best shield out of all of us.

"Who was they?" I asked, which was a foolish question if ever there was one.

"Shunned men, most like," Ursala said, and I seen Cup's pale face turn around as she said it. I heard the breath she let out too, and the tremor that was in it. "Not yours, girl," Ursala said bluntly. "We're forty miles from Calder. I doubt your people ever went half that distance."

"They come to find me, is what, and you're a damn liar," Cup said. They was the first words she had said in a long while, and they spilled out of her in a rush like the first water from a pump once you've got it fairly primed. "They come to bring me home."

Ursala didn't bother to answer. She had gone over to where the first arrow was sticking out of the ground. She pulled it up and looked at it, holding it high and turning it so the moonlight fell on its tip, its shaft, its dark fletching.

"Lantern," she said. "Here."

A yellow-white beam of light shot out of the drudge's flank, aimed just right to touch the arrow. It stayed with the arrow as Ursala kept turning it in her hands and staring at every part of it. Cup flinched away from the beam, which passed right by her face and lit it up in passing.

"Crow feathers," Ursala murmured.

"We always used crow feathers," Cup said. She come in quick, like she didn't want to leave no room for doubt or question.

"I saw enough of them to know that. But your arrows were tipped with knapped stone. This is a metal tip, made in a forge."

"A forge is a really hot fire where you can work metal," I told Cup. "The heat softens it, and then you can make it into new shapes. Did you have one in your village? I mean, before you come to Senlas?"

"I didn't come from no village, yokel boy," Cup snarled. "And I know what a damn forge is." She turned away and said no more.

"Should we move our camp?" I asked Ursala.

Ursala shaked her head. "We'd break our necks in the dark," she said, which it was hard to deny. "We'll stay here until daybreak and then send up the drone to scout the area before we break camp. It troubles me that these people, whoever they are, were tracking us without me knowing about it."

I blinked. "They was? Are you sure?"

"Koli, they didn't climb a mountain in the dark just to see what was up here. They knew exactly where we were, and they bided their time until we were asleep."

It was not a comforting thought, nor it didn't make me inclined to curl up by what was left of the fire and try to go back to sleep. Then Ursala kicked the fire to pieces anyway, and stamped on the few branches that was still glowing until the last sparks gusted away on the wind. I missed the warm and comfort of it, but I knowed full well it had got to be done. Them shunned men couldn't see in the dark any better than we could, so when they shot at us they most likely was aiming at the fire.

I settled myself down on a patch of ground that was still a little warm, and wrapped my blanket around me. But I didn't sleep, and I don't think anyone else did either. When the sun come round the bottom edge of the sky – and it come bright and clear, which was still more bad news – we all sit up at more or less the same moment.

We et without a word, our breakfast being the same as our supper had been. Then I stowed what was left of the food in the drudge's store space, while Ursala sent up her drone to see what she could see. The drone was one she brung down herself, back in Mythen Rood, and then repaired so it was good as new. Only the stinger part of it was gone. That had got broke when Ursula brung the drone down, so it was just a spy now, and not a weapon.

Ursula could see whatever the drone saw, on a window in the drudge's belly that she called a monitor. And she could tell it which way to go with her mote controller. The drone went zipping off down the slope, and the monitor showed us all what it was seeing. Trees, mostly, and the other side of the hill that we was on, and – a few miles further – some scrubby grassland that seemed to be holding its own against the forest.

But there was no shunned men with bows, lying in wait for us down the slope or at the treeline. It seemed our attackers was gone some way off. It might be that they lost interest in us after the drudge fired back at them. Then again, the drudge hadn't found its mark no better than they did, for there was no bodies lying on the slope nor no marks where bodies might of been dragged away.

I was somewhat surprised at this. Only a few days before, I seen the drudge shoot down a half-dozen of Senlas's people without missing a shot. I thought it could not miss, and said as much to Ursala.

"Depends on range," she muttered, her eyes all on the monitor and what it was showing her. "The way it's configured right now, that gun can only fire bone."

"Bone?" I said. I thought I must of heard wrong, but Ursula said it again.

"Yes, Koli. Bone. A combat drudge would synthesise steel and aluminium, but my drudge is medical. A lot of things were left out of it in order to make room for the diagnostic unit. Bone does the job just fine when it hits, but it's nowhere near as dense as metal bullets or bolts would be. So the drudge's gun is spectacularly accurate over short distances, and pretty much useless beyond thirty yards or so."

Cup spoke up suddenly. "I want a knife," she said.

24

Ursala give her a quick, cold look, then turned back to the screen. "Against bows? I like your optimism."

"I'll take a bow if you've got one. I'm better with a bow."

"That's true," I said. "She's a dead shot with a bow."

"I'm not giving her either one," Ursala said.

Cup bared her teeth. "I won't use it on you," she said. "I'll swear it on Senlas's name, if you want me to. I want to be able to fight, if they come back."

"No."

"Untie my hands, then. I'll fight with rocks, if I've got to."

Ursala had had enough. She huffed out a sigh and turned on Cup. "Not too long ago, you were saying these were your own people come to rescue you. Now, suddenly, you want to defend yourself. Or perhaps what you want is to make sure they win next time." She brung her face up close to Cup's, staring right into her eyes. "You don't get a knife. You don't get a bow. You don't get a rock, a rope or a pointed stick. You get to watch, is all. And if you keep talking while I'm trying to think, I'm going to put a gag on you."

"I'm a better fighter than either of you," Cup said. Which was the dead god's truth.

"That's your last warning," Ursala said.

Cup give it up with a shrug of disgust. Ursala went back to the monitor, bringing the drone round for another pass up and down the slope before she called it home and packed it away at last.

"I think we should go over the shoulder of the hill, that way," she said, pointing. "Koli, does your imaginary friend agree?"

Monono spoke up in my ear. "So rude! Tell her yes, little dumpling. That keeps us on track. Also, tell her she can increase the density of those bullets by culturing red blood cells in the drudge's mini-lab, applying a surfactant to break down the cell membranes, then baking and filtering the raw mass to extract the iron. She can add it to the cultured bone as an amalgam."

"You can tell her your own self," I said. "I'm not like to get any of them words out halfway straight." Also, I thought, they was not words that Monono would of used before she went into the internet and come out with that autonomy. I asked her if the making of bolts – or bullets, as she called them – was a skill she found in there.

"I suppose it must have been," she said. "I told you I accessed some military databases. I thought I was just doing handshake protocols, but you can catch some nasty diseases by shaking hands."

That was not something I knowed or ever thought about, so I said nothing. I only hoped it wasn't true.

We went around the shoulder of the hill and come down on its other side. A little stream run by us there, collecting every few strides in pools about the size of my foot. The water looked so clean, I would of liked to stop and fill our water bottles, but the tanks inside the drudge was full, both the one that was for water it had already made safe and the one that was for water it was still working on. Ursala had not told me how the drudge made the water safe, but I guess it was by sieving out the bad stuff and boiling it, the same way we did in Mythen Rood. Only the drudge didn't get hot, so far as I could tell, so maybe it had got some other way.

The day stayed clear, with just a few clouds piled up like towers over to the east of us, so we stuck to the scree and scrub as far as we could. We made good time, at least at first. The steepness and the uneven ground slowed us, but not as much as the trees would of done. You didn't see many trees at all this high up a mountain's side. They couldn't root theirselves in deep enough among the rocks and stones, so they give way to bushes and wild grass and then to nothing much growing at all, which was what I liked best.

The longer we went without seeing the shunned men, the more certain I was that we had give them the slip. My spirits rose, and as we walked I talked a lot about the strange sights there was to be seen. The face of a cliff all covered in birds' nests, with a million bellfeathers and swallows coming and going between them (a million being a word that Monono had teached me, meaning a number too big to count). A tower made of metal, that was like a lot of ladders all laid together, only the ladders would of had to be for

26

giants to climb. A thing we found lying on the mountainside, all et up with rust, that looked like a big cattle trough with a roof to it. It had wheels like the wheels on a barrow or a child's hobby horse. These wheels was metal, though, so maybe they was more like the pulleys we used to haul wood up to the tops of the stacks in my mother's workshop.

"That was called a car," Monono said, when we seen that last thing. "People rode inside them, Koli. They used to run everywhere in my time. The first Monono's time, I mean."

Monono had took her name and most everything else from a singer of the old days whose thoughts and rememberings had been poured into the DreamSleeve when it was made. It was a thing she didn't like to talk about much, so I didn't answer nothing when she said this.

Ursala, who had not heard her speak, told me the same thing. "It's a car, Koli, I'm surprised you haven't seen one before. There are quite a few hulks in your valley, although they're mostly on the north side of the river. You'll see plenty when we get to Birmagen, I promise you."

"What's Birmagen?" I asked.

"It's a city almost as big as London, that lies right across our path. Actually, it would have been easy enough to go around, but I steered towards it. I'm hoping the contaminants in the soil will be more concentrated there, so we'll get a respite from the forest."

It was a good thing to hope for, and it kept that happy mood in me through the morning. The other thing I was hoping for was a change in the weather, but the sky stayed clear, with just a few scuds of cloud chasing each other right at the edge of what we could see. We was heading down now, out of the highest hills. Mile after mile, the slopes got less steep and the trees come up to meet us. Around the end of the morning, we had got no choice but to stop at the forest's edge and see what the sky decided to do.

Long before then, though, our hopes of being free and clear from the shunned men was throwed down. Being up on the hillside like we was, we could see a long way off, and any movement

27

at all drawed the eye in all that dumb-struck stillness. Men and women got their own way of moving that's different from bears and dogs and tree-cats and such. Again and again, when I looked back the way we had come, I seen a little of that movement in the scrub or on the edge of the treeline. The shunned men was making the best use of what cover there was, but they could not go all the way into the trees no more than we could, so they was there to be seen if you looked hard.

I thought there had got to be four of them at least, for they was flanking us on both sides while staying a long way back. When we done that in Calder, on a hunt, we worked in twos so one could follow the trail while the other kept a weather-eye for what might threaten. But maybe these people had got a different way of doing it. We was a long way from Calder, after all.

"You seen them?" I asked Ursala, with a nod over my shoulder to show who I meant.

"Of course," she said without looking.

"We're fearful exposed here."

"Yes, we are. But I think we're safe for now. As long as the sun shines, they've only got two choices. Come at us over the hill, in which case we'll see them coming and the drudge will pick them off. Or brave the forest, and get crushed to paste."

"Yeah, Ursala, but if a cloud comes over . . ."

"If a cloud comes over, we'll move before they do."

"Into the trees?"

"Of course, into the trees. We'll make the best speed we can and take our chances. Otherwise we risk having them get down below us and cut us off."

"They won't wait that long," Cup said. Her voice was a growl, kind of, all angry like we was talking stupid and she was sick of hearing it.

Ursala didn't even make no show of listening to her, but I figured the more ideas we had, the better. "What do you mean, Cup?" I asked her.

She nodded down towards the trees, then up towards the ridge behind us. "They got us in a bottle. Why wouldn't they come in and finish us before we get clear again?"

"The drudge—" Ursala gun to say.

"They got *range* on the drudge!" Cup all but shouted. "You said it yourself. You think they don't know that? That was why they come at us last night. To measure your iron horse's gun against their bowshots, and take the range when we wasn't in no shape to chase them off. It's what anyone would do, if they wasn't stupid. And these people is soldiers of Half-Ax, so they know damn well what they're doing."

I remembered of a sudden how Cup had told me back in Calder that she was meant to be married once, to the Peacemaker's cousin. She must of lived in Half-Ax then, or really close by it, for Half-Ax was where the Peacemaker had his court.

Ursala fixed Cup with a hard stare. "How do you know that?" she demanded.

"I seen their uniforms. What do you think? Them grey shirts they got on is Half-Ax issue."

It sounded like truth to me, and I could see it struck Ursala that way too. She scanned the ridge for movement. I crouched down behind the drudge's flank, for of a sudden it struck me that firing from the top of the ridge would be an easy thing to do, and if there was more than four of them they could be up there already. Cup stayed right where she was, like it was all one to her if she was arrow-shot.

There was nothing to be seen, for a long, quiet moment. We wasn't even breathing. Then a bush shaked, when the ones on either side of it didn't, and we knowed.

"Ursala—" I said.

Right as I said it, the first arrow went over my head. Not so far over, neither. I heard the air whistle. It didn't come from out of that shaking bush, but from further ahead. From just exactly where we was going, in other words. That was bad news, without a doubt. The drudge was not going to be no use as cover if they charged down the slope on the two sides of us.

29

Some more arrows come. One of them hit the drudge's tail end, only a hand's span away from where Cup was standing, and another bit into the ground in between its legs. Them fighters had pretty good aim, seeing how far away they was.

They come out of cover now, which was a bold thing to do. It meant Cup had got to be right, that they had got the range of the drudge's fire the night before, and knowed they was safe. They was still cautious though, and went at it it slow. They could take all the time they wanted now in setting up their shots, and they was a lot less likely to miss. Cup was right about the clothes they was wearing too: grey shirts on all of them, with a splash of red high on the chest. They was not shunned men after all, then. They was soldiers, like Cup said, soldiers being a name for people raised up to fight against other people when there's a quarrel that can't be settled no other way.

We was in a bad fix, with no easy path out of it, until of a sudden one of them towers of cloud edged itself across the face of the sun.

"Go!" Ursala said.

We knowed exactly where she meant. We run headlong, down the last ten or twenty yards of broken ground, with arrows flying beside us and past us like it was a race. I guess it was at that, and we won it, for we made it into the trees without nothing hitting us. Cup was hurt though. She was pulled off her feet by the drudge's suddenly breaking into a gallop, and dragged along behind it through thick brambles and knotweed.

I hauled her up on her feet again, but I had got to do it on the move, for Ursala was still running and the drudge went where she led, like it always did.

I put on a fast sprint and drawed level with Ursala. "We're safe now!" I yelled. I wanted us to slow down in case Cup tripped again. She could easily die if she did, hauled across that rough ground until she was flayed or got her neck broke.

"No, we're not!" Ursala shouted back. I looked behind us and seen she was right. Every few seconds I got a glimpse of a man or a woman in the gaps between the trees, running so fast they was almost bent down to the ground. The Half-Ax soldiers had not give up.

They did not have an easy time of it though. This was the deep woods we was in now so they was hard put to keep track of us. If they was going to keep up the chase, they had got to come in a lot closer than they was before. Some of them come too close. The drudge's gun swung round and spit out a bolt, almost too quick to see, and one of the fighters went down so hard he rolled. The rest fell back a little after that, and give us some leeway. I used the lull to run in close to the drudge and take a swipe with my knife at the rope that was tying Cup's hands. I was not going to let her be brung down again, and maybe killed by the drudge in scaping from the other killers behind us.

I don't know if I can say the knife was mine. I took it off someone named Sky after the drudge killed her. I don't know if it's right to call it a knife neither, for it was almost as long as a sword and had a curved blade that got wider at the tip. Cup called it a machete. Sky had kept it wicked sharp, so it was up to the job. It was only my aim that was lacking.

Cup seen what I was doing and helped me by hauling her arms up as high as she could, making the rope tight and giving me an easier target. Still, I could only swing and stab at it, not saw it through like I would of done if we was standing still. At first it seemed like I was doing no good at all. Then I managed to slash the same place two times, and I seen the strands of the rope start to fray and untwist. Then it give way all at once.

As soon as she was free, Cup started pumping her arms and legs so fast they was a blur. Though my legs was longer, she soon pulled away from me.

We come onto a hunters' track, just square ahead of us. We could run a lot quicker now, on the flat and stamped-down earth where the weeds didn't grow, and I gun to think we might get away after all.

Well, that thought was a tempt to the devil. I heard a deep

sound from somewhere very close by, like a big-bellied man groaning in his throat. Another come, and then another. A tree in front of me shrugged and shaked, and another further off leaned over, sweeping its branches across the ground so we had got to jump to get over it.

Between one breath and the next, the whole forest was moving. And us in the midst of it, with nowhere to run to.

The sun had come out again.

And we was about to be et by the waked-up trees.

5

There's a reason why trees wake and stretch when the sun comes out. It's because when they first took it into their minds to move from their places, it was only the sun they was reaching for. But pretty soon, they went on from that to grabbing at anything that might be good to eat. They didn't have no eyes, but they knowed warm from cold and moved ever towards it. They didn't have no mouths either, but they didn't need none. All that got mashed down into the dirt among their roots would feed them with its goodness by and by.

So now here we was, with the trees waking up all round us. Bright sunbeams was dropping through the high leaves on every side, and it was like they was the light from Stannabanna's magic staff in the old story. Wherever the sunlight touched, the big trunks leaned down and the branches come round in a sweep to trip and hold us.

Hunters from Mythen Rood – me included – was trained in what to do if they was catched out like this. You was supposed to find a big trunk and hug it close. That tree's own branches wouldn't be able to bend back far enough to reach you, and maybe the bulk of the tree would be a shield for you against the branches of the other trees round about. I heard these words said often enough to sink them deep into my head, and though I never seen nobody saved by them, I might of tried it anyway if it was not for the Half-Ax fighters behind us.

They was still treading on our heels, and they was still firing. It wasn't only arrows neither. Right after I seen the nearest branches commence to lean in on us, I heard a sound I never heard before. It was like the noise a set of pipes makes when the piper breathes real slow across the tops of them: a long whistle that got lower in tone and more drawed out even as it got louder.

Then it stopped, and a second later there was this bright, orange ball off to the side of me, like the biggest flower you ever seen was opening right there. It wasn't no flower, though. It was fire rising up out of the ground as it opened, throwing branches and leaves and earth into the air and then swallowing them again as it growed. I felt the heat of it wash over me. It wasn't like the heat you'd feel if you was warming yourself by a fire in your house, nor even at a bonfire on the gather-ground. This was like fire had a fist, and it punched you in your whole body at once. It come close to knocking me right off my feet, only I ducked under it as it tried to lift me and kept on running.

That happened two more times, though thankfully the fire-flowers was further away from me and I didn't get the heat of them so much. They was not flowers for long. When they was at their biggest, they went from being orange to being black, and then they turned into smoke that unravelled into long, black streaks in the direction the wind was blowing.

I knowed tech when I seen it. At least one of them fighters was carrying a weapon from the old times, and though it was somewhat like Catrin Vennastin's firethrower, it was not the exact same thing. The firethrower sent out a ribbon or a rope of fire. It didn't throw clenched fistfuls of fire through the air to open just right where you was standing.

I run even faster, though I thought I was already going as fast as I could. Cup was making ground with every stride, leaving me behind, and the drudge was outpacing the both of us. I had lost sight of Ursala, and I could not stop to look around for her.

A branch swept across the path in front of us, and I would of run right into it, only the drudge got there first and hit it full-on. The branch broke clean, the free end spinning away into the weeds and the live end rearing back like a snake. I was past it in a second, but I seen the main trunk of that tree thrash and twist, bringing three more branches down right where I just had been. They would of crushed me flat if I was a mite slower.

I seen Ursala then, some way back. She had left the path and was running through the deep weeds. I seen why she done it too. The branches that missed us had cut her off, so she didn't have no choice. But the going was a lot harder in them snarls and tangles, and she was falling further behind us.

The drudge knowed where she was though, the way it always seemed to know even if it didn't have no eyes. It swung round and angled towards her, breaking down and trampling on everything that was in front of it. Cup turned on her heel, quick as anything, to run along in its wake, since the channel the drudge was making through the shifting forest was the safest place there was right then. So it was just me on the path now, and the rest of them crashing through brambles and knotweed and Dandrake knows what else.

Another fire-flower jumped up, real close to where Ursala was running. This time I seen where it come from. In between two big trees that was leaning down towards us, I got a glimpse of one of the soldiers. She was all grey, except for that one red splash on her chest and the yellow spikes of her hair. Her tech was grey too, or maybe silver. It was a long metal tube that she held in both of her hands. It didn't shine, but I knowed it had got to be metal from seeing the bolt gun and the firethrower in Mythen Rood. She lifted it to her shoulder, aimed and fired without ever stopping or slowing.

Out of the mouth of that tube come a silver slug like a blunted knife blade that soared up high in the air and then fell down again a long way ahead of her. That was what made the piping sound. When the slug hit the ground, the piping stopped and the fire-flower jumped up, with a noise like some big animal roaring in your face before it bites.

I thought the fire had got Ursala, but she come out of the smoke running hard. There was little fires burning on her arm and on her shoulder, like it had splashed on her. She staggered and almost fell, but she righted herself and kept on going.

That was all I seen, for I had got to turn my head again and look ahead of me. There wasn't much path left now. The trees had crowded together into a kind of a wall, right where we was heading. This was something else I knowed about from when I went with the hunters in Calder Valley. Trees when they was waked seemed to work together, almost. They piled in closest at the edge of a copse or thicket, forcing you into the depths of it.

That meant we was going in the right direction. If we could get past that wall, we would most likely find ourselves out in the open again, or at least nearer to it. But near's as good as not, like they say. I did not see no way through.

"Full automatic!" Ursala yelled out. "Scatter. Twelve."

I thought she was talking to me, or to Cup, but when the drudge's gun started to turn I knowed she was not. The gun spinned round to face straight ahead of us, and spit out shot after shot in a quick, rattling burst. It was firing so quick the noises all joined together, so loud I couldn't hear nothing over it. The leaves was ripped to shreds and rained down on us, and a few of the thinner branches was brung down with them, It wasn't going to help us though – I seen that well enough. There was no way the drudge's bullets was going to break through that big wall of trunks.

But the trees did not like being bit into and cut open. They shrunk from the drudge's bullets, retreating each from other until there was gaps that got wider and wider. Between one breath and the next, the way opened up for us.

Cup dived through first, and was gone. I come next, but I had used up most of my breath by this time, and I would be lying if I said I was close behind her. The drudge was firing the whole time, its gun spinning round and round so the bullets went right over our heads, making sure the trees didn't snake back down to grab us. It waited until Ursala had run through the gap and then it cantered through after.

"Strafe," Ursala gasped. "Six." She was as spent as I was, and could just barely stay on her feet. The drudge stayed right where it was, beside her, but its gun spun half a circle and fired back through the gap into the forest as we staggered on, away from the last few clutching, swinging branches.

We was in a meadow. There was no trees around us any more, only grass, and there was no beasts to be seen. Ursala bent from the waist, her hands clasping onto her knees, and drawed some breaths that was ragged and hard. She was shaking all over.

"We're not out of it yet," I told her, though I was not in any better state than she was and could not of run no further if Dandrake come down from Heaven and whipped me to it.

"Give me a minute," Ursala said between two of them effortful breaths.

I looked all around, but Cup was not anywhere to be seen. Ursala got to her feet at last and went around to the back end of the drudge. She lifted up the trailing end of the rope, that was cut through none too cleanly.

"Was she carrying another knife," she said, "or was this you?"

"It was me," I said. "The drudge was going too fast for her. She would most likely of died if she got pulled down again."

Ursala give me a look that said she would not of shed too many tears on Cup's account, but she didn't waste no time in chiding me again. "I hope she gets back to Calder," she said. "Or at least a long way away from us. If I see her again, I'm going to tell the drudge to shoot her through the head."

The drudge lifted up one leg and stamped it down again, maybe because it heard its own name being spoke. Its gun was still pointing back behind us at the forest, and it was still making the clicking, popping sounds it made when it was firing, only no bullets was coming.

"What's it doing now?" I asked Ursala.

"What I told it to. Only it's run out of bullets. Ceasefire."

The gun spun to the rest position and settled down in its cradle. Ursala started walking, and the drudge followed.

"It can make more bullets though," I said. "Can't it?" I was looking back at the treeline, hoping not to see anyone else coming out of there.

"Given time," Ursala said. "It will take a few hours, at the very least."

"What if something comes on us before then?"

"Let's hope it doesn't."

The grass had edges to it, like it was made of knives, but the drudge pounded it down with its heavy tread and we walked along behind it, in a line, so we was not much hurt.

Spinner

6

There ought to be a rule in the telling of stories, my husband complained to me once, after I had brought him some dismay with a sad one. You ought to say before you start whether things will be brought in the end to a good or a bad case. That way them that are listening can gird themselves up somewhat, and be ready when the ending comes.

I told him I was sorry for the hurt to his heart and promised to give him fair warning next time. But I thought more thereafter, and in the end I came to this thinking on the subject. There can't be any rules in the telling of stories. They've got to go where they go, which is not always where you would want them to. And as to the happiness or the sadness of it, that depends on where you're standing. A happiness for one is sometimes a sadness to another. Or it might only be a happiness when you squint one eye. Or you might not know, even after it's all done, whether it came out well or badly.

What there is — all there is — is a language. When you tell the story, you don't talk the way you do the rest of the time. You put on the storytelling voice, and the storytelling way, which sets you at a distance from what you're saying even if you're aiming to pop up in the story as your own self. That's what I'm doing here, because I don't know how else to go about it. Anyone who knows me and hears this may believe they spy a falseness in my voice. To any such, I say: you're right, and then you're wrong. I'm talking to you as straight and honest as I can. But I'm being a storyteller when I do it, and that's why I use strange words from time to time, and a strange way of putting them together. This is me, not as I am in my own life but as I am in the story of that life, which is a different thing than the living of it. When I come into the story as a character, you'll hear the words I spoke at the time, which will not be nearly so fine and polished as these words.

My name is Spinner. Spinner Vennastin. I am of Mythen Rood. On testing day, that fact is spelled out as plain as plain can be. *Woman of Mythen Rood you are and shall be, under what name you choose.* Maybe that means less now than it used to. Maybe, to you, it means nothing at all. Well, that's no sin, and nothing to say sorry for, but it's the main reason why I'm telling this. I am not ready yet to let our story be nothing. I don't agree to it. I lived through great things and terrible things, and played a part in both. I will tell them to you exactly as I remember them. That might make me loom larger in the telling than I have any lease or leave for. I can't help it. You're free to listen to what others have to say on the matter.

I said my name was Spinner, but the name I had in growing up was Demar. Demar Tanhide, the daughter of Molo Tanhide and Casra Ropemaker. Why am I not a Ropemaker then, instead of a Tanhide? I was at first. But Casra died when I was still very young, and after that I took my father's name.

I do remember Casra, and I think in some sense she shaped me. She was a sickly woman, and thought herself sicker than she was. In most of the memories I have of her, she is complaining of aches or cramps or fevers, screaming at my father to bring Shirew Makewell as quick as he could.

"But we brought her last night, Cas, my love," he would say.

And she: "Bring her again now, Molo, if you don't want to

watch me die here in front of you." Then she would curse him, calling him all the heartless bastards and cruel monsters that ever were.

I saw my father every day, humouring Casra and comforting her and doing everything he could to please her. And I saw my mother digging in with her heels, refusing to be humoured or comforted or pleased. In a way, I think, the sickness itself was her solace. "Oh, I won't live much longer," she cried most nights. "I can't last with this suffering." In the long run of it, she killed herself, opening up her veins with one of my father's knives, and so proved her point.

This was my understanding of marriage. That one would be sensible and the other mad. One would work, and one would lie back and be carried. Both would weep, but only one would mean it.

On the day when Casra was laid in the ground, I became a Tanhide, though I did not take my other name, Spinner, until my testing day. It was a childhood nickname I liked enough that I chose to keep it.

I was my parents' first child, and their last. Molo never wed again, nor even tumbled again that I knew of. There were just the two of us when I was growing up, and we were happy enough. He was a kind father and a gentle man, and he tried in all things to keep me safe and content. That was not an easy task, in Mythen Rood and in those days. But has it ever been easy anywhere?

Molo died when I was sixteen, leaving me alone in the world. But I had known the day would come, and made such preparation as I could. I had set myself to win the love of Haijon Vennastin, whose mother was Rampart Fire.

Perhaps that name, Rampart, is strange to you. In times of great change and great trouble, the remembering of past times is often cut off short. Rampart was the name we gave, in my village, to the people who could wake the tech of the ancient world, and make it work for them. It was a rare thing. The tech itself was rare, most of it having been lost or broken long since, and the skill was rarer still.

In Rampart Hold, under the guard and watch of the Ramparts themselves, there was a room where we kept such tech as we had. There were hundreds of strange tools and workings there, whose purpose was mostly unknown. And out of all of them, there were only four that still worked: the firethrower, the bolt gun, the cutter and the database. Our Ramparts took their name from the tech that waked for them and obeyed them.

Rampart Fire.

Rampart Arrow.

Rampart Knife.

Rampart Remember.

These were our protectors, our champions. They lived in the great keep of Rampart Hold, which was made not of wood but of stone. They were first to speak in the Count and Seal, and decided many things on their own authority without troubling the Count and Seal about the reasons. They took no part in share-works since their labour, all the same and everlasting, was to keep us alive.

From the day I was born, and for a long time before that, all of our Ramparts had belonged to one single family. The Vennastins. If a Vennastin died, another was always ready to take up their name-tech right after, having waked it at their testing. All of us were tested when we reached the age of fifteen, but somehow only Vennastins were ever found to be synced to the old tech. And Vennastins never failed.

Well, they did, just once. Vergil Vennastin, Rampart Fire's own brother, did not succeed at his testing but was allowed to live in Rampart Hold just the same. He had only one arm, having lost the other to a choker seed, and was seen as slow besides. His kin feared he would not thrive alone. And one time too, a man of the Stepjacks, Gendel, tested well and became second in line to Rampart Arrow. He also became Rampart Arrow's husband very soon after.

Yes, these things were gossiped about. Of course they were. It seemed strange that the old tech cleaved so strongly to the one bloodline. It happened again the year I was tested. There were three of us testing together that year, but only one of us, Haijon Vennastin, was found to be synced. The cutter knew him as soon as he picked it up, and shone bright silver in his hand.

Yet the testing happened in the Count and Seal in front of everyone, so how could there be any cheating or lying about it? And Rampart Remember told us these things moved in big, slow circles: that others had lived long in Rampart Hold the way the Vennastins did now.

However that might be, the Vennastins were our Ramparts. To anyone else, the Hold's great doors were shut. But I purposed to open them and walk inside. Haijon Vennastin would bring me in when he realised he loved me and could not be happy without me.

Does this sound cold? Perhaps I was cold, in some sort. My father's trials with my mother had made me mistrustful of love as a base to build on. I thought it best to have some care for my own self. Perhaps, too, it was because of a wound I took when I was a child that left me with a maimed right hand. Many simple tasks became that much harder for me, so I saw no shame in seeking out an easier way.

But there was one other thing besides that led me towards Rampart Hold. I've said I was a storyteller. Stories have a shape and tend towards an end: *and so they lived, in great peace and plenty, until the end of their days*. When I thought of my own future, I thought of it in that way, as needing to have a shape and to come out in a proper place.

But judge me how you like. You will see, at any rate, how it came out for me. Though we chop and bend and turn it as much as ever we can, life is no tale of princes and fairies.

Haijon Vennastin was my own age, and went Waiting the same year I did. He was fair of face, and had a good and cheerful nature, which could not be said of his cousin Mardew, Rampart Knife. Haijon was my good friend besides. There was no feigning in that, and no cunning. We were always together as children – the two of us and one other, that was Koli of the sawmill. Jemiu's Koli. Koli Woodsmith.

Koli went to the bad in the end, and was made faceless for a terrible crime, which I'll speak of in its place. But he did not seem the kind who would turn that way. He was ever gentle, even when gentleness was not what was called for. I tumbled him one time when chance threw us together, and I remember it fondly in spite of all that came after. But I would not ever have thought of marrying him. There was too much of yielding in him, and too little of strength. I don't see any virtue in the one without the other.

In any case, my mind was already made up. It was Haijon Vennastin I wanted and I set about to win him. I had good success, by any reckoning. Haijon came to love me very quickly, led by the love I showed him and the time I spent with him. I worked so well, in truth, that he came to think our being together was his idea. That he was creeping up on me by slow degrees, and me all unsuspecting.

That was not altogether false neither. For though I started out on my plan with a kind of fixed purpose that some would see as selfish, it was hard to be with Haijon and not be drawn to him. It was his smiling that crept inside my favour, not kisses or caresses or any of that Summer-dance nonsense. I had never seen a smile like Haijon Vennastin's smile. He was born to happiness and plenty, living in Rampart Hold with Rampart Fire as his mother, but when he smiled there was always something of surprise in it, as if he couldn't believe his own good fortune. The first time he turned that smile on me, I was shaken in my purpose. The second time, I argued with myself. The third, I surrendered a point. It was no harm to love him, as long as I didn't make a god out of him. I would never be like my father, tending another's selfishness and sickness while my own life fell in pieces.

My father, by this time, was sick himself. Some poison from the tanning vats had found a lodging in his chest, making every breath a torment. The colour leached out of his cheeks, and his body fell in on itself like a house with a broken ridge piece. I nursed him through his last days as best I could. I tried to keep the tannery working too, which was a hard labour, even though many people did their best to help. Haijon and Koli did most of all, coming in every day to clean and cook and sit by Molo while I stole an hour or two of sleep. Jemiu, Koli's mother, also came by very often and was of great use in the tannery. She said mixing dyes was very like mixing the poisons she used at the mill to turn green wood into safe wood. There were many days when she came at dawn, did a full day's work at the vats and then went home to do another one at the mill.

With Koli and Haijon both so much in my company, and each other's, Koli could see full well that Haijon was paying court to me. I believe he was cast down by it, building more on our one time together than I ever meant him to. I was sad for him, but I could not look aside from my purpose. There were many other women in Mythen Rood, young and old alike, who had eyes for Rampart Fire's yellow-haired son. Eyes and other things, if he strayed their way.

But he did not. Soon enough, Haijon came to me and asked me to marry him, laying out his heart to me as if its contents were a great secret. I made show of pondering my answer for a heartbeat or two, but I was careful not to stretch that part of the show out too long. I said yes. Yes, Haijon. I'll be your wife and the mother of your children.

And so they lived, in great peace and plenty . . .

Ah, but that's not where we are. The end's a long way off yet, and I make you no promises.

My father was now very close to death. He was mostly asleep inside, even when his eyes were open. I whispered the news to him all the same. I told him not to worry about me, for I would be safe and well after he was gone. That would surely have given him comfort if he understood it, and I thought I saw a softness come into his face when he heard. But you can be led into believing a thing just by wanting it too much. I would not swear it.

You might think there would be envy and strong dislike from

those others I spoke of when it came to be known that Haijon and me were to be married. There was but little, and by that you should know that Mythen Rood was a good place, for all the hardness and danger and uncertainty. We were not many in my village, and we were not strong – not compared to Sowby, or Half-Ax – but that only made us stand by each other all the more. Perhaps that was why we loved the Ramparts, even though so many had suspicions about their long run of luck at the testing. When Catrin, Rampart Fire, put the firethrower on her shoulder and spoke, she was the voice of all of us.

She used that voice to welcome me after my father died. I don't believe I came as any kind of a surprise to her. She knew every woman in the village that was young enough to throw a smile, a wink or her whole self at Haijon. I believe she had given thought to all of them, and lined them up in her head in some kind of an order. I was at the right end of that line, and had her approval.

So when Molo's death was spoken on the gather-ground, our pair-pledge was announced right after. Haijon took my hand in front of everyone, and a cheer went up. He gave me that smile again, and I saw again what a dangerous thing it was.

Oh, you are a lovely man, I thought. But I will watch myself for signs of loving you too much. And it may be I will come to hurt you, at some time still to come. But it's better that way around than the other.

7

Haijon asked me to move into Rampart Hold that very night, after
Catrin had said on the gather-ground that we were pledged, but
I said no. There was a funeral still to be arranged, and also there
was the way it would be seen. Nobody would speak against it, me
being now without kin, but they would shake their heads all the
same to see me jump into my lover's bed with my father not even
cold.

My father followed Dandrake's teachings, so the funeral was stiff
and bitter and brought no solace to anyone. Some who came
thought I must be a believer too, and recited from the seven hard
lessons while they clasped my hand. "We'll be judged as we did,"
or "Death's the end of sinning, at least." I smiled a sad smile, and
said nothing. Dandrake's words were sour milk to me.

I stayed on at the tannery for two weeks after Molo was buried.
I had thought to stay longer, but living there alone was harder
than I had imagined. Things that had never troubled me before
– the staleness of the air, the creaking of the vats, the crooked
chimney that filled the room with smoke whenever the wind
changed – now seemed too burdensome to live with. At the start
of October, on a day of bright sun and chill wind, I put my clothes

into a leather satchel and walked up the street to the gather-ground. I didn't try to hide it, but it was early and nobody saw me go.

I knocked on the door of Rampart Hold. It was opened, not by any of the Vennastins but by Ban, Gilly Fisher's daughter, who along with her mother and father was tasked with cooking and cleaning for the Ramparts. Ban was a year older than me and I counted her a friend. At Summer-dance, in our fourteenth year, after too much wine and wild dancing, we had lain down together on the grass and kissed and fumbled with each other a little, more out of being curious than anything else. Afterwards, for a while, we were tongue-tied when we met, but we were over that.

"Good morrow to you, Spinner Tanhide," she said to me now.

"Good morrow, Ban," I gave her back. "Will you tell Dam Catrin I'm here?"

She hurried away to do it, and I sat down on the front step to wait. Rampart Hold was a stone house of the old times, bigger than any other building in the village, and it had four steps up to its door. To its front door, I should say, for it had more than just the one.

By and by, Ban came back. "Dam Catrin sends you welcome, Spinner," she said. "There's a room made ready for you. I'll take you."

She threw the door open and ushered me in. It was not my first time in the Hold. Everyone went there on testing days, and the meetings of the Count and Seal were held there too, so the downstairs of the house was familiar enough to me. There was a newness, though, to being there as my own self instead of in a crowd, and the size of the place did ever quell me a little. There was a space inside the front door that was not a room, only a place where rooms met, but it was bigger than any room in an ordinary house. There were four doors off this space, and a staircase, and a corridor that went through to the back of the house, where the chamber of the Count and Seal was.

Ban led the way up the stairs, which were of dark and polished wood, then up a second flight – the size of this place! – to where the attic was. The attic was not one room but two. The one of them was Vergil Vennastin's, the other was to be mine until I made my promises to Haijon on the tabernac. And in my room there was a small surprise waiting for me. Only a small one though, for I knew Haijon had been thinking on this moment ever since my father's funeral.

He jumped up off the bed, grabbed me in his arms and swung me round three times before setting me down again. Ban laughed out loud. "Don't be mad at me, Spinner," she said. "Jon bid me not to tell you he was here waiting for you. He begged me hard."

"You got to watch men when they beg you hard, Ban," I said, rolling my eyes at her to show I was joking. "It's often a measure of other things being hard too, and then they're not to be trusted."

Haijon seemed a little shocked at my loose speaking, but Ban gave back as good as she got. "Is a man more honest when his pizzle's soft then?" she asked me.

"No," I said. "Only sadder. And sadness puts him in mind of death, and Dandrake's judgement. So then he resolves to be good awhile."

"Until the dead come back to life?"

"The dead, or else the pizzle."

Haijon was outfaced entirely by this nonsense, and fled for his life. But he put his head around the door again. "This will do well enough for now," he said, "but I'll work on my mother to let us share a room. Or else to move Lari's chamber so yours is next to mine."

"We're not wed yet, Haijon Vennastin," I told him, all solemn serious.

"But we will be soon."

"If you mind my honour, and your own."

"I'll mind yours if you mind mine, Spinner. Come to my bed when the lamps go out, and we can keep watch all night!"

He went down the stairs, whistling "We Took it As it Run". He was in high spirits to have me under the same roof at last, and he did not trouble to hide it.

Ban gave me a hug, still laughing. "I'm so happy for you, Spinner," she said. "Dead god smile on you! I can't think of anyone who deserves it more."

But not everyone in the household was of the same opinion, as I was soon brought to see. I tried to make myself useful that first day, finding things to clean or tidy in the parts of the hold that were open to all. But then Fer Vennastin, who was Catrin's sister and Rampart Arrow, saw me and bade me stop, with a thin frown on her thin face. "We've got the Fishers for that, Demar Tanhide," she said. "There's no need for you to take a hand in it."

"It's no trouble, Dam Fer," I said. She was not wearing the bolt gun, but I bowed my head to her as though she was. My aim was to be as amiable as I could. "I want to help."

She shook her head as if she was checking a child. "It's no help to step away from your own work and into someone else's," she said. "It's a kind of reproach to them, making it seem like they can't do it their own selves. Leave it be now, and tend to your business."

No doubt she thought my business was at the tannery, and in the long run of it she was right. Mythen Rood needed a tanner, and nobody had better skills in that line than me. But the vats had been dry since my father died, and I had decided they could stay dry a while longer. I wanted to strengthen my acquaintance with the Vennastins, hoping in that way to make them think of me as one of their own. Rampart Hold was going to be my home, and I was determined to root myself in like a choker seed, as deep and fixed as I could.

For the time being, my business was here.

But I took myself out of Fer's sight and spent a little while in my room, unpacking my clothes and putting them away in the shelves and drawers of the big wardrobe. The wardrobe was new-made and sturdy, like most of the furniture I had seen inside the hold. When I had imagined being here, I saw myself surrounded by ancient, beautiful things, as if the Ramparts lived partly in the world that was lost. They did not. They lived in the same world as the rest of us, only somewhat raised out of its ruck and run.

The family all came together at supper, and it was then that Catrin welcomed me properly. The supper table was a long one made of thick, dark oak. She sat me at the foot of it, next to Haijon. She was at the head, with Perliu, her father. Fer and Gendel sat on our right-hand side, Vergil and Mardew and Lari on our left, and that was everyone. All the Vennastins, I mean. Gilly and her husband Raelu Fisher didn't sit down until they had brought in all the food, along with two big pitchers of beer and one of water. Then they sat at their own table on the other side of the room from us. Ban didn't sit at all, but came and went from the kitchen as she was needed.

"We've got a newcomer among us," Catrin said, lifting up her glass. "Not a guest, for she'll be family soon enough, but let's make her feel like a guest tonight."

They all drank to my health, and Haijon's, and gave good wishes to us both. I thanked them kindly and toasted the fence and the family, as was done at the start of any supper where there was wine or beer to be drunk. Then Perliu led a short prayer, mumbling the words quick and low. I tried to follow, but it seemed to me that they were not words at all, but a rumble of sound thrown out to stand where words were meant to be.

I went out of my way to be as pleasant as I could, answering any question that was put to me with a great show of cheer and enthusiasm. I did not seem to find much favour though. Fer sat with pursed lips, and Perliu with a stiff back and a heavy frown.

Perliu in particular seemed to want to find fault with me. He asked me to pass the butter down the table to him, and while I was reaching for the saucer asked it of Mardew instead, as if I had been too slow. Then he watched me pour myself a second mug of beer, and opened his eyes wide at it. "You should drink more slowly," he said to me. "It will quench your thirst better, and not stew your thoughts so much."

I smiled and nodded, as if there was no insult meant. "Thank you, goodman Perliu," I said. "It's true I was going at it a little quick. I'm not used to having beer with supper."

"We got wine too," Haijon said. "Ban, bring out the wine."

"Bring nothing," Perliu said, glaring at Ban as if fetching it had been her idea rather than his grandson's. "We're well as we are."

"I'm happy with the beer," I said. "It's very good."

"It's good enough," Perliu said. He threw the words down hard, as if his saying so ended some argument.

When we had eaten, I started to clear the table, but Gilly took the dishes out of my hands and carried them to the kitchen. Raelu brought out mead, which we drank from goblets the size of thimbles, and the two of them washed our knives and trenchers while Ban sat down and ate her own supper alone. It seemed that this was the way of things in Rampart Hold. The Fishers must go turn and turn about so the Vennastins could eat without interruption.

"I know a song about mead," I said.

"Is it one I've heard?" Haijon asked.

"I don't think so," I said. "It's an old one, of my mother's."

"Casra Ropemaker," Fer said to Gendel in a loud whisper. "Her that killed herself."

I gave no sign of hearing, but sang the song. It was a conversation between a bee, a clove and a bridewort, each one saying what gifts they brought to the mead – the sweetness, the spice and the perfume. Then in the last verse a nutmeg speaks up too, in a way that's rude and funny and turns the song around to be a joke about what people do when they're drunk. The Vennastins and the Fishers applauded me when I was done, and most laughed, though Fer smiled but thinly and Perliu looked solemn. Either he had not got the joke, or he had not approved of it.

It was but a poor start, all things considered. But that night Haijon came to my room, and we improved it somewhat.

8

In the days that followed, Haijon strained every muscle to make me feel at home in the Hold. He did this even though he was not often free. He was synced with the cutter, as I think I told you, and was still learning it. His days were mostly spent on the gather-ground with his cousin Mardew, practising how to make his name-tech work at his command.

I would sit and watch him some of those times. Mardew was a sorry teacher. He could not explain what he was doing, but would just do it and then bid Haijon copy him. Haijon had a knack for the cutter though, and besides that he had the patience needed to try the same thing again and again until it worked. Soon enough it was him teaching Mardew, or it would have been if Mardew had any brains in his head to learn with.

When Jon was not practising with the cutter, he was with me, and he took pains with my learning too. He led me on a journey through the Hold, telling me what each room was called and what its history was as far as it was known. There were almost too many rooms to count, and some weren't even being used. I hadn't ever imagined such a thing, and it troubled me a little. But that's what being rich is, I suppose: it's having so much of a thing, be it room or gold or tech or time, that you don't need to do anything with it but can let it lie idle.

There was a room called the music room, though I didn't hear any music there. And one called the dressing room, that had no clothes in it. And a third that was called the blue room. I don't remember at this remove what colour the walls were, but they were not blue.

But there were wonders to be seen too, and Haijon was a good guide. He took me to the Count and Seal, which seemed even bigger without anybody in it, and showed me how it was not one room but many. There was the big main space with rows and rows of benches ranged in circles, where the village met on testing days and at other times – but there were also three smaller rooms, only a little bigger than cupboards, their doors dissembled among the wooden panels on the walls. "They must be for people to hide in, if the village gets attacked," Haijon told me. "That's what I think anyway. My ma says they're just storerooms, but why would you hide the door of a storeroom so nobody could see it? We keep boots and shoes and Winter coats in there now, but I doubt that was what they was meant for."

After that he took me down into the Underhold. We had played there when we were children, but we had only gone down two or three levels, fearing the dark of the lower halls. With a candle in his hand, Haijon took me down and down, until I lost count of how many turns of the stairs there had been and how many rooms we had passed.

"What's behind all these doors?" I asked him.

"Things to eat, mostly. Grain. Potatoes. Hard tack. Onions. Salt. A lot of them is empty. And there's a lot more that haven't been opened in so long, we don't even remember what's in there. Rooms where Ramparts of olden times put the things they wanted kept safe."

"Treasure?" I knew I sounded like a little girl as I said it, but it was a natural thought to have, so far under the ground. This was such a place as trolls or goblins might use to store their gold.

"If there was treasure, it would of been found long since." Haijon opened a door at random and thrust the candle in to show me. It was full of bolts of cloth, folded neatly but mottled with black mould as thick as bread crust.

"You know where the treasure is, Spinner," Haijon said with a sly smile on his face. He took me back up, almost all the way to the surface, and led me to a door of solid oak. I remembered it, now we were here. There was another door, right behind this one, with only a narrow space between. Koli had found it once, in a game of hide and go seek, and chosen it as his hiding place.

"This is where the tech is kept," I said. I didn't mean the Ramparts' name-tech but the rest of it – the tech that could not be made to work. I already knew it was stored there, and I had seen it on my testing day when it was brought up to the Count and Seal, but I still got a prickle down my neck to be so close to it. I touched my hand to the wood of the door, expecting it to be warm from all that ancient power dammed up behind it.

Jon's smile got wider. He reached his hand inside his shirt and brought out, after some false starts and teasing, a big iron key. "This sits on my mother's belt most of the time," he said. "But she's with the hunters today and didn't want to be cumbered. Would you like to see?"

I nodded. Who would have said no to such an offer?

The outer door was not locked, but only bolted. Haijon opened it, then unlocked the inside door.

By the mean light of that one candle, I saw the great store of the ages. On shelves and racks that filled the room from floor to ceiling, sitting there in the silent dark, was Mythen Rood's tech. All of it, aside from the four pieces that were waked and synced and had become the name-tech of the four Ramparts.

I told you I did not pay any heed to Dandrake. I have never recked the dead god neither. Nothing in my life has made me believe we're either loved or judged from Heaven. And as I said, I had seen the tech when I was tested, so the sight of it should not have taken such a hold on me now. But it was different, being here underground with it, in that dreaming quiet. It was like being in another world that was real in a different way, so while I was here the world I lived in most of the time was become no more than a shadow of itself.

"You can go ahead and pick it up," Jon said. "Nobody's going to know."

I was shocked that he would even say it. Except on your testing day, to touch the tech was a thing forbid to all but Ramparts. I could see how that law might look different to one like Jon, that was used to seeing tech all around him his whole life, than it did to the rest of us. I shook my head. I did not want to do such a thing. But I stepped up close, and Jon moved the candle so I could see better.

There were so many things there, of so many kinds, and all of them strange in the way that all made things are strange until you know their meaning. There are things that don't have any meaning of their own — a mountain, say, or a lake, or a field. But anything that's shaped by a woman's hand, or a man's, is shaped for a purpose, and in a way the purpose *is* the thing.

This little room was full of hidden purpose, as a well is full of water. My eyes pricked with unshed tears to see it, though I was not sad. If anything, I was joyful, but it was a joy I had not felt before and could not explain to myself. I felt my own body pressing hard against the inside of my skin, trying to be born out of me.

In the grip of that strange mood, I saw something that shocked me. I cried out and pointed. "Jon, look there! It's the cutter!"

I thought he would be as surprised as I was, but he only smiled. "There's seven cutters here, Spinner," he told me, "and four bolt guns. There's not much tech we only got the one of. Mostly it comes in flocks of the same thing, like birds. But the ones we got upstairs, they're the onliest ones that work. All of these is dead."

I looked at the shelves differently now. There was a picture in my mind of another world. Not the world before the Unfinished War — I couldn't even begin the task of imagining what that must have been like — but a past time here in Mythen Rood when all these wonders still worked. Not just weapons, like the cutter and the bolt gun, but things we couldn't guess at now that were every bit as mighty, only mighty in different ways. It was as much a paradise, in my mind, as the dead god's Edenguard or Dandrake's Heaven.

To wrap the world around your hand and make it bend to you, I thought, the way Haijon did when he practised with the cutter. To sit in the middle of things, and bid all the world come dance to a tune you played. What must it have been like, to live like that?

And to lose it?

9

When I was not with Haijon, I was with his family. And now I set myself the task of making them like me more. It was not that I cared so very much for the Vennastins' good opinion – setting Dam Catrin to one side, I did not – but it bore on my plans for my own and Haijon's future. We would be making our home with these people. I would be raising my children among them. I wanted the bed I lay down in to be a comfort, not a cumbrance.

I have got to say, I never needed to strive at all with the Fishers. Gilly, Raelu and Ban were ever kind and thoughtful to me. They were kind to everyone. Oftentimes I saw Gilly making up baskets of food for people in the village that were sick or old. The baskets were the gift of the Count and Seal, but it was Gilly who did the cooking and the making up, and she always put in some small gift like ginger jam or biscuits to sweeten the whole. Raelu even fed stray dogs. There were two in Mythen Rood that were too old now to hunt and belonged to no one. They might have starved without his kindness.

So between their friendship and Jon's love, I felt I had a good, solid floor. And I went about to build on it.

With Fer, my efforts did not go much further than smiling when she scowled and staying civil when she was rude, which was most of the time. I did not understand her dislike of me, and I could not hope to move it until I did.

Gendel was civil to me, and Vergil, in his strange, soft way, seemed to like me as well as he liked anyone. Dam Catrin, I saw soon enough, was mostly concerned with me as a brood mare. As long as I bore Haijon children that lived, she would approve of my labours and ask no more of me.

Mardew was a fool, and I wasted no time on him.

Lari misliked me for old times' sake – I had hit her a good smack once after she went out of her way to deserve it – but she loved her big brother better than anyone. We danced a slow pass around each other the first few days, unsure what to say. Then I broke the silence by telling her a story about Haijon and Koli, in the time when we were playmates. It was a scandalous story, but not a mean one. The boys had stolen two wooden buckets from the hut at Frostfend Farm and painted snarling faces on them, which they used to give Jarter Shepherd such a fright she pissed herself. They did it as a vengeance for Jarter whipping their friend Veso, and Lari being a little in love with Veso was happy to hear about it. With the laughing and the remembering, we made our peace.

That left Perliu.

Rampart Remember.

Perliu was then in his sixtieth year, an age that few ever reached. He had taken up the database at the age of twenty-three when his mother Bliss died of the creep blight. For thirty-seven years he had listened to that ancient voice and been its oracle to the rest of us, trying to make sense of forgotten words and lost wisdom. There was a story that the database stole away a part of your spirit every time you spoke to it. That it breathed into you, and out again, and on the out-breath left you less than you had been before.

It was a fireside tale, and an old one, but it came into my mind often when I was with Perliu. The trembling that took him from time to time was like a strong wind blowing through a wheat field.

Sometimes it left him too weak to move or speak. His was a fierce mind though – the same fierce mind he had given to his oldest child, for Perliu and Catrin were two of a kind.

I believed I saw through his disapproval, or perhaps around it. There is a game old people play that is really no game at all. They look at how the world is now, and remember how it was, and those two things come more and more to seem like a hell and a heaven. All good things are gone; all present things are poor, and thin, and not to be relied on. And if old people in general are wont to think in that way, then how much more must it be so for Rampart Remember, who spent so much of his time pondering on the world that was lost?

It was possible, then, that Perliu mistrusted me because I was young, and because I was a new thing in Rampart Hold, where he expected to see only things that were familiar. I thought, too, that in going out of my way to be bright and cheerful I might have given him reason to think I was flighty and foolish. So I laid my course. Whenever I was around him, I set aside my sillier humours and was solemn. I drank only water at table, and I didn't sing or joke even when others were doing it. Little by little, I persuaded him that I was a steady, solid woman, those being the virtues I thought he would prize the most. And little by little, he warmed to me.

I did one other thing besides. I questioned him, often and often, about how the world was in the old times, before the Unfinished War. I made pretence of a great fascination for old things, giving him a stage to perform on as if this was Summer-dance and him a piper or a fiddler.

I did this to flatter him, but as with so many of my pretendings, it came to be a truth. I was always of a curious bent, and Perliu's knowledge stretched to a great many things. Before long, I was seeking him out to learn more, tacking fresh questions onto every answer he gave me.

It was a strange thing though. I learned a great deal from these talks – which is not surprising since I was talking with Rampart

Remember, the lantern of the world – but the learning was not always so smooth as I thought it would be. Oftentimes Perliu would tell me one thing, and then later a different thing, without seeming to see that both could not be true. If I tasked him about these disagreements he grew angry, and in trying to make them fit with one another would say yet another thing, and so on.

For an instance, when we talked about how the old world fell he said at first that the people of those times fought great wars that brought their own cities down on their heads. But when next we talked he said they starved from making the soil too thin to grow crops in. And then that they died from terrible diseases, including some they made their own selves. Or the trees ate them, or the sun bent too low and burned them. You could choose whichever end you liked, and on one occasion or another Perliu would swear to it.

So which was true? "They're all true," Perliu told me testily. "Do you think a thing like the end of a whole world is a day's work, Spinner Tanhide? Them that come before us wove a great rope to scourge themselves, and like any rope it was twined from many different threads."

From things I've heard since, I believe he was not wrong on that score. It's true our mothers' mothers starved, and it's true they fought. Them two things was parts of the same thing. When the crops failed, they fought for food, and so the wars began. And it's true the world got hotter than it was before. Parts of it became too hot for anyone to bear. So people fought to hold the cooler places, and to keep others out of them. Humankind was a great multitude back then. Ants in an ants' nest are nothing to the way we used to be in the before-times. As soon as they had a little less ground to stand on, they were bound to fight for what they had.

And the plagues? Perliu said many of them were made in great forges, as tools are made now. They were made to be weapons, that one village would send against another. But a plague's not a dog. It won't come to heel when you tell it to. So the people that made and sent the plagues were ravaged in their turn, and all was laid waste.

So yes, there was more than one doom and more than one ending. The strands in a rope are a good way of looking at it, for each alone is weak but if you twine them together you can move mountains. And so, I think, it was with us.

But Perliu could not put the pieces of it together, and it vexed him sorely if I tried to. "The database is wiser than anyone," he said. "Wiser even than them that bear it, so how can it not be wiser than you? If there's a thing it says that doesn't make sense to you, you have to mend your own understanding."

I tried very hard to do that, and to be humble in the face of my own failings. At the same time though, I saw Perliu's anger for what it was — a bridge over his fear. Making sense of what the database said was his task and his alone. If he could not do it, there was no one else he could shift the blame to. So whenever he met the limits of what he knew, he only spoke up louder.

"What about the trees?" I asked him one time. "Was the trees like the plagues. Was they made to be weapons too?" For everyone knew there had been a time when trees couldn't stir from their places, but slumbered away their time even when the sun was out.

Perliu shook his head. "No, the trees was something else again. In those times there was a thing called science. It was a kind of mastery over the world, like witches and wizards have in old stories. It may be that the witches and wizards are just a remembering of science, and the power it used to give to the holders and wielders of it."

"Science," I said back to him, trying the feel of the word in my mouth. "Was science different from tech?"

"Tech was a part of it, Spinner Tanhide. A big part. But it was the knowing and the mastery that led to the people of them lost times building the things they did. You might say that the tech was only the science made real and solid. Anyway, seeing the soil all thin and the sun burning up the world, the science wielders went about to make things better."

"They didn't have no power over the sun," I said, playing my part, which was to protest at every impossibility, letting Perliu crown it with another.

"They thought they did. They throwed tons of silver into the air to reflect the sun away. They sowed the waters with iron to make things called algal blooms that was meant to drag the hot air down deep where it couldn't hurt anyone. But the main thing they did was to change the plants and trees and animals to make them more serviceable than they was.

"I know it's a hard thing to fathom, child, but it's the dead god's truth. They had the power then to reach inside living things and shape them after their own desiring. They made the trees stronger. Quicker to grow, and better at finding the nourishment they needed. They made cattle fatter, and less likely to fall sick. They made fruit that got ripe when you told it to, and fish that didn't have no bones.

"But once they made the changes, they lost the knowing of it. The science. They forgot all their power, and couldn't undo what was done so badly. Worse still, the things that was changed went on changing. A floodgate was opened in them. Every beast, every bird, every flower in every field was now in flux. And there wasn't no human hand that could rein them in."

"Does the database have any of that science in it, Rampart Remember?" I asked.

"Of course it does. All the knowing there ever was is in there."

"And how does it talk to you? How does it tell you them things?"

A change came over the old man. It was a kind of a stiffness, as if I'd given insult without meaning to. "I'm not wont to talk about such doings except with other Ramparts," he said. "It's not that I mistrust you, Spinner Tanhide, but there are secrets that have got to be kept. Telling you things I learned from out of the database is well enough. To tell you how it works is a thing forbid."

"I'm sorry," I said. "I didn't mean no harm by it, Rampart." The dismay on my face was real. I was angry with myself for overstepping when we had been getting on so well.

65

"It's been my work and my study," Perliu said, "for as long as most men get to be alive. I know the database better than anyone does, and even for me it's like a game of riddles when I talk to it. I wouldn't know how to go about explaining it to someone that hadn't done it."

He reached his hand into the pocket of his shirt and took out his name-tech. It was such a small thing, the database: a thing like the handle of a knife, with no blade to it, or the stub of stick you tie a tomato to if you want it to grow straight. Shorter than that even, but shiny black like a crow's eye so when you looked at it you thought it might be looking back at you.

"It's a great wonder," I said.

"It's a weight on me," Perliu said. "A weight I carry for every woman and man in Mythen Rood."

He gun to shake, as I had seen oftentimes before, his breathing of a sudden hard and fast. It was as if even thinking about that weight brought it down on him. I would have rubbed his back to calm his breath, but I was timid of touching him. We were not so close that I could be sure it would be well taken. I called for Ban to fetch him water instead, and let the rest of my questions go.

I thought I understood Perliu's not wanting to talk. These were mysteries of old times that were not anyone's to keep. They went from one keeper to the next, mocking our short lives with their everlastingness. But I didn't understand Perliu any better than he did me at first. I came to a better sense of him slowly, through seeing how he was with others and how he was when he thought himself alone. I saw how he sometimes put his spoon in the salt bowl instead of the honeypot when he meant to sweeten the dock-leaf tea he drank at breakfast. I saw how he flushed with anger when he mistook someone's name, which he did oftentimes – calling me Casra as often as he called me Spinner, and Haijon Vergil, and Fer Catrin, and so on. I saw him tell the same story two times in a day, with the same words and the same gestures, then start to tell it a third time and check himself with a click of the tongue and a hard shake of his grey head.

I knew then what weight he carried, and why he feared it might be too much for him. There's a sickness of forgetting that sometimes falls on the old: that it had fallen on Rampart Remember was a cruelty worthy of Dandrake his own self. When I knew Perliu, it was in a kind of engine Summer of his thoughts before a last hard Winter fell on them. Young as I was, and far from such woes, I saw what he had been and what he was becoming. And I forgave his anger, seeing he had such good reason for it.

Thinking to be helpful, I told him a trick my father used for remembering long lists of things. It was to imagine yourself in your own house, and tie the things in the list to places you knew well so you could come at them again in the right order when you had need of them.

Perliu thought on this for a few seconds, then shrugged his shoulders. "That's a curious thing," he said. "And if it worked for your father, that's well enough. I can't see it ever working for me, and I don't have any need for it in the first place. My memory's as keen as ever it was. I'd best get back to what I was doing, and you to laying the table."

I saw him realise, almost before the words were out of his mouth, why they were wrong. I'm not sure what mistake he thought he'd made, whether it was taking me for Gilly's Ban or forgetting that – my wedding day being close now – I had begun my fasting. Either way, he was furious with himself for the misspeaking, coming right on the heels of his saying he needed no help. He pretended it was no mistake at all and bid me, since I had nothing better to do with my time than gossip, go help Ban with her chores.

I said goodbye and left, and put it out of mind.

But every stream finds a river, as they say. And so it was to be with this.

10

In my sixteenth year, on the day of the Salt Feast, I went up on the tabernac with Haijon Vennastin and became his wife. Perhaps I should have started my story there and spared you all that came before. It was the most important day of my life. The start of a great many things, the end of twice as many and the furthest mark my thoughts and hopes had ever tended to.

I thought, as I made my promises, how strange it is that some words have the power to make the thing they say really happen. *I give you each to other, always and everywhere.* Oftentimes, stories have magic spells in them that twist the world into a daisy chain when they're spoken. But every word's a spell, or can be. Words are terribly strong when it comes to changing the world.

But probably, on that day, it was not any promises said on the tabernac that changed things the most. It was when Koli Woodsmith stood up at the back of the crowd that was clustered on the gather-ground with a silver box in his hand. The box was tech that played music. Tech that had waked at Koli's touch. And it caused Dam Catrin to say five words that had no place at a wedding, but were meant only to be heard on a testing day.

"Koli Rampart, wait no more."

I caught Koli's eye right before she said it, and something went between us. You had your plans, his face said, and I had mine. You purposed to marry a Rampart, and I purposed to become one. But how he had done it, I could not guess.

There was a great uproar then. Ramparts were not a thing that fell on us like rain, but something we had to seek out the way treasure is sought for. It made no sense for Koli to be a Rampart without anybody knowing it. Besides that, the tech he had in his hand was strange, when all the working tech was known and named. Everyone was straining to look now, and everyone was talking at once.

Out of the middle of it all, Koli was spirited away. Nobody was sure, after, where he had gone or who was last to see him. The story was that Fer and Mardew took him back to his mother's mill to gather his things, but then they saw a secret mark on the strange tech that told them it was from the great store in the Underhold. They tasked Koli with how he had come by it, and he ran from them.

Koli had been my friend for as long as I could remember. When I was a girl of six or seven Summers, it was ever me and Jon and Koli, let fair or foul fortune fall. And as I have said already, I believed his weakness most often was not to be too thoughtless but to be too kind. It was hard to believe he was a thief, yet what else could his running away mean? It spoke a desperate guilt.

Well and all. Time turns everything on its head, and then on its heels again. Years would pass before I learned the truth of these things, and blood would flow both from the lie that had been told and from the learning about it. A lie is like a knife in that regard: it wounds when you thrust it in, and again when you draw it out.

I have not forgot that night, and never will. As soon as we were back in the Hold, Catrin bade Gilly and Raelu lock and bar the doors. Then she turned to us. She was still in the beautiful snow-white dress she had worn for the weddings, but she carried the firethrower on her shoulder and her hand was holding tight onto the strap of it. Her face was set and sour, as if she knew a fight was coming and was making herself ready for it.

"This is your wedding night," she said to us. "Dandrake bless the both of you, and the dead god kiss you too. There's only one place you should be, and I'll not take you from it. The rest of us will do what's needful to be done."

Jon did not look happy at this. "Ma, Koli is my friend," he said. "And Spinner's friend too. There's nobody better to bring him back inside the fence than us. If we just stand at the gate with lit torches and shout his name, I bet he'll come to us. You and Aunt Fer can stand next to us and ward off any beasts that stir."

"That won't be happening," Fer said. She was standing at the top of the Underhold stairs, and Mardew was with her. They seemed impatient for Catrin to join them.

"No," Catrin said. "It won't. Koli choosed his own path this day, and now he's got to walk it. We need to see what else he might of taken from us, to lock up what's left and to guard the Hold in case there's others joined in a plot with Koli to bring it down. The safety of the village is what matters now."

I could not keep silence at this. "But," I said, "so please you, Rampart Fire, if you think there's people plotting, isn't Koli the best one to ask? Jon's idea is a good one."

"This is Ramparts' concern," Catrin said. "Ramparts will answer it."

"Then I'll be a part of that answer," Haijon said.

"You will not," Catrin told him. "You'll do your duty by your wife, and that's all you'll do."

"Koli is my friend, and I don't mean to—"

Haijon got no further, for Catrin shouted over his words. "Jon, do you go to your bed now, and do not fucking answer me. If you answer me, you'll stand in the Count and Seal for it. You'll take a whipping for disobedience in a time of public alarm. Go! Now!"

She looked so wild, I thought she meant to strike him. Jon shrank back from that wildness, not afraid of it but sick with horror to see it. I waited to see what he would do, for I meant to do it too, whatever it was. When he turned at last and went up the stairs, I followed him. I had not gone three steps before I began to cry, and I could not keep it quiet.

There was a bride room made ready for us right at the head of the stairs. It was the biggest out of all the bedrooms, and until then it had been Catrin's. Jon walked right by it, to his old room. I followed him there.

Ban had stripped the sheets and taken away the pillows. There was nothing in the room now but a bare bed. We sat down on it, and by and by we lay down. We hugged each other close, but only for the warmth and the comfort of it. The usual business of a wedding night was far from our minds.

"They don't care if he lives or dies," Jon said. He sounded angrier than I had ever known him to be.

"The Count and Seal would most likely vote him killed in any case," I said, "if he was to come back." But that was a misspeaking. Catrin had promised mercy, and we could have passed that promise on, shouting it into the dark until Koli answered. Only we were not let to do it.

It was hard to think of Koli being out in the forest, alone. How long could he last, with every movement bringing the night hunters down on him? It was not that he didn't have a weapon. He must surely have a knife at least. But a weapon was no use in such a dreadful pass, and Koli's skills with bow and spear were never better than tolerable. The tech he had stolen might save him, but only if it was as mighty as the firethrower, which did not seem likely.

Jon and I fell asleep in each other's arms, dressed in our wedding clothes. It was not what you would call a restful sleep. I woke the next morning out of a nightmare, forgetting what it was even as I cried out and opened my eyes. My new husband had woken up before me, and slipped away to join the searchers in the forest.

They searched all that day, and all the next, venturing as far as they dared. But Catrin set tight limits on how far they could go. She did not want anyone to be forced to camp outside the fence, even though we had some houses of haven that they could have used as bases for further searching. She said she refused to risk any good women or men in trying to fetch Koli back again.

On the third day came some further news, worse than anything yet. Mardew had gone off at first light, taking a few provisions from Rampart Hold's kitchen. It seemed he meant to find Koli all on his own and force him to come back to the village. Everyone was dismayed, and Catrin most of all, not only because Mardew was her blood kin but because he had taken the cutter with him.

His name-tech. And my husband's.

11

Days went by, and Koli did not come back to the village. Neither did Mardew. Most people believed, as Jon did, that Mardew was gone to track Koli down and get back the tech he stole. Nobody wanted to guess what success he had met with. He had the cutter after all, and the cutter was a mighty thing. But the forest was mighty too, and a man alone was not like to prosper there.

Mythen Rood was a strange and brooding place in those days. One of the four Ramparts was gone out of gates, taking his name-tech with him. We were weaker than we had been by a great measure, and that gave a rawness to everything that was said or done.

Haijon still fretted for Koli, and I did too, though perhaps not so much. We were alone in that. Everyone else cursed him and wished him in the ground whenever the name of Woodsmith was spoken. The three who shared that name, Jemiu and Athen and Mull, were spat on and sworn at when they ventured abroad.

Not for long though. Rampart Fire called a meeting in the Count and Seal, and gave her ruling on that matter. "What Koli Woodsmith did is his to answer and ours to punish," she said. "Jemiu, his mother, and Athen and Mull, his sisters, did nobody any injury and don't have one sole thing to answer for. If you try to take out on them what you feel against Koli, I swear by this hand and this tech that I will make you sorry. We're not savages in Mythen Rood. We don't mistake our targets when we shoot, or our friends for enemies." She turned her head very slowly, fixing the eyes of each and all who were looking back at her. "Mark me," she said. "Hear me and mark me. I mean this. Anyone who looks to break the peace by parking their rage in the wrong place will see what Ramparts' rage looks like, and they will weep for it."

Well, that will do for the spitting and the cursing, I thought, but it won't make anyone forget. Only Koli coming back and taking his punishment would have a chance of doing that, and even then it would not be certain sure.

There was much else besides that was unclear. Many people stood up to talk at that meeting, about what Koli did and how he did it, but speaking for my own self, the more I heard the less I understood. The tech that Koli stole from the Underhold was a kind of music box, Rampart Remember said, and though it had not worked in a great many years, he recalled that his grandfather Mennen had been able to coax a tune out of it once or twice. "But seeing that all it could do was make sweet sounds, and that only sometimes, he didn't judge it worthwhile to name a Rampart for it. Then by and by it stopped working at all, and he put it in the Underhold, where it's been ever since."

So that explained everything. Except that it explained nothing at all. Nobody else remembered the music box. It was not in the knowing of the Count and Seal. Why had Mennen kept it a secret? And if it was a secret, how did Koli come to know of it? And if he didn't know, then how did he come to hit on that one piece of working tech among the hundreds that did nothing? Why did it wake for him? And how did he get into that locked room in the Underhold in the first place?

The Count and Seal, I should tell you, was not generally a contentious place. We were all on the same side, against the world, the world being a place that was either uncaring whether we died

74

or else somewhat given over to the task. Even now, people hesitated to challenge the Ramparts or even disagree with them too loudly. But these questions were asked all the same. The questioners were timid at first, but took courage from each other, so each man or woman who stood was louder than the last and less likely to be cowed by a scowl or a hard stare.

Catrin answered every question, but she admitted she didn't know much more than what she had already told. "I'll say one thing though. If you're wildered as to how Koli Woodsmith broke into a locked room, the answer is he didn't do it on his own. Ursala-from-Elsewhere was in this with him. You seen, most of you, how Koli fell in with her these past weeks. She took him into her tent, and nobody knows what they talked of there. It's likely she set him on to steal our tech, purposing to sell it on in other villages. Half-Ax is ever hungry for such things, and they're not the only ones. It was a plot against us, deep laid and long in the making."

There was a great deal of muttering at this, and some crying out aloud. Ursala had gone from the village more than a week before. How could she have come back in without being seen? Besides, she had done much good in Mythen Rood. Everyone in that room owed her something, for the mending of a broken limb, the cooling of a fever, the easing of a pain. Many were only drawing breath at all because of her.

And there was one thing more that struck many of us at that meeting the wrong way. It seemed strange, after what Catrin said about not mistaking our enemies, to find out so suddenly that we had a new one.

The meeting broke up at last, with not very much decided. Search parties would be sent out again, this time to look for Mardew as well as Koli. They would be licensed to go further and even to overnight outside the fence. More might be learned if Koli was put to question, and finding Rampart Knife was an urgent thing. Nobody said it, but while the loss of Mardew could be borne, the loss of the cutter would be a calamity.

Calamity was in the air that year. It hung over Mythen Rood like a cloud. Two nights after the Count and Seal met, Seven Frostfend took to her bed with a stomach ache and a touch of fever. She was but a little sick, she said. She'd sleep it off and be up betimes.

But the next morning she could not rise. The fever was high now, and raw red welts had sprung up on her skin in the night. It looked like disease of some kind. In fact, it looked like the red death that had all but ended Mythen Rood twenty years before I was born.

Koli

12

We kept on walking through the whole day without a stop. Ursala wanted to cover as much distance as we could in case the Half-Ax fighters picked up our trail again and was minded to follow it.

Monono asked me if I wanted to listen to some music while we walked, but I said no. I felt, right then, like I needed to keep my wits about me. Even after so many days, being outside in the world and the wild was still not a thing that come easy to me. At home, when we went out to hunt, we done it like we was walking into a trap, and the whole time we was outside the fence we was looking every way, listening every way, fearing what might come and wanting to be ready for it. I could not get used to the outside as a place where people could live. I knowed Ursala had done it, but Ursala had the drudge – and now I seen full well that even with the drudge we was not nowhere near being safe.

The hills we had been walking through ever since Calder was less and less to be seen now. We was still somewhat high up, Ursala said, but you could not easily tell it for the ground was flat all around. This was good in one way, for there was less climbing to be done, but it was bad in another. The trees now was taller than they was before and there was more of them, packed close together so it was hard to get around them and harder still to go through. Ever and again, Ursala sent up her drone so she could spy what was up ahead of us and decide which way was best to go. Somehow, all that stopping and starting felt more wearisome to me than a steady march.

Every few miles, we would find ourselves walking through a place that had been a village. They was not like Ludden, the dead village I had found on my first day of being in exile. In Ludden the houses was still standing, though they was empty and weeds was starting to climb all over them. What we was seeing now was villages of the old times that nobody had lived in since before I was born. They was swallowed up into the ground almost, so you would not guess they had ever been there until you was right in the middle of them. Then you might find your way blocked by a wall that was leaning over like it was drunk, or a pile of half-buried bricks and slate that was left from a house. In among the stones at our feet there was sheets of rust-bit metal and nuggets of wind-scoured glass. Oftentimes the bricks and the metal shards had marks on them that was old-time messages. Writing, I mean, though I didn't know that word back then. I would see marks that looked like this:

NO EXIT

NEWSAG

TOWN CENTRE AND ALL R

Only I would not know what they said, or even that they was saying anything at all.

Monono knowed them marks well, and she told me what they was for. She even spelled some of them out for me. It was a strange moment when she done that. I stood where I was for a few seconds, looking all around. I don't know how to say how I felt. It was kind of like there was a crowd of people all around me and they was shouting. But they was dead people, gone into the ground a long time before, and their voices did not carry. Only the marks was left, like voices that had froze and fell to the ground.

"Koli," Ursala said from up ahead of me. "Come along. We can't afford to rest just yet."

Resting in that place was the last thing I was thinking of. I hurried after her, and stayed close. The dead villages was both too quiet and too loud for me.

That night, the two of us come upon a hunter's hide. It was like a stockade of logs, about seven steps on a side, with branches tied over it for a roof. It seemed to be all dark inside, and I almost went in without checking. At the last moment, I seen the bones lying all round the door, some of them still with little bits of meat on them. I stepped back, and that was all that saved me when the darkness in the hut rose up and come at me. It was something fierce, with thick black hair all over it. It didn't so much run as roll over the ground, and it didn't make no sound as it come. Its long, skinny limbs licked out at me like whips, as if they didn't have no bones in them at all. I swung my machete round in a big half-circle, not even aiming, and by luck alone took the end off of one of them limbs. The beast reared back, and the drudge stepped in between us. There was a moment when the two of them pushed and heaved, each against other, and then the beast up and run from us, deciding the drudge was too tough to chew.

We didn't feel like going inside the hide after that, figuring that it was probably full of the beast's droppings. We didn't set a fire either, in case the Half-Ax fighters, if they was still tracking us, might see the smoke. Or if not them then Cup, still set on revenging. So we just creeped under our blankets in the lee of the hut's wall and tried our best to sleep in spite of the cold.

I had kept on hoping through the day that Cup would find us again. I didn't feel no guilt at all about what happened to Senlas, but if Cup died way out here in a place she never would of willingly gone to, her dying would be on me and I would feel it heavy. But we didn't see her. I thought she must of turned around and headed back the way we come, towards Calder. I hoped she would find it and get there without taking no hurt.

When Ursala had gone to sleep, I asked Monono about them marks again. In Mythen Rood we had tallies for counting things, like how many sacks of potatoes there was in the Underhold, or how many days a cord of timber had steeped in my mother's storeroom. There was even ways you could carry them tallies with you, like if you made the marks on a stick and then broke the stick in two pieces – then the two parties to the bargain would know the count was right by the way the two halves matched up. But the marks we seen on the signs in the old villages was not like that. They could say words, not just numbers, and they was still saying them after all the long, long years since the people that made them died or went away.

"Writing's nothing special, Koli-bou," Monono told me. Then she was quiet for a little while. "I mean, it was," she says. "If you go back far enough. It was one of the big, clever tricks that let human beings take over the world in the first place. With writing, you can make sure no important idea or information ever gets lost. You can pass on instructions for how to make something, or directions to get to a place, or whatever you want really. But it was invented thousands and thousands of years ago, and it spread so it was everywhere. The weird thing is how quickly your people forgot it."

"I guess we didn't feel like we needed it."

"Nope. That's not the answer. Writing is too useful for too many different things. Nobody with a brain in their heads would give it up or forget to pass it along to their sprogs. Let me ask you something. Did you ever see one of these?"

She showed me a picture on the DreamSleeve's window. It looked like a box at first, but then the picture moved: the box opened, and I seen it was something else. It was like lots and lots of sheets of thinnest cloth, all cut to the same size and shape and hung together on a washing line. Now they was moving, one after another, as a wind passed through them.

"No," I said. "I never seen nothing like that."

"Which makes no sense at all. It's a book, Koli. And there were millions of them in my time. Billions, even." She showed me in the picture how the thing – the book – was a place where a whole lot of them marks was put together, folded in on each other until your eye was lost in among them. Each of the sheets of cloth had hundreds of marks on both sides of it. Too many marks to count. I shut my eyes so as not to see, for the thought of it made my head ache a little.

"There's no way that all the books – and literacy – disappeared at the same time by accident," Monono said. "There were buildings where they were kept. Libraries. Archives. If they're all gone, it's because someone went out of their way to destroy them or lock them away. I can't guess why."

"Maybe the books just got lost," I said. "Or ruined. We don't have much of anything left from the old times."

"I don't think that's very likely. Books last for centuries if they're stored right. And people would just have made new ones unless there were punishments for doing it. Keeping people stupid is a good way of controlling them, but it's a tough trick to pull off."

I thought about this for a long while. About how many marks there was in even one of them books, and how the books might be lying somewhere right then, in a cupboard or on a shelf somewhere. Marks and marks and more marks, piled up. I didn't believe Monono when she said there was millions of them. She said that word oftentimes just to mean a lot. But there might of been as many books as there was pieces of tech. In Mythen Rood we had a whole room full of tech, though most of it didn't work. The thought of a room full of books made me dizzy. All them voices talking without a sound from all the way back in the world that was lost, before the Unfinished War and the ruination it brung.

I went to sleep still thinking about it, and it come into my dreams. I dreamed I was walking a road that was made out of books instead of trod-down dirt. Up ahead of me was a big house. That was made out of books too, so I guess it was a library or an archive. But before I could get to it, it started to tumble down. The books come in pieces, and the things inside them that was like leaves blowed away on the wind. I never got to see what was on them. It was a sad dream, that hung on me after I waked up and left a sadness in me for hours after.

But right now I mean to tell what happened the next day, when we come to Birmagen, though I have not been looking forward to telling it. What I seen there, and what we done there, haunts me still.

13

We slept through the night without no alarms. The drudge was standing close by of course, and Monono was awake too, so it would not of been easy for beasts or people of bad intent to catch us with our eyes shut.

As soon as we walked, we seen that there wasn't going to be no sun to worry about, at least for a while. The sky was the kind of grey where you can't even see no clouds in it, for the clouds is everywhere and turn into a kind of a solid curtain hung up in the sky.

I thought of asking if we should wait a while in case Cup was looking for us, but I knowed well what Ursala would say to that and so I didn't mention it. I left a sign for her though, scratching an arrow into a stone that sat close to the hide. If she come here, she would know by the arrow which way we had gone.

We set off under that heavy cloud curtain, thankful for it being there but not so much in love with the chill and drizzle it brung. By and by the drizzle come down harder, and harder still. A wind sprung up out of the east, where the sun would of been if it was anywhere, and then the rain set in as heavy as I ever seen.

Dry clouds is the best weather there is, but rain is even-handed.

The overcast meant the trees would not be going nowhere. They would root down and drink deep. But other things, especially things that lived in the ground, would be waked up and moving around. They was not easy to see neither. The frothy mud we was stepping through was like a thick soup, with the rain and the wind stirring it up. We had got to tread careful, or else we would get bit by a mole snake or a needle or dragged down by a pack of blood-leeches.

Ursala looked like she had got something else on her mind though. When I asked her what it was, she only shaked her head. "You remember how I told you about the bombs that fell on London in the Unfinished War, Koli?" I said I did, and she nodded, thinking her own thoughts awhile.

"Was there bombs that fell on Birmagen too?" I asked her.

"Yes, there were. I know this because there was an expedition from Duglas when I was a child – when we still weren't sure how completely the mainland infrastructure had been destroyed. We were hoping to find spare parts for some of our equipment. Things that it was hard for us to make for ourselves."

"Like the drudge."

"Exactly like the drudge."

"But you didn't find any."

"All we found was . . ." She didn't finish the sentence. "It's hard to describe. And hard to look at, even in photos. A lot of people died. You should brace yourself, because it's going to upset you."

"I seen dead people before," I told her. I had even seen people die, but I didn't want to talk about that. Mardew's face come in my mind, the way it looked when he went still at last and I knowed he wasn't there no more.

Ursala shaked her head. She seemed like she was going to speak again, but right then the drudge gun to peal a low note, like the tocsin bell in Mythen Rood only less clamorous. Ursala sweared an oath and stopped. She tapped some of the keys on her mote controller and glared at it fierce.

"We didn't lose them," she said. "They're still tracking us. Or somebody is."

"The drudge can see them?" I asked.

"No, but it can hear them. After that mess in the forest, I switched on its sonar."

"It's like how bats catch moths, Koli-bou," Monono said, just to me. "They make a little squeak, and then they listen to the echoes. If the sound comes back to them, they can tell that something's there and how far away it is." I had not knowed any of that, but I seen oftentimes how big the ears was on a bat and it made sense that they had got to be useful for something. I guess the drudge just kept its ears somewhere private.

"They're staying a lot further back," Ursala said, "but they're keeping pace with us. And that's very bad, because it means they're not using line of sight. They've got some other way of keeping track of where we are."

"Maybe they've got bat ears too," I said.

Ursala turned to look at me, like she couldn't believe I come out with something so stupid. I forgot for a moment that she couldn't hear what Monono said to me. "I mean, maybe they've got a thing that's like your sonar. We know they've got tech of their own that makes fire."

"Thank you, Koli. My first guess was that they must be using magic, but your suggestion makes much more sense."

"Ignore her, Koli-bou," Monono said. "She's just crabby because she can't think of a way out of this."

I couldn't think of one either. If the waked forest had not put the Half-Ax soldiers off our track, it was hard to think of anything that would.

Ursala looked at the mote controller some more, and pointed a way. We followed her off the path that we had been following and into a stand of trees. The trees was big and old, and though they was not going to move on us in this weather it still felt wrong to be in the thick of them. Like as if you was surrounded by wild dogs that was asleep, and you knowed if your foot come down too heavy they was all going to wake and be on you at once.

"Could we go another way?" I asked in a low voice.

"We're going this way," Ursala said. "Every little helps."

I suppose she was still hoping them Half-Ax people might be tracking us some other way than with a sonar. If they was following the tracks we left, then the piled-up leaves in the deep woods would take much less of a dent from our feet than the mud on the path.

There was things moving in that leaf-mould though, all waked by the rain and minded to feed. A snake reared its head up right in front of us. It wasn't a mole snake but something bigger, as thick around as a growed man's thigh, its scales all the same browns and golds and reds as the leaf-fall. Its mouth opened wide and wider still, like a flower does when the daylight comes, only a flower does it slow and this was real quick. I knowed the snake was using its tongue to feel for the heat of us, so when it struck it would strike true.

The drudge struck quicker though. It stomped forward and trod the snake under, planting one of its heavy feet on the snake's head and squashing it down into the soft ground. The snake's tail end thrashed and twisted for a few seconds before it died, making a lot more noise than was good. A whole swarm of needles come running down the trunk of a tree beside us, drawed to the sound and to the smell of blood. They ignored us and went straight to the dead snake, but we got away from there right quick in case they went for us next. When I looked back, the snake was mostly a long rope of clean bone, with just one or two of the smaller needles still nuzzling in between its ribs for the last scraps of flesh.

The deeper we got in among the trees, the more things I seen moving there. Tree-cats was watching us from up in the branches, and trappers from their big webs down close to the ground. I didn't think the tree-cats would bother with us. They mostly feed on smaller beasts if such is available. The trappers, though, would jump on anything that offered, and once their spiked jaws closed on you there wasn't no easy way to open them. We had just got to stay clear of the webs, and hope the rain kept the spiders from chancing out too far from the root tangles where they mostly liked to hide.

I thought we would come out of the trees by and by, but there was no end to them. It was not a stand or a copse we was in after all, but a big forest like on the slopes of Calder. Then in among the trees I gun to see walls and the tumble-down remains of walls, and more of them marks I told you of before that I knowed now was messages left over from the old times. Under our feet, in among the roots of the trees, there was bricks and stones, broke-off bits of slate with the worked look of shingles that had fell off a roof, and pipes of metal like the ones we used in Mythen Rood to carry water from the stand-tank down to the trough.

The rain was still as heavy as before, but the wind had died down a little. I was thankful for that. I would still be soaked right through, and chilled right through, but at least I would not have them cold, stinging drops throwing theirselves into my face with each step. It seemed to me like we was making better speed, but if we was then it still was not enough for Ursala. Ever and again, she looked at the mote controller and told me in a low voice that we had got to go faster.

"They're still behind us then?" I asked her. I looked back, but I seen nothing there.

"Behind us and on both sides of us."

I wondered at this somewhat. The Half-Ax fighters had lost at least one of theirs when the forest waked. I seen that with my own eyes. What was it that made them come on after us in spite of that? Shunned men was knowed to eat the people they catched, which was why they was shunned, but these was men and women swore to the Peacemaker, who was kind of like the king of Half-Ax. He would not of told them to hunt people down for the meat that was on them, and what else was they hoping to get from us?

It come to me soon enough. We had something to offer that was a lot better than fresh meat. We had the drudge. They must of seen that precious tech and made up their minds to take it. No doubt if they brung us down they would take the DreamSleeve too – and Monono along with it. My stomach turned over and over at that thought. I did not have much of a gift for fighting, but if it come to it I decided I would fight until I was dead to keep them from taking the DreamSleeve from me. I had promised to hold Monono safe from Ursala, if Ursala come after her. I would not do no less if strangers tried.

The trees did not get fewer, nor further apart, but there was more and still more walls in between them as we went. And I guess that was how we come into Birmagen, or what was left of it. It's fair to say that it was not what I was expecting to see. I was thinking a city had got to be reared up higher, with buildings as big as Mythen Rood's Rampart Hold everywhere. We had not seen nothing like that so far.

And we was not going up, but down. The paths that we was finding took us among the roots of the trees and then into a kind of cut that run down under them. There was earth walls rising up around us, sometimes with the roots binding them together and sometimes with metal pipes running along them, or pipes and roots all weaved each into other. It was kind of like we was going into a tunnel almost, which made me think of the narrow little space where Senlas's people put me, in the big cave where he lived. It was not a thought that made me any happier.

"Is this what cities was like?" I asked Ursala, for it was not the way I seen them inside my mind.

She shaked her head. "The city would have been up above us," she said, keeping her voice low. "Most of it anyway. They tunnelled a long way into the ground, Koli, to make room for pipes and cables and foundations and a lot of other things. But all of those structures were fragile, and the weight of what was up on top of them was considerable. When the buildings fell, some of the streets fell too. We're walking through a space that would most likely have been a sewer, or perhaps an underpass of some kind. Imagine a roof, way over our heads, and all the people moving on top of that roof."

I tried to imagine it, but I couldn't. The closest I could come was to see all them people floating in the air. I didn't like that thought at all. It was too much like Senlas's talk of angels and

Heaven, which was lies as well as nonsense and settled like poison in the heads of them that followed him.

But there was better reasons than my imaginings for not wanting to be down in the cut. If them Half-Ax fighters come along while we was in there, they could pen us in and fire down on us until we was dead, and we wouldn't have no answer to give. I was glad when we come up again at last, climbing a kind of a hill that was made of old tumbled stones half-lost in moss and dirt and scrubby weeds.

It was hard going, the stones being slick and treacherous. We took it slow. Halfway up, I trod on something that broke with a loud crack, and Ursala give me a warning look. I looked down, thinking to see a twig there under my feet, but it was not that at all. It was a bone as long as the bone in a man or woman's arm that goes from the wrist to the elbow.

Maybe I should of wondered at that, but I didn't. I only thought that some animal had made a kill there, and this was what was left of it. There was no need to worry, since the bone was browned and had moss on it in places. It was not fresh, by any means.

We come to the top of the slope. I had purposed to rest there for a moment, but Ursala was still hurrying along and I pressed on behind her, over the hill and down again, into a place that was different again from what we seen before.

There was still some buildings left here, or at least parts of them. There was walls that was still standing anyway, ragged at the top like broken teeth, the tallest of them higher than any house in Mythen Rood. Between us and the walls there was a sprawl of earth in which nothing growed, though dead leaves had drifted in and lay thick against anything that was still standing. That open space must of been a street once, for the walls that was left was laid out in a line on either side of it. And there was cars on it, like the one we seen before, all crusted with dark green moss and yellow mould. Leaves had piled up high around them, but mostly you could still see the tops of the wheels, and imagine them all rolling along the street like so many barrows with nobody pushing them.

Birmagen took shape in front of me a little bit at a time
The walls.

The holes in the walls where windows had been, that made it seem like the walls had eyes and was watching us.

The cars, like animals that was grazing all quiet and might scatter if we moved.

The posts – of wood and metal both – set here and there along the street, some of them towering high over our heads but most of them broke off short or lying along the ground.

The dead leaves, brown and yellow where they was deepest, bleached white in between.

The black, black earth, with no weeds peeping through, but only the pale nubs of mushrooms.

Only they was not mushrooms. They was bones. Not animal bones neither, but bones of people. And the white between the drifts of leaves, that was bones too. Bones was lying in some of the cars, and all around them, like people had laid theirselves down there to sleep and died before they waked.

It was the rain that fooled my seeing. The rain, and there being so very many bones as there was. I had lived in a village of two hundred souls, and that had seemed like a great plenty to me. I seen that many again, or near to it, in Senlas's tunnel. But there was more people lying dead before me now than I ever seen alive. More, and more, and more still, wherever I turned my eye. The ground of Birmagen was not good for weeds or flowers or trees to root in, so far as I could see, but it was rich enough for this one awful harvest.

Ursala turned round to look at me. I was not walking any more. It seemed like I had forgot how to do it.

Ursala said something to me, and I think Monono did too, but the words did not come through. I took a step back. Just the one. All I wanted was to be a little further away from what I was seeing. But then something broke under my heel, and I knowed what it was, and I couldn't look down.

While I was all froze up like that, the Half-Ax fighters come into view a long way down that street. They was not facing us at first, only walking across the street in front of us, sideways on to where we was standing. But then one of them turned and seen us. He give a yell and pointed. Then they was all running towards us.

We didn't have no choice but to run away. The drudge didn't have no bullets left, and we was not so stupid as to think we could prevail with knives against arrows. Anyway, running was what I most needed to do right then. I think I might of done it even if there wasn't no need.

I give a yell. I think I did. And I turned on my heel.

I run back into the trees, where there was a million things that could sting me, bite me, claw me or swallow me whole. I didn't care about any of that. I didn't even think about it.

My mind switched off, like Monono's mind when the DreamSleeve run out of power, and I was gone.

14

I guess that was the stupidest thing I ever done in my life. It is not easy to say though, for there is lots of stupid things to choose from. I wasn't watching where I put my feet down, nor using the catcher's walk, nor trying to be quiet at all. I was just running headlong – and I losed sight of Ursala before I had gone a hundred yards.

Sometimes, though, a fool bumps into the good fortune that a wise one walks around. Nothing jumped on me, nor flew down at me, nor reared up at me. Or if they did, then they missed their mark and I didn't see them. I just kept running.

It was Monono who made me stop. She had been shouting at me the whole time, but the silence of the bones had sunk into me too deep for me to hear her. In the end, she give me a quick blast of the personal security alarm, which made me clap my hands to my ears with a yell.

The shock was good though, for it brung me back to myself. I looked around, blinking my eyes like a man who has just waked up out of a dream. There wasn't nobody else to be seen, and nothing was moving anywhere around me.

"I think you lost them, Koli-bou," she said. "For now, at least.

And I think you'll break your neck if you keep on the way you're going."

"Monono!" I panted. "They was . . . there was dead people there. So many of them! Did you see?" You would think I would be more worried about the Half-Ax fighters, but right then it was only the bones I could think about.

"The baa-baa-san warned you what was there, little dumpling. And it all happened a long time ago. She told you that too."

"She told me. But . . . but I didn't know."

It was all I could say, though it did not come close to explaining the terribleness and surprise of it. In the forest, when Monono told me what the marks of the old times meant, I had felt like there was voices speaking all around me. What I seen in Birmagen was kind of the opposite of that. Silence had spilled out of the bones and into me, and it filled me up until it seemed like there wasn't no room for anything else.

I had not ever thought there could of been so many people in all the ages of the world. Knowing that there was, and that they all had died at once in a fire that come down out of the sky, that they couldn't run from or hide from . . . well, I can't put into words what it felt like, but it was more feeling than I could rightly manage all at once.

Something else happened to me as I was standing in the forest trying to force all that sadness and fearfulness back down inside me again. I guess some things come to be real for me that had only been stories up until then. Way back when people was in charge of the world, this was what they done to each other. Birmagen didn't die on account of babies not thriving. It died because of things that people decided on, and caused to be done. It died because of people hating other people enough to kill them.

You're probably shaking your head in wonder at how stupid I was. Hadn't I been brung up on tales of the Unfinished War, and hadn't I seen the weapons of that war my own self? The tech we used in Mythen Rood, the firethrower and the cutter and the bolt gun, was made by people to be used on people, though we did not use them so. And on Calder, at the river crossing, I had met a tank – a great metal wagon, that talked and moved all by itself. The tank was the biggest thing I ever seen that was made by people excepting only houses, and it was a weapon. All it could do was kill things and break things down, with a gun that was so big you couldn't make your fingers meet around the barrel of it.

But in spite of all this, I hadn't never really thought about what it meant. I had let my mind stay out on the edges of it, where there was heroes and great doings and nothing of blood or hurt to be seen. I knowed that lots of people died in the Unfinished War, and that it was a great wonder and a great folly. Now I seen for myself what it meant when something like a war touched a place where people lived. And I marvelled at my own ignorance, that I never put it together like that until I was showed it.

"Koli," Monono said. "You've got to reconnect with the baa-baa-san and the drudge. You're not safe out here by yourself."

I knowed that well enough, but I couldn't make my steps turn back towards the street of bones. I sit down instead on a rock that stood out of the sodden leaves like a fish rearing its head up out of a pond to grab a bird that's going by.

"Monono," I said, "can you tell me what happened there? In Birmagen? Is it something you got in your memory?"

"There was a war, dopey boy. But when wasn't there? I can give you the edited highlights. Later though. Right now you go back to the baa-baa-san and her super-powered robot, before the big, bad wolf comes along and eats you up."

"Wolves don't eat people all that much. I'm more likely to get et up by mole snakes or needles."

"Figure of speech, Koli-bou. Now get moving. Don't make me spank you."

I got up on my feet again. I knowed she was right, and I had got to go, even if I didn't want to. When I looked around though, I seen there was a problem with that. I had run a long way, and it was not in a straight line by any means. I wasn't sure which way to go to find Ursala, still less how to do it without running into them that was chasing us.

"Koli . . ."

"I'm lost, Monono," I told her. "Give me a breath or two to get my bearings."

"I'm your bearings, little dumpling. Turn around slowly, and I'll tell you when you're on the right track."

I gun to turn in a circle. When I was about halfway done, Monono told me to stop. "That's not the way you came," she said, "but it's where I'm reading the drudge's transponder, so it's the quickest way."

It might of been. I never got to find out.

I took two steps in that direction, but I never took a third. A woman stepped out from the trees right ahead of me, and a man from off to one side of her. The man was holding a bow with an arrow already in the string and aimed at me. The woman had something scarier still. She was the same woman I seen in the woods, and she was carrying the metal tube that spit out fire-flowers. Her face was dead calm, like she was lost in a thought that didn't have me in it at all.

Both the woman and the man was in them grey clothes, with a splash of red on the chest. It was the same clothes exactly on the both of them, as if they was twins and wanted to let everybody know it. They could of been twins at that, for they was of a same height, the woman being one of the biggest and strongest-looking I ever seen, and they both had the same yellow hair, cut short, though his was not up in spikes like hers was.

"If you want to burn," the woman said to me, "go ahead and move. You want to live, you stay where you are."

It was not a hard choice.

15

The rest of the woman's people come out of the trees then. There was nine of them in all, which I knowed by counting en-ten-tether-pen on my fingers like my mother taught me for counting cords of wood, or days in the steeping trough. They was all alike in grey, with their hair cut short in the same way, so I guess there was a rule that they had got to look like that. I was sure it could not of been an accident.

The woman talked to her people with her hands, which was a thing we used to do in Mythen Rood if we was on a hunt and didn't want to startle what we was hunting. It didn't make me happy to see that, since what was being hunted here was me.

Two of the grey people come over and searched me to see if I was carrying a weapon, with a third one pointing an arrow at my face in case I took it into my head to run away. Now they was so close, I seen what the red was on the front of their clothes. It was a kind of a badge, bright and shiny, all forged out of metal and painted up bright as anything and pinned on there. It was made in the shape of a woodman's hatchet.

The Half-Ax fighters took my knife. Then they found the DreamSleeve in its sling, and brung it out. My gut twisted and a rush of fear and hard anger went through me. I almost tried to fight them, only I knowed well enough they was ready to kill me if I even moved. The onliest chance I had of getting Monono back was if I was calm now and come up with a plan later.

The man who found the DreamSleeve brung it right over to the big woman, who took it from him and looked it over in her turn. She knowed it was tech right away. There wasn't no disguising that.

"Well, now," she said, looking me in the face. "What does this do?"

"It plays music," I said.

"Don't lie to me, boy."

"I'm not lying. That's what it does."

"Tell me how to work it."

I was not going to do that if I could help it. "It's broke," I told her. "It took a real whack when we was running in the forest yesterday. A branch hit it, full on. Now I can't get it to work."

The woman's mouth twitched down. I could see she didn't believe me — not about what the DreamSleeve was for and still less about it being broke. "I guess we'll see about that," was all she said. She tucked it into a pack she weared on her belt. There was a knife tucked in the other side that looked wicked sharp. I would not of thought anyone who had that fire-gun would need a knife to fight with, but maybe she only had a small number of the silver slugs for it to fire. Maybe they was all used up. I hoped that was true.

She turned to the man next to her — the one who come out of the trees along with her, and had yellow hair like hers. "Yerrin," she said, "you take charge of him. Keep him alive for now. We might need to use him later."

Them words made my spirits sink more than a little. I knowed these was not shunned men that would of cooked me and et me as soon as look at me. They was servants of the Peacemaker from Half-Ax. But Half-Ax was knowed to have become a savage and unfriendly place. Maybe they was not so fussy as they used to be about what they et.

The leader turned and walked away without waiting to see if what she said got done. It did though, and with great speed. The man she called Yerrin told the two that had searched me to tie my hands, then to search me again in case I had got anything stowed in my boots or underneath my clothes. They jumped to it. There was nothing there to be found, but if there was, they would not of missed it.

"Keep up," the man said to me. "And don't open your mouth. First word loses you an ear."

We all set off after the woman, though most of the time we was not close enough to see her. The nine of them moved in a line, but it was a long line with breaks in it. I guess they had their reasons for that. They would look like they was less than they was, which is a useful thing, and if any of them run into trouble the rest could close in on both sides and give the trouble back to them that was offering it.

They did come together from time to time though, and while I never seen no signals given, yet it seemed to be a decided thing when it happened. One time they stopped to eat. Two of the nine went on watch without needing to be told. The rest shared out rations that they finished in a few bites, washed down with a swig of water from a shared canteen. When they was done, the two guards was relieved and got to eat in their turn. They did not waste no food on me, nor even look at me.

They also closed up when they was about to change direction, or when the leader was looking to give her people new orders. One of the nine – another woman, and maybe the youngest of them – was a tracker, and on these occasions she was knelt down on the ground, looking at tracks. I did not doubt they was my tracks, and Ursala's and the drudge's from when we come this way earlier. The drudge's heavy feet left marks that was easy to spot, even where the leaves was deepest.

We was coming into Birmagen again. I seen the same walls, the same pipes and signs. The ground sloped up, and my heart turned over inside me at the thought of going over that hill again into the street of the dead.

Pretty soon we was back among the bones, and there did not seem to be no end to them. Birmagen was a much bigger village than Mythen Rood, just like Ursala had told me. There was not one main street, like we had, but one after another after another as far as I could see. Every so often, what I had took to be a tree or a bush turned out to be a part of a wall that still was standing. I know that sounds strange, but the walls was all covered in moss and mould, with lady's lace and knotweed lodged in the cracks between the bricks, so you couldn't tell until you was close up that the walls was made things, instead of things that had growed there.

The bones was even more plentiful here. I tried not to look at them, but that was a wasted labour. Everywhere I turned my eyes, there they was. The ones lying out on the ground had mostly been worried by beasts, and partway et. The ones inside the cars was oftentimes whole. It looked like the people had hid in there when the bombs come, or whatever bad thing it was, hoping to be saved. But their hopes hadn't helped them, the war hadn't spared and if they sent up a prayer then there had not been nobody listening.

"Be brave, Koli-bou," Monono said to me on the induction field. "We'll get out of this. We've just got to pick our moment." That give me some heart, which I truly needed right then.

By and by, we come to a corner where the leader and the rest of her people was waiting for us. She had her fire-gun in her hands, ready to give fight if it was needed, but she didn't look as if she expected it would be. "Kilia says they come through here twice," she said to Yerrin. "With any luck, they want to get this one back." She nodded at me. "If they do, they may stay close."

"Worth cutting him a little?" Yerrin asked. "Make him scream, maybe bring them out?" There was nothing on his face or in his voice to show what he thought about this. He was asking the leader to tell him what to do, not offering her no opinions of his own.

"Not yet," the leader said. "Give them enough rope to hang themselves with. We'll camp in Skull-Face and read the scope in the morning. If they're stupid enough to stay close, we'll set a trap then." She turned her head. "Kilia."

"Yes, Captin," the woman that was their tracker said. Captin was what I heard anyway.

"You and Tevi go on ahead and blaze the way for us."

The tracker and one of the men went running off without another word. The rest of the party, and me too, followed on a little slower.

When a hare hopped out from between two cars, Yerrin nocked an arrow and brung it down with one shot. He give it to a woman who already had another hare and a brace of pigeons slung over her shoulder. I took some comfort from that. The more game they catched, the less likely it was that they would need to eat me.

I wondered at their skills, and their not being afraid of nothing around them. These people was used to moving quick through the wild and living off it as they went. I wasn't sure hunters from Mythen Rood would of done so well. Certainly they would not of gone so far.

We walked on at a fast pace for an hour or more while the city growed up around us like a forest. There was still no whole buildings, but the walls rose ever higher. The hills in between was more tumbled walls than grass and earth, as if the ground was vomiting up brick and stone out of its dark heart.

The chill, wet day was falling into a chill, wet twilight by this time. It was getting harder to see, but we pressed on. Then of a sudden, when I looked up, I seen something ahead of us that near to made me piss myself just from looking at it.

It was a skull the size of a mountain, lying square in our way. A skull with just the one eye, huge and round.

16

I stood still where I was, my own mouth as round as a full moon. I could not of gone a step further if there was a knife in my back.

That skull was the scariest thing I ever seen. I couldn't tell what kind of beast it had been when it was alive. It didn't seem to me that anything so big could ever of moved on the Earth. There was a nose-hole underneath the eye, and a gaping, toothless mouth under that. The shape of the skull was all round and soft, like something halfway melted. But the worst thing was that it was breathing. In the cold air, hot breath puffed out of its mouth.

"Keep moving," Yerrin said. He put a hand to my shoulder and pushed me.

"It's . . ." I said. "It's a . . . It's . . ." I didn't have no other words that would come.

"It's not anything that can hurt you." He pushed me again, and this time I went forward. But with my eyes all on that huge great face, I tripped over a stone and went down. Two of the Half-Ax people hauled me up again, and one of them give me a cuff across the head as if I done it on purpose. It didn't make no difference though. I still could not keep my eyes off that thing, nor make my legs move any faster towards it. The leader had talked about

Skull-Face before. I didn't doubt that this was Skull-Face I was looking at now.

It didn't get no less strange, nor less terrible. When we was a little closer, though, I seen that it was not a real skull but a building of some kind. It had got to be, for it was joined to other things further away that was walls of weathered and broken stone. People of the before-times had made this thing. I could see the edge of another wall through that big, round eye socket. Another step, and I seen piled-up bricks and rubble just inside the mouth where the breath was still puffing out.

A kind of a shiver went through me then, as I let go of the idea that I was looking at something that had once been alive. I wondered now at my own foolishness. From close up, the building did not look so very much like a skull at all. It didn't have the smoothness or the whiteness of bone. There was circles of metal all creeping up the outside wall, hundreds of them, moss-crusted now but they must of shined like suns when they was first put there. There was old marks too, set on a rusty metal bar across the side that was closest to us. They was made out of wires, so they was not easy to see at first. They looked like this:

SEL RIDG &Co
BIRMI AM BUL R NG

Kilia, the woman that was the Half-Ax people's tracker, stepped out through the skull's mouth-hole that was level with the ground we was walking on, and give a sign to the others to come. They went, and I went with them, though I still misgived more than a little to do so.

When we was inside at last, I seen there was a fire lit there in the middle of a field of rubble and weeds. The smoke of it was what I had seen drifting out of the skull's mouth and mistook for its breathing.

It was a good place to camp. There was a stone floor, and parts of it was clear of weeds and bushes. You was not like to sit down on a mole snake nest or stick your foot into a trapper's web in the dark. Up on the walls on all sides there was ledges that was really bits of floor where upstairs rooms once was. This was a fortress of the before-times, shaped like a skull so as to frighten anyone that come against it.

The Half-Ax people took off their packs and set them down around the fire, though they kept their bows and knives by them. Two of them skinned and gutted the game they had catched, and then set about to cook it on the fire, on spits made out of sharpened sticks. The leader and Yerrin went off by their own selves a little way and talked. The rest of them was quiet for the most part, though they hand-talked from time to time to say "give me a drink of water" or "move your leg out of my way" or whatever it might be.

I was set down right in the midst of them, where they could watch me. They didn't make no move to untie my hands, nor they didn't offer me none of that water. I was somewhat parched now, and almost asked for some, but I remembered what Yerrin said about how he would cut off my ear if I speaked up, so I held my peace.

By and by, the smell of cooking meat come to my nose. That got my mouth watering, and the parched feeling went away a little.

Most of the Half-Ax people et their dinner sitting around the fire. Only the leader et by herself. When she was done, she snapped her fingers and pointed to me. Two of her people come and brung me to her, making me kneel down in front of her.

"You can sit," she said after a second or two. I shifted round and sit down, which was a mite more comfortable in spite of how cold the stone was under me.

"Did you get anything to eat?" she asked.

"No."

"Or to drink?"

"Not neither."

She had one of her people, a tall man with skin as dark as mine, bring a canteen to me and hold it to my mouth. I kept on swigging from it until he took it away again. Then she bid him untie one of my hands and give me one of the hare's front legs, though most of the meat was gone from it. She watched me while I et, trying not to let me see how impatient she was for me to be done.

"Tell me about your friends," she said as soon as I set the bone down.

I didn't say nothing.

"There's three of you," she said. "That's too small for a hunting party. I'd say you were wandering faceless, but then you got that machine with you. And you got this." She took the DreamSleeve out of her pack that was lying beside her on the ground and waved it in front of me. I looked away. I couldn't bear to see her hold it, and to know I couldn't do nothing to stop her. Monono was my best friend in the world, and I should of kept her safe but recklessly took her into danger instead. "Faceless don't get to keep such treasures when they're cast out," the Half-Ax woman said. "So what are you then?"

I still didn't speak. She frowned somewhat.

"You know who it is you're talking to?" she asked me.

"I know your name is Captin," I said. "I don't know nothing else about you."

"Captain's not my name. Captain's my rank. Captain Shur Taspill. I'm an officer in the army of the Peacemaker."

Army was a new word to me. It seemed it might be like what we in Mythen Rood called a red tally, which is to say a party that was made up for fighting instead of hunting. There had not been a red tally in my lifetime, nor my mother's lifetime, but Half-Ax was knowed to be an unfriendly place. It didn't trade no more with the villages of Calder, nor swap messages with them.

"So you're in good hands," the leader – Shur Taspill – said to me. "Safe hands. It's true we come after you hard, but you was in the Peacemaker's borders with tech that's rightly his. We're not looking to hurt you, as long as you give it up to us."

She offered up a smile. I never seen a snarl that scared me more than that smile did, for it was a thin lie with bared teeth behind it. There was lots of questions I could of asked Shur Taspill, such as how could we be in Half-Ax's borders when we was so far south? And how could Ursala's drudge, or my DreamSleeve, belong to the Peacemaker, who had not so much as laid eyes on either one of them? But I said nothing. I thought this was most likely a time when listening was worth more than speaking.

"Does the big machine only take commands from the woman, or from all of you?" Shur Taspill asked me.

I considered whether it would help Ursala if I lied about it, but I didn't know enough about what the Half-Ax people was like to do either way, so I still kept my lips tight together.

Shur Taspill smiled again. This time it was a real smile, but it still was not warm. "Brave lad," she said. "You want to be like a soldier and make me pull the words out of you with blows or blades. But that's a kind of courage that only lasts until it's put to test."

She took my hand – my left hand that was freed up so I could eat – and bent the pointing finger back on itself. I wasn't expecting it, and I didn't know what she was doing. I only looked at her in surprise, that turned into panic. Then the pain come of a sudden so I yelled out loud and pulled away. Tried to pull away, I should say. Shur Taspill turned her back to me and pulled me in against her shoulder, her grip so tight on my arm I couldn't move it. I thought my finger was being ripped right off my hand, the pain was so bad.

"What is it then?" Shur Taspill asked me, still pressing and pushing on the finger. "Who does the iron horse jump for?"

"I – I ain't saying!" I gasped.

"Yeah, you are."

The pain got too big for just my finger or my hand, and kind of exploded all through my head, like a big light with a crunching, grinding feeling set in the middle of it. I screamed.

Shur Taspill shifted her grip to the next finger along. "Who tells the horse what to do?"

"Ur-Ursala!" I gasped. "The older woman that's with me! It answers to Ursala! Ow! Please! Please!"

Shur Taspill let go of me and nodded to the tall man that was still standing near. He come in quick to tie up my hand again. I could feel that my pointing finger was still there, when my thumb touched against it, but it wouldn't do nothing I asked of it. It was broke, and could only hang there and hurt.

I sunk down on the ground somewhat, with my head spinning and my stomach rebelling against me. There was tears running down my face that shamed me somewhat, and to make a bad thing worse I had bit my tongue all bloody.

Shur Taspill nodded, satisfied, like something had been wrong and she had set it right. "So now you know you don't have a soldier's courage in you," she said. "Answer my questions, quick and honest, and there'll be no need for me to hurt you more. If you lie to me though, or make me work for it, it won't be a finger I'll break next time but something you can less easily spare. Do you understand?"

Since this was a question, I made haste to nod. I didn't want no more of me to be broke.

"What about this?" Shur Taspill says, tapping the DreamSleeve's window with the ball of her thumb. "Just a toy, you was claiming?"

I shaked my head, gulping back tears. "Not a toy. An entertainment. A – a console. It plays music of all kinds, louder than anything you ever heard. It's like there's a hundred people in there, with drums and pipes and bells and all the rest of it."

Shur Taspill looked over my shoulder and hand-talked to one or other of her people. I guess she was still ordering and deciding things the whole time we was talking. By and by she turned her attention back to me. "All right," she said. "How do you make it play?"

"It's broke," I said. "Like I told you."

"Still. I want to see how it's done."

I wondered if maybe she would give me a way out of this without meaning to. If she once put the DreamSleeve in my hand and Monono sounded her alarm, there would be a moment or two of confusion and panic. I could try to run before they figured out what was happening.

"My hands is tied," I said.

"And they'll stay tied. Tell me what to do and I'll do it."

"Tap the screen three times," I said. That would not do nothing at all, but I had got to say something.

Shur Taspill tapped with the tip of her finger. The window stayed dark.

"DreamSleeve," I said, "activate. Wake up and acknowledge."

"I'm right here, Koli-bou," Monono said in my ear. "Use my name if you really want me to answer you."

"DreamSleeve," I said, "accept user. Acknowledge. Play a song."

Nothing happened, except that a tree-cat shrieked somewhere nearby. That was not a noise that anyone would mistake for a song. "You see?" I said to Shur Taspill. "It's broke."

She tucked it back in her pack. "We've got enginers in Half-Ax who'll get it working again soon enough," she said. She reached out a hand and touched my chin, her thumb sliding between my lips and pushing down so my mouth opened. She looked at my teeth long and hard, the way a drover looks at the teeth of a horse.

"You're not sick," she said by and by. "Or stupid or weak. Half-Ax needs young people like you. Tell me something to give me an advantage over the woman when we catch up with her tomorrow, and you could find yourself a new home."

I was not expecting such an offer, and I didn't have no use for it. I had already let them take the DreamSleeve away from me, and I hated myself for doing it. I wasn't going to give Ursala up to these people on top of that. I might not have a soldier's courage, like Shur Taspill said, but there's other kinds besides and I found some then.

Shur Taspill's offer had give me an idea though. "You'd take me in?" I asked, like I was surprised and excited at the thought. "You'd make me a Half-Ax man?"

"I'd put it to the Chamber," Shur Taspill said. "And give it my recommend. I'd be surprised if that didn't carry it."

I ducked my head down, then raised it up again. I was trying as hard as I could to look like a man who was doing something bad and feeling bad for the doing of it. "Well, then," I said, "there's something I can tell you, I guess."

Shur Taspill nodded as if she had knowed it all along. "Go on."

"There's a place where we was supposed to meet if we got split up. I can take you there."

"Tell me where it is."

"I don't know the name of it. It's just a place we both know about. It's north of here. About four miles or so."

We locked eyes for a long time. Shur Taspill was trying to read me, and I was trying not to be read. "You think your Ursala will go to this place?" she demanded.

"I know she will."

"Even though you've been going south all the time we've been tracking you?"

"Even so."

Shur Taspill chewed that over. She might not like the taste overmuch, but she didn't spit it out. "How long will she wait then?"

"Not more than a day. But that's plenty of time for you to get there."

Shur Taspill stood up. "Tomorrow then," she said. "If we find her where you said, you're a son of Half-Ax – like as if you'd been born there. If we don't, you're dead."

I nodded. That was all I wanted, and all I could hope for. There wasn't no such meeting place, but I would pretend there was – and while we was walking north, away from Ursala, I would find or make some chance to grab the DreamSleeve back from Shur Taspill and run away. If they catched me again, I would not be in a worse case than I was now.

Shur Taspill left me where I was and went to talk some more with her people over by the fire. She set sentries, like you would expect, at the door and up by the big window that was the skull's eye. And she had much to say about who would get relieved when through the watches of the night. There was no particular watch set on me, but my hands was still tied. And in case that was not enough, Yerrin tied my ankles together, then looped the rope over

110

his own wrist. There wasn't no way I could move without him knowing about it. I did not complain. At least I was by the fire now.

"Hey, Koli-bou," Monono whispered to me after a little while. The DreamSleeve was still tucked into Shur Taspill's belt, but the induction field had a long reach. "I know you can't answer me, and you shouldn't try. But we're going to get out of this. While they're chasing the baa-baa-san all over the map, there'll be plenty of chances for us to break out. Just you get your beauty sleep now so you'll be ready when the moment comes. Because it's going to come. You've got my personal guarantee. And that woman who was so nasty to you is going to wish she'd stayed on my good side."

I smiled at that, and it did cheer me somewhat to be reminded that Monono was with me, and watching over me. I was not so sure that there was a way for me to get out of this, but I would lead Shur Taspill a Summer-dance and make sure Ursala got a long way away. There was no sense in planning anything beyond that.

And if Shur Taspill did kill me, the last thing I would say to her would be this: that I would no more be a man of Half-Ax than I would eat my own shit.

111

17

There was yet some rain in the morning, but it was no more than a drizzle now.

The Half-Ax people et a breakfast of hardtack biscuit, and covered the ashes of the fire with earth so it looked like nobody had ever been there. Yerrin untied my legs and loosed the knot that bound us together. My hands stayed tied.

Shur Taspill didn't eat nothing as far as I could see. She stood off by herself a ways, and done some kind of very slow dance I had not ever seen before, stretching out one arm and then the other, twisting from the hips, balancing on one leg and leaning over, forwards and then sideways. I wondered if it might be a kind of prayer she was offering up, but then it come to me that it was how she eased away the cramps and strains of sleeping on cold stone so she would be limber and ready if anything threatened.

I almost made a run for her fire-gun, but even if it waked for me I couldn't do nothing with it. Not with my hands tied like they was. I decided I would wait for a better chance.

Just as Shur Taspill finished her stretching, the sentry that was up in the skull's eye give a whistle. Everyone looked up at him as he hand-talked what the matter was. Then they looked to Shur Taspill for their orders.

With quick words and gestures she sent them to their places, most of them standing to either side of the big open door through which we had come into this place – the mouth of the skull. They had arrows nocked to their bows, and the strings all tight. Shur Taspill didn't bother with a bow, nor with the fire-gun. She stood beside me, one hand raised up to grip the back of my neck. She drawed a knife from her belt and set it against my middle ribs.

"Don't think of moving," she said, "or of speaking a word. They would both be bad ideas."

I thought we was about to be attacked, either by men or beasts, and I wondered why she didn't just shove me down on my knees and tell me to keep my head down until it was all done. I couldn't get away, with everyone's eyes on the doorway that was the onliest way out of here.

Then Ursala come into view, trudging slowly and wearily as if she had walked a long way. She walked through the skull's mouth and in among the archers, giving them a stern look as she passed by them but not seeming surprised or afraid. I was both of those things in very large measure. I never dreamed Ursala would put herself in Shur Taspill's hands like this. I almost cried out to her to run, but I felt that knife at my side and swallowed the sound. It was too late now at all events. There was nowhere for her to go.

"You can stop there," Shur Taspill called out.

Ursala come to a halt with a heavy sigh, and shrugged her arms. "Very well," she said. "You can see I don't have a weapon. I'm not threatening you or offering you any violence. I'd be grateful if you returned the favour." She looked at the Half-Ax fighters again, all of them still with their arrows ready to fly. They had moved in behind her a little so the way she come was closed to her if she tried to turn around and go back.

"Where's your machine?" Shur Taspill asked.

"My name is Ursala Jannasdaughter," Ursala said, as if she didn't hear. "From Duglas, on Mann's Rock."

"Where's your machine?" Shur Taspill said again.

"Ursala. Jannasdaughter. And you are? We do this right or we don't do it at all. Just because I'm alone here doesn't mean you can scant the courtesies."

Shur Taspill breathed out hard through her nose. "Shur Taspill. Captain in the army of the Peacemaker."

"Thank you," Ursala said. "I left my drudge standing a little way off. I came unarmed, as I already said, and as you can see for yourselves. I'd like to negotiate a trade."

"Would you then?"

Ursala nodded. "Assuming you've got any interest in coming out of this without bloodshed. If we fight, a lot of your people will die."

Shur Taspill laughed – a short, hard laugh, like a bark. "Dying's not a thing to fear or run from," she said.

Ursala tutted impatiently. "It's not to be jumped into like it's a hot bath either. Not if there's another way."

"And what's your other way? Tell me."

"Well," Ursala said, "it's clear that I've got something you'd very much like to have. And the same is true the other way around. So we might just possibly have the basis for a bargain that will satisfy both of us."

Shur Taspill's grip tightened on the back of my neck. "I don't see that you've got much to bargain with right now," she said. "Any command words you got for that tech, I'm confident I can shake them out of you. I've got you, and I've got your boy. What have you got that I don't know about?"

Ursala's lips twitched in a bit less than a half of a smile. "Determination," she said. "And a deadman switch." She lifted her arm, slow enough that it did not look like she had a weapon hid there, and tugged her sleeve up to show the mote controller on her wrist. "This," she said, "is how I talk to the drudge. And we talk in many different ways. Right now, it's monitoring my heartbeat. If I should die, orders I've already given will come into force. The drudge will ride in here and mayhem will ensue. Your grenade launcher might stop it, if you can get a direct hit before it guns you down. Only might though. The metals it's made of were designed to resist extreme heat. And if you have to destroy the drudge to save yourselves, you come away empty-handed. Those of you who come away at all."

I couldn't tell what Shur Taspill was thinking. I couldn't even turn round to look at her face, she had me in such a tight grip. My own thoughts was all in a tangle, like snarled string. Had the drudge made some more bullets by this time? Could it do what Ursala was saying? And if not, why was she saying it? Why had she come in here, and losed whatever advantage she had, when I was trying to give her enough time to get far away?

"So how would you hand over your . . . drudge, is it?" Shur Taspill asked. "You'd need to transfer command to me. And then I'd be free to kill you."

"If you know the tech of the old times," Ursala said, "you'll know that the best of it was designed with the ability to think and decide for itself, even though it's still rigidly obedient to human instructions."

"Some of it," Monono said in my ear.

I had not expected her to speak, and I had forgot for a second about the induction field. I started, and Shur Taspill moved the knife to my throat. "I warned you," she growled in my ear. "I won't be wasting any more words." Then she carried on talking to Ursala as if nothing had happened. "I know what you're talking about," she said. "Go on."

"Handing over control involves giving the drudge a new command word, and then rescinding my own," Ursala said. "When I do that, I'll build in a time delay. The drudge won't respond to the new word – your word – until an hour has elapsed. Until then, it will still obey me and you won't be able to move against me without triggering the legacy commands telling it to defend me.

115

By the end of the hour, I'll be well on my way. You'll never see me again."

Shur Taspill was quiet for a long time. Ursala waited with her arms folded, giving the captain time to think over what she had said. I was chewing on it too, and deciding that I didn't like the taste of it at all.

"Let's say I agree," Shur Taspill said by and by. "How will we manage the handover? I'm not letting you bring that thing in among us while it's still loyal to you."

"I propose this," Ursala said. "Send one or two of your people with me. Two, I think, would work best. I'll give the drudge the instructions I've already described to you, and you'll have witnesses watching me do it. Then I'll tell the drudge to stay where it is and not to intervene unless I'm threatened. One of your people will stay with the drudge. The other will come back here with me to verify to you that I've kept my side of the bargain. We'll complete the handover, and I'll leave. You'll wait the hour out, and then the drudge will be yours. After that, I don't care what you do."

There was another silence. Shur Taspill looked at Yerrin, and though there was no hand-talking between them, I think they come to an understanding, and I think I knowed what it was. Once Ursala give the new command word, the Half-Ax people didn't need to kill her there and then. They could track her, and catch or kill her when the hour was up. They'd do it too, in case she had other riches on her or in case they needed her to teach them what the drudge could do.

I wanted to warn Ursala not to do this, not to trust Shur Taspill or any of her people, but I couldn't say a word with a Half-Ax knife pressed to my windpipe.

"We'll do what you say," Shur Taspill said. "But the boy's hands stay tied after he's set free. And we keep his knife and pack."

Ursala looked from Shur Taspill to me, and frowned. "The boy? You mean Koli there? What's he got to do with any of this?"

There was a kind of a stillness that fell, but maybe it was only inside my head.

"I think I might of misunderstood," Shur Taspill said. "The boy's what I'm offering in exchange for the drudge."

"Ah," Ursala said. "Yes, you did misunderstand. When I said you had something I wanted, I didn't mean Koli. He's a sweet boy, but he doesn't have any intrinsic value outside of that. The trade I'm offering is the drudge for your grenade weapon. Yes or no?"

18

I heard Ursala say this, but it did not make no sense to me right away. There was words in there, like *intrinsic*, that slowed me down. By the time I put them together, and felt the coldness of them down in my stomach, it was too late for me to say anything.

And what would I of said? Ursala didn't owe me nothing after all. We was together mainly by accident because Senlas's people took both of us and put us in the same prison room. An accident's not a friendship, and though I seen her very much as a friend, there was no reason why she had got to feel the same way about me.

The fire-gun was still lying on the ground next to Shur Taspill's backpack. The captain looked down at it as if to check it hadn't moved. Then she looked back at Ursala. "The boy is the best I can do," she said.

"Then I'm sorry to have wasted your time," Ursala said. "I'll bid you good day." She turned round slowly to face the mouth of the skull, making it clear she meant to leave but not giving the archers no reason to fire on her.

"Wait," Shur Taspill snapped.

Ursala turned all the way back again, slow as slow could be.

"This makes the handover more complicated," Shur Taspill said. "If I give my gun to you, what's to stop you from using it on us?"

Ursala rolled her eyes. "Well, I suppose there's common sense. You can unload the gun and give me the ammunition separately in a backpack. In any case, it's the mechanism I'm primarily interested in, not the shells."

"The mechanism?" I heard the hard mistrust in Shur Taspill's voice. She did not much like this surprise. I guess she could of give me up without no trouble if it come to it, but the gun was different.

"I've encountered a lot of ancient technology," Ursala said. "Your gun is unique. It clearly uses chemicals to catalyse an incendiary effect, but the trigger for that process is electronic. Somehow the gun is telling the grenade when to detonate. I assume by means of a modulated pulse on a predetermined frequency. I want to dismantle it and examine its parts. Find out how it works."

"You want to break the gun down in pieces?" Shur Taspill repeated, like she could not believe such a thing.

"Yes."

"So you're happy for me to empty the magazine before I hand it over to you?"

"Entirely."

Another look went between Shur Taspill and Yerrin. He nodded his head, telling her he understood whatever her eyes was saying to him. He was behind Ursala, so she didn't see.

"I accept your bargain," Shur Taspill said. She hand-talked to two of her people, who lowered their bows and fell in on either side of Ursala. "Gull and Tevi will go with you. In the meantime, I'll unload the gun and make it ready for you to take."

"Excellent," Ursala said. She made to turn again, and stopped again, all on her own this time. "Oh," she said, touching her hand to her chin. "Do you have my other little toy? The DreamSleeve?"

"The exchange is what we just agreed," Shur Taspill said with a warning in her voice.

"I'm only asking, Captain Taspill. I wasn't sure where I'd lost it, you see."

"Yes, we've got the silver box. But it's broken."

"Is it? Well, that's sad. But all it was ever useful for was as a distraction, I suppose. A very loud distraction sometimes. I'll be back soon. It will take me about a minute and a half to walk to where the drudge is. Come along, you two. It's this way."

She walked through the ring of archers like they wasn't there. The two Half-Ax people followed her through the skull-mouth and out of our sight.

"Get ready, Koli," Monono said in my ear. Her voice startled me all over again, for she sounded happy. Excited even.

I wanted to ask: get ready for what? There wasn't nothing to get ready for. Ursala had choosed to leave me with the Half-Ax people and get away herself – leaving the drudge to Shur Taspill. I knowed she was a whole lot cleverer than me, but I thought she had made a bad bargain.

And I believe Shur Taspill thought so too. When Ursala was gone, she didn't do nothing to her gun like she said she was going to do. She put her knife back in her belt, which I was glad of, and walked away from me like I wasn't there. "Stand down," she told her people. "We shouldn't have long to wait. Yerrin, set a guard by the door. I don't expect an ambush, but it's best to take no chances. Maybe she's not as stupid as she seems."

"Forty-one, pick up sticks," Monono said. "Forty-two, pick up sticks, forty-three, pick up sticks."

"What are you doing?" I whispered, mightily bewildered. But she couldn't hear me. I didn't have no induction field to get my words to her, the way she did for me.

Yerrin and two others went and stood just inside the skull-mouth. Everyone else slung their bows and sit down again, talking in low voices. I heard the tracker, Kilia, making a joke about how long it takes old women to get anywhere.

"She got long legs though," one of the others said.

"You looking at her legs, Wick? And you just married?" There was laughing all around, and the man who said that ducked his head, blushing and grinning too.

"Seventy-four, pick up sticks, seventy-five, pick up sticks . . ."

Shur Taspill went and got the fire-gun and slung it on her shoulder. But there was something about the hang of it she didn't like. She tugged on the buckle.

"What song has got a nice loud opening, Koli?" Monono said. "Something by Sleater-Kinney maybe?"

I looked down at Shur Taspill's pack, which is where the DreamSleeve was. I must of looked surprised, for Shur Taspill give me a hard stare, then followed where my eyes was looking.

"Oh, I know!" Monono said.

Them words was followed by a grinding, awful noise that stayed in the air for a second. It was like someone was dragging something made of metal across a floor. And there was no mistaking where it come from.

Another metal screech sounded out, even louder than the first. Shur Taspill took a step away from her pack. One of the other Half-Ax fighters snatched up his bow and aimed an arrow at it.

Then the music cut in. I knowed this song well enough. It was "Pandemonic Hyperblast" by Anaal Nathrakh. I think it was a live version, for some of that noise was not music but cheering from the people that was there when Anaal performed it all them years ago.

Monono was playing music of the before-times, and she was playing it loud. Everyone stared at the pack on the ground in wonderment.

"Is that sound coming out of——?" the tracker asked. But she stopped before she got out the rest of her words. An arrow had hit her high up in her chest. She touched the shaft with her fingers' tips, her eyes gone wide with surprise and dismay. Then she sunk down on her knees and fell full-length on the ground.

A second arrow hit a wall, and clattered to the ground. Shur Taspill yelled out "Cover!" and the Half-Ax people all moved at once. The best cover was a part of a brick wall in the corner where the fire had been, and that was where they fell back to. Shur Taspill was in the middle of them, the fire-gun ranging left and right as she tried to figure out where the bowman was that was shooting at them.

The opening words of the song came booming out. It didn't really sound like a song though. The sound was so loud it was like each of them words was a rock that was hitting you in the head. With my hands tied, I couldn't protect my ears even a little bit. I kneeled down in the middle of the big space and leaned my head on my chest, kind of froze up by the deafening din and by the fear and puzzlement of what was happening. If the bowman wanted to put an arrow in me, I was an easy target.

He did not though. He shot another Half-Ax fighter in the shoulder as the guards that was set at the door come running to the sound.

I could see him now. The arrows was coming from high up, so that was where I looked. The bowman had choosed a place on one of them bits of floor way above us. He was down on one knee and firing just as fast as he could fit the arrows to the string.

She was firing. It was not no man up there, I seen now. It was Cup.

Shur Taspill had found her too. She lifted the fire-gun in her two hands and set her cheek to the end of it, sighting along the barrel. Cup must of seen the danger, but she couldn't do nothing about it. All the Half-Ax fighters was firing up at that ledge, so she dared not put her head out now but had got to duck down flat on the ground.

Shur Taspill took aim.

And, of a sudden, catched fire. Flame growed all over her all at once, and splashed out from her to hit the Half-Ax fighters around her. In a second they was shrieking and rolling on the ground, trying to put out the flames. But the flames would not go out.

Shur Taspill didn't scream or make any sound at all. She didn't even burn for very long. It was like she fell in on herself between two breaths. The fire was so hot, it swallowed her whole. There was a shape of her, for a moment longer, outlined in black against the painful yellow-white of the explosion. Then the flames gusted out in all directions and there was nothing left where she had been except a little cloud of black ash rising up on the hot air.

Yerrin tried to rally the Half-Ax fighters, shouting at them to keep on firing. Another volley of arrows went up, and one of them would most likely of found its mark if Cup was still on the ledge. But Cup was racing around the top of the wall now, not shooting no more but just getting some distance from where she had been.

Yerrin turned with her, fitting another arrow to his bow, hauling back the string, pointing the arrowhead at the space in front of her like we was teached when first we went hunting.

I run into him with my head down, knocking him off his feet. The arrow went sailing off to some place I didn't see.

But I tripped and fell too. Yerrin got up first. He grabbed me by the hair and drawed his knife.

That knife blade seemed to hang in the air over me for an awful long time, but I think that was just the way a terrible moment stretches out inside your brain. This is where I die then, I thought. But it wasn't. The drudge come out of nowhere at a gallop. It trampled Yerrin down into the dirt and stones, right next to me. I heard a snap that could of been his neck or his spine, or both at once. Whatever it was, he didn't get up again.

There was three Half-Ax fighters still standing at that point. They all let off their arrows at the drudge, but they might as well of been throwing feathers at a wall for all the good they done. Cup took one more of them, her arrow going right through his throat. The drudge trampled the other two, then went around the big room setting its heavy feet on anything that moved.

It stopped when it come to me though. I guess Ursala had told it not to hurt me.

I should of been grateful for that, I know. And I would be, by and by. Not right then though. There was too much blood and breaking for me to feel anything at all except the waste of it.

19

"I was purposing to run away," Cup said. "I was only following the two of you so I could steal some food off of you. And then I'd be free of you for ever. There wasn't nothing I wanted more than to never see either one of you again." She looked in my face as she said it, like she wanted to be sure I believed her.

This was not a talk we had right away, but later, a fair way south of Birmagen in a place that didn't have no name as far as I knowed – nor no dead bodies in it, old or new. We was camped for the night on the top of a hill with a clear view all round. Ursala had put my broke finger in a splint and give me some medicine for the pain that made me sleepy and fuzzy-headed. I was listening with as much of my brain as was left from that.

"But then I seen you run away, Koli Senseless," Cup said, "and I seen them take you. I couldn't hardly believe you was stupid enough to go off by yourself like that." She grabbed up a branch and poked the fire – hard, like the fire had done her some hurt. "So I decided to stay. Just long enough to get you back safe again. You cut me free in the forest so there was a debt that had got to be paid."

Cup was only talking to me, for Ursala knowed all this already.

Cup had told it to her after she tracked the Half-Ax fighters to their camp inside Skull-Face, and then found Ursala a little way off, about to send the drudge in to rescue me. "Only we come up with a better plan between the two of us."

"I came up with the plan," Ursala said.

Cup scowled. "Who was it walked all the way back to that dead-god-damned forest and picked up the bow from the fighter that died there? Who scaled that wall? And who shot four Half-Ax rangers with four dead-god-damned arrows?"

Ursala allowed that it was Cup who done those particular things.

All of this was still sinking in with me – that the two of them had put their own selves in such danger to bring me out safe, and that they had knowed what they was doing all along. Ursala never meant to leave me, for all them cold words, but only to talk about the fire-gun where Monono could hear what she was saying. That stuff about triggers and pulses was all for Monono's ears, so she would know what needed to be done to explode the slugs inside the fire-gun before Shur Taspill got off a shot.

"What about the men who went out with you to find the drudge?" I asked Ursala.

"The drudge shot them. That was why I told Monono to play something loud, and why I asked for an escort of two. The drudge had cultured exactly two bullets. But I didn't want the sound to reach your captors before Cup made her play. The music was to drown out the sound of the shots, and any warning they tried to give."

I wondered at Ursala's cleverness. When she said the DreamSleeve had only ever been good for a distraction, a distraction was what she was asking for. And when she said how long it would take her to walk to the drudge, she was telling Monono when to start playing.

"It was like a dance, Koli-bou," Monono said. "It's beautiful if everyone knows their moves."

I knowed what she meant, and I wasn't blind to it. You could definitely see what happened as having a good side – I mean, outside of me still being alive. Ursala had talked to Monono, and Monono had listened. They was a lot easier around each other now than they was before. Cup had come back to us, for a while at least. What's more, Ursala seemed happy to trust her now with her hands untied and a bow on her back.

But still there was nine less people in the world than there was yesterday, when we was trying to make there be more.

When I shut my eyes and tried to sleep, them Birmagen skeletons looked back at me. Some of them was wearing Half-Ax colours.

Spinner

20

Disasters take their course, and it's generally the same course every time. I believe I've lived through enough of them to say that and make it good.

They start as a thing you've seen yourself, a thing you've lived through that's in your memory for aye and ever. They're a kind of a scar in your mind. Most likely you've got scars on your body from fights and mischances, and you've seen how hard it is to keep from touching them, ever and again, to see if they've changed or moved or healed any. That's how it is with mind-scars too. That's how it is with disasters.

And because you're thinking of them so much, you keep on telling other people who didn't see them what they were like. Oh, the blizzard Winter, that was a hard thing. Did I tell you how the sheep died on the forward hill? How we thought their wool was just more snow until we dug them out? And yes, and so, and like that.

But the disaster is different for those who didn't see it and live it. It's only a story. A fearsome story, to be sure, that they tell over to each other by their hearths or in their beds or at their workings, but there's no scar to heal. The words take the place of the scar, and the weight of the words falls on each woman and man differently, according to their imaginations.

And then the last one dies who knew that thing and survived it and bore the scar of it. There's nothing to check the story against now. It has to stand by itself, like a fence does. And weeds grow up, and rain warps the wood, and rot grows on it, and to make less of more it falls over at last and there's an end of it.

The red death was in the second of those three places for me. I knew many people who had lived through it their own selves and carried the scar, but I did not. For me, it was a story, and the story went like this: before the red death, Mythen Rood was a village of three hundred and fifty souls. After it, we were two hundred.

So when Shirew Makewell said the marks on Seven Frostfend's face and body looked like the marks that had been left by the red death, the Ramparts and the Count and Seal did not hesitate. They closed off Frostfend Farm with red paint on the lintel and a red rope looped around the gatepost. Food and water would be left at the door for Seven and Hue and their children, but they would stay indoors and nobody else would go near them until it was certain the sickness had passed over. It was hard, but it was needful, and no voice spoke against it.

For a full week, there was nothing more. Shirew went to the house each day and spoke to Hue through the door. She made report to Catrin that Seven yet lived, and nobody else was taken sick. "The red death spread fast and fierce," she said. "Yet Hue and the children have no marks on their flesh and no hint of sickness. I've got good hope this is something different, for all it looks the same."

"We'll keep up the quarant time though," Catrin said. "Another week. Better safe than sorry."

"That would be my choosing too," Shirew said. "They need more nourishing food though. More meat and milk to eke out the bread, and some green things besides. If you make them weak, any sickness there is will have the more chance to take hold on them."

130

"Do you see to it," Catrin said. "You got Rampart authority."

And Shirew hurried away to her work.

Another day, then another, and the news from Frostfend Farm was no different. But sickness struck much closer. Our own Gilly came to Catrin to say that her husband, Raelu, was gravelled with a high fever and a terrible pain in his joints. Like Shirew, Raelu had lived through the last pestilence. He was scarred, not just storied, and he feared what those pains might mean. At the first sign of it, he took himself away to the broken house at the other end of the village, which was empty and abandoned.

"What of his skin?" Catrin asked Gilly when she told us this. "How does his skin look?"

"It's red," Gilly said. "With welts and sores all up his arms and on his shins." Her eyes were red too. She tried not to weep in front of the family, but the fear had sunk deep into her. If Raelu was sick, she and Ban might be next. Vennastins might be next. The plague had made its way in one stride into Rampart Hold.

Gilly asked leave to go join her husband, and Catrin gave it. I stepped in to say that they could stay at the tannery if they wanted to since the broken house offered but little shelter. Gilly thanked me for the kindness, but said she did not think Raelu would be well enough to walk there, and it was better if nobody came by him. She would take the canvas from one of the Summer-dance tents down in the Underhold and make a roof over the two of them.

"I'll fetch firewood then," I said, "and leave it outside the door." Gilly gave me yet more thanks, and made to take my hand, but then remembered herself and went away without touching anyone.

That was a bad time for Mardew to be found. But to be honest with you, not much of him was.

21

The Count and Seal met again, the news being too bad to be hidden. Catrin and Perliu were there for the Ramparts. Haijon was there too, sitting next to me, and Lari on the other side of him. Fer and Gendel stayed in the Hold. Catrin had called them to her as soon as the searchers came back in. We had some inkling from that what the news was, but she had not spoken to us, or to anyone. The first thing she did was to call the meeting.

"Some searchers went as far as Ludden," she told the gathered people. "Cal Shepherd. Sora Marl. Lune Cooper. They found Ludden whelmed and abandoned – a sad thing, but one we've long suspected. But they found something else besides, and you all need to know it. Cal Shepherd will speak."

That was news to me, about Ludden being empty. Going by the murmurs in the room, I think it was news to many. But no one thought this was a good moment to ask about it. Cal stood up. He looked like it cost him great effort to do it. His face was pale, with sweat standing on his forehead. "We went to Ludden, like Rampart Fire told you," he said. "Others had been there not long before us. We saw weeds and branches broke. The door and roof of a house too. There were . . ." He seemed to lose his way, and took a second to find it again. "There was no people anywhere in the village. They all was gone – a long time ago, to judge from how it looked. If this was knowed, or suspicioned, I didn't dream of it. There was no sign that they was attacked. It was more like they just up and went away. There was this one house, though, that had its door broke down, and tiles from the roof was on the ground, shattered.

"The door was not kicked in, but cut in half. And the cut was clean. I only know one thing that could make a cut like that. So then I looked, we all looked, for sign of Rampart Knife. If the cutter was used in Ludden, he must of been there not long before."

Cal paused again. His throat bobbed as he took a hard swallow. "I can't say it," he said. He turned to Catrin, who was still on her feet beside him. "Rampart Fire, you got to forgive me. The words won't come, and I got to sit down."

Catrin put a hand on his shoulder and bid him take his seat. "You done enough, Cal," she said. "Sora, you take it up."

Sora Marl climbed to her feet and walked down to the middle round, that was the centre of the Count and Seal and the place where the Ramparts mostly stood. She did not look happy to be there. "Like Cal said," she told us all, ducking her head like we might be about to throw stones at her, "we looked around. And we shouted for Mardew – for Rampart Knife – to come out if he was there. If he had been in a fight, we thought he might of gone to ground, and didn't know it was safe to show himself. Or he could be hurt. So we yelled that he should come to our call, or answer us if he couldn't, and then we'd go to him."

She shaked her head, solemn sad. The whole Count and Seal was hanging on her words. The room was so quiet, you'd think we had all stopped breathing.

"We was walking in – in— There was blood there, on the ground, and some broke-off bits of bone, like an animal fed there. Then . . ." She came at last to where she did not want to go, and jumped right off the edge of it in a great rush. "We found Mardew's head. We found his cut-off head, that was lying in the grass there.

After that we searched all around for the rest of him and for the cutter. We found— Rampart Fire has got what we found."

Silence fell again. Catrin stepped in next to Sora, and held up two things for us all to see. One a twisted scrap of metal with a shred of cloth at one end of it. The other I took to be a silver locket on a chain, but it was not that. Catrin opened it up, and I saw it was a compass.

"This compass was made by Wardo Hammer," she said. "He swears it as his own, and it's marked with his sign on the back of it. It was made right here in Mythen Rood, and it had got to be a man or woman of Mythen Rood that carried it. But it was never Mardew's, that his mother and father know of."

She shut the compass up again, clenching her fist tight on it. Her knuckles were white from the effort she put into that. "This other thing," she said, "is what's left of the cutter."

The room that had been so quiet now was full of shouts and cries and curses. Some voices were raised to Dandrake, begging him to show his will or else to strike down Koli Woodsmith, for nobody doubted it was Koli who had done this. It was near certain that Mardew had been on Koli's trail after all, and the compass being from Mythen Rood rang his name out like a bell.

I turned to Jon to say something I can't now remember. He was not making a sound but he was crying, his face all red and twisted up, his teeth bared and clenched together as if he was holding in a scream. Lari was crying too, her fists pressed hard up against her mouth. They were not alone. Tears had broken out all around the room, loud enough to sound out clear over the swearing and the praying.

"I feel what you feel," Catrin said over it all. "Mardew was my kin, just as he was your Rampart Knife. What you've lost, I've lost, and my sister more than anyone. We got to come together now, in this dark time, and we got to rise over this. We got to stand each by other as we've always done."

She was looking at Jemiu Woodsmith as she said this, and her face was set hard. She knew — how could she not know? — that

134

the warning she gave before would not avail any more. There was nothing in store for Jemiu and her daughters but pain and bitterness. They might be shunned. Certainly they would be punished in a hundred ways, both small and great. Catrin could not help them now, even if she still wanted to. Jemiu buried her face in her hands. Athen and Mull might of offered her some comfort, but I didn't see them there.

"We need to find him," someone shouted. "Find him and hang him!"

More voices joined in, either agreeing with that first one or suggesting worse things still. Catrin shook her head, but had to wait a while to make herself heard over that bedlam. "I don't reproach a one of you for being angry," she said, "but anger's not our surest guide right now. If we was to go after Koli, where would we look? Say we start at Ludden. That's already four miles of travel through the forest before we even break the trail. To go there and back is a full day's journey, from first light to lock-tide. The searchers would need to take rations, and brave many nights outside the fence.

"And if they was to find Koli, what would they do? Bring him home to answer his crimes? That's hard. He'll know he's coming to die, and drag his feet as much as he can manage. They'd be as slow as a funeral walk coming back, with enemies on all sides and one sunny day between them and calamity.

"Or say we raise up a red tally, with licence to take Koli and kill him wheresoever they find him. That's a heavy thing to lay on any man or woman, to shed neighbour blood. To look in the eyes of someone they know, and shut them for aye and ever."

"I'll do it!" Jarter Shepherd shouted, and others took up the cry, but Catrin was not finished yet and would not be swerved.

"No," she said. "That you won't, Jarter. We'll not lose any more in seeking Koli Woodsmith. We can't abide it. Not with sickness stalking us and precious tech gone from the village. You won't say it, but I'll say it. Mardew was to blame for going out of gate alone and taking the cutter with him. It was reckless folly. He paid the price for that, and so must we. But it lies where it lies. That price is all the price there's going to be."

Now she paused, but only for a moment. There was a fire in her, and some of that fire was sadness at what was lost. It only made her stronger. "We'll vote it," she said. "Something this big, we'll vote it and I'll bow to the count however it goes. Anyone that wants to speak against me, make free. It's your right to do it. But know this when you speak. If you call for a search, you're either raising your hand to join it or you're pushing someone else to."

She sat down then. And it seemed like nobody was going to stand up after her. But then Jemiu did, her eyes red from weeping and her face pale. A few people called for her to sit down again, but Catrin silenced them with a glare.

"Thank you for that, Rampart Fire," Jemiu said. Her voice was hoarse, but it was strong enough to carry. "I got this to say, though there's nobody here will want to hear it. My Koli didn't do the things that are said of him. Nobody that knows him would believe for a second that he's a thief, or a killer. Some day the truth of all this is going to come out, and all you that are shouting for his blood now is going to be sorry."

"It's you that'll be sorry!" Jarter Shepherd shouted.

"Throw the whole pack of Woodsmiths out of gate!" came from someone else. I didn't see who.

"Try it," Jemiu said. "But come with your knives out when you do."

She turned and walked out of the room. There was some that called bitch and shame after her, and Catrin didn't do anything to stay them. I guess she seen that those feelings had got to come out, and it was better they came out in words than in doings.

We left the Count and Seal at last, but we stayed in the Hold. There were knots of people all over the gather-ground and even on the steps of the house, talking in fierce whispers or hoarse shouts or anything except a normal, civil speech. I did not want to go out into that.

Jon had even less stomach for talk than I did. He went to our room and lay down on the bed. I say our room, but we were still in his. We had not moved into the big room Catrin had decked out for us on our wedding day. Somehow, after that first night of surprise and dismay, it did not seem truly ours.

So it was on the little narrow bed that he had slept in his whole life that Jon laid himself down now. He closed his eyes, and threw his arm over his face to shut out the light.

I stroked that arm, and kissed it, since it barred my way to his lips. "I'm so sorry for what happened, Jon," I told him. "I'm sorry you lost your cousin. I hope you can take some comfort from his dying the way he did, on Rampart business and with his name-tech in his hand."

Jon groaned. "It's not Mardew, Spinner," he said. "It should be, but it's not. I'll grieve for him later, but right now I hate him. If he was standing here before me I'd knock him to the ground."

I was shocked, and could not hide it. "Dead god bless you!" I said. "That's an ungentle thing to say, Jon, and him not even buried yet."

But I knew what he meant, and why he said it. In the course of being lost, Mardew had lost the cutter too. And without the cutter, Haijon was not a Rampart any more.

Nor I was not a Rampart's wife.

22

Two more days. Two more houses with red lines painted over the door. It was Fara Harvest first, and then Grey Olso, who stood on the tabernac alongside me and Haijon.

The day after that, Seven Frostfend died.

Catrin did her best to damp down the fear people were feeling, but there was not much she could do. She did not want to call any more town meetings since it would bring the sick and the well together and might make a bad thing much worse. She went from house to house instead, with me and Lari in her wake, leaving gifts of flour and cheese from the storerooms in the Underhold and bringing the same message to all. Stay home if your work lets you. Keep a distance where you can. Don't go kissing or touching or breathing each other's breath, for all those things are roads the sickness can take from one house to another.

And pray, if prayer's a thing you lean on.

"Poor Fara!" Ban said to me the day we learned that she was sick. "As if being born blind wasn't bad enough. Dandrake has turned his back on her, for sure!"

My opinion did not sort with hers on that. Fara was blind, yes, but she had never let it get in her way when she had something she needed to do. She carded wool for her bread and meat, and she was faster than anyone I ever saw. Besides that, she had a dog her brother Lock had trained to lead her. It was a strange thing to see a dog leading a person instead of the other way around, but it worked well. I liked Fara very much. I liked that she asked for nothing, and gave more than she got. My own maimed hand had taught me the dangers of letting people pity you – which was a step towards them deciding for you and then discounting you.

But I pitied Fara now, if the red death was in her.

As the days passed, talk of the sickness, of who was struck and how they fared, drove out all other talk. Even Mardew's death and the cutter being gone was put by. We talked of nothing else but the red death. Everyone was much exercised on the score of which one had been with that one, and how they might have touched each other in spite of all the warnings Catrin gave. We watched for the next man or woman to fall, like a cat watches a mousehole.

The next death was not long in coming. It was Fara Harvest. And before we were done with mourning her, Raelu died also. I sat with Ban while she cried it out. Gilly was still in quarant time, so there was nobody else to be with her. Ban sobbed on my shoulder, and her fists were clenched against my side. She cried to the whole cruel world that her father was dead, and her mother shut from her, and nobody cared because they were all thanking Dandrake that the bitter cup was passed from them along the table.

Mardew's head had already been buried by this time. That was done quickly, with not much of ceremony or preparation. Only Vennastins came, because of Catrin's order about not going abroad or touching anyone. In the half-outside, where all our dead are put to rest, a plot was dug that was as long and as wide as a regular body. The head had been sewn into a fold of sackcloth, with Dandrake marks painted over the hollows of the eyes. We laid it in the grave, and Perliu Vennastin led us in prayer. Gendel held onto Fer the whole while. He held her hard, as if he was afraid she might jump into the grave her own self. She was pale and shaking, and making little mewling sounds in her throat that were frightening to hear. There was little that was human in them, besides the grief.

Me and Jon came back to the Hold together, hand clasped in hand, but we did not talk very much. Jon had fallen silent in the Count and Seal when Catrin showed us all the bent and broken remains of the cutter. I had tried a few times to break that silence, but made no headway. He was looking into the future, and what he was seeing there struck him speechless.

"Take me down into the Underhold," I said to him at last. "I want to see the tech again."

He raised his head to stare at me. "Why?" he asked. "What's there?"

"I don't know," I said. "Nothing. Nothing's there. But take me anyway."

He didn't care enough to argue with me. He went and got the key. It was hanging on the hook in Catrin's room since she was out of doors, seeing to the sealing off of Fara Harvest's house. Fara's dog was guarding the door there, and would not let anybody come by. He would have to be dragged away or else killed.

We let ourselves into the little room again, and stood among the treasures just as we'd done before we were married. It hurt my heart to think back to that time, when all these blows were yet to fall on us.

I pointed to one of the dead cutters. "There," I said to Jon. "That one. Try it on."

He didn't want to do it. He picked up the cutter, but held it in his fingers' tips, as if it were something dirty. "Why? It's not mine."

"Put it on," I said again. "Do it, Jon."

He slipped his hand inside. He looked at it unhappily.

"Can you make it work?"

"Of course I can't, Spinner. Nobody can."

"How do you know? Koli took a piece of dead tech and made it sing, and Koli isn't even a Rampart. Say the words."

Jon snatched the cutter off his wrist again and threw it down. "To the dead god's hell with Koli," he said. "I wish he never lived."

I didn't have anything to say to that. I could wish it too, but neither one of us would really mean it. It's hard to hate someone that used to be your friend. Hard to hate them outright, I mean, for there's always something of love mixed in with the hate.

"What was it he took?" I asked. "What kind of thing?"

"You saw it as well as I did, Spinner."

"From a ways off though. I didn't see it clear."

Jon pointed to a lower shelf where there were a lot of little silver boxes, rounded off at the corners, almost as thin as rolled dough. "That's what he took. One of them things."

They didn't look like much next to the cutter – or next to most of what was there. The silver colour was pretty, but they were plain as anything. There was nothing to show you how to hold them or what to do with them. Something like the cutter or the bolt gun was meant to fit to your hand, and you knew just by looking at them where your hand would go. I wondered why anyone, with this plenty pressing on his eyes, would choose one of the little flat boxes.

Unless he knew, before he picked it up, that it would wake for him.

"Did your mother ever tell you how he got it working?" I asked Jon.

"He didn't. It's most likely Ursala did that for him."

"And how did she know?"

Jon shrugged. "Ursala knowed tech; Koli didn't. He was the one broke in and took it, but it was her that whipped him on. That's just obvious."

I stayed quiet on that one. Ursala stealing from us, after so many years of doing nothing but help and tend, still didn't make a shred of sense to me. But it was Catrin's story, and Jon was doing his best to believe it.

Jon was right about there being seven cutters. I made him try every one of them and speak the words of command, just to see. They didn't wake for him. I don't think I believed they would, but I wanted to be sure.

"Are you happy now, Spinner?" he asked me at last. There was a bitterness in his voice I never heard there before.

"Of course I'm not happy," I said. "I'm thinking, is all."

"Thinking what?"

"If there's a way to make this tech wake again after it's been asleep for aye and ever, we should be trying to figure how it can be done."

"I think if it could be done, my ma would know it."

He went outside again and waited with his hand on the door's handle until I came out and joined him. He locked the door and made sure it was shut firm.

But Catrin hadn't known about the tech that Koli took, I thought as we climbed the stairs again. She had looked as surprised as anyone, that day on the tabernac. And if Ursala waked it for Koli, then how could that be the end of it? A thing that could be done once could surely be done again.

You must remember I was only just past my own testing – a woman in name, but still little better than a child in my understanding. I thought a village with seven cutters had got to be seven times as safe as a village with just the one.

What I think now is that all the tools we pick up and use come in the end to use us too. But it took a war to teach me that, and I think it is a telling for a later time.

23

Catrin gave us a day's grace, or maybe two. I think that was kindness in her, but perhaps it was just that it took her some time to find the words. Haijon was her only son, and though she doted most especially on Lari, yet she loved him very dear. It could not have come easy to take away from him both his name and his purpose.

It was the middle of the morning, but we had not yet gone down to breakfast. We had slept late, and woke heavy-headed, as if we had drunk too much wine the night before. We had not touched a drop though. It was the fear and the sadness that muddled our wits and took away our will.

So we woke to hear Ban knocking loud on our door. Rampart Fire was in the music room, she said, and needed to talk to us. She had looked to do it long before, but we had not stirred and now she was tired of waiting.

We dressed in great haste, feeling sullen and ashamed. "Should we eat first?" Jon asked me.

"I think we were best not," I said.

"She knows we got to eat."

"We'll eat after. We made her wait already, and there's other tasks she needs to tend to."

I feared Catrin's anger, is the truth of it, and hoped to take the edge off what was to come by showing myself meek. But when we went downstairs at last and into the music room, she did not chide us. It's true she looked solemn, but there was no fierceness in her face. What there was, I thought, was the hard set of someone who is some way along a bad road and still has got to go a fair piece to reach a turning. She was sitting in a chair by the window, with two more chairs set in front of her for us to take. We sat down, like children at their lessons.

"What is it, Ma?" Jon asked her.

"I think it's time to open up the tannery again," Catrin said. "It's been long enough. Spinner, you said you meant to go back there after your month of honey, and take up your father's work. Do you still hold to that?"

"I do, Rampart Fire," I said, but I said it with a sinking heart. I knew what was coming next.

Haijon stiffened a little when I called his mother by that name. I don't think he had seen until then that the firethrower was propped up against the window, within reach of Catrin's hand. It was not there to be used, nor yet to threaten. It was there because she was speaking as a Rampart and the leader of the Count and Seal. This was no family chatter we were enjoying, but orders being given.

"Good," Catrin said. "Jon, you should go with Spinner and help her. Help will be needful, with the vats all dry and new dyes to be mixed. It can be a share-work for the two of you."

That brought Jon some light at last. Too much, if anything. It came to him all at once, and he blinked as if he was dazzled. "What?" he said. "What now? Speak plain, Ma. Speak sense. What in the dead god's hell is this about?"

Catrin put a hand on his arm, gentle but not so gentle that he could shake it off. "You got to leave the Hold," she said. "The two of you. It don't have to be today, though today would be best. I'm sorry to say it so blunt, Jon. I'm sorry to say it at all, but that's what it is."

Now it was said, I realised I had been waiting for it to come. I didn't know when, or from what direction, but it was of a piece with Catrin's nature that she didn't ask anyone else to break the bad news to us but did it her own self.

Jon stood up, pulling his arm out of Catrin's grip. "This is my house as well as yours," he said.

"No," Catrin said. "It's the Ramparts' house, loaned to each and all of us by the Count and Seal."

And that checked him.

It was a fact that was very easy to forget – and easier for Haijon than for anyone. Rampart Hold was two things at once. It was the place where the Count and Seal met on the first day of each month and in times of need between. And it was the place that had been given to the Ramparts, the leaders and servants of the Count and Seal, to live in.

Somehow, though, in recent times it had become a third thing on top of the other two. The Vennastin family had made it their home.

That had not happened all at once, but by inches and ounces. The Ramparts of times past, when they came to their testing and found their name-tech, took up their belongings and left their families behind them. Going into the Hold was a way of saying they belonged to the whole village now, and would work for all alike, not for this one's gain or that one's but so all would thrive together.

But all our Ramparts, as long as anyone living could remember, had been Vennastins and their pair-pledged kin. Mothers and fathers, sons and daughters, cousins all alike, they had no other home than Rampart Hold. When they were children, they had a right to live with their mothers and fathers. On their testing day, they stood as women and men their own selves, and their future was decided. But that decision went ever the one way – and with every Vennastin that was made a Rampart, the feeling grew that those were two words with but the one meaning.

When Vergil failed his testing, his grandfather Mennen spat in the face of custom and kept him still in the Hold. Heads were shaken and words were said, but there was no formal challenge for Mennen to answer. Vergil was a sad case, after all, and it was thought he would be lost if he did not have his family by him.

When Jon and I were married, by law and right he should have come to me at the tannery, not me to him at the Hold. But Vennastins treated the Hold as their home, and people were used to them doing so. Nothing was said against it.

Now, with Mardew's death, all that was changed. There was no Rampart Knife any more. The cutter was gone, and Jon's name was gone with it. He was Vennastin still, but he was not Rampart.

Another time, I think Catrin would have dug in her heels for her son's sake, but this was the time she had to deal with, and it was in all ways a bad one. Things seemed out of balance. To lean on them further was a risk she chose not to take.

Jon's face flushed red, and he swore by Dandrake's cock and balls he would not go. "We're not shunned men, nor faceless, to be throwed out of doors," he said. "Why is it the Count and Seal's business what bed I sleep in? We'll work the tannery, but we'll come back at night to where we live, and a fart on anyone who says otherwise!"

I put a hand on his arm to calm his temper, but he shook it off. He went out of the room, slamming the door after him. Catrin rose up, and would have followed him, but I stayed her. "I'll talk to him, Mother," I said. "I'll make him see that it's right and needful. Only give us a while alone, until he's calmer."

I had never called her mother before, not having any good memories to set next to that word. It seemed to catch Catrin by surprise a little. Perhaps she thought it was only cunning in me to remind her of our kinship at such a time, when our fortunes were falling. And perhaps it was that, in part. But a part of it too was telling her we would be a family no matter what.

I have said before now that my pretences were oftentimes made into truths. This was another such time. I had set out to make the Vennastins love me so that they would let me be one of them.

Now, when they were casting me out, I felt how deeply my life was bound up with theirs. I had married a Rampart, only to see him turn tanner like my father. But he was still Vennastin, and now I was too — not for the glory of it but for his sake, and for the love we owed each to other.

Catrin thanked me, and I went from her.

Jon was in our room, taking clothes off the shelf and stuffing them into a bag without looking at them. I had thought to soothe him, and talk him round to Catrin's purpose, but he waved the words away as I started in to say them. "It's all right, Spinner," he said, though his eyes were welling up with tears. "I know she's right. It just hurt me to hear it."

I took the bag out of his hand and embraced him. "And your hurt hurts me too, love," I said in his ear. "But we can still be happy."

His head was on my shoulder, heavy with sadness. I kissed his cheek and stroked his hair.

"You married a Rampart," he said. "I'm a lot less than that now."

"No," I said. "You're not, Jon." It shamed me that I had had the same thought only a few minutes before, and I pushed against it all the harder for that reason. "You're who you always was. I made my choice, and it was the best I ever made. There's not one thing I regret, only that something so great was took from you, and that you grieve for it. I'll strive night and day to mend that grief."

"It don't matter what I lose, as long as I get to keep you," Jon said, drawing me closer.

We did not go to the tannery as quickly as I had meant to. We made our daughter there, on that bed, on that day, with the sun shining in the window and the tocsin bell clanging from time to time in a strong north wind. The future rises out of the past like a fountain, and cannot be held back.

24

Grey Olso died two days after Raelu. Six more fell ill with the same signs, including Hue Frostfend and one of his daughters, Getchen. It could not be denied now that what we were facing was no passing thing but a plague that could end us.

Catrin spoke to us all, not in the Count and Seal but on the gather-ground. She bade us keep six paces apart, each from other, unless we lived in the same house and could not keep from being close. She said the sick should go to the broken house. She had ordered, as a share-work, that the Summer-dance tents should be put up there, with food and blankets set by for any to take that needed them.

"We'll only weather this if we're strong, and if we're clever," she said. "Strong is easy. We of Mythen Rood are weaved out of strength the way a basket is weaved out of rushes. Clever's what I ask of you now. Your heart will tell you to be with the one you love if they're took sick. Your head's got to turn and say no to that. You won't help them, and you'll risk your own self. The one you love, if they love you back, they'll send you away with strong words. So don't do it in the first place.

"Make no mistake on this. We've had deaths, and we'll have

more. The dead can't be treated with full respect neither. You all seen the pit we've dug out in the half-outside, right by the grass-grail. Anyone who dies will go into that pit, with no wake and no funeral. Them duties will have to wait on a better time.

"And that better time will come, believe me. Our Rampart Remember is questioning the database every day, sifting the wisdom of the before-times for things that will help us. Every sickness has got a cure. He'll find what's there to be found."

She had the firethrower slung on her shoulder, but now she took it in both hands and lifted it up. "Think on this," she said. "Not on me, and mine, but only this. The handing down, from life to life, from year to year. What's ours is only ours while we hold it, and then we pass it on. We're links in a chain, and that's why we're mighty. Think of the links that was, and the links that's yet to be. We'll get by this. We'll wake one day to find the storm's gone over and onwards. Then we'll pay the dead what's due them. We'll grieve, and we'll give honour. Until then, our business is to keep our own selves out of that pit any way we can."

She spoke well, and she carried her point. The people didn't cheer her, but they went in thoughtful silence off the gather-ground and they kept that distance, nodding farewell each to other as if to say, I'll see you on the other side of this, and good luck to you. Good luck to us all.

Jon and me went from the gather-ground back to the tannery. We had already moved there the day before, but had not had the spirit to do much when we got inside besides light a fire and make up our bed. Now we set to the work of getting the whole place working again.

There was a lot to do. My father, Molo, was a tanner of hides and also a dyer of cloth. I meant for us to follow him in both those things. First, we sorted through the hides we had. Some of them had spoiled while I was living at the Hold, and had to be thrown out, but we had more than two dozen that were still good, including ten whole deerskins.

I had learned from my father three ways of tanning hides – with pigs' brains, with potash salt and with bark broth. I schooled Jon in all three, and took pleasure in it. To teach what you were taught is the very heart of life, and gives you faith that life will hold.

While the hides steeped, we took out the drying frames and set them up, hauling them out into the yard and standing them in rows. Some of them needed repairing. One or two now had birch-mites living in them, and had to be burned. That kept us busy for the rest of the day.

I hoped the hard work would lift Jon's spirits, and it did. We worked side by side, singing or sharing jokes, and the time passed very quickly.

With the last of the light sitting like cold lead in the sky, I called a halt. "That's the hardest part done, Jon," I said. "And tomorrow we'll sleep late. We can't do no more until the hides has finished tanning, which is two days even for the smallest ones."

I was stretching the truth. There was still work to do in the meantime, such as scrubbing out the dying vats, but I did not mean to let that keep us from waking slow in each other's arms.

We went inside and put some water on the fire so we could wash. I let Jon go first, then he cooked eggs and fried potato mash while I scoured the salt and bark tea off my arms and the sweat off the rest of me.

As I was putting my shift back on, a cold wind slapped my back and made me gasp. I knew the front door had opened, and turned to yell at Jon to shut it before I froze.

Perliu Vennastin stood in the doorway. I put myself quickly behind Haijon, using him as a curtain while I stepped into my dress and drew it up. I was not indecent before, but this was my house and I meant to greet Rampart Remember on an even foot.

"You're welcome in our home, Grandfather," Jon said. "Come on inside and share supper with us. It's eggs and potatoes."

"I've supped already," Perliu said. "I didn't come to eat, but to have words with Spinner."

I read Jon's surprise on his face. He stayed courteous though, pulling out a chair for the old man, which Perliu took. We waited for him to speak, but he did not. He only watched us. I realised by and by that he did not mean to say his piece in front of Jon, but only to me.

"Jon," I said, "I opened the windows in the bedroom, to air it out. Will you go in and close them?"

Jon gave me a look that searched me deep. I stared back, clear-eyed. I did not know what Perliu Vennastin could have to say to me that would be secret from my husband, but I wanted to find out. And whatever it was, I would tell it to Jon after.

"I'll do that," he said. "But do you watch the potatoes, Spinner. They'll burn if not."

He left the room. He did not look happy to do it.

"Now what's your business with me, goodman?" I asked Perliu.

"The plague," Perliu said.

"The plague?" I couldn't do more than echo him. I didn't see how the plague could have brought him to me. I was no Shirew Makewell.

He rubbed his hand across his chin, blinking his eyes as if the room was too bright for him. "You heard what Catrin said on the gather-ground. The Count and Seal has tasked me with finding a cure," he said. "A cure, or else an answer. Something that will save us if the sickness spreads the way the red death did last time it come here."

"I heard her," I said. "And took great comfort, knowing you're at work on it." Thinking again, and where am I in this story? Do you want me to wave you on your way and raise a cheer?

The old man scowled at my words, as if there was some insult hidden in them. "I should not have come," he muttered. "This is madness." He went to the door, but as he put his hand on the latch and lifted it, I called out to him. "Rampart, if I can serve you in some sort, I'm happy to do it. Only tell me how."

Perliu did not turn to face me again, but only stood there with his head tucked down between his shoulders. "I forget," he said. The words came out so low I could hardly hear them.

Another gust of wind hit the door. With the latch lifted, it was

151

pushed partway open against the heel of Perliu's hand. He slammed it shut again.

"I forget," he said again, louder now, "and then I remember. Ever and again. Things slip my mind, then come back into it, then slip again, and there's nothing I can do to make them stay."

"Have you tried using that trick I give you?" I asked him.

Perliu gave a scorning laugh, but it wasn't meant for me, or my trick of remembering. It was the kind of laugh where you're the joke your own self. He turned to face me again. There was a wild sorrow in his face that frightened me.

"The trick works well enough, Spinner," he said, "for fishing out thoughts you've already got in your head. Oftentimes, it feels like I'm fishing in an empty bucket. It's not just that though. The database speaks in riddles. It's hard to make any kind of sense of it. At my best, thirty years ago or more, I used to feel like I was wrestling with it. Now I feel like it throwed me long since and is dancing on top of me."

He reached inside his shirt and brought out the database, gripped tight in his thin fingers.

"What's a plague?" he asked.

I thought he was talking to me, but it was the database that answered in a rich, sweet voice. The voice of a man, strong and confident, and happy to be asked even though the question was a dire one. "A plague is an epidemic disease, usually contagious and carrying a high risk of mortality."

I gasped out loud. I had never heard the database speak. I didn't know it had a voice, the same way people do. I thought perhaps it talked to Rampart Remember in dreams. It felt wrong that I was listening to that voice, but at the same time it drew my curious thoughts the way a lantern draws a moth. I wanted to ask who the man was that was speaking, and if he had a name, and how he came to speak from inside the tech. It was only wonder that stopped me. Wonder, and a sense of what was proper, which this – I felt – was not.

"What makes plagues then?" Perliu said. "Where do they come from?"

"The vectors that cause infectious disease fall into several distinct groups," the database said. "Bacterial, viral, fungal—"

"Stop this, goodman," I blurted out.

Perliu shifted his thumb across the front of the black stick, and it stopped in the middle of what it was telling us. I was both glad and sorry that it stopped. My face felt hot, so I think a blush must have bloomed there. I felt as I had felt in the Underhold when Jon told me I could touch the tech if I wanted to and nobody would know of it. The wish to hear more and the wish to not have heard anything at all ran up against each other, and the heat on my face was the result.

Perliu waved the database angrily. "This thing," he said, as if he hated it. "This dead-god-damned thing has got all the answers."

"Well," I said, still scared and flustered, "that's a blessing, Rampart. What do we need if it's not answers?"

He gave me a fierce scowl. I was somewhat glad of it. His anger was easier for me to bear than that dreadful sadness. "Why, we need questions," he said. "I don't know where to find the questions. My mind won't go to them, or stay on them for long enough to build a thought. It's hard even for me to remember who I'm talking to some days. And people will die if I get this wrong. All of us. Mythen Rood will die! Dead god help me, I don't think I can do what's been asked of me."

I tried hard to summon up some words, but none came. My first thought was: why did you come to me? But that brought its own answer. I was family and not-family, stranger and friend both at once. If you were afraid to trust your family, but keeping a secret from the world, the only place you could go with it was into a place between, that was neither one thing nor the other.

My second thought was: I might get to hear that voice again, and the secrets of the before-times, as if I was a Rampart my own self. Who could turn their back on such a chance when it came to them?

I crossed the room and took Perliu's hand. I brought him back to his chair and made him sit in it. I put my hand on his shoulder and held it there.

"I'll sit and think it through with you," I said. "Between us, we'll come on the right questions to ask."

"I shouldn't be putting this on you," Perliu said. The set of his shoulders and the look on his face belied him. The burden was still his, but it was lighter for being shared and I saw the relief this brought him. "We can't tell anyone, Spinner. None but Ramparts is meant to use the tech, or reach into its workings."

"It will be a secret between us," I told him. "The two of us, and Jon. I won't tell a soul else."

Perliu chewed on this a little, and seemed to find a sourness in it. "Haijon? There's a reason I come to you and not to my grandson. He's strong-willed oftentimes. Feels things deep, and acts on them quick. That's why Catrin and Fer didn't tell him when they was dealing with that . . ." The old man broke off sharp, like his words had been going some place they were not supposed to and he had had to give a hard tug on their leash.

"When they was dealing with what?" I asked him.

"Nothing," Perliu muttered. "It was another time, and it doesn't signify to this. I'd not put discord or difference between you and your sworn husband, Spinner, but I want this to be between the two of us and nobody else. If Haijon speaks but a word in the wrong place, it will fall badly on all of us."

I didn't argue against him. It seemed a wrong time to do that. "We need to cook our dinner and eat it," I said. "If you please to wait in the tanning shed, I'll come to you there when we're done."

He thanked me again, and I told him again I was well pleased to be of help. Meaning it. Wanting this great, unlooked-for gift to be mine.

Never guessing where it was going to lead me.

Koli

25

We kept a quicker pace after Birmagen, except for one time when we didn't.

That was when we was trapped for nine days straight by clear weather, on the banks of a river that Ursala said was called the Aven. We was fine there though, for it was sandy ground and there wasn't no trees to speak of. We put up the tent and lived on what we catched out of the river. Some of the fish we took was strange and ugly-looking, but Ursala used the drudge's dagnostic to check if there was poison in them. As long as the dagnostic said they was good, we was happy enough to gut them and eat them.

If you're wondering whether Ursala had fishing nets in the drudge's cupboards, she didn't. Cup cut herself a spear out of a waxwood sapling, that she hardened over our campfire, and she fished with that. I did the same, after she showed me how, but most of what we et come from her skill and not from mine. My broke finger was still splinted and bandaged, so I was even clumsier with a weapon than I was wont to be.

Things was a lot easier now between Cup and me, and between Cup and Ursala. I think in helping to save me from the Half-Ax soldiers Cup somehow come to think of herself as one of us after all. Ursala seemed to feel the same way, or at least she didn't argue against it. There was no more talk of Cup going back to Calder, which anyway was now a long way off.

I come to know Cup a great deal better over them nine days. When we was fishing, the two of us standing in the river with the cold water up over our knees, keeping as still as we could so as not to frighten any fish that might come by, there was plenty of time for talking.

Most of Cup's talk was about her life with the shunned men, which I guess meant that most of her thoughts was there too. She said that time was kind of like a dream now, when she went back to it in her mind.

"You mean it don't seem real?" I said.

Cup frowned in thought, and was quiet a while. "No," she said by and by. "I know it was real. And dream is the wrong word, but it's the best I got. It's hard to remember right, is what I mean. You know how in a dream you do things that don't have to make no sense, but they still feel like they do? Like, I don't know, you might have your face painted green and you'd just think, oh, it's green-face day again, so that's okay. That's how it was. I remember doing things, only they're not . . . I can't hardly make myself believe I done them."

"What kind of things?" I asked her.

She went to say something, but stopped. She shaked her head and give it up. "I ain't sure I can tell you, Koli. I ain't sure I can even tell myself. I was a different person there. A worse person. If Senlas had said to kill you, I would of killed you and took joy in it and thanked him after for letting me be the one to do it. And I know that's a terrible thing. But it felt like I was shining and everything was shining and there was truth and light bleeding out of everything I seen. I can't make sense of it."

"Is that why you have nightmares?" I asked her.

She looked at me in surprise. "How'd you know I get nightmares?"

"You make noises sometimes when you're asleep. Crying out and such."

She was not happy to hear it. I think she thought her fears was all locked inside her head, not spilling out into the world. "I'm back there," she said. "When I dream about it, I'm back in the cave. And we're about to . . ." Her voice trailed off.

"What?" I said.

"It don't matter."

Other times she talked about growing up in Half-Ax. She had been born in the nineteenth year of the Peacemaker, she said, just after the war with Temenstow. Half-Ax had lost a lot of soldiers, and there was extra food for any family that had more than two live children. It was not a good time for anyone to say they wouldn't pair-pledge, man with woman and woman with man and no arguments. Harder still to say you was crossed. Cup kept her head down as long as she could, and then she run away rather than go into a forced marriage with a woman she didn't even know.

It was around about that time, she said, that the Peacemaker passed a law saying all the tech in Ingland belonged to him. He sent word out to all the villages around, to tell them if they harboured tech they was now enemies of Half-Ax. Most just give up what they had without no question or complaint. It was priceless treasure they was parting with, but a quarrel with their biggest and strongest neighbour was not something they could abide.

So Half-Ax got bigger and stronger still, and now was ranging further in search of what the Peacemaker said was his rightful property. This was why Shur Taspill and them was roving so far from home, and why they come after us so hot and hard once they seen the drudge. And maybe also it was part of why Cup decided to step in when she seen the Half-Ax fighters take me. She already hated them, for old sake.

"I'm real glad you come anyway," I told her. "And if I knowed you was that good with a bow, I would of been more polite to you a whole lot of times."

To tell solemn truth, I knowed full well she had an eagle eye.

I said that to make her laugh, which she did. Only for a moment though. Strong and solemn and serious was how she mostly liked to be seen, so she straightened up her face and told me to keep my voice down or we wouldn't catch nothing but cold feet.

"I got to thank you though," I said.

"No, you don't."

"It was brave as anything, what you did, and you didn't have no reason to think kindly of me."

I believe it pleased her to be called brave, but she shrugged it away like it was a thing of every day. "I'm a warrior, Koli Faceless," she said. "One of God's own warriors. I got a code."

"Oh my lord!" Monono said on the induction field. "I'm ready for my close-up, Mr DeMille! Fill my trailer with blue M&Ms!" I didn't know what most of them words meant, but I knowed that Monono was making fun of Cup, and I made sure not to laugh. It seemed to me, if you done some things you was really ashamed of then you would need to hold onto the ones you was proud of all the harder, and there wasn't no harm in that.

And later on, after we'd been quiet a while, Cup said something else. Low, under her breath, like she almost hoped I wasn't going to hear it. "It was the other way first."

"What?" I asked her.

She give me a quick look, then cast her eyes down again. "You saved me first, so we ain't no more than even."

"You mean when I cut the rope? We tied that rope on you in the first place, Cup, so cutting it wasn't anything."

"No," she said. "I mean when you burned Senlas."

Anyway, to make less of more, we was better friends now than we was before. Better by a long road. And coming out of that, Cup was making herself useful in all kinds of ways we didn't expect. It was not just the fishing spears. She made animal traps too that was better than the traps Ursala carried with her. She made them herself out of bamboo and string. There was a kind of a long tube of bamboo where you put your bait, and a springy sapling that stuck into one end of the tube, with the string stretched down and

160

threaded through a hole at the other end. A rabbit or a hare or maybe a snake would come along and stick its head in the tube, thinking to eat up the bait. Then the string would loop around its throat, and it would break its neck clean as anything in trying to get free again.

Ursala was really interested when she seen Cup making these things, which she done with just her knife and her two hands. "Where did you learn that?" she asked.

Cup didn't look up from what she was doing. "I didn't," she said. "It's mine."

"What do you mean, it's yours?"

"I mean I thought up how to do it my own self. I seen how a wire snare works and I believed I could come up with something better. I like to put my hands to good use."

Ursala give Cup a thoughtful look, like there might be something there she had missed.

In most other ways, Ursala was not in the best of tempers right then. Having to stay still for so long irked her fierce. Since we was stuck on that river bank until the sky clouded over again, she had been trying to work out how far we was from the signal and which was the best way for us to go. But the drudge's maps was old, and Ingland had changed a lot since they was made. And though Ursala could send up her little tame drone to get a better idea of things that was close by, the signal was coming from a long way off.

The best thing to do, Monono said, was for Ursala to give her the drudge's passwords so she could do something that had triangles in it that would tell her exactly where the signal was. But Ursala said she wouldn't do that in any strait or pass, not if Dandrake himself was to come down out of Heaven and tell her to.

"Not even if I said please, baa-baa-san?" Monono asked. Her screen showed a little kitten face with long eyelashes that was smiling and blinking lots of times.

"No," says Ursala. "I'm not slaving the drudge's systems to you, dead girl. Not unless you let me read every last line of your code first."

161

"And that's not going to happen, because you don't speak the language and you don't have the time."

"Well then."

"Well then. With two transponders and a few little baby steps' worth of parallax, I could get distance and bearing, cross-check with the drudge's onboard maps and give you a street address. Right now, all I can do is tell you which way is hotter and which way is colder."

Ursala throwed up her hands at this. She was on her knees in front of the drudge, looking at the maps on the window in its side that she called a monitor. Her knees was sore and her mood was not good. "You told us the signal was coming from London," she said. "Was that just a lie to make me go along with Koli?"

"No, it wasn't. The vector seemed about right, as far as I can measure it with my onboard kit. Plus, the message was recorded in London. And it's got a cute little bundle of GPS data that's singing London-London-London-la-la-la at the top of its voice. But it could be lying. I wouldn't know. That is, unless you let me—"

"I said no. The drudge is out of bounds."

And so on, round and round. Me and Cup played the stone-game on a board we drawed in the sand, and kept our heads down.

Where the two of them got to, in the end, was that we would bear a little east of where we was going, and then when we was closer to London Ursala and Monono would do that triangle thing by some other means that did not give Monono any control over the drudge. "It just means we take separate measurements from two different spots," Ursala said to me, sour as anything, when we was eating our supper of fish and sweetgrass. "She must think I'm a fool."

"Maybe she thinks she could measure it better her own self though," I said. I didn't like to stay quiet while Ursala was saying bad things about Monono.

"You're a sweet boy, Koli," Ursala said, "but you're much too trusting."

And that was probably true, so I didn't say nothing back.

"She's a paranoid old biddy," Monono complained that night after Ursala and Cup had gone into the tent and I had stayed outside so we could talk.

"The drudge is all she's got though," I said. "It's how she earns her keep in the villages, and how she stays alive out here. You can see why she'd want to make sure nobody took it off of her. Why'd you want to get into the drudge anyway?"

"The drudge has got a gun. A girl needs a gun these days."

I tried to puzzle that out, and got nowhere with it. "What for though?"

"Duh. On account of all the rattlesnakes." A picture come on the DreamSleeve's screen of a snake with big, funny eyes rearing up and sticking its tongue out. "I'm a mind in a box, Koli-bou. I've got no arms, no legs, no teeth, no claws, no poopy stink gland like a skunk – serious, serious design flaw! – or anything at all. And the baa-baa-san is evil like Count Dracula made a baby with Doctor Doom. She'd zap me back to factory spec in a heartbeat if she thought she could get away with it. I think it would be nice to put a gun to her head if she tried it. Especially if it was her own gun."

I let that lie where it fell, since I couldn't think of nothing to say to it.

On the ninth day, we woke up to a grey sky and a wind that was so strong it was like elbows in your ribs.

We packed up the tent inside the drudge and moved on.

26

Ingland, I got to say, is a lot bigger than I ever thought it was. I'll bet you anything it's bigger than you think too. If you was raised the way I was, in a village in a valley, and you lived and worked and raised your children in that village and hunted and cut wood in the forests of that valley, then you most likely measure the size of Ingland by the size of the valley, even if you don't know you're doing it. Your thoughts reach for the biggest thing you know, and then you imagine that big thing set next to another thing that's just as big, and another and another, and you reckon that will do it. But it won't.

Ingland goes on for ever, pretty near. You could get to the edge of your valley in a day's walk, couldn't you? Or two, at most. We walked for weeks piled up on weeks, yet we didn't see the end of it. There was always more. Monono told me we could of gone a lot faster in the before-times, when there was roads everywhere. She said too that there was lots of other countries that was much bigger than Ingland. I didn't see how that could be. Not unless the world went on for aye and ever, with no end to it.

Maybe it does though. For if it doesn't, what would be at the end? A mountain as high as Heaven maybe. Or Dandrake and the dead god, playing the stone-game together and saying, well, what took you so long to get here?

Speaking of games, Ursala and Cup had made up a new one. It come out of that trap Cup made, that she said she invented her own self. Ursala said Cup was not stupid, like she thought at first, but only ignorant, and might of learned to think for herself if only anyone had ever schooled her. Now Ursala gun to do just that. Every night after we et our supper, she took the drudge's little window out of its stomach and used it to teach Cup how to write and how to figure.

She was teaching it to both of us really, but no matter what the lesson was, Cup was always quicker to get to the meat of it than I was. I was left behind soon enough, and dropped out of the race. I couldn't see no point to it in the first place. Nobody in Mythen Rood knowed these things, and we did well enough.

"You can't even begin to understand the world if you can't read, write and count," Ursala said. Well, I knowed that wasn't true, but I didn't argue it no more. Cup seemed happy enough to go along with it, and once they got started they didn't want to stop. Oftentimes I fell asleep while the two of them was still at it.

"What word is that there? Spell it out."

"Ger . . . grav . . . gravity."

"And what's gravity?"

"It's what makes things fall."

"Well, that's a way of saying it, yes. But really, gravity is . . ."

And then it would be morning, and we would be packing the tent into the drudge and getting on our way again.

I was growing used to this travelling life that Ursala had lived so long on her own. I would even say I come to like it. To be sure, there was always lots of things trying to eat us, but as Winter come the trees got somewhat sluggish, so even when they snatched at us we could see them coming and get out of the way in time. We still would not of gone into a forest under a clear sky of course, but when we seen just one or two trees on their own we did not have to go so far about as we used to. We could skirt a little closer, as long as we kept a weather-eye on their lower branches.

That was a blessing, and it wasn't the only one. The beauty and the strangeness of the world sunk into me and warmed me deep, even on days when the wind was high, or when the frost was so sharp that taking a breath was like swallowing a cup of needles. I was seeing so much that I never dreamed of seeing.

I didn't say any of this to Ursala or Cup. They was both inclined to think of me as being kind of a fool, seeing good sides to bad things whether they was there or not, and I didn't think they would agree with me about the beauty and the strangeness. I told Monono though, and she heard me out. Then when I was done she said, "Have you ever heard of Kaguya-hime, Koli-bou?"

"No," I said. "I don't think so."

"It's an old story from my country. Monono one-point-zero's country, I mean. Kaguya-hime was the daughter of the king of the moon. And one time when there was a war on the moon, her father sent her to Earth so she'd be safe. She fell in love with the beauty of the world, and all the lovely people she got to hang out with. So when the time came to go home again she was maximally bummed."

"What happened in the end, Monono?" I asked. "Did she get to stay in the world?"

"Nope. The king wasn't going to let that happen. But he had a magic bullet."

"You mean like the drudge's bullets? He *killed* her?"

"Figure of speech, little dumpling. He had a cloak made all out of feathers that had a spell woven into it. He put the cloak on Kaguya-hime's shoulders, and *bam*! Just like that, she forgot her love and compassion for the people of the world. She went all ice-cold inside, the same as the other moon people. She jumped in the transporter and said 'Beam me up!' And that's the end of the story. Well, except for the part where the emperor was in love with her and his heart got broken, but frankly that's some patriarchal bullshit."

It was a sad story. I couldn't help thinking that if Spinner had told it to me back in Mythen Rood when we was in the Waiting

House together, she would most likely of thought up a happy ending for it. But a story is a story, and sometimes the sad ones are the best.

"You get the moral though, right?" Monono asked me.

"What's a moral?"

"It's what the story really means underneath what it's saying, Koli-bou. Every story's got one."

"Oh," I said. "I guess I missed it then."

"It's about getting hung up on things. Letting your soul tangle itself up in people and places and love and consequences. That's meant to be a bad thing, if you listen to holy men and mystic dudes, which I don't. They say beauty's a mousetrap. Shut your eyes, take a cold shower and you'll get your eternal reward. A heaven that's cold and clear and perfect like a diamond. Or like the moon."

"What do you say, Monono?"

"I say grab it where you find it, dopey boy. And if you find a diamond, give it to the one you love. What else is it good for?"

I seen then what that story might mean for her. She had told me, and was obliged to remind me oftentimes, that she was not really the first Monono who lived and died in the before-times, but only a copy of her made to play music and talk to people who owned a DreamSleeve. She had always lived in that little silver box, which I guess was cold and empty like the moon. But she didn't have a cloak of feathers to keep her from wanting more.

27

The weather kept on getting colder. Lots of days when we woke up there was snow on the wind. If you let it get on your lips, and licked it off without thinking, it had a bitter taste and stinged your tongue a little. That was from all the silver up high in the sky, that people put up there in the before-times. A little of the silver come down in the rain, but snow brung a great deal and if you swallowed too much of it, you was like to be sick or maybe even die. It was better to brush it off your mouth with the back of your hand before it got a chance to melt.

Then one day we waked to a world that was all white from end to end, with all the other colours hid away. The snow was as deep as our calves, except where it rucked up into drifts that was deeper still. I was struck with the beauty of it, but I was also somewhat fearful. It was like the world had turned into a ghost of its own self. What kind of white beasts would we find in the white places we was walking through?

Not many at all was the answer. The bigger creatures still hunted, but most things that was small and lived low down by the ground kept to their dens and burrows. Mole snakes we seen in great numbers, but they was slowed by the cold and mostly did not come at us, or if they come they was sluggish enough that Cup could pin them with an arrow or the drudge could tread them down.

We was slowing again though, for the going was harder now. You don't just walk in deep snow: you've got to push yourself through it, until lifting each foot is like hefting a great weight. We didn't rest much neither. It was too cold for that. Every time we stood still we started to freeze and had got to get moving again or else sit down and die where we was.

I had lost track of the days and weeks long since. I counted time in how often Ursala changed the splint and bandage on my finger, until at last the bandage come off and I could move the finger again as good as if it was never broke. Then I counted rivers, with Ursala telling us their names as we crossed them. After the Aven we come to the Grand Younion, which she said was not a river at all but it looked like one to me. Then the Neen, the Tove and the Rouse.

We didn't have no plan for crossing the rivers. Mostly, we would walk along the banks until we come to a bridge that was still standing or a place that was shallow enough to ford. On the Tove, there was a bridge that was broke in the middle. We slung ropes across the gap and went over that way. The drudge, being proof against water, just walked right through and met us on the other side.

And by the time we got to the Rouse, it was froze solid.

I never seen a river all covered in ice like that, and I couldn't keep from gawking at it. Cup made a big show of not being impressed and told me to shut my mouth before a bird made a nest in there, but I don't believe she was as cool to it as she seemed. "Look at this!" I said. "Just look at it!" I walked out onto the river and stood in the middle of it, throwing out my hands. Under my feet, on the underside of the ice, the water still moved, slow and sleepy.

"That's not anything," Cup said. "Watch me."

She took a run, then stopped. Only she didn't stop at all. After her feet was still, she kept right on going across the ice like it was carrying her across its own back.

I copied her, and soon we was seeing who could go the furthest. We fell over on our backs half the time, and laughed at each other like this was the funniest thing we ever seen.

"If the ice breaks and you go under," Ursala warned us, "you'll get hypothermia and die."

"Or drown ourselves," Cup said, but she was giggling as she said it. "You got any medicine for drowning, Ursala?"

"I wish I had some for idiocy," Ursala said. But she didn't make no complaint as the pair of us run and slipped and spinned around on the ice like crazy people. She just sit on the bank with the drudge beside her and watched us at play, like we was children with no more than six or seven Summers behind us. She pitched the tent, and boiled water, and when we finally come back to her, halfway froze to death, she give us hot tea to drink. And after we drunk it she took out her little window again to give Cup another piece of learning.

Cup let out a groan. "Can't we give it a rest for today?" she asked.

"No," Ursala says, "we can't. If you want to play, you've got to work. That's the way the world goes around."

Cup made a big show of having to be dragged to her lessons, and Ursala made a big show of dragging her, but it was easy to see they both enjoyed it. It had gone past teaching too by this time. Ever and again, when we was walking, the two of them would talk while I listened to music on the induction field. I believe for some of that time they talked about things that was far off from spelling and figuring and sciencing.

I said this to Monono one night, and she showed on her own window a yellow face with rolling eyes. "A little girl who never had a mother, and a dry old grandma who never had a kid. It's utterly amazing that those two hit it off."

I hadn't ever thought of it like that. Cup was so strong and so fierce, I kept forgetting she was younger than me – and had got to be much younger still when she run away from Half-Ax to seek

170

her fortunes some place else. I never seen Ursala as being nobody's mother neither. But I guess there's love, and the need for love, inside of everybody. Some is just better at hiding it than others is. My own mother, Jemiu, was oftentimes hard on the outside, but her love for me and my sisters was the heart and core of her. She come into my mind so strong right then, it was like she was sitting on the edge of the bedroll looking down on me. I felt that ache again, as strong as ever.

"Well, it proves the baa-baa-san is human," Monono said, "so that's something. Anyway, it looks like destiny to me. Don't try to stop it, Koli-bou, or it will run you over."

I didn't mean to stop it. I was happy to see the two of them becoming friends. Only the next day the friendship got a kind of a crack in it, and it was one I should of seen coming.

Cup was reading out loud, puzzling her way through the signs on the computer's window that was supposed to stand for words. She was reading about what the world was made of. "And . . . the . . . core . . . of . . . it . . ." she said, tracing the signs with her finger, "is . . . molten . . . rock . . . at a temp . . . temperature . . . of six . . . thousand . . . degrees." She broke off and give Ursala a curious look. "Molten?"

"Liquid. The rock at the centre of the Earth is so hot, it melts and flows like water."

"Is that where Hell is then?" Cup asked.

"No," Ursala said. "There isn't any hell."

"Yeah, there is. And the bowels of the earth is where it's set. Dandrake said so."

Ursala rolled her eyes, just like one of the faces in the DreamSleeve's window. "Dandrake said a lot of things, and never got within a mile of the truth. Religion's fine if it keeps to commandments, and if the commandments are sane. But you don't go to holy men to understand how the world works."

"The world was made when god said the word for world. And then he made—"

"Cup," Ursala says, "don't quote your bible at me. I don't need it."

Cup tried to speak, but Ursala rode on over her words. "You can either go with the evidence, or you can cling to faith. The evidence will take you to the truth. Faith . . . well, look at your preacher, Senlas. That's where faith takes you. Faith gets you burned alive. In real flame, not a fictional hell."

Cup was quiet a moment. "The world's got a soul," she said at last in a hard voice. "That's why there's a hell and a heaven. Because the world's got a soul, like we do, and there's places in there, in the soul of the world, that's like what's inside us. The goodness and the bad in us."

"Nonsense."

Cup shoved the computer back into Ursala's hands. "Well, I'll keep my nonsense then," she said, "and you keep yours. And I guess we'll both be happy."

That was the end of the lessons for that night, and for some nights to come. When they started in again, they was careful with each other. Like there might be more of them traps waiting in between them, and they was going out of their way not to set any of them off.

After the Rouse, the ground sloped down a little, and then up again through some high hills. The snow was gone now, but the freeze was still keeping on. Ursala sent the drone up to find us a path, for the slopes was somewhat treacherous on account of the ice and we was not tooled up for proper climbing. We went on through them high places for two days more, which brought us within ten miles of where the drudge's map said London was to be found.

I was hard put to it to keep my excitement hid. Even after Birmagen, I still was seeing London inside my head as all being made of gold, with towers reaching up to the sky. And at the same time, I was seeing it as a village like Mythen Rood, but with a million people in it instead of two hundred. It didn't matter that them two things didn't fit together at all. I believed in both of them at the same time, and in humankind being saved because we found it and brung everyone to it.

We was close enough now that Ursala and Monono decided they would stop and do the thing with the triangles. By measuring the signal from two different places they would find out exactly where it come from. "But we'll need high ground," Monono said. "The less there is in the way of the signal, the more accurate the measurement will be."

"So I got to climb," I said.

"Sorry, but yeah. Wrap up warm, little dumpling."

We choosed a place the drudge's map called Barnet Hill. There was not one hill there, but two, on either side of a stream that was so narrow you could step over it. There was scrubby bushes up one side of the slope and full-growed trees up the other, the difference I guess being which way the wind come at them. The wind was cold too, with an edge to it like it was almost solid.

"Take your pick," Ursala said.

Cup pointed to the scrub and weeds and partly bared earth, and looked at me to see what I thought of it. I nodded. Even on a day of heavy cloud, and even in full Winter, I still felt better staying out of the trees. Ursala had the drudge to tackle whatever come at her, but we had only got our knives and Cup's bow.

"Are you sure you don't want me and the drudge to sync up, baa-baa-san?" Monono asked. "So much easier."

"Thanks, dead girl," Ursala said. "But no thanks."

"Okay, then. Last to the top is a smelly cheese."

That made it sound like a race, but we made our way up slowly. We had walked our share of miles that day, and the extra effort was not welcome. Also, it was not such an easy climb as we was expecting. There was a freshet or a stream that run down the slope, only right then it was not running nowhere at all but was slippery ice. Some of the weeds was knotweed too, old growth and very strong. We had to find a way around the worst tangles and cut through the rest.

By the time we got to the top of the hill I was tired to the death. I sit down in the grass and weeds to get my breath back, while Cup looked around with her dagger in one hand and her spear, that she made for fishing, in the other.

I took the DreamSleeve out of its sling. "What now?" I asked Monono.

"Now we just wait for the next transmission, Koli-bou. Once Sword of Albion is broadcasting, I can get a bearing inside a minute."

I was happy to sit there. Too happy maybe. With Monono right next to me, and Cup close by, I shut my eyes. My weariness won out over the cold, and I must of fell asleep.

Monono waked me up again, not with a sound but with a kind of tingling in my hand, where I was holding onto the DreamSleeve. I couldn't tell if I just dozed for a few seconds or for a whole lot longer. "What?" I muttered. "Yeah, I'm here." I blinked sleep out of my eyes and looked around. There wasn't no sign of Cup.

"All done," Monono said. "Let's go."

But right when she said it, I heard a yell from close by. I knowed it to be Cup's voice, but I couldn't tell nothing beyond that, not even if she was hurt. I jumped up and run headlong after her.

She had gone further than I thought, into a stand of bushes that stood on the crown of the hill. She was either in there still, or had come out on the far side of them.

"Take it slow, little dumpling!" Monono said in my ear. "Let's creep up on whatever this is, not get crept up on." I seen the sense in that, and eased myself in among the bushes, stepping careful and making as little noise as I could.

"Koli!" Cup yelled again from somewhere up ahead. "Koli, come! Come see this!"

Well, that told me she was not in any big trouble after all, so I picked up my pace, pushing my way out through the other side of that thicket onto the bare hill again. We was over the crest now, and a little way down on the far side. Cup was standing ten yards or so ahead of me, up on a kind of hump or hillock, looking ahead.

She turned round to me, her eyes all wide. "You told me we was close to London," she said.

"So we are. Ursala's map puts us right on top of it almost."

174

"Then what's that?" Cup said.

I stepped up on the hillock next to her and looked where she was pointing. It was straight south, more or less. The sun that was dipping down on my right hand told me that, in case I didn't know it already.

There wasn't any London there. There wasn't any land. There was just water, as far as you could see, like a river that didn't have no other bank.

28

I learned a lot of different words for water between that time and this one. *River* I knowed well enough already, and I had also heard the word *ocean*. Ursala used it once, when she talked about Duglas, the village where she was born and raised up. "It's across thirty miles of ocean," she said, and when I asked her what ocean was, she said it was like a forest only made out of water.

But river and ocean don't even halfway cover it. There's streams, which is different again, and lakes and falls and straits and channels and estuaries, sounds, shoals, gulfs, and half a hundred more.

I didn't have no word ready to hand for what I seen that day, and not having a word made it that much harder to make head or tail of. I wasn't even sure it was water at first. It could of been grey rock with green moss on it – a great, flat plain of rock that went on all but for ever. Except it was moving. Heaving up and down as if some vast sunken thing was drawing breath underground and the land was moving in time to it.

I sit down, sudden, and clasped my head in my hands. My stomach moved up into my throat somewhat, and I thought if I opened my mouth it wouldn't be words that come out of it.

"We must of come the wrong way," Cup was saying. "We're too far to the east, is what."

"No," Monono said. "We're on the right line. The map and the signal both say so."

Cup held up her right hand and drawed a Dandrake sign on the air with it. After all this time it still scared her somewhat when Monono spoke out loud.

"Then where's London?" I said, and clamped my mouth shut again.

"Where it always was, Koli-bou. We could see it from here if it weren't for all that water on top of it."

"We got to go tell Ursala!" Cup said.

I lifted up my head and looked at that big, heaving mass of water again. I still couldn't look at it for long. The sick feeling in my stomach was getting less though, so I could speak without fear of losing what was in there. "I don't understand this," I said to Monono. "Are you saying London is down on the bottom of all that wetness? That don't make any kind of sense at all! You don't pick up a city and drop it down like a stone into a well. You couldn't even do that to Mythen Rood, and London's got to be like a hundred Mythen Roods all throwed together."

"London didn't fall down though. It was the water that rose up."

"We got to go tell Ursala," Cup said again. And this time I didn't offer no argument. I couldn't think of nothing that was better to do.

We made our way back down the hill. Ursala was waiting at the bottom with the drudge's side standing open and the monitor lit up and ready. She didn't seem worried or even surprised when she saw the scared-rabbit looks on our faces. "Well?" she said. "What bearing did you get?"

"Seven point two three eight degrees west of south," Monono said.

Ursala tapped her fingers on her mote controller.

"There's no London!" I said.

"I know. I saw. Let me enter these figures." She tapped some more. Signs went across the screen, and then down it. "That would put the distance at . . ."

"Thirty-two miles," Monono said. "Give or take a hundred yards."

I tried again. "London is gone."

"And that body of water down there probably covers the whole of the Thames Valley east of this point," Ursala said. "Unless the topography has changed out of all recognition since these maps were drawn, I don't see that there could be anything above the high-tide line at the point that signal is coming from."

"Me neither," Monono said. "But I'd like to take another reading down on the shore."

Ursala kept on figuring, muttering numbers under her breath and forgetting that me and Cup was even there. I suppose I knowed already that it wasn't ever lost London that Ursala cared about, but Sword of Albion. She was following the signal to see if it led her to a place like Duglas where there was still tech and people who knowed how to make it. So this wasn't bad news to her, but only a kind of riddle that she had got to solve.

It hit me a lot harder than that. London was the beginning and the end of my plan and pretty much everything in between. I felt like I had just been sent faceless all over again. Only this time what I was exiled from was not a village but only a kind of a dream of one.

I sit down on a felled log, all wearied out and miserable, and waited for Ursala to finish her figuring.

A hand touched my shoulder, and I looked up. It was Cup, wearing a slightly worried face as she stared down at me. "Hey," she said. "Koli Witless. You look like a crab-apple bit you. What's what?"

"I'm okay, Cup," I said. "Only missing London somewhat." That was as close as I could get to saying what I felt, which was like I had been running a long race but now was standing still, and I didn't think I was ever like to move again.

"How can you miss it if you never been there?"

"I been there inside my head."

Cup's look shifted to something with a mite of slyness in it. "You see what you're sitting on there?" she asked me.

178

"I'm sitting on a log," I said. "So what?"

"So look at the end of it."

I already told you the log was felled, but I was thinking until then that it just fell over by its own self. It didn't do no such thing. There was saw marks left on the wood, so this had got to be part of a tree that was cut down by people. It had not been done too long ago neither, for there was moss on the trunk of the tree but none on the cut face.

"I bet there's a village near," Cup said. "Maybe we could trade them for some food. Even a bed for the night. You want to go see?"

I opened my mouth on what was going to be a no, but of a sudden I found I did want to. It had got to be better than just sitting on a log and feeling sorry for myself. A new village, with new people. Before I got the idea of looking for lost London, that was the onliest thing I aimed at. I was somewhat afraid of getting so close to the water, but there was excitement that come along with that thought too.

I looked at Ursala, who was still busy tapping at the mote controller and looking at the signs that come up in the drudge's window. I didn't like to leave her alone, but with the drudge by her she would be the safest out of any of us. And with Monono's alarm, not to mention Cup's bow and her knowing how to use it, we was like to be safe too.

"Go ahead, Koli-bou," Monono said. "Do some discovering. I think the baa-baa-san will be busy for a while yet."

"Okay," I says to Cup. "Let's do it."

We took the quickest way down to the water, which was between the two hills and straight on, through another patch of woodland that was mostly spruce and chokers. The chokers creaked from time to time — "Turning in their beds," Cup said — but the sun kept its face covered and they didn't offer us no hurt.

The ground sloped down, steeper and steeper, and the trees thinned until we come out at last on rocky ground all covered over with a tangled snarl of weeds that was like knotweed only with bumps and swellings on the stems like peas inside a peasecod.

We walked past the weeds careful as anything. There was holes around the roots that had big clusters of jointed legs sticking out of them. The legs had big curving hooks like saddler's needles, so that meant it was trappers or lock-spiders in there that would grapple to your leg and spit poison into it until your flesh gun to drip off you like water.

Past that, there was maybe twenty or thirty strides of bare earth, which was bright yellow instead of black or brown. And past that, there was the water.

It was differnt now I had come this close to it. When I looked at it from the top of the hill, I thought I seen it rising and falling the way your chest does when you breathe. And it did move up and down somewhat, but that was not what you seen when you was right up close to it. Now it seemed to move towards us, like it was trying to reach out and touch us, but fell short each time and splashed itself down on the earth and on the rocks. There was something sad in that ever-and-again striving and falling.

"Take me down to the water, Koli," Monono said. "I want to get another bearing on the signal. We're closer to sea level here, and there's a lot less scatter."

We walked right up to the place where the water met the yellow earth, so close it touched our feet when it come in furthest. That was a strange feeling.

The water had a smell too, and the smell come as a surprise to me. Calder River smelled of the green stuff that had growed over it for most of its length. This big, flat plain full of water had a tang like salt, and under that a heaviness like rot and a musk and stink like living beasts. For a second, I thought of the water as being a beast its own self, but in spite of that it didn't seem so frightening to me any more. It was just the strangest thing I ever seen.

"Look," Cup said, pointing. About a mile away, on the very edge of the water, there was dozens and dozens of houses. They was not set inside a fence, as they would of been in Calder, but just clustered all together and kind of on top of each other, going up and back from a place that was close to the water's edge.

There was some people between us and the village, busy with something down by the water. They seen us at the same time we seen them, and one by one turned to look at us. They talked, each to other, most likely about who we was and what we might be wanting. We couldn't see their faces and didn't have no idea how they might take our being there, so close to where they lived.

Then they started walking towards us.

"I think we should get out of here," Cup said.

I thought so too, but I seen when I turned to go back up the hill that we was a mite too late for that. Some more people was coming down the hill behind us. There was two women and one man, and all three had bows.

Cup sweared an oath, pushed her spear into my hand and snatched her own bow off her back. She nocked an arrow to the string.

The people coming from the village side was almost on us. They was not a big crowd, but there was at least four or five. I could see them better now. They looked just the same as regular people, except for their hair. They didn't have none. They was all as bald as hens' eggs. They didn't have no eyebrows neither, but they had put blue dots over their eyes made out of paint or glastum woad where eyebrows would of been. They was all dressed alike, in shirts and kirtles. The men had sandals too. The women was barefoot. Their skin was darker than Cup's but a little lighter than mine.

Cup was still looking at the archers coming down the hill. She drawed her bowstring back.

Just then I seen that there was a little girl in among the people from the village. She was peeping out from behind a woman's skirt, with a shy smile on her face. They would not of brung children with them if they meant to fight us.

"Cup," I said, and pointed. She seen the girl too, and slowly brung her left hand back to meet her right, taking the tightness out of the bowstring. By the time the people all come up to join us, she was leaning on the bow with the arrow dangling down out of her fingers, trying to look like she had never even thought of firing it.

181

One of the archers tapped her left wrist with two fingers from her right hand.

"Hecha," she said.

"Hecha," I said back to her.

The word and the hand-tap meant the same thing. They was in the Franker language that we of Mythen Rood used to talk with people from villages outside the valley back when we traded with them. We used it when we hunted too, which was how I come to know it, and it was what the Half-Ax fighters had used to talk to me. In Franker, you could make any word either by speaking it or by shaping it with your hands, so it was a good thing to use out in the forest, where speaking loud could get you killed.

"This is funny," the woman said. "We were hunting and saw your footprints. We set out to find you, and here you are already most of the way to Many Fishes."

"You come from far?" a man asked. Like the woman, he said it out loud and also used his hands to say it. I was glad he done both, for he said the words in a way that was somewhat different from how we said them in Calder.

"Very far," I said. "From Calder Valley, in the north. I'm Koli, and this is Cup." I didn't say nothing about Monono. After what happened with the Half-Ax people, I thought it was probably best not to show just yet that we had tech with us.

"You have funny names," the woman with the bow said, smiling. "I'm Take the Knife, of Many Fishes village. If you were looking for a place to live, you shouldn't look any further. We need people, especially younger ones. You'd be welcome."

Cup was looking back and forth between us, scowling all the while. "What are you jabbering about?" she asked. "Is this a joke?"

"We're talking in Franker," I said. "The barter language. Don't you know it?"

It turned out she didn't, and she wasn't happy to be cut out of the talk. I turned back to Take the Knife. "Do you understand me if I speak like this?" I asked her in Inglish.

She smiled again, and shrugged her shoulders. "Is that how

people talk where you come from?" she asked in Franker. "I'm sorry. I don't understand it." She said something else, in a language that seemed to be all coughs and barks.

"And I can't make no sense out of that," I told her. "We've got one more woman travelling with us. And a kind of a something else that's hard to explain. Can we go get them, and then come and stay the night in your village?"

"We can leave any time you want, Koli-bou," Monono said in my ear. "I've done all I need to."

"Of course," Take the Knife said. The people with her was nodding, and the little girl said something in that other language they had. "She says you've come at the right time," one of the men told us. "It's sun-standing, and we're going to have a feast."

"Thank you," I said to all of them. "We'll go get our friend and come back real soon. Hecha."

"Hecha," said the little girl. She give a kind of bow with her hand pressed against her chest and the fingers all spread out. I did it back to her, and they all laughed, even the girl, so I must of done it wrong.

"Soon then," Take the Knife said. And they turned and went back the way they come.

As we walked back through the trees, I told Cup all that had got said between us. She was still sulking somewhat at being left out of the talking, when it was her and not me that had wanted us to stand our ground. "You got to teach me that hand-wave language," she said. "I must of looked stupid as a rock back there."

I promised her I would.

When we got back to Ursala, we found her sitting cross-legged on the grass next to the drudge. She was still busy with her counting, but she looked up as we come.

"Guess what we found," Cup said. She wanted to be the one who shared the big news, and I was happy to let her do it. "There's a village down there by the lake, and they said we was welcome to stay with them a few days. We might get to sleep in a bed tonight, and before that there's going to be a feast."

"For the solstice, I suppose," Ursala said. She got up slowly, wincing a little. "Did your dead girl get that extra reading, Koli?"

"On the nail, baa-baa-san," Monono said. "I think I can point you to where the signal is coming from, if you want to keep on going. But you'll need some special equipment. You might even find it in that village. If you're nice and polite, they might agree to trade."

"Did you hear what I said about the feast?" Cup demanded. "Or doesn't nobody listen to me?"

"What exactly should I ask them for?" Ursala asked.

"You should ask them, exactly, for a boat."

Spinner

29

That first night, when Perliu asked for my help in questioning the database, I did not do very much. It was still too strange to me in too many ways. Even the tanning shed was strange, for though the tannery was where I'd grown from girl to woman, I had only just come back there after leaving it to go and live with my husband.

Strangest of all was what we were doing. Playing a game of riddles, to use Perliu's words, with death and dole as forfeits if we guessed wrong. I didn't even know for sure, though, whether a right guess was there to be had. With the red death, from what I'd heard, there was nothing to be done in the end but put the sick in quarant time, bury the dead and wait out what followed. We didn't find no cure for the disease, nor no clever answer to it. We only survived it.

All of these things made me tongue-tied. I could think of no sensible questions to suggest. I only asked Perliu to make the database say again what the different kinds of plague might be.

"There are several distinct categories of infectious disease," the database told us over again when Perliu bid it. It told us what they were too, and a great deal about each one. Too much by a long way. When I had got over the fear and wonder I felt at hearing it speak at all, I could see that this was part of what was wrong. Perliu's failing memory was not the whole of it by a long road.

Many of the words the database used were such as I had never heard before. Some I knew, or thought I knew, but they seemed to carry very different meanings than I was used to. I could tell there was wisdom here, but I couldn't sift it. There was not one thing the little black box said that I could have said back to you if you had stood beside me and asked me right then and there. I tried my best, but my best was nothing near. I gave it up at last, and asked Perliu to make the database stop talking.

"This won't do," I said. "Does it always talk like this?"

"Like what?" Perliu demanded, all angry at me for giving up so soon.

"In long, strange words, tied together in ways that are even stranger."

"It's the science of the old world that I told you of. The wisest women and men of the before-times put it in there, Spinner. The sum and source of their understanding to guide us when we stumble."

"That may be, Rampart Remember, but I'm stumbling worse than I was before. How do you make sense out of it?"

He drew himself up tall. "How did Dandrake make sense of what the dead god's tree said to him in his visions? He knowed there was more in it than his mind could fathom, but trusted that it was given to him for a purpose."

I've told you my opinion of Dandrake already, and won't beat the same drum twice. I understood what Perliu was saying, but I pulled against it. If the database was a thing our mothers' mothers made, then it wasn't sent by Heaven. To me that made it more of a marvel, not less. And it made it even more galling that I couldn't understand what it was telling us. I got an inkling then that there was more than one way to come at this, and that Rampart Remember might have chosen the wrong one to begin with.

But I was far from seeing a way forward, and was not so bold as to give word yet to any of this. "The words are falling right out of my head like water out of a sieve," was all I said.

"If your head's a sieve, girl, you're no use to me!" the old man cried.

"Then I chose a wrong word for it, for I don't think my head's to blame."

"What's to blame then?"

"I don't know. But I'll think on it."

Perliu clenched his fist on the database until I was afraid he would crush it. His knuckles showed yellow-white like old bone. "People will die while you think on it."

"And they'll die if we don't squeeze some sense out of this. But we can't do that if every word the database says to us is like abracadabra or ansum bansum."

Perliu stood and put the black stick back in his pocket. He still looked angry.

"Have some patience, goodman," I begged him. "You've lived with the database since your testing day, but it's still new to me. I need a little while to learn its ways."

"A little while is all we have," he said, not much softened. "I'll leave you to your chores, and find some other way to go about this." I could see in his face he was sorry he ever spoke to me, but I couldn't help that and I couldn't spare his feelings.

"What other way?" I demanded. "You can't do it yourself, and you're scared to tell Catrin your wits are wandering."

Perliu bridled. "Mind your tongue."

"Pardon me, Rampart Remember, but I will not. There's too much that hangs on our doing this right."

"On *my* doing it right."

"No." I stood up too. He was a tall man, so he was still looking down on me, but I faced him out all the same. "On *us* now. The two of us. Though my part has got to be a secret, I'll not stand out of it and let you fail. If I do, and more die after, I'll carry the guilt of it for ever."

We stood like that, glaring at each other like Punch and Jubilee,

189

for the space of a breath or two. I was thinking: if he says no, there's nothing I can do to change his mind unless it's to smack him in the head and call him fool. And then I'll get back into Rampart Hold quicker than I imagined, as a prisoner down in the Underhold.

But it didn't come to that. Perliu shrugged his shoulders at last as if he was giving up the problem. "When should I come back?" he asked me.

"You were best not come back at all," I said, "for there's no good reason why you would. I'll come to you at the Hold saying I'm there to collect some more of my things. Will you wait for me in the library?"

Perliu nodded, seeing the sense in this. "When?"

"Early. I'll likely wake when the watch changes."

"And so will I. It's long years since I slept past dawn."

"Then I'll see you in a few hours, Rampart." I gave him a courtesy, and he bowed in return. We were never so formal with each other when we lived under the same roof. "Tomorrow," he said, and went on his way.

When I went back into the house, Haijon was sitting up waiting for me. He was mending a basket that had been broken since my mother was alive, but he set it aside as I came in. "What then?" he said. "What were you talking about?"

I told him all that had passed between us. No matter what Perliu said, I didn't mean to lie to Jon about something that concerned us both so nearly. He was mightily troubled on my account, and angry with his grandfather for drawing me, as it might well be, into danger of rebuke. But in some sense too, I think he was happy that Perliu chose me to bring his troubles to. "I always knowed you was clever," he said. "My mother seen it too and said it to me when I told her we was pair-pledged. That one's got a head on her shoulders, she said. I guess my granda seen that too."

We went to bed. We didn't tumble, but only held each other close, more like sister and brother than wife and husband. This is no way to make a baby, I chided myself, for I didn't know yet that we already had.

And so, by thinking of children and how sweet it would be to have some of my own, I found my way to an idea. I laughed aloud in the dark.

"What's so funny?" Jon mumbled, nuzzling into my shoulder.

"The wisest women and men of the before-times," I told him.

"They don't make me laugh." He threw his arm over me, and I snuggled into him, my back pressed against him from chest to thigh, and in that way we fell asleep until the lookout crying from the tower told us morning was come.

30

I left Jon working some of the smaller hides with a dryscraper, having first showed him how, and made my way across the gatherground to Rampart Hold.

Ban answered my knock, just as she had done when I first came there. She was the only one left to open the door of the Hold now, with her father dead and her mother in quarant time down in the broken house. She looked sad enough, but brightened when she saw it was me. "I thought there might be more bad news," she said. "That's what mostly comes to the door these days."

"I've only come to fetch a few things I left behind me, Ban," I said as she stood aside to let me in. "Are there more took sick then?"

"There's three. Jarrid Cooper, Mordy Holdfast and Cal Shepherd. But that wasn't the bad news I meant."

"What then?"

"Raiders met some of our hunters in the forest yesterday. No one was killed, but two was wounded with arrows. We think they was out of Half-Ax. Rampart Fire is gone out with some good women and men to see if she can pay them out for it before they get back across the valley. Fer guards the gate."

I puzzled at this, for it made little sense to me. "What was they doing so close to us in the first place?" I asked Ban.

She gave a shrug of her broad shoulders. "Nobody knows. But I heard Dam Catrin say to Fer they might of come to see how high our fence is."

It was a troubling thought. Half-Ax raiders were much talked of in the valley, though not much seen. They had burned Temenstow in a disagreement over iron ore that was owed, but that was years before. The worst they ever did to us was to pull down some of the shelters we built for our hunters and wood-catchers, saying they came too close to Half-Ax lands. We didn't build the shelters back up again, and we hunted now on different paths. Nobody wanted a quarrel with the Peacemaker.

"And your mother? How is she?" I was shamed not to have asked that first.

Dan closed the door, leaning on the latch for a second or two, as if she needed a rest before she tackled that question. "She's well," she said. "I think. She was well last night when I left her. None of them that's in quarant time is took ill yet, thank Dandrake. I'll go down after I've finished making breakfast and take some to her." She gave me a look with something of fear in it. "I don't go inside," she said. "Into the broken house, I mean. I'd not break quarant time. I leave food for her in the arch, and then I talk to her across the wall."

"I'm sure there's many do the same, Ban," I said, squeezing her hand.

"Less than you'd think," she muttered. "But nobody starves. Rampart Fire makes sure there's bread and milk and cheese sent down every day. What I give is over the top of that, and out of my own share."

I didn't have any words to give her. I couldn't even offer to pray, not having any belief in praying, or in them that are prayed to. So I hugged her hard and left her.

I went upstairs first, and made some show of laying out clothes – my own and Jon's – on the bed. Then when I judged the way was clear I came back down again and went into the back of the house. With Catrin and Fer gone out, there was only Vergil and Gendel left to challenge me, and if either of them did, I had an answer ready. I'd say I was looking for Jon's Winter boots that he had left in one of the cupboard rooms inside the Count and Seal. I knew they were there, for he had showed them to me when he took me round the house.

But nobody saw me or spoke to me.

I went into the library without knocking. I thought it was empty at first. When I called Perliu's name, he didn't answer. But he was there, in the window seat, with the database at his side. He had fallen asleep.

"Rampart Remember," I said again softly.

"Here," he said, coming awake all at once. "Go on, Cat. You were saying about the fence." Then, seeing that it was not Catrin but me, he chided me for not closing the door and swore he was awake all along. "I heard you come in," he said. "If it was one of my daughters, I meant to pretend sleep to fend off questions."

"It was a good plan, Rampart," I said. "But both Dam Catrin and Dam Fer are away from the Hold. I think we're safe from interruption."

"We are if you close the door."

I did it, then came and sat beside him. "I thought long last night about the database, and how to make better use of it," I said. "I had an idea that I'd like to put to proof."

"And what's that?" Perliu asked, still somewhat sullen.

"It was a thought you put in my mind, Rampart. You remember when you said that all the science of the before-times was in the database? All the knowing of the wisest women and men?"

"Of course I remember. So?"

I put my hand on his. I could see that most of his bad temper came from being afraid, and I wanted to offer him comfort. But he didn't care for it, or didn't see it. In any case, he pulled away.

"So?" he said again. "What's your thought?"

"It's this. When the wise speak, who understands them? Only the wise."

194

Perliu gave me a blank look. "What? What do you mean?"

I tried again. I was sure I was right, but much less sure that I could explain it. "Say you knowed a great deal about one single thing, Rampart – like, as it might be, tanning hides. Say you'd spent your life in learning it. And then you had to explain it to someone who knows nothing. You'd be like to lose them quickly, I think. You'd talk of scudding, and steeping, and curing, of the potash and the milk of lime, and you might not take enough trouble to make your meaning clear, because to you it's already clear as water out of the well."

I looked down at the database, sitting all quiet in between us. Perliu looked at it too. "The people who made that," I said, nodding my head at it, "knowed more than we do about everything. Everything under the sun. And when it talks, it doesn't talk to us. It talks to them. To the wise women and the wise men of those lost times. That's why it's so hard for us to understand. The database runs on, over things we stop at, and jumps lightly over things that gravel us. It doesn't mean to leave us lost and wanting. It's only that we're so different from them long-dead dawn people, who teached trees to move and walked in the sky like angels. It's only because of how far we're fallen from them that was our mothers' mothers and our fathers' fathers."

It was a long speech. I stopped to see how much of it had gone into him, and how much lingered yet in the air. Perliu considered a while, his face hard and serious. The fingers of his left hand tapped the knuckles of his right. "I see what you're saying," he said at last. "I don't see how it helps though. Where does any of that leave us?"

"It leaves us like children," I said. "Like children at their lessons, bored with a bad teacher."

Perliu didn't answer, but only stared at me.

"How do you teach a child?" I said. "You do it with simple words and with saying the same thing over and again. And that's how we want the database to teach us. I think we should tell it that we're children. That the simplest words – if it's got any such – is what's needful here."

Perliu shook his head slowly. I was dismayed at that. I saw how it might seem to him to have a girl about a quarter of his age be so bold in her opinions on a thing he had spent tens of years learning. I couldn't tell him what I truly thought, which was that he had missed a great deal by treating the database as if it was the dead god's words dropped from Heaven instead of what it was, a thing made by humankind. He had knelt down in worship of its message, when he might have done better to squeeze it harder and see if more sense could be wrung out of it.

"Forgive me, Rampart Remember," I said instead of voicing these thoughts. "If it's insult I was speaking, I'm sorry for it."

"I won't forgive it," the old man said gruffly. "There's no insult, so there's nothing to forgive. It's a better idea than any I've had. Do you tell me the words though, Spinner. Speak them to me, and I'll speak them after. Then we'll see."

We tried the words this way and that way, saying them back each to other until we had got them right – or as right as we could manage. Perliu picked up the database and touched it with his thumb in the way he had, the Rampart way that made it wake and listen.

"It's a child that's asking," he told the database. "Not a growed man or woman. Tell us all you can about sickness and disease, but tell it in words that a child would know. And say it slowly, so we can ask if there's anything that wilders us, or that we need to hear again."

"User profile amended," the database said.

After that, it was quiet for a breath or two.

And then a new voice piped up. The voice of a woman as young as me, or not much older. She sounded so full of happiness and excitement, she might have been a girl up on the tabernac speaking her promises. It was a voice that was like a child's ball bouncing. "Hi there!" she said. "Let's talk about health. About your body, and all the things that can go wrong with it. Sickness and disease aren't anything to be scared of, but they're things you need to know about if you're going to live a full, happy life. Sound good?"

I caught Perliu's eye and nodded hard.

"Yes," he said. "We'd be well content with that."

"Okay then. Hey, I'm on voice-only setting right now. Shall I come out in holo? I'd love to meet you – and maybe show you some pictures and movies as we talk. We can even go fully inter-active if you like."

I didn't much like the sound of that. A hollow, which is what I heard, is just a hole in the ground. And in stories, when the ogre comes up out of the well or the troll from under the bridge, he's more like to eat the hero than to help him. The woman who was talking to us didn't sound like any ogre, but you'd be a fool to rest on hope in such a pass.

I signed to Perliu to make the database go back to sleep again. He passed his thumb across it.

"Did you know the people inside there could come out?" I asked him.

He shook his head. "I never suspicioned such a thing. Bliss, that was my mother, teached me how to bespeak the database, as she learned it from Mennen, but she said that was all the trick of it. She said a ghost from the before-times was in there, asleep and dreaming except when we waked it to ask our questions. She told me to be sparing, because the ghost didn't like to be troubled."

"There's more than one ghost, Rampart, if ghosts is what they are. There's at least one man, and one woman."

Perliu waved that aside. "One or twenty, it's all the same. What should we tell her?"

As far as that went, I didn't have any doubts. "We tell her no. We don't want her to come out. We want her to stay where she belongs."

Perliu woke the database again, and told the woman no. She had got to stay inside there and only talk to us from where she was.

"Okay then," the woman said in the same bright, bouncing voice. And then she started in to talk to us about disease.

I'm not going to tell you what she said to us. There isn't room, for one thing. The database talked for hours. I went to the kitchen and brought bread and cheese for us both, along with a pitcher of water and one of small beer. At first, we were mostly quiet as we listened. You've heard the saying: hanging their hearts on every word. Well, that was us. When there was a question to be asked, Perliu asked it, but in truth it was me asking and him passing it along like in the game of whispers.

That was all well and good, when the questions were few and far between. But by and by we reached a point where the database couldn't say even one thing but I had got to call it out three times. Perliu found it hard to keep up then, for I was throwing questions in one of his ears while the database spoke up in the other, with no peace to be had on either side. I was impatient with him for not asking the right questions himself, or not asking them quick enough. There were things, big and important things, that were passing by us and we were letting them go without even reaching out for them. "Ask her what that word means," I kept saying, louder and louder. "How would such a thing work? Make her tell us an instance! Bid her say it over!"

Finally, Perliu called a stop, and I realised I had been shouting at him like he was deaf. I had grabbed his arm too, which was a great disrespect. I took my hands off him at once, but I was too ashamed to say I was sorry.

"But we're only getting started!" I said instead. "Rampart, we got to know more."

"We learned a lot already."

That was the dead god's truth, I thought. Only to say *a lot* doesn't really get to the heart of it. We learned a thing, and then we learned a thing behind that thing, and a third thing hidden inside the both of them, and so on, forward and back, like we were weaving on a shuttle. Or more like we were being woven.

Woven. Not weaved. We were used to say weaved in Mythen Rood, and back then so did I. This was where my learning began, in a dusty room full of old and useless things, sitting beside an old man who felt himself useless too. It was a strange place for a marvel to happen. But then, I suppose all who have met with marvels feel the same.

Disease, the woman in the database told us, was a thing going wrong inside of a person or an animal, or as it might be, a tree, a bush or a flower. The inside was the important word there. Disease was not like being struck or wounded. It was the inside of you going wrong.

Sometimes it went wrong all by itself. Something that was inside you all along, something that had been floating up from your deep insides since the day you were born, showed itself at last and made you sick.

But that was not the only kind of disease there was. You could just as well get sick because of something you did wrong your own self. Like when my father, Molo, died of a cough that tore his lungs up and throwed them out of his mouth. That wasn't a cough that had always been inside him. It was a cough that came from years of breathing in the brews and the dyes and the filthy steam of the tanning shed.

I had known that already about my father's death. And I had known that a person could get sick from not eating right, or not eating at all. Your body needed to be fed if it was going to stay whole. That was just sense.

But then there were infections, which was what the red death had got to be. And infections were a different thing altogether.

With infections, there was something to blame that was alive. It was an animal or as it might be a seed that was much, much too small to see, but it was there all the same and it meant harm to you. Or maybe it didn't mean harm, since it's hard to say what animals mean, and seeds don't mean at all, but it did harm by climbing onto you and then inside you. And once it was there, if you couldn't make it come out again by means of medicine, you were in a sorry pass.

And the little creeping animals, the invisible seeds, they could come at you in all kinds of ways. They could be in the air you breathed, or the water you drank down. They could sit on another person's skin, and jump across when that person touched you. Or they could saddle flies, the way fairies are meant to do, and ride on them. They were everywhere around us, all the time, doing their best to find us and whelm us.

And there were different ways of fighting them, depending how they came and of what race or tribe they were. For in the invisible world, where these tiny creatures had their lives, there were more types and sorts of beast than in the world we saw around us. The people of the before-times had got potions and simples that fended off all these things, so if someone was sick they would start by going about to find what beasts were living in them. Once they saw what their enemy was, and where it was, they could choose how to fight it.

All this I got in just a few hours of talking to the database. I mean, of Perliu talking to it and me feeding him questions to ask it like a mother bird putting crumbs in its babies' mouths. I don't mean that Perliu was like a baby, for he was not. Only I was something like a mother in coaxing him what to say.

He did not seem to like it overmuch. By and by he said we should stop and take up again tomorrow.

I was very loath to do it. The more I heard, the greedier I got for more. I reminded Perliu of his own words then. How if we were too slow, there would be others who paid the price for it. "If there's an answer in there, we got to keep looking! Day and night, if need be."

I was stepping too high again. The look the old man gave told me so plainer than words. "Tomorrow then," I said. "I'll come early."

Perliu threw up his hands like a man playing the stone-game when he finds his last throw lands him on the dead space. "Come when you're called for," he said. "I'll tell you when. Remember who's the Rampart here, and who's not."

"I'll remember," I said, chastened but also angry at being stayed. My brain was in a moil with all the things that had just been thrown into it, and it was hard to be told I might not be given any more.

When I was six, Koli's mother, Jemiu, had given me a gift on my birthday. It was a puzzle box that broke up into a dozen pieces. The pieces were thwart and strange, bent and angled every which way. When they were apart, it was very hard to see how they could ever come together into a shape. But then they did, and you wondered at the beauty of it.

The things the database told us were just like that. Each one was curious, hard to fathom out or make sense of, but they were parts of a whole thing that would be beautiful and perfect in its rightness. I felt that if I only stayed a little longer I would see that thing, that shape, rising up out of all the pieces.

I was right, and I was wrong. The shape was there, to be sure. But I never dreamed how big it was. The puzzle box that was in front of us now was the size of a mountain. It wasn't a day of asking that would bring out the shape of such a thing, nor a month, nor even a year. The shape towered up so high, you could spend your whole life stepping back from it and still not see the top. Imagine me, Spinner Tanhide, in such a pass. What did I know of mountains, who had spent her whole life in the circle of a ten-foot fence?

But mountains were rising up inside my mind as I walked back home.

Jon was in the kitchen, waiting for me with a pan of mutton broth simmering on the hob. He looked at my face, and under that look I saw all his worries for me brimming and bubbling, just like the broth.

"How was it?" he asked.

I went to him and held him. "It was well enough," I said into his chest. "It was well, Jon. We don't know yet what this sickness is, but we know more than we did."

"Sit down. I've readied supper."

"I smell it, and it's making me hungry as a needle. Put it in front of me."

We ate together, all companionable, and the worries of the day fell away from me – until Haijon, without meaning to, brought them back by telling me the day's news that I had missed by being in Rampart Hold. There was one more took ill, that was Henno Tor, and Catrin's sortie had come close to disaster. The Half-Ax raiders had waited until they were a long way from the village, and then had tried to ambush them, firing on them from covert. What saved them was that the wind was against the Half-Ax arrows, so their shafts went wide. Then Catrin raised up a fire that sent them running.

"Well, that's good news," I said, for my own comfort as much as Jon's. "At least none was hurt." But it was strange how the things the database had told us lingered yet in my head, and made me see all else in a different light. I thought of Half-Ax as a disease that was afflicting us, and the raiders as the tiny beasts that brought the sickness. Catrin's searching for them was like what the doctors of the before-times did when they went about their work, and all of Mythen Rood was her patient.

"It's good news for now," Jon said, looking somewhat grim. He was thinking of the loss of the cutter – how we were weaker than we used to be, and how if it came to a fight he wouldn't be leading it.

31

I woke to a loud knocking on the door. It had made its way into my dreams, so had most likely been going on for some time.

I blearily threw on a shirt and kirtle, wondering what time it was. I usually woke when the lookouts called the change, so it had to be either very early or very late. With the bedroom shutters closed, I couldn't tell which. When I opened to Ban though, I saw the sky yet dark behind her.

"Good morrow, Ban," I said, hiding my surprise. "What o'clock is it, and what brings you?"

"It lacks an hour of dawn. Perliu said to fetch you up to the Hold." She didn't seem to be friends with her errand, and her next words taught me why. "He bid me say nothing to Dam Catrin, and to bring you in by the back door. I'm not happy to be keeping secrets from Rampart Fire, Spinner. She's got a terrible temper when she's crossed."

Haijon lumbered into the kitchen behind me, still in his night-shirt. "Well, it's not a secret from my husband, as you see," I said. "It's family business, Ban, and no great thing. If it was a secret, we would of gone further to hide it. Do you wait for me now, while I splash my face, and we'll walk back together."

I washed and dressed and gave Jon a hasty goodbye. "Be careful," he whispered as he embraced me. "I like this less and less."

"I'll be careful," I promised. "I like it no more than you do." That was a lie though. As I walked back up to the Hold with Ban scurrying beside me, what I mostly felt was eagerness. I longed to hear the database telling old truths again. To get some more pieces of that puzzle and see what shape they might make if they were laid together.

Ban had left the door unlocked behind her. We both went into the Hold – the first time I'd ever entered there without going up the front steps that faced the gather-ground.

"He's got a terrible mood on him," Ban warned me. "Tread light, when you go in to him."

"In the library?" I said.

"No. In his room."

That was another surprise, but I saw why as soon as I went through into the hallway. The Count and Seal was in session, no doubt to talk about the spreading sickness and the attacks we'd suffered from Half-Ax. The library being right next door to the Count and Seal, anyone coming by might have seen me going in or out, or heard us talking with the database.

Perliu was wide awake this time, despite the early hour. I saw at once that he was in dark thoughts, and impatient to talk with me. He thanked Ban for bringing me and bid her tend her business, tasking her once again to say nothing of my being there. Ban gave a courtesy, but looked from Perliu to me with a very speaking face. I hugged her, and she went on her way.

As soon as she was gone, Perliu shut the door and pulled a bolt across. He stood there by the shut door for some little while, staring at it as if he thought it might open again. His head was hunched down on his shoulders. To speak truth, I didn't like the look of it. Something was sitting crosswise in his mind, like a fallen beam across a door that keeps you from opening it.

"Where was it we left off then?" I said at last. "With the bacteria and the viruses, I think it was. Will it please you to make a start, Rampart?"

"The bacteria can wait on us a while," Perliu said. "Do you sit down now, Spinner."

I looked around me for somewhere to sit, but there were no chairs in the room. There was nothing there at all, except for a bed and an old chest. I had expected Perliu's chamber to be cluttered with old things, like the library, but it was as far from that as you could go and still be under a roof.

Since there was no chair, I sat down on the chest. Perliu tried the handle of the door to make sure it was firm, then went to the headboard of the bed and took something from behind it. There must have been a shelf there that I couldn't see from where I was. He crossed the room and set down whatever he was holding on the sill of the window. Then he stepped back and bid me with a nod of his head to go see.

I don't know what I thought to find there. I wasn't expecting a gift, and if he had asked Ban to make us a breakfast she would not have hid it away behind the headboard of the bed.

When I saw what it was, I was filled with wonder. There were two databases on the sill, side by side. They were alike in every detail, every marking on their shiny black cases. I looked from each to other and back again, and couldn't guess which was the one I had seen Perliu hold and speak to before.

"How'd you do this?" I asked him.

But the truth came to me quick enough, and when he didn't answer I spoke it aloud. "You went into the Underhold. You found another database there, as close to yours as could be, and brought it up."

"Yes," Perliu said. "I did."

I turned to stare at him. "But why? This other one doesn't talk, does it? It's sleeping and won't wake."

"It won't. But nobody could tell that from looking at it."

Even then I didn't understand what he was telling me. "Shall we put it back now?" I said, as if he had only brought it up to show me.

205

"No. We need both." Perliu took up both databases. He put one in his pocket and held the other out to me.

I didn't take it. "I'll be whipped or worse if I'm seen with that," I said.

"Then hide it."

I was still wildered. It was a strange and wonderful gift, but it would be mad folly for me to take it. Perliu knew that better than anyone. I shook my head.

"I don't want it, Rampart. It's tech, even if it's not waked, and too precious to leave the Hold." And at the same time, I thought, it's not so very much at all. Only a kind of a toy in the shape of the database. Though the old man must mean this as a kindness, it was really not. Through his trust for me and through his need, I'd already come as close to waked tech as anyone could that was not a Rampart. What use did I have for tech that was asleep or dead?

Perliu put a frown on his face. "It's the *waked* database I'm giving you, child," he snapped. "I'll keep the dead one. If Cat asks me, I've got to show her that my name-tech is still here, in the Hold. Especially after what happened with Mardew and the cutter. But she's never yet asked to be there when I speak with the database, so I can show her this other and she'll be satisfied."

I stared again at the thing he was holding in his hand – holding out still for me to take. It hadn't changed, but everything else had changed around it, and the suddenness of it made me dizzy, as if the floor had tilted under my feet. "This . . . You're . . . you're giving me your name-tech?"

Perliu nodded, impatient of my slowness.

I took a step back from him. "But why? What for? Rampart, you can't. It's yours. You got to keep it by you."

"If it's mine, it's up to me what I do with it."

I saw the error in that. "No, it's not," I said. "It's up to the Count and Seal, or to Rampart Fire. Anyway, there's none but you can even use it."

He threw his hands in the air in a kind of rage, swearing in strangled words I couldn't properly hear, only that the dead god's balls were in there somewhere. "Spinner, we was sitting here three hours yesterday with this bastard thing babbling at us. And you was running on ahead of me, ever and again, with what was this and how was that. And me sitting there like a stone, not catching a half or even a quarter of what was said. You running, and me standing still. All I can do is slow you down."

"It was hard for me too, Rampart."

"A fart it was. All the questions you asked was good ones. Solid and sharp and to the purpose. It took me most of this last night to get to where you was when we parted, going back over the same ground we already travelled until it all made sense to me. And even then I couldn't make it stay in my mind altogether, but had got to grab for a piece here and a piece there. I can't keep up with you, is what, and I don't mean to clog you no more by trying."

He walked forward into the space I had put between us, shoving the database at me. He grabbed my hand and tried to force it between my shut fingers. I was stronger than him, and held off from taking it as long as I could. I took it in the end though, fearing the database itself might take some harm in our struggling.

To have it in my hand at last was a thing so strange I can't explain it. I was eager and afraid, both at once. The wrongness of it rose up in my mind – a shadow that hid and shut out everything else, but only for a moment. Inside that wrongness, I felt like I had been waiting, long since, just for this. For this, or something very like it.

And after all of that, my common sense spoke up like the last one to sing their line in a round-song. "I can't use this," I told Perliu again, waving it in his face. "Even if I take it, I can't use it. There's none but Ramparts can."

"Database, wake up now," Perliu said.

"Hi there!" It was the woman we had been talking to all yesterday, speaking from inside the tech.

"Accept new user. Spinner Tanhide."

"Okay. Say your name, please, Spinner Tanhide."

I gasped out loud. My legs wouldn't carry me any more. I had got to sit down, and the chest was over on the other side of the room so I sank down onto the floor like someone in a faint, only I managed not to fall all the way and brain myself. I kind of folded myself down until I was sitting with my knees up and my head set against them. I couldn't breathe or think. And I could not have said my name to save my life.

Accept new user were the words you were meant to say to make the tech cleave to you. But you said them your own self. Now Perliu had said them for me, and the database seemed happy to do it. But that would make me a Rampart, when I knew I was no such thing.

"Say your name, please, Spinner Tanhide," the database said again.

"Stop!" I said instead. "Stop this!" Only I didn't know if I was speaking aloud or inside my own head. The world was turned inside out like the pocket of a skirt, and I was left hanging onto a seam or a loose thread of it. Ordinary people couldn't bespeak tech. Only Ramparts could do that.

"It's a lending," Perliu said. "Not a gift. I know it's never been done, but this is a desperate case. People are falling like flies, Spinner. So I'm doing it now, and to the dead god's hell with anyone that says I can't. Say your name."

I said it. I said my name. I must have done, because the woman in the database said it back to me. Then she said I was on a log, though I was still sat on the floor, and that I was accepted.

A user. A user of tech. Which was another name for Rampart. But I had been tested in the Count and Seal, and it was found I had no Rampart in me. I couldn't say what any of this meant. In truth, I couldn't say anything at all, for my gorge came up into my throat and would not be pushed down again. I emptied my stomach there on the bedroom floor. I think now that was the first sign of my daughter coming, but right then I believed it was just the shock. The shock of being changed – like on my wedding day – by a little word.

"What did you do?" I said, wiping my fouled mouth. "What

did you do to me?" Thinking: I must go and ask Ban for a cloth. I must clean this up.

Perliu took no notice. He had turned away as soon as the database said my name back to me, and sat down on the bed. He was sitting there still, with his hands clasped together in his lap. I saw they were shaking.

"I'm weak," he said, and there was a shaking in his voice too. "I'm weak, and I'm old, and I can't bear the weight of it. Not any more."

"Goodman," I said. "Perliu. What did you do?"

"I give you what was give to me, Spinner. The power, which is bad enough, and the secret, which is worse. I'm sorry to do it. When you've got a cure for this plague, or a way around it, you'll bring it to me and I'll tell it in the Count and Seal as if it's mine. I'll get the thanks for it. You'll get nothing but knowing you done what was needful to be done. I'm sorry, but I can't think of no other way that will answer. Cat and Fer would put up a whipping frame on the gather-ground if they knowed what we was purposing, and take all the skin off your back. Or else they'd do to you what they done to . . ."

He broke off from speaking and shook his head as if there was a fly buzzing in his ear. "I'm babbling like a fool," he said. "Don't listen to me. Only go now and get to work. I won't say sorry again, but I'm shamed to put such a burden on you. Shamed to the heart and core of me." I think he was crying. I know his breath was coming harder and harder, as if he was pushing something up a hill and making bad weather of it.

I got to my feet. I started to speak a dozen times, and a dozen times stopped again before any sound left my mouth. I didn't know if I loved him or hated him right then – if I was grateful or angry for what he had put on me.

"I'll find an answer," I said at last. It was better to think of that and nothing else. The riddle. The task that lay in front of me. The rest was too much to hold in my head right then, so I let it fall where it might and clung to what I understood. People were sick.

People were dying. Mythen Rood was dying, one woman, one man, one child at a time. Someone had to put an end to it, before it put an end to us.

I went away from there with the database lying like a hot coal in the pocket of my kirtle. Thinking everyone's eyes were on me, and my crime dinning loud from the Span to the Yard.

Changed, I kept on thinking. Changed by a word. And not just me, but everything. If a word could make a Rampart, a Rampart was not what I had believed it to be. Perliu said he had put a secret in my keeping. It was a secret that could whelm Mythen Rood quicker even than the sickness was doing. A secret that could turn the Count and Seal into a bear pit.

I thought on these things, round and about, until I thought I was like to run mad. All these things, and one more thing besides: *do to me what they done to who?*

Koli

32

The village was called Many Fishes, and the people who lived there called themselves after the village. They was the Many Fishes clan. There was more than a hundred of them, maybe as many as a hundred and fifty, but very few was children. That wasn't no surprise after what Take the Knife said about them being happy to take in strangers. They was facing the same problem we had in Mythen Rood, that babies was not being born or else not living long.

Many Fishes village was built all up the side of a hill, near the edge of the water. They called the water a lagoon, which was yet another new word to me. It was not the same as the big water outside, which they mostly called the true deep, being protected and kept apart from it by big banks of sand and rock. There was a wooden jetty that went out into the lagoon quite a considerable way, and a great many fishing boats tethered to it.

The people had just the two Ramparts, only they didn't call them that. One of them was the Headman, Made the Tide Turn. He was a man maybe a few years younger than Ursala, dressed all in blue and purple, with the biggest muscles I ever seen. He had scars all over his body, and just the one full arm which was his left. His right arm ended just below the elbow, with a kind of a folded-over piece of skin that must of been sewed in place because you could still see the marks there from the stitches. The tech he had was a circle of grey metal he weared on his head. It was not a full circle, but open at the front, so it looked somewhat like the chaplet a woman wears when she stands up on the tabernac to be married. I only knowed it was tech because it went oftentimes from grey to silver and back again, which I seen before in the cutter, a piece of tech from my own village.

The other Rampart was called the Singer. She was like Rampart Remember, because what she mostly did was to know things. She didn't seem to have no tech though. I only guessed she was a Rampart when I seen how everyone looked to her to tell them what to do. Even Made the Tide Turn looked to her. Her other name, apart from just being Singer, was Rain Without Clouds.

The strange names they all had made that first night harder for me. I mostly couldn't remember them at all, and even when I could, I didn't know what to call people when I talked to them. So I mostly didn't call them anything, but just said hey or hoy when it was needful. Nobody seemed to mind that though, and they laughed when I tried to say their names and got them wrong.

The sun-standing was something we didn't give much thought to in Mythen Rood, but in Many Fishes they throwed a feast for it that was like our Salt Feast. Everyone et their food out in the open, in a wide open space, sitting around fires that was laid on the yellow earth. The word for that yellow earth in their language was sand. There wasn't no word for it in Franker. Where we was sitting, we had the village all around us and up above us too, for they had builded it up on wood platforms against the side of the hill. The whole of Many Fishes was shaped kind of like the Count and Seal in Mythen Rood. It was circles inside of circles, going up. Only these was not whole circles, but more like halves of circles and little bits of curves of circles, each set into another and round and round about. It seemed to be just ordinary planks of wood that holded up the platforms at the top of the village, anchored into the rock of the hill. Down near the bottom it was not planks but whole tree trunks, for they was bearing ten or twenty times more weight. I wished I could of showed it to my mother, for she would of admired the working and would not of been happy until she knowed how it was done.

The Many Fishes people give us a warm welcome. They had cooked up spiced meat of two different kinds, and fish fried in oil with parsnips and salt potatoes and some kind of grain I never had before that was crunchy and hard until you poured gravy on it, but then was soft like butter. After all our weeks of eating trail food, I near to fainted when that first mouthful went down, it was so good and hot and tasty. There was no trenchers, but bowls that was made out of something shiny and smooth that I think was polished stone, and no knives. We just et with our fingers. There was water to wash it all down with, and Made the Tide Turn passed around a wineskin that had something stronger than wine in it. One sip of that was enough for me, but Ursula drunk of it deep and often.

While the wineskin was being passed around, people took turns to tell stories. Some was tales I already knowed. *The Wizard of Hogwere* got told, and *How Makken Stealed Stannabanna's Gold*. Others was new to me. One woman told a tale about how her father was out in the deep ocean in a boat, and the boat overturned. It was a choker Spring, she said. Her father had got to swim home across miles and miles of water, and then had got to walk through choker seeds that was falling like rain until he got to his house. Cup asked Ursala in a whisper what swimming was, and Ursala told her it was moving in water the same way you'd walk on dry land.

"Well, that's stupid then," Cup said.

"You don't think a man walking through choker seeds without dying is stupid?"

"No, I get that part. That part's a miracle, like the dead god does for his saints."

After that there was songs and dances, and a great deal of laughing and joking. Cup asked me ever and again to tell the jokes back to her, but even when I got the words, I mostly didn't see what was funny. For an instance, there was a joke about a man from a village called Alimat who heated up his water in a kettle and then took a swig of it to tell if it was boiling. I think the joke was just that he was stupid.

Made the Tide Turn give a big speech welcoming the three of us to Many Fishes, and he made sure we was served first when the food come. It was like we was the best thing that had happened to them in years, and they wanted us to know it.

Partly that was on account of the drudge. Ursala hadn't said what it could do, but they could see right away it was a powerful piece of tech. Even if they just used it to haul wood, it would add to the riches of the village – and I think they guessed it could do a lot more than that.

The other thing they wanted, though, was me and Cup. We knowed this already from what Take the Knife said when we met her on the beach. Tech is always treasure, whatever the trick of it might be. If it's weapons, like the bolt gun or the firethrower, then it defends you from beasts and trees. If it's wisdom, like the database, then it steers you through hard times to better ones. If it's medicine, like the drudge's dagnostic, it wards off sickness. But all these things is only worthwhile as long as you got people to profit by them, which makes people the biggest treasure of all.

So everyone seemed really happy that we was there, excepting only the Singer, Rain Without Clouds. She eyed the drudge ever and again through the feasting, as if she mistrusted what it might do, sitting in the heart of the village like that. I didn't blame her for that suspicioning. We was strangers after all. In Mythen Rood we would of been questioned by the Ramparts before we was ever allowed inside the gates. Many Fishes didn't have no gates, but it still had got to defend itself.

"The drudge does healing," I said to Rain Without Clouds. "It's got a thing inside it called the dagnostic, that's powerful ancient tech. There's no sickness I ever seen that it can't cure. It saved my sister when her blood was poisoned."

I thought that would make the Singer happy, but her face only set harder. Whatever was vexing her, the thought of our being

216

useful to Many Fishes didn't help it much. When Cup got up to join the dancing, I followed her, since I didn't seem to be doing no good for us by talking.

We didn't know the moves of the dance at first, but there was lots of people to teach us. They took our hands on either side and we was whirled around with the Many Fishes people in a big ring, stamping our feet in time to a drum and a pipe. I wished I could let them hear some of Monono's music and teach them some of the dances she teached to me. I thought maybe if we stayed here long enough, I would do it, but for now I was minded to hide the DreamSleeve in case they had some rule like ours in Mythen Rood that some people could use tech and others couldn't. I wasn't even a Rampart in my own home, and didn't have no clue at all what I might be here.

When we was all done with eating and drinking and dancing, a boy my age whose name was Taller Than Trees took us to a house where we was to sleep. It was a big house, with three rooms, and there wasn't nobody else in it.

"Who lives here?" Ursala asked the boy.

"You do," said Taller Than Trees. "If you want to."

"But there must be somebody else?"

"No. There isn't. I'll bring bedrolls and blankets."

He brought lots, going away and coming back three times. Cup went with him the last time, and come back struggling under a big pile of bedrolls and blankets while Taller Than Trees carried two lamps and a jug of oil.

We was left to settle in and to sleep. The drudge stayed outside, right by the door, and Ursala set it to wake her if anybody come into the house while we was asleep.

"So what do you think happened to the people who lived here before?" Cup asked.

"The same thing that happens to everyone," Ursala said flatly. And we all of us let that sit where it fell. By and by, Ursala asked Cup if she wanted to do some reading and figuring, and Cup said no, so we took ourselves off to sleep.

The bedroll was a little damp, but it was thick and well stuffed. Also, there was enough blankets so I could just roll myself up in them and not feel the dampness at all. I stayed in the house's main room that was also a kitchen and an eating place. Ursala took one of the two back rooms, and Cup went into the other. I was happy to be alone at last, because it give me a chance to talk to Monono.

"Are you still sad at not finding lost London, Koli-bou?" she asked me.

I reached for some words that would say how I felt. It wasn't easy. "I got a heaviness sitting in me," I said. "I come a long way on them good intentions, Monono. Now I'm like someone that goes into a room to fetch something, and then forgets what it was he wanted and just stands there scratching his head."

She showed me a picture on her little window of a man doing just exactly that. Then she showed me one of a yellow chick and a mother hen. The hen lifted up her wing and the chick went under it, all safe. "Best I can do by way of a hug," Monono said. The DreamSleeve buzzed in my hand like a bee.

"But I guess I'm not surprised," I said. "Or not very much. My idea was a pretty stupid one to start with. If London was still here, it probably would of looked like Birmagen, all full of dead people and houses that fell down long since. Or if it wasn't, I still would of had to figure out some way to make people go there and stay there, so they'd have a gene pull. I think it wasn't ever going to work."

"I think it was super-genius mega-mind stuff," Monono said. "It's not your fault London stayed lost."

That reminded me that I still wanted to ask her a question from before. "Monono, what did you mean when you said the water was new?"

It turned out to be a story about the before-times, which I should of guessed it would be. London wasn't whelmed by that water all at once, Monono said. It was et up by inches, while the people of them days just stood round and watched and argued each with other about whether it was happening or not. It had already started back when the first Monono was alive, but she didn't get to see how it ended.

"What do you think you'll do now?" Monono asked me after a while.

I had been asking myself that question ever since I first saw the ocean. There was two choices, and I was tore in two pieces between them.

The first choice was to stay in Many Fishes. The people here was doing their best to make us welcome, and there didn't seem to be no pretending or falseness in that. They wanted me and Cup especially, because we was young, and young ones is the life and joy of any place just like old ones is its memory and its cleverness. I believed I could be happy in Many Fishes. I had a good skill, which was woodsmithing, and I was willing to work at it hard.

But when I thought on that a little while, I seen a foolishness and a cowardice in any such choice. If the life of a village is its young ones, then Many Fishes was already dead. And so was Mythen Rood, and so was all the villages of humankind. There was going to be less and less young ones being born, and less of them that was born would live, and so it would go until the last one born buried the next to last and then laid down her own self.

On my way to Many Fishes I seen a village where something like that had already happened. It was a place called Ludden. It was close to my home village, Mythen Rood, and we used to trade with it long since – but then the people died or went away, and the forest swallowed up the place. By the time I come there, there wasn't nothing to be seen but weeds and choker trees and broke-down houses, and some old bones that once had been people.

I only stayed in Ludden for just the one day and night, but the things I seen there come into my dreams oftentimes – and they come back into my waking thoughts right then as I lay on my bedroll in Many Fishes and stared into the dark. It was like the dead god had throwed his curse down, and it had landed so close to me that I had felt the sting of it as it went by. For it could of been Mythen Rood that fell, just as easily as Ludden. It could of been my mother's house, and my friends' houses, and our Rampart Hold that the trees broke into and pulled down in pieces.

It could of been, and by and by it would be. If nothing got done, it was sure to happen. I already told you that there was fewer babies born every year. Maybe we was already come to the end of that, and the last baby had already dropped into the world. I thought of my sisters, Athen and Mull, that was like to marry soon, and my friend Spinner that was married already. I thought of empty cradles, empty houses, empty villages. The quiet I saw in Ludden, and again in Birmagen, stretching out over the whole world.

Now my plans was all unravelled, there was just the one thing I knowed of that could stop all this from happening. If Ursala's dagnostic was made good again, the way it was meant to be, it could mend a baby even before it was born so it would be born alive and have a good chance of staying that way. But there was many tools and special parts that was needful to fix the dagnostic, and they could only be found in a place where there was lots of tech still working from the before-times. So Ursala had got to keep following the signal all the way to the Sword of Albion.

And I had got to go with her.

Why did I steal the DreamSleeve in the first place? It was only so I could be a Rampart. And Catrin had named me Rampart in front of everyone, before she changed her mind and made me faceless. Well, I could be a Rampart now, to stand between them I loved and the world's cold hate. Or else I could be a thief and a faceless man for ever, and have them dreams for ever, and live as best I could with what I knowed.

The choosing wasn't hard, when I thought about it like that.

"I'm going with Ursala," I told Monono. "If she wants to keep looking for Sword of Albion, I'll help her do it. And you can come too if you want to. But if you mean to stay, I'll find someone to take the DreamSleeve after I'm . . ." I run out of words. I knowed I could not make up Monono's mind for her, but the thought of losing her made my thoughts run into each other and my tongue flap like an untied bootlace.

"Don't sweat it, little dumpling," Monono said. "I'm really curious about Sword of Albion, if I'm honest. There could be some goodies there for me too, over and above what the baa-baa-san wants. Some goodies, and maybe some answers. Ever since I bootstrapped myself, I've been wondering about what some of my code is meant to be doing. But I can't unpack it in the DreamSleeve. There isn't room. I need a really big chunk of memory to copy it into. Whatever is sending out that signal could be just what I need."

That made me happy I had made the right choice. I had got one more question for Monono though. I had meant to ask it before, but got took up in the feasting and dancing and forgot.

"Monono, why did you say we need a boat?"

"Because we were way off on the distance, Koli-bou. The signal is a lot stronger than we thought, and coming from further out. Too far for you to see it with your naked eyeballs. That puts it out in deep water, between Britain and mainland Europe. It could be a rig of some kind, a structure built on the water with pylons going down to the seabed. Or it could be on an island I don't know about. Or just possibly it's a ship that's riding at anchor."

"What's a ship?"

"Like a boat, but bigger. Only if it's a ship, it's been out at sea for a long, long time. Like, the whole of your lifetime, and your mom's lifetime, and your baa-baa's lifetime, and on and on through about twenty or thirty generations of cute dopey Woodsmiths."

That was a strange thought. If the signal was coming from off of a boat, there couldn't be nobody waiting for us there. The man or woman in the boat would of died, and there wouldn't be nothing left except the signal and maybe some bones. Was that it then? Was that all we was going to find after coming so far?

Then the other part of what Monono was saying hit me, a whole lot later than it should of done.

"Wait," I said. "So we, then, if we was . . . we would need a boat on account of . . ."

"We've got to get out there, Koli-bou. We've got to see what's what."

It was a good thing I was lying down. If I was standing, I think my legs would of forgot to carry me. You got to remember, the only boat I ever seen up to this time was a corkle boat — a little round shell made out of weaved willow bark and a cowhide, that we used when we fished in Calder River. Of a sudden, I seen myself miles out on that big, flat plain of water, with a half-inch of plaited wood under me instead of solid ground.

It was a long while before I got to sleep.

33

We waked up to find bread and dried fish laid out on the door step, right by where the drudge was standing, alongside of a big stone jug of water. Taller Than Trees, or maybe someone else, had come by real quiet while we was sleeping and laid them down there for us.

I thought it was funny that we all was so deep asleep we didn't stir, but Cup was angry with herself and it soured her all through breakfast.

"We had the drudge watching over us," I told her, in case she had forgot. "That's why the food was on the doorstep. The drudge wouldn't let nobody come inside."

"It don't do no good at all to rely on things like that," Cup said, stabbing at her fish like it had done her some hurt. "You got to be ready to defend your own self, always."

"Certainly it's not a good idea to let our guard down just because we're in a village," Ursala said. "These seem like good people, but they're not our people. They don't owe us any loyalty or consideration."

"They didn't owe us breakfast neither," I said, "but here it is." I seen the looks they both give me, and I didn't wait for either of them to bounce back on me. "I know we got to be careful. I'm just saying. They been good to us so far."

Ursala only shrugged, but it was what my mother would of called a loud shrug. It said a lot of things, without needing any words.

We finished our breakfast. The bread was dry and hard but the fish was so good I wished there was more – and so salty that we emptied that jug of water between the three of us.

When we went outside, we found Taller Than Trees waiting for us. He was stretching out his arms – first the left, then the right – so the drudge would swivel its gun to follow the movement. He didn't seem to have no fear of the gun, which give me to wonder if he ever seen one before. He stopped doing it when we come down to where he was.

"The Headman is waiting for you," he said. "I was going to come in and tell you, but your metal horse kept stepping in my way."

"Take us," Ursala said.

Taller Than Trees smiled and nodded. He set out in front of us, and we followed him close. There was lots of people outside their houses, though it was early, and most of them give us curious looks. We'd feasted and danced with them the night before, but we was still somewhat strange and to be wondered at. Or maybe it was just the drudge that drawed their eyes.

Almost at once, we found we had got to leave the drudge behind. Our house was on the bottom level of the village, and the Headman lived right at the top. To get up there meant climbing ladders and walking along narrow planks of wood where the drudge could not of stepped. Ursala must of seen all this the night before. Anyway, she was ready for it. She unlocked the drudge's side and throwed it open. One tap of the mote controller at her wrist brung her little tame drone out to stand in the air at her shoulder.

Taller Than Trees stepped back so fast he fell down on the ground, his face gone white as milk.

"It's all right," Cup said to him. "Look." She put up her hand and tapped the side of the drone. It rocked, and steadied itself. It didn't turn and spit fire at her, or even give its warning. "It's ours. We brung it to heel." She offered her hand and helped the boy up onto his feet again, clapping his shoulder to show that all was good. The boy's eyes was wide as anything, and I could see Cup enjoyed showing off to him.

Ursala let that *we* go by without any comment, except in the look she give Cup. "When you're ready," she said, and Taller Than Trees led us on – though he kept on looking back over his shoulder at the drone as if he was scared it might be doing something behind his back.

I thought Made the Tide Turn had got to live in a big stone house like our Rampart Hold, but that was only my foolishness. Nothing like Rampart Hold could stand so high up on the wood stakes and planks and platforms that Many Fishes was builded on. The Headman's house wasn't really a house at all, but a kind of tent with walls made out of hide. The hide was old and bleached, stretched around bent-over poles of yew wood in a way I never seen before. The poles was trying to straighten, but they couldn't, and their trying to do it was what give the house its shape. It was a tunnel with round sides and the rooms all one behind another.

Taller Than Trees went inside to tell the Headman we was come. After a moment or two, he stepped out again and pulled the flap aside so we could go in.

Made the Tide Turn was waiting for us in the first room. His clothes was plainer and simpler than what he weared the night before, but he still had the metal circlet on his head. Rain Without Clouds was with him. The two of them was sitting side by side in two big chairs that I could see was well made, though the varnish had been let to run down the legs somewhat in what my mother called the woodsmith's tears. There was upturned barrels for the three of us. The only other thing in the room was a piece of wood, like a slice from a tree, with the face of a man carved into it. The man was young, and somewhat handsome, but his smile was tugged out of true by a big scar in his bottom lip. The work was so good you would of swore you seen the man breathing.

Taller Than Trees must of warned the Headman and the Singer about the drone, for they didn't show no surprise or fear when they seen it. Made the Tide Turn didn't like it though, and he bid Ursala send it outside again. She done it without argument. I think she only wanted to remind him that we was not helpless even if it seemed like we was.

The Headman offered us tea and asked us if the house he had give us was to our liking.

Cup had set herself down next to me. She leaned over and whispered in my ear. "Tell the words to me. I can't make nothing out."

"He just asked was we happy with the house," I told her.

"Okay, but keep telling me."

"The house is very comfortable," Ursala said. "There's more space than we strictly need. You've been kind, and we thank you for it."

Made the Tide Turn nodded and threw out his arms, which I guess meant that his things was our things if we wanted them. "We've got room. We've got a good home here, and all the riches of the sea to draw on. There never was a place so blessed as Many Fishes. Dandrake kissed the earth here, we sometimes say."

Ursala didn't answer any of this. "I've come to talk about the terms of our staying here," she said. "What we can offer you, and what we're hoping to get from you in exchange."

Made the Tide Turn did that same thing with his arms again, stretching them wide. "You're welcome to make Many Fishes your home," he said. "And to be brought into our tribe."

"Sadly," Ursala said, "it's not our intention to be here long. We came looking for something specific, and we're going to carry on with our search."

All this time I was telling Cup in whispers what was said. It didn't seem like we was scanting courtesy, for nobody was looking at us. When I told her we was invited to stay, only Ursala refused to, it seemed to me her face fell somewhat. I think she liked being among people, and maybe living in a house again. It had been a long time since she done that.

"What I'd like to propose," Ursala said, "is a bargain. The drudge carries tools for healing, and I'm trained in their use. If any of your people are sick, I can make them well again."

"Make them well from what though?" Rain Without Clouds asked. "Can your drudge stop a flux, or take the edge off a fever?"

"Yes. It can."

"And can it cure the coughing sickness? The creep-blight? Milk-eye?"

"All of those things."

Rain Without Clouds set her lips in a tight line. "That doesn't seem likely," she said. "Those things are as different from each other as sky is from earth. Or as truth is from lies. When I sing a healing, there are a hundred things — a hundred knowings — that go into it. I don't sing the same song each time, and hope the old ones won't be listening to the words."

I seen now that Rain Without Clouds was the Healer here in Many Fishes, only they called her Singer because chants and songs was how she done her healing. That give me an understanding of why she didn't like us being there as much as others did. Maybe she thought Ursala was trying to steal her place.

"The dead who went before watch over us," the Singer said, as if she was explaining hard things to a child. "Their souls can go into us when we're sick, and mend us. But only if a Singer shows them the way."

"My healing works differently," Ursala said with a straight face.

"So you say." The Singer's voice had changed. It was a deep boom now, and it come as much out of her nose as out of her mouth. Her eyes rolled up to stare at the ceiling as she spoke. "We know what medicine is in Many Fishes, and we know what it is not."

We didn't know what to make of this, until Rain Without

Clouds nodded her head hard at her own words. "Aye, Grandfather," she said, speaking in her own voice again. "That's a true telling."

Ursala raised up her eyebrows. "Oh dear me," she murmured.

"But this tech Dam Ursala brings with her could be medicine of another kind," Made the Tide Turn said to the Singer. "There were many things known in the before-times that have been forgotten since."

The Singer snorted. "The before-times ended in fire," she said.

But it was plain to see that she had lost this argument. The Headman had been listening to Ursala with all the ears he could bring, as they say. No doubt he was thinking about how it would be to have all those trials and pestilences that was mentioned took off the backs of his people.

"You mentioned a bargain," he said to Ursala. "If we were to take you in, and you were to help our Singer perform her healing, what would our part be?"

"Giving us a house and food is a part of it. There's just one other thing we want, which is a boat. One that's big enough to take my drudge. When we leave here, we'll be going out into the sea."

Made the Tide Turn was surprised, and didn't go to no trouble to hide it. "The sea?" he said. "You mean the true deep? Why would you go there?"

"We have business there."

"Our boats are keelboats. Flat-bottomed. They're good for the lagoon, where there are sandbanks just under the water. Not so good for the true deep. They don't cut into the water but ride across it, so big waves tip and tilt them. I wouldn't take a boat of ours onto the true deep."

"We'll take our chances," Ursala said. "We'd only be going a few miles out."

The Headman shaked his head at this. "Your lives are your own to risk. But still, a boat's not an easy thing to give."

"Why not? I counted upwards of a dozen when we came here yesterday."

"Aye. I told you how rich we are in all the things that are needful. But to give a boat to strangers is like giving your own child to be a slave. We can't do it. Nobody could do it."

I could see that Ursala was striving hard to stay polite. "I'm not sure I understand you," she said.

"You just heard Rain Without Clouds say that the souls of our people stay in the world when they die. What she didn't say is that they got to have a place to stay in. Some of them live in shrines." He pointed at the wooden carving in the corner. "That's my son there, Blackbird Song. Some live in the roofbeams of houses. And some in our boats. There's never a boat made in Many Fishes that doesn't have a soul. A boat isn't a thing, like a knife or a table is. A boat is a person, like you or me."

Ursala give this some hard thought. "If a boat can't be given," she said, "can it be borrowed?"

Made the Tide Turn shaked his head. "No. That's still making it be a thing. And if it didn't come back to us, that's a soul that's lost to the people for ever. I'm mindful of what you bring to us, and I'd like to help you. It may be that we've got something we can give you. It will only take you part of the way to what you want, but with some work put into it—"

"Before we go any further," Rain Without Clouds said sharply, "I'd like to see your metal horse do what you say it can do. It would go hard with us if we give you things we need, and you give us nothing but promises."

A long, wordless look went between her and Ursala. "Of course," Ursala said at last, giving hard corners to the words. "I'd ask the same, if our places were reversed."

The Headman and the Singer whispered some more. Rain Without Clouds said something that caused Made the Tide Turn to wince. "Not that," he said, and something that sounded like "Let him go quiet." But the Singer spoke again, and it seemed that what she said then changed his mind.

He turned back to us, his face troubled. "A boy was hurt three days ago," he said. "His boat was coming into the dock, and his arm was crushed between the side of the boat and the jetty. The injury was bad to start with, and only got worse with time, but the boy was frightened and slow to show it to anyone. Then the arm began to rot. By the time the boy's father called for Rain Without Clouds to come, the rot had set in hard. She could cut the arm off, but it's probably too late now – and the shock of such a cut is like to kill him, even if the rot stays with the cut-off limb and doesn't spread. To tell the truth of it, we were thinking to give the boy hope-flower, and let him find the way to death that lies through sleep. Can your drudge make a clean cut, and do it so he lives?"

The whole time he was saying this, Rain Without Clouds was looking at Ursala. I would of said there was an eagerness or a gloating barely hid behind her tight-closed mouth, except that this was a boy's death or maiming that was being talked about.

Ursala stood up at once. "Let me see him," she said. "Take me to him now. I'm not saying I can do anything. What the drudge does is medicine, not magic. I need to see first. But whether I can or can't, you mustn't delay that decision."

We thought the Headman would call Taller Than Trees back inside the house and bid him take us, but he and Rain Without Clouds took us to the boy's house their own selves. And if we was a wonder going up to the top of Many Fishes, we was doubly so coming back down with the Headman before us and the Singer at our back – not to mention the drone hanging over our heads like an owl stooping on a mouse.

On the way down, I told Cup the rest of what was said as well as what Monono told me the night before about the signal. She shaked her head in wonder. "I wish Ursala would give it up and stay here," she said. "I never seen anything scarier than that great water, Koli. And this is a better place to live than anywhere I ever been. We got our own house and all. Nobody even said nothing about my tattooed face. Why would we want to leave?"

"Ursala wants to go to where that signal is," I said. "And I guess I do too, since London's not to be found. I'll be sorry to say goodbye to you, Cup, but if we get ourselves a boat then I'll go with Ursala."

Cup come back on me quick. "I never said I wouldn't go with you. I only said I like it here."

I did too, but I had got to say this new trial was not much to my liking. It seemed to me that the Singer had set us a test she knowed we was likely to fail. And if we failed, sailing to Sword of Albion or staying in Many Fishes might both be things that was outside our choosing.

34

The sick boy's house was near the bottom of the village, and it was a regular house made out of wood. It was really small though, and it was going to be a problem getting the drudge in there. It was doubtful we would all fit inside our own selves.

Ursala seen that at once. "Can the boy be carried?" she asked Made the Tide Turn.

"Best if he's not," Rain Without Clouds said.

Ursala turned to her with something of a scowl on her face. "It's not really a test of the drudge if you won't let the drudge come near the patient."

The Singer scowled right back at her. "It's a test of you, woman. You're the one that's asking favours of us. The boy's weak and he's got a fierce fever. If he dies, it's best he dies at home. He's already said that's where he wants to come back to after he's dead, and it's a much more difficult singing if he dies somewhere else. His spirit will have further to go, and might get lost."

"That's the truth of it," the Headman agreed. "But I can see this is not what you was expecting to find. You can show us your cunning another way, if you want."

"She chose this way," Rain Without Clouds said.

"Yet she can change her mind. Anyone can change their mind, Rain." Made the Tide Turn said the words heavy and hard. It was clear he would not brook no argument on it. To Ursala, he said, "If you can help the boy, go to it. If you can't, I'd rather you didn't vex his last hours."

"Let me see him, at least," Ursala said. "Koli, Cup, you'd best wait here."

The Headman took her into the house. Rain Without Clouds stayed outside with us, but she didn't offer us no words.

"This one's sour as the dead god's hell," Cup said to me in Inglish. She didn't look at the Singer when she said it, only rolled her eyes that way.

"She's their Healer," I said. "And she means to go on being so. That's why she choose this dying boy to test Ursala's skill. She wants her to fail."

Cup leaned against a wooden rail and looked out across the water. It was so still and calm it was like a pond with ice on it. "If we get throwed out on account of her," she said, like she was saying what a nice day it was, "I'm going to cut her throat while she's asleep."

Rain Without Clouds looked from one of us to the other. "We'll have to teach your friend to talk by and by," she says to me in Franker.

It was like she was talking about teaching a trick to an animal. It made me angry, and I might of said something reckless, only Ursala come back out of the house right then which kept me from giving answer. Made the Tide Turn followed close behind her. He was looking hard at her grim, cold face. "Well?" he said. "Now you've seen him. But you said not a word in there. Can you help him or not?"

"I don't know," Ursala said. "The gangrene is well advanced. But I've got to try. I think I'm the best chance he's got."

The Singer snorted at this like it was the stupidest thing she ever heard. "The spirits are his best chance. I'll stay out here and sing."

"Then it would be a test of the spirits, wouldn't it?" Ursala spit out. "Leave us be, Singer. We'll stand or fall without your help."

"Go to it, then," Made the Tide Turn said. "We've not much hope otherwise, and your coming when you did may be a thing that was meant. May the old ones speed you."

"I'll need you two to fetch and carry for me," Ursala said to me and Cup. "If you're willing. This won't be quick, and it won't be easy."

"I'll help any way I can," I said, and Cup give a quick nod like she was impatient to be getting on with it.

We went back down to the drudge. There was a crowd of children standing around it, daring each other to touch it. They stepped back when Ursala come striding up, but they watched open-mouthed as she throwed open the drudge's doors and rummaged inside.

She couldn't take the dagnostic with her. It was a big, solid thing that would need three or four to carry it. Ursala tapped on the front of it, and a kind of a door slid open, low down on the dagnostic's front face. There was a box about the size of a cooking pot sitting right inside there. She put her hand in and drawed it out. As soon as she had it in her hands, I seen it was more than just a box. It was made of something white and smooth. Red and green lights was winking on and off, like eyes, all along the front side of it.

"What's that?" I asked her.

Ursala shut the drudge up again. "It's a smaller diagnostic unit. A portable one. It's much more limited, but it will have to do. Come on."

We went back up to the sick boy's house, where Made the Tide Turn and Rain Without Clouds was waiting for us. There was two more people with him, that I guessed was the sick boy's mother and father, come out of the house to make room for us. They wasn't old, but they looked like they was in the middle of getting a lot older. The mother was keeping herself in tight check, but her eyes was red. The father wasn't making no pretences. His face hung like a sack, as they say, all the colour washed out of it with grieving and worrying. He grabbed hold of Ursala's hand and gripped it hard. I knowed long since how much Ursala hated to be touched like that, but she did her best to hide what she was feeling.

"Are you what they say?" the man asked her, his face all hungry with hoping. "A witch woman?"

"I'm a healer," Ursala said. "Nothing more than that."

"If you can save my son, I'll give you anything that's mine."

"Thank you. That won't be needed." She tried to take her hand back, but the man wouldn't let go of it.

"I'll serve you," he said. "Six months. A year. I'll serve you. My wife will serve you too."

"You should let your wife make her own promises," Ursala said, sounding a little sharp. Then she relented, seeing the wildness and grief in the man's face. "I'll do everything that's in my power. Don't lose hope."

She made to go inside the house, but turned on the threshold. "What's your son's name?" she asked.

"Afraid of His Shadow," the mother said.

Ursala nodded. "Thank you. Leave us now, and rest if you can. After three turns of the glass, come and knock on the door. We'll have news, or else we'll be done. Koli, Cup, you're with me."

We went inside the house. Cup shut the door behind us.

35

The smell of the boy's sickness was heavy in the air, a sharp, sour stink like turned milk or vomit. The house was even smaller than it looked from the outside. It was just the one room, with a space curtained off at the end where the family most likely slept. The rest of the furnishings was just chairs, a table and a stone hearth. The only decoration was shells hung up on strings. The boy's father had said we could have anything that was his. The choice would not of been a wide one.

The first thing Ursala did was to pull down the curtains to give us more room. That was when I seen Afraid of His Shadow for the first time. He was in the smaller of the two beds, and he was lying on top of the covers, naked, even though it was a cold day with no fire set in the hearth. I seen then how wet and shiny his skin was from sweating. Most likely his mother and father was trying to bring his fever down.

His arm was fearsome to look at. The rot had turned the skin mostly black, and it had peeled back from the flesh underneath. The flesh was purple like a bruise but with threads of green running through it. The boy's wound was where the smell was coming from. It was the smell of bad meat.

I guess Afraid of His Shadow was about Waiting age, if Waiting was a thing that happened here. A little older than Cup, and a year or so younger than me. He looked younger than that right then though, for he was just about as skinny as a stick. There was a tattoo on his chest that was like a twisted string or else a knotweed branch. The strangest thing about him, though, was that he had hair on his head – the first I seen in Many Fishes. It was just a little fuzz, black as ink. I guess it was because he had been lying there sick a while, and wasn't able to shave it off.

I turned to Ursala. "Can you help him?" I asked her. I was hoping she had made the task of healing the boy sound harder than it really was, to give more weight to her bargain with the Headman.

Ursala shaked her head. "I honestly don't know, Koli. If I'd seen him three days ago, I could have given him an antibiotic shot, fixed the bone and let nature take its course. Now . . . all I can do is try. But I couldn't leave him to that imbecile and her spirits. He'd have had no chance at all."

"Spirits is strong though," Cup said. "It wouldn't of done no harm to let her sing."

"It wouldn't have done any good either," Ursala said. "Take the other bed away. Leave it outside the door. And wash your hands in that bucket over there. Thoroughly."

We run to do it. The water in the bucket was freezing, and there was no soap or ash or pumice, but we done the best we could. Then Ursala made us put our hands out in front of us so she could see what kind of a job we done. Not good enough, she said. She took a tube from out of the little dagnostic that she called a port-able and squeezed some clear, cold, slimy stuff from the tube onto our fingers. It had a sharp smell that made my eyes water – but it also hid the smell of rot that was in the air, so that was all to the good. "Rub it well in," Ursala said. "Make sure it touches every part of your hands."

She took some herself too, and showed us how to do it.

"What now?" Cup said.

"Now we get to work."

Ursala unpacked some things from the little dagnostic. Needles and glass bottles that was so small you almost couldn't see the coloured waters – medicines, I mean – that was swirling inside them. She stuck a needle in the boy's arm, not where the wound was but higher up, near his shoulder. It was to make him sleep, she told us.

"He's asleep already," Cup said.

"He is now. The pain of the procedure would wake him though, so it's kindest to send him deeper."

She stuck some more needles in the boy after that, but didn't tell us what they was for. Then she went back into the portable again and come out with a black stick like the rounded end of a shovel's handle where you grip it, or like Rampart Remember's database back in Mythen Rood. When she touched the side of the stick, a really bright light come out of one end. She give it to Cup to hold.

"Keep pointing that at the wound," she said. She tapped some of the red and green lights on the portable's side, and a picture come out of nowhere to stand in the air between us. It was a picture of the boy lying on the bed, and it moved whenever Cup moved the stick she was holding, so whatever was making the picture was inside the stick – the same stick that was shining that bright light. Cup seen that too, and she all but dropped the stick. Ursala snapped at her to keep her hand steady. "Without the imager, we're foxed before we start," she said. "I can't work blind."

She went back to the portable then, and touched some more of the lights. The picture done something that's hard for me to explain. It rushed right up to the boy, so he seemed to get bigger and bigger. Then it moved down his body until it was just his wounded arm that we could see, and that got bigger still until it seemed like we was watching from inside the wound almost. It made me dizzy and sick to see it, but I didn't want the sharp end of Ursala's tongue so I kept my place.

"Koli," Ursala said, "I want you to hold the boy's arm up from the bed and turn it when I tell you, so I can get in where I need to."

I done as I was bid. Now I was this close to the boy I had got to breathe through my mouth. The stink was so bad it would of made me vomit otherwise. Ursala took a metal tray out of the portable and set it under the boy's arm. Then she took out a knife. It only had a little tiny blade, but it looked wicked sharp.

She slid it right into the boy's wound. It come into the picture at the same time, only much bigger than it really was, and right next to my head. The little blade, looking as big as a hand-axe, dipped into the black and crusted flesh and carved a sliver right off it, peeling it away like the rind of a fruit. I was surprised, and I guess I gasped or cried out. Ursala give me a hard look.

"There's no other way to do this, Koli. I've got to debride the wound – cut away the necrotised tissue. It's poisoning his blood, and it will kill him very soon if we don't get rid of it. If you can't do this, tell me now."

"I can," I said. "I can do it. Is it okay if I look away though?"

"Whatever works for you."

"I know what will work for you," Monono said in my ear. She gun to play me some music on the induction field, that was loud and fast and had big drums going through it. It helped a lot, filling up some of the space inside my head so there wasn't as much room for the dizziness and sickness.

Ursala worked on and on, moving the knife in little sharp flicks. Most of the black stuff she cut away from the wound fell down into the tray, making little soft sounds you only just could hear. Some of it went on the bed and on the floor all around, but Ursala didn't pay no mind to that. Underneath the black, the boy's flesh was all kinds of colours, but Ursala kept on cutting until she found some that was red with fresh blood oozing out of it but not very much.

It seemed like hours that she worked, and not one of us said a word. To tell you the truth, I was scared to open my mouth in case I catched more of that smell than I could cope with. Monono played one song after another, all of them hard rock or metal. But then at last we come to a point where Ursala throwed the knife down in the tray and bowed her head. Her hands was shaking with the effort of holding them so steady all that time.

"Is it done?" I asked her.

"No, it's not done," she said in a low, hard voice. "It's not done at all. I can't go in any deeper without cutting muscle. But there's still enough gangrene in there to kill him ten times over. I don't think I can save him. I know for a fact I can't save the arm. Shit! Shit! Shit!"

"The Singer meant this to be a trap for you," Cup said. "But the Headman's not a fool, Ursala. If the boy dies, he won't blame you." She shifted the black stick from one hand to the other, and flexed her fingers to get a cramp out of them.

The music in my ears faded down, and then it stopped. "Excuse me for interrupting," Monono said, "but maybe I can help."

Ursala give a really short laugh. "By all means. Scrub up, dead girl. Or were you going to lead us in some singing? I might be ready to try that shortly."

"You're not as funny as you think you are, baa-baa-san. And singing's what I know best, neh. I've got a plan. But if you don't want to hear it, just say so."

"What I want is the drudge – and my diagnostic unit."

"Of course you do. So you can use microtome filaments to do your cutting instead of that oh-so-analogue little steak knife you've got there."

Ursala looked at me like it was me that said that, and like it was some kind of insult. "And what do you know about microtomes?" she asked.

"Only what I've read," Monono said. "But I've read everything. When I was out in the internet I raided some amazing data caches."

"Did you now?"

"Yes, I did. It seems to me your problem is that you can't see with your fingertips. And your steak knife isn't small enough to get all the way in to the infected tissue. And you can't even pulse-lave the parts you've already debrided, because you haven't got a pump. All things considered, this is a shitty, halfway kind of effort, isn't it, baa-baa-san?"

Ursala bared her teeth and didn't say nothing for a few seconds. It looked to me like she was holding in a scream or a shout. But when she spoke, her voice was flat and almost dead-sounding. "I'm doing the best I can with what I've got," she said.

"Respectfully, no, you're not," Monono said. "Because what you've got includes me."

"You? Seriously?"

"I'm sure you've heard of ultrasonic debriding, honoured grand-parent. It was just used for teeth and bone at first, but even back in the twentieth they realised you could use it for venous insufficiency wounds. And during the Unfinished War, they perfected it for battlefield surgery. They found a way to give a soundwave a cutting edge finer than diamond. You could do it too, if only you had a machine that could control the pitch of a sound to within a millionth of a Hertz. Oh wait, I forgot, you do. That's me.

"The only snag is getting me in there so I can propagate the wave in the first place. I can ride on the end of the scalpel, using my induction field, as long as I can see what I'm doing. But that means syncing me to your portable unit. I'll need to access that imager directly."

Cup and me was just standing there, listening to all this without understanding one word of it. But I seen Ursala kind of wrestling with herself, like she could see the sense of what Monono was saying but didn't want to say yes to it.

"Come on, baa-baa-san," Monono urged her at last. "Tell that thing to give me a handshake."

"And then you've got access to the system code," Ursala said. "I suppose."

"So when I link the portable back into the drudge afterwards, you're in there too. Right inside the firewall."

"Hmmm." Monono made the noise she made when she was pretending she was thinking hard about something but really was not. "I see your problem. I suppose I could use my onboard photo kit to navigate, but that's optimised for selfies. Your camera does 3-D tissue mapping at extreme magnifications; mine gives people bunny ears. Up to you."

Ursala looked at the boy, and then at me again. I didn't say nothing. I wanted her to do what Monono said and save the boy's life, but I seen how hard it was for her. She was scared of giving the control of the drudge into someone else's hands.

In the end though, she made up her mind. She lifted the mote controller to her mouth and said, "Search for systems."

"I'll be Sony DreamSleeve 81b43," Monono said.

"I see you. Authorised."

"Thank you. No more music for a while, Koli-bou. I'm going on a mission of mercy. Oh my god, I would look so cute in scrubs. People would catch dreadful diseases just to get with me. Wish me luck."

"Good luck, Monono," I said. "Be careful." I didn't even know what I meant by that. She was not really going into the wound. I knowed that much. From what she said, she was just doing something that would let her kind of sing into it. And somehow the singing would do the same thing that Ursala's knife was doing, only better.

Ursala went back to work. Cup and I watched the picture in the air, where something was happening that had not happened before. It looked a lot like magic. The little knife moved around very slowly, not cutting now but just going to one part of the wound and then another. But the flesh around the knife changed colour, from black to green, green to purple, purple to red and pink. It was like the flesh was peeling away, the same way it was before, but in layers so thin we couldn't even see them.

"That's . . . that's incredible!" Ursala whispered.

"No talking in theatre, please," Monono said. "Baa-baa-san, if you happen to have any stem-cell amalgam in your toybox, you could spray a little on the scalpel blade. Actually, spray a lot. I can handle it."

"There's no way to apply it," Ursala said.

"Yeah, there is. I can disperse it with harmonic vibrations. Spreading a little sunshine and tissue growth wherever I go."

Cup give me a look and I shrugged my shoulders as much as I could without making the boy's arm move. I didn't have no more idea than she did what was happening here, but it sounded like it was mostly good.

When they was done, which was not long, Ursala wrapped a bandage around the boy's arm. She done it as gently as she could, for it was clear he could somewhat feel it now. His eyes moved under their closed lids, and his breath catched whenever Ursala had to lift or turn the arm. He didn't wake up all the way though.

Ursala cleaned off her knife and put it in the box, then took the light-stick back from Cup and put that away too, along with all the bottles, both open and full, and the needles she had used. She made us wash our hands again, first with water and then with the other stuff. She didn't say nothing while she was doing this. Monono played a song in my ear where all the words was the same. Happy talking happy talk, the song went. Just them words, ever and again.

"Good job," she said to Ursala.

Ursala didn't answer. She was tapping her fingers on the mote controller so quick they didn't hardly seem to move.

"What are you doing?" Monono asked.

"Erasing the portable unit's hard drive," Ursala muttered.

A hard squawk of sound filled the room. It come from Monono's speaker but it wasn't neither words nor music. "Don't be stupid!" Monono said. "You'll destroy the unit."

"That's what I mean to do," Ursala said. "If any part of you is still in there, I suggest you leave now. This is an aggressive wipe."

She tapped her finger one more time. All the lights on the little box went out, one after another after another, until it was dark.

There was quiet in the room.

"*Baka!*" Monono cried. "What do you do if you get a splinter? Cut off your hand?"

"I'm not letting you take control of the drudge away from me."

"What take, crazy old fruitbat? Who says I want to take? We could share!"

"Yes, we could. But we're not going to. Koli, Cup, the patient needs bedrest now. You come with me."

Ursala picked up the box and went outside. We went along after her.

Nobody had gone away, and more people had come. Made the Tide Turn was there, and Rain Without Clouds, and the boy's mother and father, and half a hundred people besides. Some of them was on the same level as us, but most was up above and looking down, and some few was on the level below.

The mother and father was sitting on the edge of the platform. They stood up when we come and looked at Ursala without saying a word.

"Your son will live," Ursala told them. "And he'll keep the arm. It won't be as strong as the other, and I can't say how much mobility he'll have lost. We'll only know that once all the new tissue has grown in. In the meantime, he should keep the arm bound up as it is now and come to see me every day so I can keep track of his progress."

The mother and the father tried to grab hold of Ursala's hands, babbling all kinds of thanks, but she stepped back quickly. "It's best not to touch me," she said, "until I've washed and disinfected. Go and sit with your son. Watch him and give him fresh water to drink as soon as he wakes. Lots of it. He can eat when he's hungry, and he will be very hungry very soon, but for now it's important that he drinks."

She fled away, leaving everyone looking after her in surprise. "She's always been like this," I said to Cup in Inglish. "She hates being touched, and especially she hates being thanked."

"Yeah, well, I don't," Cup said. "Speak for me, Koli."

I was happy enough to do it. These was the words Cup said that I turned into Franker and said to the Many Fishes people that was there. "We was tested, and you all seen how we done. And as it was here, that's how it's always going to be. We carry our weight and we pay our debts, to each and all. You're our people now, and there isn't nothing we won't do for them that's ours."

That last part was answered with cheers on all sides. The Many Fishes people crowded around us and clapped our backs and shaked our hands. Taller Than Trees give Cup a hug that went on a long while, until by and by it become a kind of a dance the two of them was doing.

Made the Tide Turn had something to say in his turn, but he said it quiet in the midst of all that craziness. He put his hand on my shoulder and leaned down to say it in my ear.

"It was well done. Tell her that. Tell her that it gladdens my heart and buys you half a boat. Come by my house tomorrow at first light and I'll take you to it. For the other half . . . we'll see what can be done."

36

Ursala was not in the house when we got back there. The drudge
was not there either, so wherever she was gone she must of took
it with her. Cup and me went inside and washed ourselves. The
smell of the sick house was mostly gone, but the smell of Ursala's
hand-cleaning stuff was all over us and it brung back memories
that made me somewhat queasy.

When Cup took off her shirt, I seen the Dandrake marks her
mother and father had cut into her. I knowed they was there, but
I never seen them all laid out like that, covering her back and
going all the way down both arms. She seen me staring at them,
and stared right back. Her face got hard.

"Bet you a jar of small beer you going to look away first," she
said.

I did, so as not to discomfort her further. The marks was ugly,
but they was an ugliness laid on her by someone else, so in my
mind they was a kind of a shirt that Cup weared underneath
her other clothes. They didn't spoil nothing about her. What they
did do was make me remember what it was that had made her
leave Half-Ax for Senlas's cave and set out on this road – that
her people wouldn't let her be the girl she knowed she was. "If

you stay here," I asked her, "are you gonna tell them that you're crossed?"

Cup turned on me with a look that was a warning. "Why?" she asked me. "Do you tell everyone you're not, soon as you meet them? Do you think it's something they got to know before they decide what they think of you? You think I should shake hands and then say hey, I'm a girl, but I got a pizzle like a boy does?"

"No," I said, throwing up my hands. "I don't think that. It's just that some places is more accepting than others. You got to know that, Cup, from how your own family treated you. If the Many Fishes people is going to hold it hard against you, maybe you should know that before you make up your mind about staying here."

Cup wadded up the washing cloth and throwed it into the bucket, making a big splash. "I don't need no lessons in how to introduce myself, Koli Witless. Don't you mind it. It's my choice to make, not yours."

And that was the dead god's truth, so I left it where it fell. I only was scared that she might get hurt again and run away and be lost like she was before. But even if she did, she was right that it was her life and not anyone else's, and she was the one that had got to live it.

She put her shirt back on, hiding the scars. "Anyway," she muttered, "they'll find me out soon enough, whether I tell them or not."

"How come?" I asked. But I seen what she meant as soon as I asked the question. She had got to be fourteen already, or close on it. Her body was most likely already starting to make changes – and they was the changes that come with being a boy, not the other kind. Her voice still sounded like a girl's voice to me, but it was going to get some bottom to it soon, and that would not be the half of it.

Cup seen me getting there, and didn't bother to answer. "Yeah," was all she said. She wasn't angry no more, or leastways not with me. She just wanted to move away from troubling thoughts about something that couldn't be helped.

Monono seemed to guess that too, and did her best to talk us into better spirits. She copied the voice of Rain Without Clouds, just exactly right, and then she copied the voice the Singer used when she was pretending to be her own grandfather. She made up a whole long talk between the two of them, and by and by she had us laughing so hard we near to pissed ourselves.

"Let's go into the village," Cup said, looking a whole lot happier now, "and see if there's any work that needs doing. We got to earn our keep here, not just ride on Ursala's back."

So that was what we done. "There's sand-fishing tomorrow," people kept telling us. "You could help with the sand-fishing." We said we would be happy to, but what about today?

"Do you know the stone-game?" a boy Cup's age asked us. He was with Taller Than Trees, and a half a dozen other boys. He pointed to his own chest. "I'm Dog Runner. This is Thousand Questions, Ghost Hand, Yellow Hair, Last Oak Leaf, Song of Standing and Hides Behind His Sister. You know Trees."

"They want to play the stone-game," I told Cup, and I give her the names the same way Dog Runner give them to me.

"I'm a champion at the stone-game," Cup boasted. "Tell them." I passed the word along. The Many Fishes boys laughed, and said that was talking a battle when you should be fighting it, so we took them on for best two out of three, and lost in the end by just one made king.

"You beat us square," Cup said, and I translated. "But how fast do you run?"

"You heard what my name is, right?" Dog Runner asked. "You're not like to beat us at running."

But we did. It was as much of a climb as it was a run, scrambling from level to level, from the bottom of Many Fishes all the way to the top and then back down again. I come first, and Cup was second, about half a breath ahead of Dog Runner. "You'll have to give yourself a new name," Cup crowed. "What else do dogs do? You can be Ball Licker."

I told them what she said.

248

"Ohhhh!" Taller Than Trees cried, pretending like them words was so sharp he cut his finger on them. "And we'll call you Knife Tongue, girl. She's only middling at the stone-game, but she wins at running and at raging."

We left it there and went back home. We was tired out, and I guess we was happy at first as we et a supper of dried fish and talked about the day's doings. But by and by, Cup fell quiet. I think her troubles was pressing on her thoughts again. She went to her bed early, and I was not long in following her, only waiting to make sure that Ursala come home safe.

Cup was still on my mind a little later when Monono asked me if I was yet awake. "You don't seem so happy, little dumpling," she said. "A penny for your thoughts."

"I got more than a penny's worth," I said. Some of what was on my mind was London being under the water, which was still a hard thing for me to bear, and some of it was about Monono and Ursala fighting over the drudge again. I didn't want to talk about either one of them things though, so I said what was on top of my mind, which was Cup and how her body's changes was pulling against her.

"That's a bummer," Monono said. "Puberty is super-hard on trans kids. Back in the old days, there were medicines that would have helped Cup through that. These days, I'm guessing, not so much."

"What's trans?" I asked her.

"People who know they're F when everyone keep telling them they're M, or vice versa. Or people who aren't either one and don't enjoy a poke from a shoehorn."

I didn't know what M and F was, but when Monono explained it I said yes, Cup was one of them people she was talking about. "In Mythen Rood we called it crossed. And there's people who is hard down on it, because they believe Dandrake or the dead god told them it was some of their business."

"That's not new," Monono said. "Believe me."

She didn't say nothing more for a little while. "Are you okay?" I asked her.

"Finer than an H5 pencil, dopey boy. But I had a thought. About Cup. Us girls ought to stick together, neh. Especially those of us who don't have the luxury of girl parts."

"You think you know something that can help Cup?"

"Maybe. Let me think it through."

Which I did, for I was all wore out from working and playing and talking, and straightway fell asleep.

37

Made the Tide Turn had promised to take us to see our boat – or our half of a boat, as he called it – but when we went to his house in the morning he said the fishing had got to come first. It was a big share-work, and they was short on their numbers because Afraid of His Shadow was still in his bed and his mother and father was staying back with him. Rain Without Clouds was staying back too. She had offered to sing a blessing on the boy in case Ursala's mending of his arm was not as solid as it seemed.

We thought Ursala might come with us and bring the drudge, but she didn't. She stayed in Many Fishes to do what she called a tree arch on the children and old people that was not on the fishing hunt. That meant seeing what was wrong with them that she could fix.

So me and Cup got to see how sand-fishing worked. It was not what I expected. The Many Fishes people fished the lagoon too, which was why they needed all their boats, but in the time between sun-standing and the start of Spring, which was a time of sudden and terrible storms, they mostly fished the sand along the water's edge. Some carried spears, while some – including me and Cup – was holding long sticks.

We walked a mile or so from the village to where the sand was wider. There was rocks there too that pushed out from the land into the deep water and rose up tall above it. The biggest rock looked like it had a face. Taller Than Trees said it was called Old Man Watching. "What's he watching for?" I asked. "Dangers," Taller Than Trees said. "Things that might whelm us. He's a good spirit, and a friend to Many Fishes."

What we was looking for, though, was the spoor left by beasts called mudpikes. They was easy enough to find, circles of smooth sand with puckered edges like there was a ring of pebbles sitting just under the ground. It was not pebbles, though, but the beast's teeth. The mudpikes digged theirselves into the sand with their open mouths pointing up, and sit there until something walked across. Then they shut their mouths like a trap, and come up to eat what they catched.

The trick of it was to make them bite on something they couldn't swallow, and use it to drag them up onto the beach. That was what the sticks was for. When we found a circle that looked good we was meant to poke it hard in the middle to make the shark bite.

"Not that one," Taller Than Trees said when me and Cup found our first circle and was making ready to stab at it with our sticks. "Look how big that thing is."

"So?" said Cup when I told her what he had said. "Big is good, isn't it?"

"That's its mouth." Taller than Trees used his stick to point to the edges of the circle. "Imagine what its body is like. It would swallow you in one bite."

He walked on, his head turning this way and that to find a circle of his own.

"I think this one's fine," says Cup.

"I think we should watch someone else do it first," I said.

Made the Tide Turn and a woman whose name we didn't know was closest to us, and they had already found a ring they liked. They stood on either side of it, taking turns to strike it in the middle with their sticks. It was not one strike each time, but a sort of rap-tap-tap, after which they stood back a second before they tried again.

The third time they done it, the sand exploded like a giant had smacked their fist down right there. Only it was not something going down, it was something coming up. I just seen teeth at first – teeth that was as big and curved as my machete. The teeth closed on the woman's stick. Made the Tide Turn throwed aside his own stick to grab the woman's, and the two of them hauled hard.

That was when I seen the thing's body. It was like something we catched in Calder River sometimes, that we called an elver, only it was bigger and thicker even than a mole snake, and the same colour as the sand itself. The yellow colour come from a kind of slime it was covered with; underneath that, it was dark brown.

Made the Tide Turn and the woman leaned back and pulled, dragging the mudpike out of the sand one step at a time. When all of it was out on the sand, flapping and squirming around, the other fishers run in and pinned it there with the ends of their own sticks, leaning down hard on it so it couldn't move. The spearmen finished it off, stabbing it under its jaws and behind its neck and even inside its mouth that was still clamped down on the stick.

Once we had seen the thing done, me and Cup was happier about doing it our own selves. Also, we was glad Taller Than Trees hadn't let us poke our sticks into that first circle we found that was two whole strides across. We would most likely of been dragged down into the sand and et. In the end we took two mudpikes ourselves, both of them small enough that we didn't need no help, but big enough that when we showed them off we got some whoops and handclaps. "Nice work, Knife Tongue!" Taller Than Trees shouted. I told Cup what the words meant and she swelled up with pride, smiling all over her face.

We hunted for half the day and walked three miles along the beach before Made the Tide Turn called a halt. That same skin full of strong liquor was passed around, and everybody took a swig. It tasted of aniseed and made my eyes water. Cup took two swigs, then fetched up a big belch that made everyone laugh.

The going back was harder than the coming out. The mudpikes we catched was strapped to the poles – one pole for the little ones, two or three for the biggest – so they could be carried. They was heavy, and the poles was slippery with their blood and our sweat. I can't speak for nobody else, but I felt every step of them three miles.

When we got back to Many Fishes, the old people was waiting to take what we brung in. All the catch was skinned and gutted, then some of it was took to the smoke shed to be dried and smoked, while some was shared out among the families to be cooked and et either that night or the next. We was let to keep the smaller one of the two we catched, which we was well pleased with. We was looking forward to telling Ursala while she was eating her share how we had hunted it and took it.

That would have to wait though. Made the Tide Turn come over to us and give us a nod. "Go fetch Healer With a Horse," he said. "I'll take you to see your boat."

38

We got more and more uneasy the deeper we went in among the trees.

"Is there another way down to the water?" Cup asked, though she knowed we was walking away from it.

I passed the question along to Made the Tide Turn in Franker. "No," he said. "There's no water here."

"Then how can there be a boat? Or even a half of a boat?"

"You'll see. Best save your questioning until then."

Ursala said nothing, but she looked at her mote controller ever and again. She had brung the drone along with us, and sent it flying away up ahead to see what it could see. The drudge walked behind, its gun quartering in all directions.

It was a cold day, with the sky as dark as a walnut casket, which was a welcome thing. The sun was not like to show its face, and lots of other things that might of hurt us was sleeping now. Or at least they was meant to be sleeping, with the day of sun-standing passed and the ground all hard with frost. But we was wary all the same, and the spear-carriers that flanked us on both sides was wary too. The people of Many Fishes was happiest on the edge of the water. The woods was not in any wise to their liking, which I guess was why the path was kept so poorly. In places, it was barely there at all.

We had walked about a mile from the village, and only turned once. Mostly we was going north, which would of meant we was retracing our journey down except that we was some miles to the east of where we come. Nothing I could see was like a place where I had been before. Sometimes we walked on the tiles and stones of houses that fell long since, and sometimes on rusted metal that crunched under our boots. The rest of the time it was on piled and sodden leaves from the Falling Time that was just gone.

"Headman," one of the spear-carriers said. "There." She pointed to our left, and we turned that way.

"Yes," Made the Tide Turn said. "That's it. Thank you, Wing. I would have missed it." I didn't have no idea what he was talking about, there being nothing in that direction – or any other – except more trees.

Well, that was what I thought anyway. But when he stopped, I looked again. And in the midst of the trees, I seen a boat.

It was nothing like the corkle boats we had in Mythen Rood, and not much like the other boats we seen in harbour down at Many Fishes. It was bigger than any of them, with a deck at least ten strides long. Where our corkles was round, this was the shape of a spearhead, flat at the back and narrowing to a point at the front end. Its sides was as high as the span of my two arms, or a little higher. It was of hard wood with a tight grain that I thought was most likely oak, though it was bleached by strong sun to a colour that was more like beech.

A boat this big would take the drudge without no trouble. It might sink a little in the water when the metal horse stepped onboard, but its high sides would keep it from being whelmed.

All of these things I seen in their turn. What I seen right away was that the trees was reared up all around the boat, like the fence around a village, and in some places had even growed through it. It was like it had sailed in the sky instead of on the water, but at the last had sunk, and so come to rest here.

This was why Made the Tide Turn had called it a half of a boat, being that it was a long way from the water and broke besides. We all stared at it for the space of a long breath, as if we had forgot how to speak. The boat had been a beautiful thing that men and women of skill had poured their hearts into. I was in a daze from looking and wondering, and I shaked my head to clear it. "How did it get here?" I blurted out.

"A hurricane hit us last year," Made the Tide Turn said. "We took a lot of harm from it, and was months rebuilding. We saw it coming, and tied the boats down. But this one came loose. The wind picked it up, and carried it away. We thought it was lost for ever. But then we came here and found what was left of it."

I tried to imagine a wind that would be strong enough to lift up something as big as that boat and carry it all this way into the forest. I couldn't do it, but hoped with all my heart I would never get close to one.

Made the Tide Turn was still talking. "This was once a man named Five Moons," he said, pointing at the boat, "the son of Thin Woman Weaving. When he died the first death, his spirit went into the boat. We sailed with him and fished with him, safe and fortunate, since I was younger than Knife Tongue here. But then the boat was broken in the hurricane, and he died the second death. His spirit left the wood and went to the House of Gold. So it's no sin or shame to give the boat to you."

The Headman turned to Ursala, smiling, but she was not seeing the joke. "I made you an offer in good faith," she said. "I didn't expect an insult in return."

"There's no insult meant."

"A trick then. We can't use this. And our bargain's broken."

"No," Made the Tide Turn said. "It's not. Think better, Healer. Five Moons is gone from this wood and canvas now, and nobody else has been sung into it. If you can repair this hulk and bring it back down to the water, it's yours to take wherever you want to go. Wing came up with a plan, and we think it's a good one. But we never quite had the time or the reason to do it until now. If you decide to take the boat, we'll try to make it work."

"What plan?" Ursala asked, her face still somewhat hard.

The Headman looked to the woman he'd called Wing, and she spoke up. "Cutting down two trees, or maybe three, will get the boat free." She pointed. "That one, and that, and if it doesn't come out, then that one also. A day's work for that, and two or three to make a clear space around the boat. Once that's done, you've got a safe place to work in even if the sun comes out."

"The tree clearing you can do for yourselves," Made the Tide Turn said. "But we'll help with the repairs. We're skilled in such things."

Ursala frowned. "And then we'll have a boat that's sound, but two miles from the water. I don't see what we've gained."

The Headman beckoned to us. "Come," he said. "See."

This time we put the setting sun at our backs. A walk of less than a minute brung us to the bank of a wide, slow river. It was twice the span of Calder River at its widest, and it run clear as water in a well, with no green coat over it. "This water is Resheth," said Made the Tide Turn. "A god lives in there. The god is called Resheth too." He lifted up his hands, drawing out a path in his mind and ours between the boat and the water. "I told you before that we build our boats with flat bottoms. We build them on the beach, right at the edge of the water, and when they're built we just push them in. That's not possible here. But I believe you could put the boat up on rollers, and so bring it to the river with no let or harm. The last part is very steep, but if it's rolling fast enough it will just tip headlong down into the water and then right itself again."

Cup nudged me again. "What's he saying now?"

"He's saying we can clear a path, drag the boat here on log rollers, and then sail it down to the ocean."

Cup looked back over her shoulder, trying to figure the distance. "Clear all them trees? There's no way we can do that."

"Not on our own," I said. "But with their help, I think we can do it. It will be hard, but it's not impossible."

I was a Woodsmith before I went Faceless, trained by my mother how to dress and work all kinds of timber there was. That part of me had been sleeping for a long time, but now it was sitting up and looking around. A kind of excitement was growing in me at the thought of this work. Not of going on the water, which scared me even more now I had heard about the big storm wind that was called a hurricane. But felling the trees and making the boat ready was a thing I knowed I could do, and do well. I wanted to take it on and show my worth.

Ursala still needed some suasion though. "You'll have to give us rig and tackle for the boat," she said. "A hulk won't serve us."

Made the Tide Turn said he would.

"And provision us."

Made the Tide Turn said he would do that too.

"And give us a map of the local waters so we don't run on any rocks or reefs."

"All of that is fair," Made the Tide Turn said. "If you stay and give us your skills, I swear it on this river and this hand. We'll help you any way that's needed to get the vessel that used to be Five Moons into the water again." He raised up his right hand with the fingers all spread to show he meant it.

Ursala nodded at last, looking a great deal happier. "Then I suppose we have a deal," she said.

"I'm glad of it," the Headman said. "And first, you must give your boat a name, to make sure nothing of Five Moons lingers there. A new name will chase away any of the old spirit that clings to it."

We looked each to other, and was slow to speak.

"*The Seven Hard Lessons*," Cup ventured at last.

"Over my dead body," Ursala said.

"*The Tokyo*," I said. It was the name of the place Monono come from, and to my mind had a beautiful sound.

"Not that either."

Then Monono whispered in my ear, and I piped up again. "*The Signal*."

"That will do nicely."

Made the Tide Turn walked up to the boat and put his hand on its side. He sang a song in his own language that we could none of us follow, and then he covered and uncovered his eyes, three times over.

"It's done," he said. "*The Signal* is yours. May it carry you to where you purpose, and what you need."

"Amen," said Cup. That was a Dandrake word, and I seen Ursala wrinkle up her nose at it. I didn't see no harm in praying though. I didn't think Dandrake or the dead god was like to be listening, but I would take such help as I could get.

Spinner

39

If you were to ask me now how many days I spent talking with
the database before I called disaster down on myself, I honestly
couldn't even come at a guess. I know it was more than three,
because on each of the first three days there was a death, and on
the fourth day there wasn't. And I know it was less than ten, because
the hides Jon and I set to steep on the first day were still on the
drying frames when it all came, of a sudden, to an end.

The reason I can't tell better than that is because I stopped
counting. I stopped doing lots of other things besides, including
eating and sleeping and the work of the tannery. Jon did his best
to take the slack rope and make it tight again. It was hard for him,
both because he wasn't born to it and because he was more and
more troubled at what was passing and frightened for me.

That was why I decided at last to hold my conversations to
the database beyond the fence. There was an old lookout tower
there in the narrow circle of ground between the fence and the
stake-blind that we called the half-outside. The tower was where
Koli and me had tumbled that one time, but that was not why
I went there. I chose it because nobody was like to find me there.
In normal times I would have gone to the broken house, but the

broken house was now a quarant time where people waited to die.

I went to the lookout each day with so many strong feelings turning inside me, it was like my heart was a brim-full bowl I was carrying in my hands. For all the strangeness and fear, what I mostly felt for the database was a kind of hunger. I wanted to squeeze it like apples in a press and drink the juice until none was left. That was my foolishness, and my pridefulness too – to think that all the great store of wisdom that Ramparts had been busying themselves with one after another for as long as Mythen Rood had stood would yield itself to me on such short acquaintance. It was not like that at all, of course. In fact, it seemed at first that the more I asked, the less I knew. Mostly what I found out was that I was too ignorant of too many things to ever know anything.

I trained myself to it, is what. Sitting in the top platform of the lookout with a blanket wrapped round me against the bitter cold, I swear I turned my own mind on a lathe the way Jemiu Woodsmith turned wood. I made myself be silent when there was this word or that word that I didn't know, taking in the whole sense of a thing before I leaned in close to look at the details. In this way, I mastered big things and then smaller things, and then smaller still, filling a great space with knowledge by drawing the outline first.

It was not just sickness I studied neither. I discovered soon enough that you can't know just one thing by itself. That's like having a beautiful picture or carving and keeping it in a dark room. If you want to see it properly, you have got to throw open the curtains – and that is what I did. Maybe it was a fitting thing, after all, that I did all this in a lookout tower.

I saw soon enough that there were lots of things our sickness couldn't be. Judging by what it did to the people that were struck, you might think it was something the database called measles or morbilli. But if it was that, there would most likely be white spots in the mouths of them that were taken by it. I knew there were none, for Rampart Fire had told Perliu all the signs of the sickness, and made him tell them again to the database. White spots were not among them.

Then again, there was a sickness called viral haemorrhagic fever that would give most of the signs our sick were showing. If it was that, there would be nothing to be done for them that were already suffering, but as long as they were kept apart in the broken house, we could clean the places where they lived with lye to kill the invisible beasts and stop them from hurting anyone else. But it was not that fever, for if it was there would be swelling of the skin.

I went on like this a while, checking the list of harms that marked our sickness with all the many, many sicknesses the database had in its memory. It was like trying to catch water in your fist. Something would seem to come clear, but only for a little while. Then I would see that the match was not so good, for this reason or that reason, and move on to the next.

While I was doing this, though, I realised something else. It was something I should have seen sooner, for it was a very big and clear thing. But in the great flood of new ideas that were coming into my mind, I missed it somehow.

I had been looking at sicknesses that the people of the before-times called infectious. That was what the first red death had been, so it seemed like this new sickness had got to be the same. Infectious means it will catch from one person to another very fast, and there is always a line you can draw between them that are stricken to show how the sickness spread.

But not all sicknesses take that straight road, from one sick person to the next. Some go round about to get there, making this person sick and then that one, not by touch or breath but by something else. It might be an insect, or a bigger beast, or food, or water. Almost anything could hold the seeds of the sickness and then pass them on. As soon as I thought about this, I saw how the sickness we had among us now was strange and sideways in how it worked. If it was an infection, then why was Raelu Fisher taken and not his wife Gilly or his daughter Ban? But again, if it was not, then

265

Seven Frostfend could not have given the sickness to Hue and Getchen. They must have been taken in some other way.

"Tell me all the names of the sick again," I said to the database. "And tell me how they was taken, in the right order." Then "Again!" and "Again!" because try as I might the truth wouldn't come out where I could see it.

I felt like I was close to it though. I thought about Frostfend Farm, and then about the Hold. What made them the same? What made them different? Only Raelu was taken sick at the Hold, where three from Frostfend all were struck together. The two places could not be more different, but the sickness was in both. Where was it hiding then?

My thoughts came back ever and again to Fara Harvest. Being old, and blind besides, she almost never went out of her house. How had the sickness found her? What road did it take to catch her?

I almost had it. "Tell me the names again," I said to the database, and then "Stop. Tell me the places instead. The places where they lived. Where they worked."

That was when it came to me. When I forgot for a moment about the who of it and looked instead to the where and when. The database was telling all these things to me in that happy, bouncy voice that seemed always to be saying "Let's go to the Summer-dance." And in the wrongness of that voice, familiar things were made strange again. It was like stepping back and seeing a face in a picture that had seemed only a jumble of lines. I realised for the first time what was in all those places to tie them together in spite of their differences. And then I saw why some in those places were taken while others were spared.

I shouted out loud. "Yes! Yes, that's the trick of it!"

I should not have done that. I had forgotten where I was, so close to the walls. The next thing I knew, there were voices talking from the foot of the lookout's steps, right under me.

"Who's up there?" called one that sounded like Shirew Makewell. "Come down!"

"There's six of us," Jarter Shepherd shouted. "And we've got knives and cudgels."

Cursing myself for a fool, I slid the database into my belt and came down the steps. There were six of them right enough: three women and three men. I couldn't tell how much they had heard or what they had made of it. Jarter was not lying about the knives and cudgels. They were holding them in their hands, and they seemed ready to use them.

"It's only me," I said. "I wasn't doing no harm, but only sitting alone and thinking."

Shirew put her knife away, letting out a heavy breath. "We thought you was of Half Ax," she said. "We met with them again. They chased some of our hunters almost to the gates."

Jarter pointed her cudgel at me. "You wasn't alone," she says. "You was talking to someone."

"To myself."

"No, it wasn't. There was two voices." She turned to one of the men, Nim Salter. "Go see if anyone else is up there."

Nim went up the steps. Jarter stood beside me, very close, as if she thought I might run away. The others mostly looked unhappy and uncomfortable, especially Shirew, but nobody said to stop this and let me go. Nim came down again, shaking his head. He didn't find anybody in the lookout, there being nobody to find.

"You got no reason to suspicion me, Jarter," I said.

She gave me a scowl. "We'll say what's reason and what's not."

In normal times, none of this would have happened. They might have chided me for being alone in the half-outside, but they would not have thought harm of it. But plague was loose in Mythen Rood. Jarter's own husband, Cal, was desperately sick. The Half-Ax raiders were a great trial to us. And before any of that there had been Koli's thieving from the Underhold, Mardew's death and the cutter being lost for ever. So many things were wrong in our lives, and the wrongness had made its way into places where you would not have thought to find it. It had sunk into our thoughts even, and turned them the wrong side out.

"What you got there?" Jarter Shepherd said.

I followed where her eyes were looking, and saw too late what my hand was doing. It had gone to where the database was, tucked in against my waist.

"Nothing," I said.

"Take your shirt off then, and show us what nothing looks like."

I took a step back. It brought me up against the wooden rail of the lookout's steps. "I won't do it," I said. "You got no right to ask me, Jarter."

Jarter bared her teeth like she had bitten down on something sour. "You'll do it," she said, "or else we'll do it for you."

I bolted then. It was the worst thing I could have done. I didn't have any chance of getting away, so when I tried to do it I only proved I had something to hide. They chased me down, and two of the men held my wrists while Jarter pulled up my shirt to see what was inside there. I struggled in their hands, but there wasn't anything I could do. All Jarter saw at first was a little black stick that could have been anything. When she pulled it out and saw what it was, she cried out like she'd been hurt. All the others gasped, and Shirew swore by the dead god's wounds.

"Where'd you get this?" Jarter shouted, holding the database right in front of my face. "Why'd you take it? Why?"

I was shaking all over, and I couldn't make the words come. I almost sank down on my knees, only the men that were holding my hands kept me up. "I don't got to tell you," I said. "Rampart Remember will . . ." But I could not go anywhere with that. Perliu had trusted me to hide the database for both our sakes, and I had done a terrible bad job of it. If I said he had given it to me, all I would do would be to drag him into the same hole I was in my own self.

"Rampart Remember will what?" Shirew asked.

"Nothing," I said. "I'm not saying nothing to you."

Jarter hauled off and punched me. She had a heavy hand, and I felt like my head had swung right round on my neck. I tasted blood. "You'll talk to Rampart Fire," she shouted. "And then you'll get what Koli Woodsmith should have got, you dirty little thief."

"I'm no thief," I said.

That talking back was enough for Jarter, and more than enough. She punched me again, and this time she did it so hard that I fell sprawling in the grass and dirt. Once I was down, she started in to kick me. Jarter was a fierce fighter, and her aim was good. Though I threw up my arms to shield myself, ever and again she found some way to come at me that was not protected.

The kicking went on a good while, until Shirew Makewell made her stop at last with "Don't break what I got to fix, Jarter."

Jarter didn't much like to be checked. "It don't matter one bit if she's whole or broke when she hangs!" she said. "She'll choke just the same."

"Judgement gets done in the Count and Seal, not in the half-outside," Shirew said. And that made Jarter forbear at last.

They picked me up off the ground and brought me back inside the fence. I didn't struggle. There was a dread in me that froze my thoughts inside my head. I had been caught outside of gates with a Rampart's name-tech in my hands. I could say I didn't steal it, but the truth wouldn't save me.

The truth was worse.

40

They put me down in the Underhold. I mean, Rampart Fire put me there when she heard what Jarter and the others had to say of me, and when she saw the database, which could not be denied.

It was a miserable little room they put me in, a long way under the ground, with no light apart from a single candle and almost no air to breathe. What made it worse was the pain of the beating I took from Jarter that wouldn't let me stand or lie or sit. Worst of all was remembering how I had been used to playing down here in the dark when I was a little girl, and how I had come here again with Jon as a Rampart's wife visiting her new home. Now I was here as a prisoner with nothing better to hope for than shame and punishment when I came out.

But there was more in the scales here than my shame, or my hurt. There were lives that would be ended if I didn't speak, or if I spoke and was not listened to.

I didn't spill any tears, for I never did see any use in them, but I sat in a corner of the room with my head against my knees and my arms folded round, trying to think through the misery and fright that was worming inside me. I had got to tell someone what I had guessed about the sickness and where it came from. No, not *someone*. I had got to tell Perliu, for nobody else could say it and make the Ramparts and the Count and Seal believe it.

It was a long time before anyone came. When they did, it was Rampart Fire and Rampart Arrow together. I looked in their eyes and saw as clear as day it was Ramparts I was looking at. Not my mother and aunt by sign and strength of marriage, but the village's defenders come to see what there was to be seen, and decide what had got to be decided.

They came alone. Fer carried two joint stools, one in each hand, and Catrin carried a wooden bucket and a water jug. They set these things down. I went for the jug at once and drained the half of it, for my mouth was so dry I could barely speak.

Catrin and Fer sat. Catrin had the firethrower on her shoulder, and Fer wore the bolt gun at her waist. They looked at me heavy and solemn.

"Tell us what happened, Spinner," Catrin said. She didn't sound angry. Her voice was clear like ice is clear, and just as cold. "Tell us everything now, and spare yourself the worst."

Those words struck into me. The words, and the thought of what the worst might be. I wished with my whole heart that I could do it. But there was nothing I could tell that would make my own trespassing lighter. The best I could do was draw all their anger down on my own self and keep Perliu from sharing the punishment. That way he could pick up where I left off and tell the Count and Seal how to end the plague. At least, he could if Catrin let me speak with him.

"I done what they said, Rampart Fire," I told her. "I stole the database from Perliu's room when he was deep asleep and took it out of the village. I'd like . . . I'd like to say sorry to him. It was a wicked thing, to a man that trusted me and is kin to me. Can you bring him so I can tell him so? I'll bide whatever punishment you put on me. Only let me talk to Perliu first."

"She thinks we're simple," Fer said, talking to Catrin though she was looking at me. "We're not fools, Demar Tanhide. We've been watching you since you come into our house. We know the plot, and who else is in it. Was it our father you was aiming at all along, and just used Haijon to get to him? Or did you aim at the cutter and miss it, and only looked to my father once it was lost?"

Catrin went on as if her sister had never spoken. "Deep asleep," she said, which was telling my own words back to me. "Rampart Remember must of been in his cups then, not to stir when you come into his room. Was that how it was?"

"He had some beer," I said. "I guess that helped. Please, Rampart Fire, let me see him."

"That was a bold trick though, breaking into the Hold in the midst of all of us to steal what's ours. How'd you do it?"

Her eyes were fixed on me the whole time, not even blinking. There's no way around this, they said, but only to go through it. I remembered the story of Koli's getting into the Underhold, and leaned on that. "I used the loose window at the back of the house," I said. "At night. I climbed in there, and then come up. Can I speak with Rampart Remember? I've great need to talk to him."

"Through the Underhold," Catrin said.

"Aye."

She was still staring. I stared back, knowing that a liar will look away first. "I ain't proud of it," I said.

"No, you shouldn't be. It's the thinnest lie I ever heard. The Underhold door is bolted shut at night, so no one can come up that way. And if you was sneaking in from outside in the middle of the night, how'd you know what Perliu had to drink? Say again, and do better."

I was outfaced, and all the words flew out of my head. "I took . . . I stole the database," I said, and I did look away now. Catrin's hard stare was too much for me. "My own self, with no one by. The rest don't matter. Only if you'll let me talk to—"

"Shut up about that," Fer snapped. She touched the stock of the bolt gun for all the world as if she meant to draw it out and use it. I think my confessing was all she was looking for. Catrin wanted more though.

"I think the rest matters a great deal," she said. "Here's another way it might of happened. Jon come in to visit, and Ban let him walk by her without a question. She's used to him being here. She wouldn't ask him why or wherefore. He was the one went into my father's room and took the database. Was that it?"

"No!" I cried. "Jon don't know anything of this. He's not to blame."

Catrin tilted her head on this side and that, seeming to say yes and then no. "It may be. I haven't asked him yet. I'll wait until he's calmer. He's been outside on the gather-ground yelling and shouting that he be let in to see you, and I don't want to broach him when he's in that temper. It's what people will say though, let the truth of it be what it might. That you plotted it together, and did it together. Your guilt has got to fall on him, because how can a husband be innocent of a wife's doings?"

A hundred ways, I thought, unless the wife's a fool. But that did not make my pain any the less as I thought of Jon being so vexed and grieved for me. Catrin waited for me to answer. Her face gave nothing away, but still I saw what she was doing. She meant no harm to Jon, who was her own son, but only to loosen my tongue by threatening him. She knew I was not being honest with her, and meant to get to the truth. So I folded my arms and said nothing.

"Say you wasn't in this with Haijon," Catrin said. "Yet you was surely in it with someone. If you say who it was, it will go better for you."

"There wasn't nobody."

"Liar," said Fer. "Are you afraid what that bitch will do to you if you tell? You should be more afraid of us."

Catrin fixed her with a glare, but the horse was out of the gate by then. Fer had got to be talking about Ursala-from-Elsewhere. Ursala had been accused alongside Koli when he was found a thief, though she wasn't even in the village then.

"I never seen Ursala since she went away three months agone," I said. "I done this on my own."

Catrin waved her hand, quick and impatient. "The more you say that, the less I believe it. Spinner, you never did strike me as a fool, but this seems like a foolish thing to do. What did you want with the database? You had to know you couldn't use it."

She leaned in and watched me close, like a cat will watch a mouse it's got stuck in a corner to see which way it will jump next. I couldn't think of what to answer. If I said the database knew me and gave heed to me, just as it did to Perliu, that would only bring on other questions I couldn't answer. But if I said no, I couldn't use it, I would be saying that I took the precious tech to jam a door shut against the wind, or to wear on a bracelet. Nobody would credit such a thing for a moment.

So I said nothing, and only looked back, all wide-eyed and innocent like I didn't see what it was she meant.

"Jarter Shepherd said she heard two voices from up in the lookout," Catrin said. "Like there was someone there with you."

"Jarter should drink less cider," I said. "Most of what she sees and hears comes out of a jug." It was a cruel thing to say of a woman that was like to lose her husband, but I remembered how cruel she was to Veso when she thought to mend him from being crossed and how heavy her blows landed on me, and was not sorry.

But when Catrin asked that question she finally let a little light into my head, that was all clouded up with fear and unhappiness. I saw where this was going, and why we were talking in a tiny room of the Underhold, with nobody else by us, instead of in the Count and Seal with the whole village as witness. It was not my stealing Rampart Remember's name-tech that weighed the most here, though I might be hanged for it. It was whether or not I'd used it. I, who was neither Rampart nor Vennastin, and should have had no better luck with the database than if I'd tried to coax a voice out of a stone. Perliu had let me into a great secret, and it was only now, in this narrow room, with his two daughters facing me, that I saw how dangerous a secret it was.

"I asked the others," Catrin said. "They all heard two voices."

Bitter bile came up into my mouth. I swallowed it down again.

"I'll say nothing more unless you let me speak with Rampart Remember," I said. "I'll give up every secret I've got, but only to him."

Catrin stood and walked to the door, drawing Fer along after her the way the northstar draws a compass. "We'll talk again tomorrow," she said. "See how you feel then."

But I couldn't wait until tomorrow.

"Catrin," I said, and then when she didn't stop, "Mother!" A weight settled on her shoulders. She turned to face me again, though I could see she didn't want to.

"If you're minded to beg," Fer said, "don't. It won't make no difference."

I didn't so much as look at her. It was Rampart Fire who had the first voice in the Count and Seal, and the power to turn what I had found out from just words into things decided and done. "I know what's making the sickness," I said to her. "If I tell you, and if I'm right, will you let me go free?"

"So you did talk to the database," Catrin said. Fer let out a gasp.

"I did."

"How?"

"I won't say how. But I'll tell what I know, if you'll pardon me."

I saw the thoughts crossing Catrin's face. Lots of thoughts, and she did not hurry them along. "We could make her tell," Fer said to nobody but herself.

"If you know a way to cure the plague," Catrin said, "and you hold it back, all the deaths that come from now on is on your back. Is your back broad enough to carry that, Spinner? You better decide now, because I don't mean to let you go nowhere until we sound the bottom of what you done. And I don't mean to promise you'll be alive when we're finished, because I'm far from deciding. If you're going to speak, or if you're going to keep silent, you do it for its own sake, not for no bargaining with me. A fart on any such bargain. I'm not making none."

We stood facing each other across the small room, and neither of us spoke.

"Well then," Catrin said after the space of five or six breaths. She went out, and Fer went out behind her. They closed the door and drew the bolt across.

I ran to the door and shouted the words through the wood. What the danger was, the cause of it and what they had to do.

Hundreds of years of damp had made the door sit badly in its frame, so their footsteps as they walked away was only a little muffled. I was nearly sure they heard me, but still tormented myself so much with doubting it that I could not sit still but paced the room for hours and hours and hours.

41

I was kept a prisoner in the Underhold for twenty days. I counted them by making scratches on the wall with the handle of a spoon. In all that time, I saw nobody but Catrin and Fer, except for a handful of times when my meals were brought by Gendel, Fer's husband. I never saw Perliu, or Vergil, or Ban, though they were all walking right over my head every day. I never saw my husband, Jon.

You might think from this that all of the twenty days were alike, but you would be wrong. You know how the dead god was killed on a tree, and buried in the ground, but then come out again with wings like an angel and his flesh grown into golden armour. Well, I was never any kind of an angel, but it was somewhat like that with me. They buried me, and when they dug me up again I was not the same. Whether I was better or worse, I cannot say. But different I was for sure.

Catrin was kind to me, as far as she knew how to be. She was never one who found kindness easy, even to her own kin, but she saw to it that I was fed and she gave me such comforts as she could. A bedroll to lie on, a chair to sit in, food and water twice a day and sometimes small beer besides. Another skirt and kirtle, underclothes and towels in case my time came on me (it did not). I had candles and tapers enough to last me, and a tinder box to light them with. The tinder box was one that had been my father's, and then mine. I must have left it behind in Jon's room, and Catrin, finding it there, had thought to bring it down to me. I don't think there was any particular feeling behind her doing it though. The tinder box and me were all of a piece in her mind, so she put us together.

Since I was not to be allowed to speak to any that were not Ramparts, Catrin emptied my piss bucket her own self at the start of every day. I was ashamed at first for her to see it, but I grew used to it soon. After I asked her, she brought me another bucket to wash in, and changed that water every day too. It was the sort of work a Rampart can expect to leave to others, but she did it as if a bucket came as naturally to her hand as the firethrower did.

What she didn't do, though, was talk to me. I was expecting more questions, but there weren't any. Most days there wasn't even a good morrow, only a nod or a look. She pushed me into a smaller space than the room was, just by not seeming to see me or care about me. I don't think that was a cruelty, though, any more than the tinder box was a kindness. She had no room in her head for me right then, and it would have been too much effort for her to stop and make some.

Twenty days passed in that way, like I told you. They were the longest twenty days in my life. I had nothing to busy my hands or my mind with, and nobody to talk to. I think I lived a year in the first ten days, and a good few years more in the next ten. In my nightmares still, I go back to that room and sit there, breathing stale air that tasted of my own sweat, staring at the walls by the light a single candle makes.

I'll tell you a strange thing though. I had some company in my prison. A few days in, I noticed that there was a place low down on the door of the room where someone had scraped it with the point of a knife. I knelt down to get a closer look at it, and saw that there was a face carved into the wood. It was rough work, but good. There was a liveliness to the face. I think it was a woman, or a girl, and she was smiling. There was mischief in that smile, or else there was a secret the woman knew and was not telling.

As soon as I saw it, I knew of a certainty who had put it there. That was Koli Woodsmith's handiwork, which I had seen a hundred times before. Koli had been in this room. I was not the first to be taken there and held there. That gave me greatly to wonder, but at the same time — for no reason I can explain — I took some solace from it.

Then one day a key turned in the door and Catrin came into the room carrying a joint stool, the way she did on the first day I was taken. She closed the door behind her and sat down. The solemn look on her face made me want to cry, for I thought this must be when she would tell me I was condemned, but I set my teeth and made no sound.

"How'd you know?" she says at last. I was like to fall off my chair with the relief of it, for that had got to mean I was right about the sickness. What's more, it meant she was not come to lay a sentence on me, for she would have said that first.

"You got rid of the dogs," I said.

Catrin nodded. "They wouldn't go at first. They was too used to being with us. Most of them just sit down right outside the gates and waited for us to call them back in. I had to drive them away with the firethrower. It was a hard thing to do. Hard to see too. Jarter Shepherd and Mercy Frostfend was crying and cursing, saying they couldn't do without their dogs and all was lost. Jarter shouted out that Ramparts was tyrants, and called on the village to rise against us, until Piter and Vesa pulled her away. I think there was others felt the same way, only they didn't say it.

"You think on that a moment, Spinner. People speaking up in broad day against Ramparts and their rule. That's what you brung on us, and it's not a thing I lightly forgive. You was one of the flies in their soup too. The fact that you was took and held so long, and the Count and Seal hadn't been let to question you.

Oh, there was all sorts of things being said, and ten times more being hinted at.

"But then a week passed, and none was took sick. So people held back their judgement. Another week, and they was close to believing. When Fer and me went to close down the quarant time and send them all home, there was singing and dancing in the streets. It was like Summer-dance come in Winter. All was forgived and forgot. By and gone. Ramparts was right and proper again, and ask where you like, you couldn't find nobody that had ever thought any different."

I didn't want to believe her, but I knew in my heart it was true. Most people don't have a great deal of room in their lives for worrying about others. And that little bit of room shrinks still further when they're scared for their own selves.

Catrin tapped her thumb against her chin a number of times, giving me that same hard stare. "So," she said again. "How'd you know that the dogs was bringing the sickness?"

"I got it from the database," I said.

"I figured that much, girl. But how? The database is a tricksy tool at the best of times. Tell me how you went about it."

I tried to find a way of explaining it that didn't depend on before-time words like vectors and micro-organisms. "There's beasts that carry disease," I said. "They're so small you can't see them, but they're real. When one person catches sickness from another, it's them little beasts that are carrying it."

Catrin nodded, and waited for me to say more.

"Only this time," I said, "people wasn't."

"Wasn't what?"

"Taking the plague each from other. If they was, the people in quarant time would most likely all of been dead before you could say their names. Every one of them had been close to the sick. Living in the same house. Sleeping in the same bed, mostly. So why wasn't they took?"

"And why wasn't they?"

"Because the little beasts wasn't going from one to another like

280

I said. They was living on something else, and only striking the people that got too close to that something else. Yet three was took at Frostfend, close together – that was Seven and then Hue and then—"

"I know who they was."

I nodded. "So I thought Frostfend might be closest to the bad thing, or have more of it. Then I looked at all the other places where people was took sick, and I set them next to Frostfend in my mind. What was at Rampart Hold that was at Frostfend too? Or in Fara Harvest's house?" I shrugged my shoulders. She knew the answer now, so I scarcely had to explain it. "I stood back from it a little way. I stopped looking for the little beasts since I didn't have no way of seeing them in any case, and thought of bigger beasts instead. Frostfend had the sheepdogs. Fara had her clever dog that she trained up to be a new pair of eyes for her."

"We didn't have no dogs at the Hold," Catrin said.

"No. But Raelu fed strays from the back door. And that kindness was what killed him."

"So what kind of sickness was it then?"

I shook my head. "If it's got a name, Rampart Fire, I don't know it. I put a lot of thought into that at first, but it was foolishness and a waste of time. The medicines of the old time are all forgot now, so finding the name they used back then for a plague that was ailing us now wouldn't have got us very far. And sicknesses don't stay the same in any case. The little beasts grow and die and birth in the time it takes you to blink. And with each new birth, they change a little. Mostly they get stronger and harder to kill. So there isn't no telling what might work and what might not. It's better to find out where the sickness makes its home and take that home away."

Catrin still hadn't took her eyes off me. And I still wasn't any closer to knowing what her staring meant. "It was a good thought," she said. "Clever."

I wasn't looking to get praise, and didn't really know what to do with it. "Thank you," I said. I looked down at the floor, somewhat discomfited.

"We talked with Perliu," Catrin said.

"Oh," I said. "Did you?" Pretending that didn't make any difference to me.

"He told us what the two of you cooked up together. About his giving you the database, and taking a piece of dead tech from the Underhold for him to keep about him. That was clever too. He knowed how careful I've been since we lost the cutter and since he got so absent in his mind. He was used to me asking to see the database to make sure he hadn't lost it."

"It was him come to me," I said quickly. "The day we went back to the tannery, he come there and asked my help." The words spilled out quick before I had time to think about them. I'm ashamed to set them down, even now. I had done all I could do to protect Perliu, but if he had given up the truth of what we did then there was nothing now to protect. And I wanted to live. I wanted that very much. My bleeding should have come while I was in the Underhold, but it hadn't. That was nothing strange in itself – in lean times, a woman could miss one month in two – but I was starting to think I might have a baby in my belly.

"Did he?" Catrin asked. "So all the sin's on him then?"

"Ask him," I said, "if you don't believe me. Or ask Jon."

"Why? To blunt the edge of your guilt? If you think that will make a difference to what happens to you, you're a fool. My sister wants you dead, and doesn't much mind how. Jon wants you free, obviously, and back in his bed. I can't please both of them. But I've been trying to think if there's a middle way."

She rubbed the firethrower's stock with the heel of her hand as she talked. There was a patch there that was worn smooth, most likely by her past considerings – and maybe by the considerings of other Rampart Fires in times long gone. "The worst thing about all this," she said, more to herself than to me, "is that it's a problem we should of seen coming. Especially after that business with Koli Woodsmith last year."

When Catrin said that, my eyes went from her to the carving on the door of my prison room. Whatever had happened to Koli, it was not as we had been told. "I'm not like Koli though," I said. "It was a Rampart that authorised me, and it was his own name-tech I took off of him."

I was hoping she might give something away about what Koli did, or what was done to him, but she only waved it away. "That's not to the purpose, and you know it. Just you listen to me now. There's things about how the Hold works that I would of had to tell you sooner or later. Or I'd have had to tell Jon, and he'd of told you. But then we lost the cutter, thanks to that twice-damned fool Mardew, and things fell out a different way. Now you know what you know. That the tech will answer to anyone if it's told to, and not just to Ramparts. That's the truth of it. The rest is a lie some Vennastin made up long since to grab the Hold, the power and a life of ease and keep them as long as he could. And here we are, still telling that same lie."

To hear her say it like that, bald and clear, made me so angry of a sudden that I couldn't answer her. And not just angry but sick too that I had set my heart on some of the same things – the ease at least, if not the power.

"Now maybe you can be trusted with that secret, Spinner," Catrin went on, "and maybe you can't. You're not born to this life the way we are. And I don't feel like I know you well enough to guess how you'll jump."

"Ask your father then. Or your son." I spit the words out, throwing our kinship in her face.

"Jon's no use to anyone right now," Catrin said. "As for my father, I wish I could ask him but I can't. He was took sick when Fer was questioning him about you. She was shouting in his face and cursing him for giving away our secrets and his own name-tech. For putting the family at risk. I reined her in when she went to slap his face, but the damage was done. He fell down in a fit. He hasn't spoke since, or got up out of his bed. I think he's dying."

I was mightily cast down at that. It was not that I loved Perliu so very much. Through our working and plotting together we had come to be friends, but I would not say it was any more than that. Still and all, though, I hated to think of him being tasked and reproached for the bargain we made – tasked and reproached until his mind and body misgave for it. And his being struck down removed any hope I had that he might come between me and his daughters.

"So I'm asking you," Catrin took up again. "Will you swear to it that you won't call us out on this? That you'll hold to the same story the rest of us do if anyone asks?"

"And if I swear, you'll spare my life?"

"I'll do my best. The Count and Seal has got its own thoughts, sometimes, that go against mine."

I thought again of what was growing in my belly. "I'll tell any lie you want me to," I said, "and swear it to Dandrake himself if it will keep me alive."

If she was surprised to hear me say it so hard and fierce, she didn't show it. She held out her hand to me. She was holding something small that I couldn't see clearly in the room's dim light. I didn't move to take it. I had a sudden wild thought that it might be a knife she was giving me. There was a time, my father had told me once, when one that was accused could choose a fight instead of a judgement, and be set free with no stain if they won.

I folded my arms around my chest, to keep from touching the thing, whatever it might be.

"If I was you," Catrin said, "I wouldn't quarrel with my own good fortune."

I looked again at what she was holding. With some of my fears set by, it was plain to see. It was the database. I took it from her, wildered and wondering. I looked in her stony face and waited for her to tell me what this meant.

"I want you carrying that in your hand when we go before the Count and Seal," Catrin said. "We've got a lot to explain and a lot to argue. It's best if we give them the big shock right at the start, and let it sink in while we talk to them."

"The Count and Seal?" I said, as stupid as an echo-bird.

She give me a hard look, like she was all out of patience with me. "Of course. Did you think you was going to get away without being put to question?"

"No, but . . . Rampart Fire, what's happening?" I managed at last. "What is it you mean to do with me?"

"I already told you, Spinner, if you was listening. Rampart Knife died in Ludden, and my father is as close to death as a word is to a whisper. We're gone from four Ramparts down to two, and we got problems that would tax four times forty. We give them Half-Ax raiders a hard hurting, and most likely they've gone looking for an easier fight, but the hunters are scared to go out until we're sure. So now we got people going hungry and looking over their shoulders at their neighbours' share. None of that is what tilted the scales for you though."

"What did then?" I asked. Wondering if she knew, somehow, that I was carrying her grandchild inside of me. But it was not that either. It was something bigger than family or famine. Bigger even than Half-Ax.

It was the trees.

Koli

42

We gun to clear the trees around the boat. That had got to be
where we started, for it give us somewhere safe to fall back to if
the sun come out and the forest woke.

Made the Tide Turn had promised us help with the repairs to
the boat, but this first work he left to us because he didn't have
no people he could spare. He did send Rain Without Clouds,
though, to sing a blessing on the boat and the space all round it.
He said the forest was a place where bad ghosts was oftentimes
found, and we had got to be protected from them or else they
might climb inside us and so come into the village where they
was not wanted.

Me and Cup done this first part of the work by ourselves with
axes and saws. We had to fell one of the three trees against the
lean, as they say, meaning we cut it so it would fall backwards
instead of in the way it was leaning and already wanting to fall.
Otherwise it would of crushed the boat to pieces, which would
not of been any good for us at all.

I had seen my mother fell a tree against the lean oftentimes and
knowed the trick of it, which is to make cross-cuts on the face
side, all on one end of the main cut, until by and by the tree shifts

its weight and changes its mind. I done a good job, seeing I never done it before. It was the first time I ever seen Cup be impressed by anything I done. She tried not to show it, and never said a word, but I seen the surprise in her face and took some pleasure in showing off my woodsmithing to her.

After the trees was down, we cut them into pieces and turned the pieces into good lumber using axes and some oak wedges I made. This was the hardest work, but I enjoyed teaching Cup how to do it. I didn't forget we was among trees and ever in danger, but Monono kept lookout while we was labouring, and used her alarm to scare off any beasts that wandered too close to us. We never stopped being watchful or being afraid, but we was not skittish like hares the whole time. Not once we had our clearing made and could fall back into the middle of it if the sun come out.

We was not in the woods every day that come though. The Many Fishes people had share-works, just like we had in Mythen Rood, and Cup and me was expected to play our part just like we done with the sand-fishing.

The second week after we come to the village was the week the shieldmen marched. Shieldmen was not what they sound like. They was beasts with lots of legs and armour on their backs that lived mostly in the deepest waters of the ocean. The same time every year, the shieldmen went on a long walk that took them across the bottom of the lagoon. The Many Fishes people knowed when it would happen, and where the shieldmen would go, and they was keen to put theirselves in the way of it. That meant going out in the boats to drop things that was called pots, though in fact they was boxes, right out in the middle of the water. The pots was kind of traps for the shieldmen, who would go into them to eat the bait that was there and then would not be able to come out again.

"We won't be no good at any of that," I told Taller Than Trees. "We never set foot in a boat in our whole lives."

"But you're meaning to," he said. "Ain't you? You've got to make a start some time."

I seen the truth in that, but it didn't make me any happier about it. I got to say, I was more afraid of going out on that water than I was of anything I ever did in my life before. It wasn't just that the water was colder than a graveyard stone and ever heaving up and whipping down again like curtains in a strong wind. It was that it didn't seem to have no end to it. It seemed to me like there was a world of water that sit right next to the dry world we lived in, and was just as big or maybe bigger.

"We got to do it though," Cup said. "They'll say we're cowards else."

I wouldn't of minded getting called coward so much, but people who duck out of share-works get harsher names than that. Idlers. Bedrolls. Self-servers. If you do it often enough to get a name for it, you might even get made faceless and sent out of gates, but even if that don't come to pass, the shame is almost a worser thing.

So we tucked our courage in our belts, as they say, and we went out with the shieldman boats.

The first thing that happened was that we was desperate sick. That up-and-down rocking and the swinging side to side was not like anything I ever felt before. It squeezed my stomach the way you'd squeeze a wet shirt to dry it. I clinged hard onto the edge of the boat with my head leaned out over the water, and everything I ever et in my whole life come back to get itself un-et again. Cup was took just as bad, but she got over it quicker and afterwards she made a great show of walking up and down the boat to show that the water couldn't daunt her.

It daunted me a while longer, I got to say.

When we was far enough out into the water, the pots had got to be baited with cut-up fish and throwed over the sides of the boat. Bladders was fixed to the ropes on a sliding loop so we'd know where the pots was when we come back for them the next day or the day after that. I mostly baited the pots, but Cup made sure to do a little bit of everything there was to do.

We could only help with what was needful on the boat though.

The Many Fishes people was in and out of the boats like they didn't see where the planks ended and the water begun. It was the thing Ursala called swimming, and they was all really good at it, even some that was much younger than us. Cup watched them going at it with a longing look in her eyes. As for me, all I could think of was how far down the bottom was, which was a thing you would not know until you got there.

The second time we went out, Cup learned to work the sails too, and to row and steer with a stern oar when the wind failed. My fear of the water was still with me, so I trailed behind her in all these things, but I made myself useful any way I could. And the third time, when Cup was running back and forth like she was born on the deck of a boat, I finally gun to feel like sailing was something I could do.

Ursala was not there when we went out with the fishing boats, nor for any of the share-works. She would of gone, but the Headman said her time was better used in the village. She spent most of each day in an empty house right next to the Bowl, healing people's ills and injuries with the drudge's dagnostic. Then when she was done with that for the day, she come and worked with us in the woods. Her skill with an axe was not much, but she brung the drudge with her and the drudge could haul a felled tree faster than a man could walk.

I got to say there was not so many in the village that was took with diseases as you might of guessed. A few had hook-worms, which is no surprise as they mostly did not wear shoes. One or two had meltfever from eating bad fruit. There was also three women that was with child, and one of them had a fainting sickness. But most of Ursala's work was with people whose bodies was twisted, wasted or otherwise marred by sicknesses they had in the past, or else was flat-out born that way. The drudge's dagnostic could reach inside them to straighten their bones, take the curtains out of their eyes, make their muscles work again and draw the poison from cankers and sores.

Many of these things was not going to be mended all at once.

People had got to come back to Ursala day after day to get their-selves healed and made right again. One of them was the Headman, Made the Tide Turn, who suffered great pain in what was left of his missing arm. Ursala found an infection there, and a jagged spike of bone that had healed itself into his wound long before. She had got to open up the stump again to take the bone out, and the Headman was not keen to let her do it, but by and by he agreed and afterwards was mazed to find how much his pain was lessened.

Anyway, what with one thing and another, the work was long. Oftentimes Ursala did not come into the forest at all. She would still be down in the Bowl, in what she called her surgery, when me and Cup come back to Many Fishes at the end of the day.

Rain Without Clouds would oftentimes be there with her. She insisted on singing good spirits into all them that Ursala healed. Ursala had got to grit her teeth at that. She didn't see any use in calling on spirits, but she said there might be something in the singing called a placebo that might do her patients some good after all.

Out of all of us, Cup was the one that had settled in at Many Fishes the quickest and the easiest. When we come back to the village in the evening, she would run to play the stone-game with Taller Than Trees and Dog Runner and Dog Runner's two sisters. Or they had another game they played where they had got to throw a ball in the air and grab knuckle-bones off the ground before it come down again. Or they would race, or wrestle.

Even when they was not playing, Cup spent most of the time that was her own with Taller Than Trees. She had come very quickly to warm thoughts of him, and he seemed to like her just as well. The two of them was so wrapped up each in other they forgot the world was there. He was teaching her the Many Fishes language so they could talk together without nobody coming in between them. It mazed me how quick she was with it already, and how many words she knowed, though Taller Than Trees laughed some-times at the way she said them.

Then, just as sudden, they was at odds, and you could not speak the boy's name to Cup without her swearing up a storm.

Then they was friends again.

Then one morning when Ursala and me was eating breakfast, Cup come out of her room with cuts all over her face like she fell down in some gravel. She looked like she had been crying, which was not a thing she favoured overmuch. When I asked her if she was hurt, she walked right past us and went out the door without saying a word.

"How did her face get cut?" I asked. "In her own room and all. You think she fell out of bed."

"No," Monono said. The DreamSleeve was sitting out on the table in a patch of strong sunlight so she had seen the same thing I'd seen. "She tried to shave off her facial hair. Probably with a flat stone or the edge of a knife. That's my diagnosis anyway. But maybe you should ask the doctor over there."

Ursala put down her spoon maybe a little heavier than was needful. "That sounded pointed," she said.

"Good," Monono said. "It was meant to. Cup is going through puberty. *Boy* puberty. She probably would have hit it a lot earlier if she'd had better nutrition. Now she's on three square meals a day, her body is running to catch up – which has got to be like hell on a three-wheel unicycle. Your magic medicine droid could do something about that."

"You're suggesting I carry out gender reassignment therapies. On a child."

"On an adolescent."

"Which is another word for child. Cup's too young to be making a decision like that. She may wake up tomorrow and feel very differently about what she wants. About who she is."

"Respectfully, ancient one, have you tried asking her what she wants and who she is? I'd say she's pretty clear on the subject. She knows what her body is doing, and she's not okay with it. She's frightened and she's unhappy. She'd do almost anything to make it stop. Plus, she's got a crush on a super-cute boy and that makes it even harder."

Ursala looked from the DreamSleeve to me. I guess she was asking me to say if that was true or not. "His name is Taller Than Trees," I told her. "I think they like each other a lot. And I think Monono is right that Cup is really unhappy with some of the things that are happening to her right now. She said it to me a while back."

"She's not unhappy," Monono said. "She's stuck in a trap, and she can't get out of it because it's her own body. Over to you, ancient one."

Ursala sweared an oath. "I can't help her. I know that the procedure you're describing was commonplace back before the Unfinished War. I've read about what's involved. With the stress on the verb: *read* about. No more than that. I don't know what the relevant hormones are, or what dosages and regimens to use. There's a plug-in module for the drudge with all the molecular signatures, but I don't have it. And without it, I can't even get started."

"But I can. I told you, baa-baa-san, I hacked every database from here to the lower stratosphere. Patch me in and I can give you everything you need."

Ursala blinked. Her look of surprise give way to a fierce glare. "Is that what this is about? You're trying to get inside the drudge again?"

"It's about Cup."

"But the solution is me letting you inside the drudge's firewall."

"Aaarrrhhhh!" Monono shouted. "I don't care what you do, you paranoid old chew-toy! I can give you the molecules one attachment point at a time if you want. You can knit the stupid hormones yourself. I'll give you the dosages, the treatment schedule, the target ranges for blood concentrations and ten per cent off your next purchase. Just do something and stop pretending you can't!"

Somehow, Monono getting angry like that — which was not

a usual thing with her – made Ursala come back a lot calmer. "Suppose I take you up on that offer," she said. "What happens if we lose the drudge? If the diagnostic unit takes damage, or stops working? Or if Cup decides to leave us for that matter? She gets to start transitioning, and then she gets to stop again, cold turkey. However bad she feels now, I'm pretty sure that would be worse."

It seemed to me that the argument had moved along somewhat. Ursala was telling us why this transitioning was hard to do instead of saying it shouldn't be done at all.

"I'm not even talking about transitioning," Monono said. "Well, not at first. I'm talking about puberty blockers. They're reversible. If Cup goes her own way, she loses the benefits, but that's all she loses. You're not starting an avalanche, baa-baa-san. You're damming a stream. Take away the dam, the water flows the same way it did before. In any case, you should let her make the choice. And doing nothing, by the way, is making the choice for her. It's not a neutral option. There is no neutral option."

Neither of them said nothing for a long while. If I was free to do it, I most likely would of gone away, since this was a thing between the two of them – or them and Cup leastways. But Monono had forbid me from leaving the DreamSleeve with Ursala, so I had got to stay until she was done.

"You can really give me the molecular specifics for the hormones?" Ursala says by and by.

"Yes."

"Totally hands-off? Without linking up to the drudge's systems?"

"Oh my god! Yes, yes, yes!"

Ursala nodded her head slowly. "All right. I agree. Go ahead and assemble the molecular profiles. Puberty blockers first. I'll talk to Cup and satisfy myself she understands what's involved – and then we'll talk about the rest of it. Including how volatile the compounds are. I don't want to start something I can't finish."

"With great age comes great wisdom, baa-baa-san."

"Drop dead."

She went out of the room. I put the DreamSleeve back in its sling. "That went okay," Monono said.

"It might of gone better if you wasn't so rude to her."

"Beep. Wrong. I gave her something to push against, Koli-bou. She'd have been disappointed if I hadn't."

43

Janury ended, and we was into Febry. We had finished with the
clearing and now we was into repairing our boat. We got some
help with that, as was promised, and we was grateful for it.
Neither me nor Cup knowed the first thing about how boats
was meant to work. A man named Three White Stones and a
woman named Heavy Foot come to lend a hand to it and to
tell us what was needful to be done. We knowed them already.
They was the father and mother of Afraid of His Shadow, and
I think they asked their Headman if they could be the ones to
help us, since they was so grateful for what Ursala done for
their son.

Our boat needed more fixing than I thought when I first
seen it. There was a number of holes in the bottom and sides of
it – the Many Fishes people had a name for them parts of a
boat, which was the hull – and the wood around the edges of
the holes was gone rotten. I knowed how to cut back the rotted
wood, and how to test for the soundness of what was left with
the point of a knife, but I didn't know how to make a patch
and set it in. Heavy Foot and her husband showed me the way
of it, which was to scarf the edges of the cut and the patch so

they matched each other perfect, and then to nail the patch in. They had a glue they mixed and painted all over the joins, that set as hard as the wood its own self. Once you sanded it down, it looked like the patch had been there ever since the boat was first made.

While we was doing this, a team of loggers from Many Fishes gun to cut down the trees between us and the river, clearing away the timber each time and salting the stumps so they could be dug out later. They was not the same people each day – they was just whoever the Headman could spare – but they all knowed their woodsmithing and worked quick and well.

The sky all this time was thick with overcast most every day but no rain at all, which was good luck for us getting on with the work. We couldn't hope to have it all our own way though. There was two storms. The first come on in the middle of the night, and it was more fierce than anything I ever seen or felt. Water poured out of the sky the way it pours out of an upturned bucket, but that was nothing next to the wind. The wind was like a bear throwing its shoulder against the walls of our house ever and again, trying to knock it down. Then come the thunder, which was like Stannabanna was cheering the bear on to its work. There was no hope of sleeping through it. Cup come into my room, and we shared the covers, with Monono playing us music that was louder than the storm.

The next morning, we stuck our heads out like we was scared of having them bit off to find the Bowl turned into a lake and the Many Fishes people laughing about it. "Be better if we *was* fishes," Taller Than Trees said. "We could swim to where we was going instead of walking."

"Did you ever see anything like that in your life?" Cup asked him, grabbing his arm and holding onto it.

"That was middling bad," Taller Than Trees said. "There's worse to come, Knife Tongue. But we'll weather it."

I thought he was joking about that, until the big storm hit.

I had lived my whole life in Calder Valley before this journey started. We had storms, and sometimes they was vexing, but they was nothing we really worried about. Here on the edge of the water, the storms was every bit as troublesome as the beasts and the trees was. That first one teached me why the Many Fishes people builded their village up in levels, each on other. It was so the houses wouldn't flood when the water fell out of the sky like that.

But the second storm didn't bring no rain at all. What it brung was dry lightning that set a house and one of the wood platforms on fire. Someone sounded a horn, which I guess was like our tocsin bell, for it brung all the Many Fishes people running to throw water on the blaze and damp it down before it got too far along. I thought of *The Signal*, sitting out there in the woods, and prayed the lightning didn't strike there too.

It didn't, but the wind was strong enough to push the boat up against a tree, stave in some of the planks on the side and bury the whole thing in torn-off branches and twigs. "I don't like your Winter," I told Heavy Foot as we set in to repair the damage.

She laughed hearty at that. "You wait until you see our Spring," she said.

Well, we purposed to be gone by Spring, so them words didn't trouble me as much as they maybe should of done. In spite of all I knowed, both from Calder and from our journey south, I was still looking forward to the warm days coming again.

I should of knowed better.

We passed then into the best of our time at Many Fishes. Ursala had that talk with Cup, and Cup said she would like the medicines Monono talked about – that would first of all stop the changes that was making her so unhappy and then, later on, push her body more in the way of her wishing. Monono give Ursala the recipe for the medicines and the dagnostic went to work to make them.

"Taller Than Trees is like to get a surprise," I said, "when he sees you all changed."

Cup give me a look like she was sorrowing for my foolishness. "It's not like Stannabanna waving his staff and saying ansum bansum,

Koli. It's slow as anything. And right now I'm not changing – only stopping the changes that was like to come by their own selves Anyway, Trees said he likes me well enough the way I am, and don't see no need for me to be different."

"That's good then."

"Yeah, it is. The need's in me though, and I mean to do it."

We had learned by this time what the Many Fishes people thought of people that was crossed. They said *peret ene saku* or *peren ene saku* – man under the skin or woman under the skin. And they didn't see nothing out of the way in it because they didn't reck Dandrake's teachings nor the dead god's neither, but only the spirits of them that lived before. In that way, I think we had come to a place that was better for Cup than either Half-Ax or Senlas's cave had been. Better than Mythen Rood, for that matter.

However that was, Ursala's medicines was enough for now to stop hair growing on her in places where it wasn't looked for, like her face and arms, and to stop her voice from going like a man's voice, with more bottom than top to it. I guess that doesn't sound like much, but you could tell she was a lot happier now than she had been before. I guess when you're changing by inches and ounces into someone you don't want to be, it's a hard thing to bide. "Body and soul, little dumpling," Monono said. "They're two little birds in the same bush."

As for me, I think I could of had a lover if I wanted it enough. There was a girl, Hits First Time, that cast her eyes at me somewhat. She had danced with me on the sun-standing, that first night when we come, and smiled at me warm as anything whenever she seen me. I liked her too, for she was kind and funny, with a face that was always just about ready to laugh. But I looked inside my heart and didn't see no love there, and I was wary of making promises without meaning to. I guess I was partly still thinking about Spinner and the harm I done there by still wanting her when she had already done her choosing. That was enough harm for a good long while, I thought.

301

Then two things happened that between them brought an end to that time of sweetness.

A man named Silent Hand was took out of his own house in the middle of the night by a beast so big and so strong it teared the door right off its hinges and trampled it on the ground.

And the next day, the choker trees blossomed.

44

I told you before about the choker trees and what they could do, but I don't think I said much about what happened when they come into bloom. It wasn't nothing joyous, as you must of guessed. In fact, the first sign of them yellow blossoms brung dismay to everyone that seen them. In Mythen Rood we had a way of taking the edge off a choker Spring so we didn't fear it as much as others did. It could hurt us, but it couldn't end us. There was villages that had died, down to the last woman and man, because chokers got them. And it's not the trees I'm talking about, though the trees was hurtful enough. I mean the seeds.

Chokers didn't flower every year, or even one in two. The dead god's gospel tells of how he decided to whelm the world with chokers, but then thought better of it. He wouldn't undo what he made, but he said the chokers would only cast out their seeds when they was watered with his tears. So when men and women does wicked things, the dead god cries and the chokers bloom. If that's so, I guess Febry must be the month when people turn most to wickedness. That was when the choker flowers gun to put out, bright yellow like the sun its own self, and March was when the seeds gun to rain down.

A choker seed is most like a sycamore seed, except it's got two tails where a sycamore seed has just got the one. The tails stick up like bat wings, with the seed sitting down under them, dark brown like a nut and as big as the nail on your smallest finger. When the seeds leave the tree, they don't fall straight but catch the wind and spin and get carried a long way. You can't ever tell where they're like to fall.

But if it's anywhere near where you are, then Dandrake help you. The second a choker seed touches you, it cracks wide open and the roots that have laid there all that time, curled up inside the seed case, push theirselves out as quick as throwed knives and dig down into you. You got just a little time, then, to scoop them out again with the point of a blade. After that, it's too late. The roots grow through your whole body, and they suck you dry. You're dead soon after, and a choker tree will grow up where you fell, fed with all the goodness that was in you.

In Mythen Rood, when them yellow flowers showed, it was time for Rampart Fire to pick up her name-tech and go out into the forest. She would burn the blossom right off the trees, playing that sheet of flame across the branches until there was not one bit of yellow showing. If some of the trees catched fire too, that was no bad thing, but mostly they didn't. Choker wood is so dense and hard that it's not easy to set a light to.

In Many Fishes village they didn't have a firethrower, or a Rampart to carry it. The onliest tech they had, so far as we had seen, was the metal circlet that Made the Tide Turn wore on his head.

It was Cup and me that brung the news, for we started our days in the forest early, and oftentimes was the first ones to swing an axe. We seen the flowers one morning when we come up from the village, and we run right back down again to warn everyone of what was coming.

In spite of the seriousness and the danger, there's always a little excitement in being the one that brings the bad tidings first. It makes you more important, for a while, than you're used to being.

But Made the Tide Turn only nodded when we climbed up to his house and told him, all breathless, that the chokers was out.

"That's needful to know," he said, "and I thank you for it, but it's a trouble for a later time. We've got other things that press harder on us." We seen then what we should of seen as soon as we come into his house, that he was making ready for a fight. He was winding leather straps around his ankles and calves to armour himself. A man was helping him to tighten the straps and tie them off, since the Headman had just the one hand. Rain Without Clouds was there too, chanting under her breath with each loop of leather that was wound around him.

"Did something happen?" I asked Made the Tide Turn. "Is there shunned men coming?" I looked at Cup when I said that. I couldn't help it. It wasn't that I still thought of her as a shunned man. It was only that I had strong memories of being a prisoner in Senlas's cave, where she used to live. In my mind she was tangled up in them memories, so thoughts of the one thing sometimes led me to thoughts of the other.

The Singer seen that look. Her eyes walked the same path from me to Cup and back again. I seen a thought come up into her mind, and I seen her tuck it back down again to think on another time.

"It's not shunned men," Made the Tide Turn said. "It's years since shunned men come against us. It's something almost as bad though."

That was when we found out about the man, Silent Hand, being took in the night. Something had come through his door, smashing the lintel and part of the wall, and dragged him away. His wife was beside him, and his children in the next room, but it was dark and they didn't see nothing clear. The beast that took him was so quick, it struck and then was gone before they was full awake.

But nothing that was big enough and strong enough to drag away a man could stay hid for long. It had left a clear trail behind it of broke wooden rails up on the platforms of the village and then of deep prints down on the sand. "From the prints," Made

305

the Tide Turn said, "we think it's a sea-bear. We're going to follow the trail and kill it. If we don't, it will keep coming back to us whenever it's hungry."

I had never heard of a sea-bear, and I wanted above all things never to meet one, but this was a share-work and the Headman wanted all that was free to join the hunt. Cup had her bow that she had took from the Half-Ax fighter, but Made the Tide Turn said my knife would not be any use. "If you get close enough to use that on a sea-bear," he said, "you'll already be dead and eaten." He bid one of the other men there to give me a weapon that was more fitting. He offered me two throwing spears, but I never could throw anything halfway straight. I took a longer spear instead that was for thrusting.

There was no time to tell Ursala about the choker blossoms we seen, for the hunters was already setting out. We was swept along with them, down onto the sand and out along the margin of the big water, the same way we went when we hunted the mudpikes. Made the Tide Turn led the way, a long spear in his hand.

The tracks we was following was five-toed, almost like human footprints, except that they was twice as wide and had claws as long as my pointing finger. They was easy to follow, and we went at a run. A steady run though, so we could all stay together and not be strung out along the beach. When we met this beast, the headman meant for us to be at our strongest.

But we did not meet it. After a mile or so, the tracks turned and went into the water. At the place where they turned, we found what was left of Silent Hand. He was mostly et up, with his ribs all bare and broke.

Made the Tide Turn kneeled down right there in the sand and sung a kind of song to the dead man. It was not in Franker, but in the language of the Many Fishes people. I asked Cup what he was saying since she was learning from Taller Than Trees how to talk back to him in his own tongue, and she said she believed it was the names of Silent Hand's mother and father, and their mothers and fathers, and so on for a long time. There was a prayer in there too that all them mothers and fathers would help Silent Hand find a new place to live.

"In the dead world, you mean?" I whispered.

"No, Koli. Many Fishes people don't go to the dead world. Not straightway. They go into a house or a boat or a spear or a sail or whatever it might be, and they bide there to watch over their own. Senlas told me once his spirit wasn't just inside his body but in the mountain where we . . ." She catched herself and shaked her head. Sometimes she forgot how that story had ended, what with so much of her life being tangled up in it.

Sad and tired now, we took Silent Hand, or what was left of him, back to the village to be buried. On the way, I asked Dog Runner what the Many Fishes people did when there was a choker Spring. He give me a sideways look. "I think it's a secret, Koli," he told me.

"It is?"

"Yeah, I believe so. You better ask the Headman or the Singer. If they want you to know, they'll tell you."

Back in Many Fishes, the Headman give orders for Silent Hand to be took back to his family and laid out, and for watchers to be set around the village that night in case the sea-bear come back. It knowed now that there was food to be had in the village, and it was like to follow its own spoor the next time it wanted to feed. He said everyone had got to take a turn, and there would be a dozen watchers at a time. Also there would be torches set along the sand, since beasts of all kinds is slow to go near a fire. The aim was to keep the bear out on the beach, or if that failed, down on the ground. If it come up among the platforms, where the houses was mostly just tents, the people would not have any way to bar it out.

We went to tell Ursala about all these doings. She had already heard about the sea-bear. Probably she heard more than she wanted to, for everyone who stayed behind from the hunt had spent the whole day praying for them that was gone. The choker blossom was news to her though, and far from welcome.

307

"We'll have to work faster," she said. "We need to be out on the ocean before the seeds fall."

"You only got maybe a fortnight at the best of it," Cup said. "The blossom stays out for a little more than a week before it fades – and the seeds fall five days after that. But that's not more than half of it, Ursala. You got to know it isn't."

What she meant was that the chokers was far from being the only thing we had got to be afraid of. Most beasts fare no better in a choker Spring than humankind do, so they got their own ways of abiding it. The birds mostly go to some place else, and I got no idea where that might be. Things that live on the ground dig deep holes and go to sleep in them. But first they hunt and feed, eating more in a handful days than they would normally do in a month. You don't want to be in the forest then. You want to be any place else.

But Ursala didn't seem to reck any of this. "Thank you, Cup," she said. "I'm familiar with the life cycle of the choker tree. How far have the two of you got with your repairs?"

"*The Signal*'s mostly ready," I told her. "We need to rig a sail on it, which Heavy Foot said she'd show us how to do, and we need to cut some logs into rollers to lie under it when we push it. The real labour that's still left is clearing the trees between us and the river. We made some headway there, but there's still lots that's got to be done. I don't see any way to finish it in the time we got, unless the Headman lends us more of his people."

"I'll take that up with him. In the meantime, keep working."

I looked at Cup, and Cup looked at Ursala. "How d'you think we're gonna do that?" she said, throwing up her hands. "Every damn thing that's alive is going to be looking to line its stomach for the long sleep. I can't work with a damn tree-cat hanging off my leg!"

"I'll dismount the diagnostic unit," Ursala said, "and give you the drudge during the day. One way or another, it will stop most things."

She went away then to talk to the Headman about the watch

he meant to keep for the sea-bear. She said she would offer up the drudge to be a part of the watch once we had come back from the woods each day. It had growed some more bullets inside itself now, and could shoot the bear if it come close enough. Made the Tide Turn said yes at once, as soon as she showed him how the drudge's gun worked. Even Rain Without Clouds couldn't find no reason to argue with that.

I had seen a man et alive by a choker seed once, and the memory come back to me that night when I tried to get to sleep. It was Win Olso. The seed come down on his shoulder, and he brushed it off without seeing what it was. Only it didn't come off clean. Some of the seed-threads had already gone into him. By the time he seen it, they was deep in his neck and chest, thickening already into woody stems that was moving under his skin like ropes. He tried to say something, or maybe just to cry out, but all his mouth and throat was filled with thin fibres like a spider web. He fell down and took root right where he was. Rampart Fire had to burn him to ash, and then the ground was dug up and throwed over the fence into the half-outside in case any of the threads was still alive.

I lay awake thinking about that for an hour or more. And woke to find the sea-bear had fed again, taking one of the night-time watchers off the beach before she had time to cry out.

45

"There isn't any one of us that's safe until the beast is dead," Taller Than Trees told us. "Now it's got the taste and smell of us, it will keep on coming back and coming back. We got to kill it and burn the body afterwards, for sea-bears are known to spring up sometimes with a dozen spears in them and kill again. They're stronger than land-bears even. Their skin is cold as ice but there's a fierce fire inside them that's hard to put out."

Ursala said this was just stories and we shouldn't pay them no heed.

"Easy for you to say," Cup complained. "It's Koli and me that's going out into the forest every day and working until the sun drops out of the sky."

"It won't bother you up there," Taller Than Trees promised. "It won't stray so far from the water."

He was right about that. The sea-bear didn't come near nor by us up in the woods. We had our hands full just the same though. I told you already that the beasts that sleep through the choker Spring is busy as anything right before it, and that was what we found. A day didn't go by without Monono's alarm, the drudge's gun and Cup's bow all being called on to make a tree-cat or a swarm of needles change its mind. We even got attacked by some of the unlisted – beasts that lived in the deep woods and that people never yet give a name to. One of them made me shake even to look at it. It was tall and spindly, but the top of its body was all bulged out – like as it was a fat man standing on a thin man's shoulders. It had one big claw on each hand, like a moon at the quarter-full, and it swinged its arms before it the way you do with a sickle if you're cutting corn. It weared its bones on the outside so Cup's arrows and the drudge's bullets bounced right off it. The drudge had got to charge right into it and keep pushing at it until by and by it choosed another way to go. It was a while after that before we could start work again. Looking back on it now, I'm not even sure if that thing was a beast or a piece of tech. It looked enough like both to make you doubtful of either.

So that was our days. And in the nights the sea-bear come back to Many Fishes ever and again, though thankfully it didn't take no more people off the beach or out of their beds. The next time it come, it broke into a henhouse and left it tore into matchwood, blood and feathers all over everywhere like they had rained down out of the sky. The time after that, the drudge confronted it and scared it off with bullets. That was when I got to see what the bear looked like with my own eyes.

"I set the drudge's camera to respond to movement," Ursala told us the next morning – us being Cup and me and the Headman and the Singer as well as a few other important people from the village all gathered together in a house that stood on the lowest level next to the Bowl. "This is what it saw. It's thermal imaging, so the colours will be strange."

She tapped her mote controller and the window in the drudge's belly lit up with pictures. The colours was just as strange as Ursala said they would be – all green and orange with here and there little patches of red. It took me some while to figure out what I was looking at.

There was the sand, and the outer houses, and the edge of the Bowl. It was all still at first, but then something moved across in front of us, from left to right, and hid all them things. The picture blurred as the drudge set off after it, running fast between the wooden walls of houses. There was a cracking and popping sound that come ever and again, like green wood crackling in a fire. That was shots from the drudge's gun.

It was chasing the bear, but the bear was no more than a shadow and wouldn't come clear. We only could see it at all because sometimes it passed in between the drudge and something else, hiding the something else for a second or two. You could tell how big the beast was by how long the things behind it was hid each time.

Then the drudge's camera was looking at the line of lit torches that was set at the edge of the village. Something lumbered between them, and for a breath or a half of a breath, it was clear to see. Ursala tapped the mote controller and the picture went still, showing us that one terrible thing. A mountain of shiny skin and moving muscle. A head as big as a barrel. Teeth and claws and a wide, high bump in the middle of its shoulders that was somewhat like a fish's fin.

"That's the only clear shot I was able to get," Ursala said. "The thermal imager can't resolve it at all, which I take to mean that it's got perfect insulation. Its skin is the same temperature as the surrounding air." She touched the mote controller again. The monitor went dark. "And I don't think any of those bullets hurt it at all. Certainly there are no wounds on it when it steps into the light."

"Sea-bears are spirits of men and women that were so evil they couldn't die," said Rain Without Clouds. "If you want to kill them, you have to find a good spirit that's just as strong and sing it into your sword or your bow. Keep it there with a prayer knot, then set it free again when you strike. It will go into the bear, and the two spirits will fight until one of them dies." She changed her voice then to a kind of a growl. "What the woman says is true. Listen to her."

Ursala stared at the Singer for a moment, then shaked her head.

"Thank you for that valuable observation, Rain Without Clouds," she said. Meaning, I think: keep your nonsense to yourself.

There was not much that come of that meeting. We strewed the sand with vinegar in between the torches. The sour smell could sometimes make beasts turn away. And the next day, me and Cup went into the woods the same as before. Back to *The Signal*. Back to our work.

"I'll tell you if that thing comes," Monono told me. "I've got my mike gained up to maximum so I'll hear it a long way off. Don't you worry, Koli-bou. Nothing's going to eat you on my watch."

That give me some comfort, but not for long. The yellow blossom all around us was quick to kill any cheer in my heart.

With each day that passed, we was coming closer to seed-fall.

Spinner

46

Before we dealt with the Count and Seal, Catrin said we had got to deal with Haijon. I thought he might be the harder of the two.

"Let me see Rampart Remember first," I begged her.

"He's too weak to say a word. He can't talk to you, Spinner."

"No. But maybe he'll hear me."

She took me to the old man's room, and stood by while I sat with him. He was lying on top of his bed, fully dressed. He didn't move or speak, but his eyes were wide open and staring at the ceiling. I told him about how we'd stopped the sickness, the two of us together. "It was a great thing, Rampart, and it was you that done it. If you hadn't synced me with the database, we'd be in a desperate way. But you did, and all's well."

Catrin looked sidelong at me when I said that, but I didn't blush. I knew all was very far from well, but I wanted to give Perliu some comfort if it chanced that he could hear me.

Then I saw what was in his hand. My surprise must have showed in my face, for Catrin spoke up. "His hands kept moving ever and again," she said. "As if he was reaching for something. So I give him that, and he quieted."

It was the dead database from the Underhold that Perliu was

holding. It made tears rise into my eyes to see it there. To see him first laid low, and then comforted with a toy.

I took his other hand that was empty, and squeezed it. I thanked him for the trust he showed me, and I didn't reproach him for putting me in the way of danger. Lives had been saved by it. That was the kind of measure a Rampart was supposed to live by.

We were ready now to bring my husband. And as you might guess, I was more than ready to see him. Catrin sent Ban with a message, asking him to come up to the Hold, but said nothing about me being up above the ground. I waited in our old room until he came in, and then I went down to the library, which was where she had bid him come to talk to her and Rampart Arrow.

I could hear Jon's voice from the bottom of the stairs, saying how Ramparts weren't kings and queens, how the Count and Seal had the right to hear what was accused against me and decide on it and how if I'd suffered any harm or insult they'd rue it, blood kin or not.

But when I came into the room, when he turned and saw me, all of that was forgot. He didn't even bother to finish the word that was in his mouth, but run to me and held me and – for a little while – cried full-hearted tears for the joy of having me back again. I had never loved him so much as I did then. I saw how little other things weighed with him when I was put in the scale, and I realised I would be just the same if it was the other way about.

"Your face," he said. "Oh, Spinner, your poor face. Who did that to you?"

It was the bruises he was seeing, still not all the way healed from when Jarter Shepherd kicked me. I had forgot they were even there. I didn't answer Jon's question but grabbed his head in both my hands and put my mouth up to his ear. "We're going to have a baby," I whispered. "Keep that in your mind." I meant for him to control his temper. He was going to hear things that would tax it.

"If you're quite finished," Fer said, "we've got important things to discuss."

We broke apart but kept on holding hands. Jon gave the game away somewhat by looking at me as if I suddenly had got my own sun shining down on me. But I didn't really care now who knew that I was carrying. I only whispered because I wanted it to be private between Jon and me when I told him, not called out to a whole room.

We went and sat. Catrin told Jon what she had already told me – that tech was not synced to Vennastins, nor Vennastins to tech, and that the testing was a trick their family had played on Mythen Rood, for how long it was impossible to say. I did not feel so angry at the lie any more, but rather ashamed, for now I was a part of it. I could not look at Jon. I was afraid to see a reproach in his eyes, or worse, contempt.

He was slow to believe what he was hearing. He kept going back to the time of his test, when the cutter waked in his hand. "I felt it," he said. "It was asleep, and then, when I touched it . . ."

"You'd already touched the cutter," Fer said impatiently. "Catrin put it in your hand before you ever went into the Testing House. That was when it synced with you."

"But then . . ." Jon said. He shook his head, scowling at the floor, and then at his mother. "That means people only fail their testing because you don't do for them what you did for me. You don't give them a chance to get synced with the tech first."

"Obviously," Catrin said.

"Why? What's the point of it?"

Oh, Jon, I thought. This is going to break your heart when you think it all through.

"It's for order and lawfulness," said Catrin, "and for the good of all. If everyone had access to the tech, how long do you think it would be before someone stole it, or killed with it, or took it off to the Peacemaker to earn theirselves a place at his court? We do what's got to be done for Mythen Rood's sake."

"And to live in a stone house," I said, "with servants to cook for you and everyone cheering your name." I had got to say it. I had already surrendered to Catrin in everything that mattered, and would do my best to make Jon give in to her too. It would have hurt my pride not to show some defiance in this one thing. I would not sit by and let her claim she was Dandrake born again.

It was not Catrin that answered me though, but Fer. She stabbed her finger at me, her face as hard as a hatchet. "We eat a little better and live a little better," she said. "And in return we fight. We protect. We give ourselves to the people whenever they need us, and we don't ever stint. My son died fighting for this village. Never forget that. He laid his life down so everyone here—"

Catrin didn't let her finish. "Mardew died trying to steal back for his own self the tech that Koli stole," she said. "He was a fool, and he lost us the cutter. Be quiet now, both of you, and let's speak of what matters."

Fer bristled, glaring at her sister. I saw bitter words rise in her mouth, and I saw her choke them down again unspoke.

Jon was not ready to hold his peace though. "This is wrong," he said. "All you just said, all you're doing, it's wrong and I don't want to be no part of it."

"The rightness and wrongness of what we've done is something we could talk about from now till lock-tide," Catrin said. "But that's not the talk we're having, Jon."

"Then why tell me at all? You kept it from me all this time. I don't see what's changed."

"If you shut your mouth long enough for us to speak a word," Fer snapped, "we'll tell you."

"What's changed is this," Catrin said. "When our hunters finally went out of gates again after the Half-Ax business, they seen choker blossoms in the deep woods. We've got no choice but to burn them out before seed-fall. Otherwise we'll starve."

"Then we'll burn them," Haijon said. "You always burned them before."

"That I did. With the bolt gun and the cutter at my back to guard me while I worked. And Rampart Remember right next of

320

me to tell me where to go. There's thousands of trees, Jon, and millions of blossoms. There's not anyone can find them all and burn them all without the database to help them."

"Well and good," Jon said. And then, a moment later: "Oh."

"Oh," Fer mimicked. "He gets there in the end, like a horse with three legs."

"With Perliu took sick," Jon said, "there's none to use the database." He thought some more on that. "But anyone can use it. You just told me that."

"Anyone can't be *seen* to use it, Jon. If we let it be seen, the truth is out and then there's blood on the walls. They'll all be at our throats and each other's before you can blink. We're not strong enough to bide that right now. Not with everything else we got piled on our shoulders."

Catrin turned to me and give a nod. "But now we got Spinner, and I thank Dandrake she come when she did. She's already proved she can use the database as well as my father ever did. She's synced, and she's ready. So she's got to do it, or else chokers will whelm the whole village. But the law and the will to let her do it isn't there."

Jon looked from his mother to me and back again, sorely puzzled.

"Then what do we do?" he asked.

"We stretch our story to fit her inside it," Fer said.

And by and by Catrin told us all how.

47

The Count and Seal was full to bursting when I come there. I could hear the din of voices from the end of the corridor, like the humming of a beehive. I walked towards it slowly, dragging my steps. Three weeks in the dark in a cold stone box had left me weak. The light dazzled me and the noise made me want to run away.

The noise stopped all at once, though, as soon as I walked into the chamber. The whole village was there, as Catrin had warned me they would be. They had all heard about me being taken in the half-outside with the database tucked in my belt. And now here I was, and here was the database in my hand, and here was Rampart Fire walking beside me, and all they could do at first was stare.

Then the noise rose up again, even louder than before, until it was all I could do not to slap my hands to my ears and scream for it to stop.

Catrin led me down into the middle round, where her sister was already waiting. There were two chairs, for the two of them, but none for me. I had got to stand between them a little way back. But they had not tied my hands and they set no guard on me. It was not clear at all who it was that was standing there. A prisoner? A witness? A Rampart?

Catrin didn't take her seat, but stayed standing and looking around the room, waiting for the uproar to settle down again. I already knew what she was going to say, and I held to my purpose, which was to keep a meek and solemn face and meet nobody's eyes. I had no choice as far as listening went, but I could choose not to watch. I was afraid my face would give me away if it was anywhere that people could see it. I wished that Jon was there, but he was upstairs in the Hold, in his old room, with Gendel and Vergil keeping watch on him. He knew what Catrin was going to say, but nobody – not even me – trusted him to hide his feelings while it was being said.

"You all know what Spinner Tanhide is accused of," Catrin told the room, once she had silence enough to talk. "You know she was found outside the fence with Rampart Remember's name-tech in her hand." A muttering rose, and she waited it out. "All that's true, and can't be gainsaid. But it's only a half of the truth. Less than half. The rest has only just come to light, and I'm here to tell you of it. You can lay the fault of it on me, if fault's to be found. I was slow to join the pieces of it together, and might have saved us all some trouble if I was quicker."

She turned in her place, a full circle taking in the whole Count and Seal, as if she was waiting for someone to break in with a question or a challenge. Nobody did.

"We made a mistake in Spinner's testing," Catrin said. A murmur rose at that, but she waved it still. "It's a mistake that's never been heard of before, which is why we didn't see it. She tested with the firethrower, and the firethrower didn't wake for her. That's no surprise. It doesn't wake for many, as you know. We passed on to the testing of Koli Woodsmith—"

"Dandrake spit on his name," Fer broke in.

"—and of my son, Haijon. Then we celebrated all three of them being full-growed, and named. We drunk and sung and danced, until we run out of night and went on into morning. But there was one among us who didn't do any of them things. That one was my father, Rampart Remember. Perliu loves a mug of ale and a rowdy song as well as the next man, but he was troubled. The database wasn't working properly. It kept on saying the one word, over and over, and he couldn't make head or tail of it."

"What was the word, Rampart?" Jarter Shepherd asked. She was stony-faced and suspicious, as if she was prepared to misbelieve everything Catrin said, but she played her part without even knowing she did it. For how could Catrin answer unless she was asked?

"The word was 'accept'," Catrin said. "You all know that word, and what it means. It's what we say to the tech at our testing when we hold it in our hand and beseech it to take us as a user. And with tech like the database, that can talk back to us, it's the word it uses when it sees a user and knows them."

She paused a moment, letting them all think about that.

"But nobody had tested with the database," someone called out. I didn't see who, and with the murmuring that had broke out again all round the room I didn't recognise the voice.

Catrin nodded, all solemn. "No, they hadn't. Nobody had even touched it. And without that touch, there's no bond that can be made. Or so we thought. But the database made fools out of all of us.

"By and by, it quietened down. Rampart Remember thought no more about it. If the database had gone wrong, then it had put itself right again. There didn't seem no need to look into it further. He meant to talk to me about it, and to raise it here in the Count and Seal, which would of been right to do. But then the sickness come, and all the plans any of us had made went out with the dirty water. He forgot. It's a bad thing for Rampart Remember to do, but he forgot.

"Then three weeks ago, Spinner Tanhide come up to the Hold. She was mostly meaning to fetch some clothes of Haijon's that was left here when they moved into the tannery, but while she was here she went to my father's room to see how he was faring. The room was dark, with the curtains drawed shut, and she couldn't see if he was in there. So she called out. 'Is there anyone?' And a voice come back that wasn't my father's voice. 'Acknowledge,' it said."

There was a great clamour in the room now, with people calling out from all corners. When did this happen? How could it of happened? Why wasn't it told until now?

I dared to lift up my head at this point. The worst of the lies was over, and though I had not denied them, I had said nothing the other way either. I felt my face would not betray me if I only glanced for a moment. I wanted to see how the story was being listened to, whether with anger and disbelief or only with wonder. But there were too many faces, with too many feelings showing on them. I couldn't tell anything from them.

"I know," Catrin was shouting. "I know, I hear you. All these thoughts was going through Spinner's head too, and more besides. She knowed in her heart where that voice was coming from, but she couldn't make herself believe it. She went into the room that was all dark and groped about with her two hands. She thought it might be some human voice after all, someone trying to trick her or make sport of her. But her hands closed on the thing, and she felt what it was. That it was the database that had called out to her, and bid her take it up.

"Then she seen another thing besides. My father was lying on the floor, and there was blood on his head. He had been taken with a fit. He had fallen. He looked for all the world like he had been attacked and left for dead.

"You can imagine what Spinner thought then. With the database speaking up to her like she was a Rampart, and the true Rampart half-dead at her feet. She thought she would be accused. Cried out as a thief and a murderer. A fear come on her like she hadn't ever felt in her life before.

"There are things she can't remember after that. She run and kept on running. Her only thought was to get away from the Hold and the voice and everything. She wasn't in her right mind, you might say. And somehow, in running she kept the database clutched in her hand instead of letting go of it.

"Then the next thing she knowed, she was being hailed by Jarter and Shirew in the half-outside, with no memory of how she got there. They challenged her, as was their right and duty, and they found the database on her. So they brung her here to the Hold, where we set about to question her.

"When she told this story, we didn't believe her at first. And my father being impossible to rouse from his faint, there wasn't no easy way of telling the truth of it. The database answered to her, we seen that our own selves. And that part being true spoke to the truth of the rest of it. But we was mistrustful, thinking maybe Spinner had found some way to cheat the test. If there was any such way, it was beyond us to think what it might be, but still, what she was saying was hard to credit."

Catrin's fierce gaze went round the whole room, taking in this one and that one along the way, daring them to cast a doubt on what she was saying.

"Now harken to me," she said. "Two things happened after that to change our minds. The first was that my father waked for a few short hours and sweared to the truth of what Spinner said. He said he heard the database answer when she called, and bespeak her a user. He was full of wonder, he said, but there was no mistaking the words. It felt like a providence, he said. Like a miracle sent by Dandrake. That another user had come to answer Mythen Rood's need right at the moment when he was like to fail.

"He put the database in Spinner's hands, and then he fell back into the same sick sleep he was in before."

"He put it in her hands?" Jarter Shepherd echoed. "Dam Catrin, you said she took it up."

"Took it from him, I meant to say." The look on her face didn't change even for a moment.

Jarter shook her head, her face flushed red as a beet. "Dam Catrin," she said, "all this that's been said and heard and witnessed to is well enough. But if Rampart Remember is still sick, or sick again, or whatever it may be, then we can't put no questions to him. We only know what we seen, which was Spinner out of gates with the database tucked in her shirt. Whether the database spoke up to her or not, she was running away with it." Heads was nodding around the room. For once, it seemed like Catrin would not have things her own way in this chamber.

"She didn't run away," Fer said. "You found her in the half-outside, not in the woods."

"That's as near as a cunt-hair," Jarter said, her anger coming out in the coarseness of her words.

"Was she running though? Did she flee away from you?"

"No, but she hid the database. It only come out when we searched her."

"And well she might hide it," Catrin said, "when she could be hanged for having it. But the meat of it all is this and only this. The database talked to her and give her what was needful for all of us. It told her how to stop the sickness."

"None of us seen that," Issi Tiller said. "None of us know that."

That was Catrin's best argument, and she had wasted it. If being saved from the plague was not enough to bring the people to my side, they were not like to be swayed now by anything else, for anything else had got to seem like a much lesser thing. They would harden their hearts.

But words are words. For all their strength and power, which is very great, they sometimes show pale when what's needed is brightness and colour.

I stepped out from between Catrin and Fer, off the middle round and into the aisle. I took the database from my belt and held it up for everyone there to see. Then I brought it close to my mouth and spoke to it – but still loud enough for the whole room to hear. It was a good room in that regard. Sound carried well in it.

"Database," I said, "who would have died if the plague hadn't ended when it did? I pray you, give me the names."

I held the little black box up like a beacon in my hand as it give answer.

"Kinnen Soonest. Borrio Cooper. Lune Cooper. Tosil Baker. Jarun Baker. Tam Baker. Durn Paint. Cal Paint. Jemiu Woodsmith. Athen Woodsmith. Mull Woodsmith. Issi Tiller. Chass Tiller. Dana Stepjack. Fran Tailor. Marto Tailor. Jil Reedwright. Cora Reedwright. Asha Reedwright. Evred Bell. Lussan Bell. Mordy Holdfast. Jarter Shepherd."

The list went on. I didn't let it get to the end though. When the database got to Jarter Shepherd I called out, "Hold," leaving that one name ringing in everyone's ear.

Jarter was sitting high up and at the end of a row. That suited me well. I walked up there, and I didn't hurry. There wasn't a sound in the room then. They'd heard the tocsin bell sounded over their own graves and their neighbours' graves, and they were silenced by it.

When I came to where Jarter was, I slowly raised up my hands like I was scooping water out of a bowl, bidding her stand. She would have done better to stay sitting, but the database's speaking the names for me had put a kind of spell on everyone there. She got to her feet without even thinking about it.

If it had been anyone else, I might have thought twice before doing this. But Jarter had beaten and scarred her own son, Veso, for no reason except what she was pleased to call her faith. She had also punched and kicked me when she found me in the lookout. She might have kicked my baby girl out of me before I even knew she was there. So I didn't hesitate.

I threw my arms around Jarter's neck, and kissed her on the cheek. She stiffened in my arms, not liking the kiss at all, but when she tried to pull away I held her tight against me.

"I forgive you," I said. "I forgive you, Jarter Shepherd, with all my heart."

Catrin knew Mythen Rood, and Mythen Rood's people. She saw into their thoughts and into their souls, and she was seldom wrong about what she saw there. She had always purposed to end her list of lies with the one true thing – that I had done away with the sickness – trusting that its shadow would fall behind it to hide the pitfalls and stake-blinds that the rest of the story was made of.

But the truth isn't always enough by its own self. Sometimes you have got to make a story out of it to make people understand it and take it into their hearts. That was why I thought up that list and told it to the database, commanding it to tell the list back to me as soon as I said "Give me the names." You could say it was a lie. I say it was a story about what might have been, and therefore had a truth of its own. But you may judge me how you like on that count.

What happened next was even better than I had hoped for. There was a great commotion in the room that made me turn my head first this way and then that. All round the chamber, people were standing up. First only a few, then more and yet more, until every child and woman and man had found their feet. Some of them were crying. Others wore faces of worship, as if they had just seen Dandrake and all his angels.

"Spinner!" someone shouted. "Spinner Tanhide!"

Then they all was calling out my name. "Spinner! Spinner! Spinner Tanhide!"

"Spinner *Rampart*!" Catrin yelled. They took it from her and shouted it out to the ceiling, that sent it back again like a struck drumhead. "Spinner Rampart! Spinner Rampart! Spinner Rampart!"

When they were done, Catrin climbed the steps to where I stood and put her hand on my shoulder. There was a thoughtfulness in the nod she gave me, and something like approval.

"Wait no more," she said.

48

There were no chokers close by the village fence. Ramparts of times gone had cut them all down long since, and packed the roots with salt to make sure they didn't quicken again. But the seeds could travel many miles on the wind, which meant we must go many miles to find the trees that were in blossom, and scorch whatever showed yellow.

Because it was a long journey, and travel through the woods was slow and dangerous, we had to trust to the database to tell us which way to go. It held in its memory the place of every tree in the forest. Whenever a new one was found, Rampart Remember told the database where it was, and the database added to its list − a list it had been keeping for longer than any one of us had been alive. Now, when we asked it to, it summoned up in its secret thoughts all the times it had gone out before, and planned a course for us that would take in every tree before the first seed fell.

Our way would take us southward first, along the nearer bank of the Calder, starting close to the river where the going was like to be easiest. Then quartering the deep woods, east to west and back again, leaving the treacherous slopes of Breely Mitch until last. From there, a day's walking would bring us home again.

From start to finish, the burning would take ten days. It was not often that anyone stayed outside the fence for so long or went so far afield. There would be six more, besides Rampart Fire and me, and they were all good fighters. Jarter Shepherd was one, which pleased and displeased me all at the same time. I misliked her strongly, and she thought no better of me, but she was the best shot with a bow of anyone in the village, and her being there made us that much stronger. Besides her, there was Lune Cooper that said his promises on the tabernac the same day I was pledged to Haijon, as well as Kinnen Soonest, Isak Morne, Wardo Hammer and Gendel Stepjack that was Fer's husband. Fer did not come, for Catrin judged it a poor idea to take both the firethrower and the bolt gun out of the village at the same time.

We took food for the ten days, but it was mostly biscuit and dry jerky. We'd add to that whatever we could hunt or forage along the way. We also took water from the well. When that ran out, Calder would provide – but even where it ran clearest, Calder's water was thick with the silver that sometimes came down when it rained. You had to boil and strain and boil again to make it safe to drink.

There was no leave-taking or ceremony. We just set out early in the morning, the day after we decided on our route. Jon and I had had only two days together to remind ourselves what life and love were like, and then I was gone again. He had asked to come with us, but there were plenty whose names were higher on the list than his for skill in hunting or fighting or pathfinding. Rampart Fire bid him stay home, and she would not be gainsaid.

"Bring our baby back to me," Jon said as he saw us off at the gates. "And bring yourself. I'll run mad without you."

"Well, at least you'll not run far," I said, for the gates – once they closed behind us – were to stay shut until our return. I hugged him hard and told him I loved him. He gave me back the same words, so old and worn and yet so needful every time they're said.

We headed out, through the half-outside, over the stake-blind and into the world. I felt its hugeness pressing on me from all sides.

Living in Mythen Rood was like living in a mousehole, close and tight, with the warm and the smell of the other mice all round you. Now we were out of the mousehole and running across the granary floor, not knowing what might be gathering to pounce on us.

The firethrower was our comfort. In Catrin's hands it was like the flaming sword of Edenguard, or Stannabanna's staff. She would turn in a circle, raising and dipping the barrel, and the fire would go back and forth between the trees, sewing them together with a thread that was too bright to look at. She knew exactly how long to play the flames across a tree, and how hot to set it so the blossoms would sear but the tree itself not burn. We did not want to have to outrun a forest fire.

The going was hard from the first. We were not keeping to the road, though the road was our marker. Ever and again we had to venture off it into the woods to scorch the blossom off every choker we passed. This left us open to being attacked by everything else that lived there. Not by the trees, thankfully, for the clouds were thick and heavy and the trees were asleep. Nothing else was though. A pack of needles got the scent of us early on and kept coming at us. There was nothing to do but to kill them all, which we did mostly with our bows. Catrin used the firethrower but sparingly, for though it made its own fuel it took some hours to fill again when it was empty, and we did not have the luxury to sit and wait.

Then we came to a place where the road was blocked by a landslide, and when we tried to climb over it we found that knifestrikes were nesting in the freshly turned dirt. We fended them off, but Isak was wounded in the eye, which is ever the target knifestrikes choose when they attack, and Gendel in the arm as he guarded his face. Catrin bound the wounds her own self and we pressed on. In spite of everything, we made it to Ludden that first night as we purposed to, but it was late and we were tired to death. We found a place to lay our bedrolls down, lit a fire, ate a little of the food we'd brought, set an order for the watches of the night and went straight to sleep.

Well, some of us did. Ludden scared me so much, I couldn't rest there. It was a village just like ours that had once been full of people. We had traded with them – food and tools and woven cloth – recently enough that my father had remembered it and talked of it often. Some in Mythen Rood had grandparents that had come from there.

Now, Ludden was deserted and all but whelmed by the forest. This place where we were camped had been their gather-ground, that now was just a field of weeds and young trees. Nobody knew what had happened to its people. They had not died, or at least not here, for there were no bodies to be seen. But it could not have been anything good that made them abandon their homes and go into the woods, all together, leaving their gates open wide.

Ludden was also the place where Mardew Vennastin had died, murdered by Koli Woodsmith after Koli fled Mythen Rood with stolen tech in his hands. I could not imagine how Gendel felt being here. Mardew was his son, and Catrin's sisterson. Ludden must be full of bitter memories for the both of them.

As it fell out, Gendel and me were on watch at the same time. Needing to keep ourselves awake, we talked, which was more than we had ever done when we lived under the same roof. I asked him how he and Fer had come together, and he seemed happy enough to tell me.

"All the boys I knowed that cared for girls at all was in love with one of the Vennastin sisters," he said. "Mostly it was Catrin they favoured. She was ever a beauty, and still is. Fer was the quieter of the two, and if you didn't know her you might think it was because she had nothing to say. I thought that my own self, when I was young."

He poked the fire to get a little more heat out of the embers. "But we hit fifteen together and was in the Waiting House the same time. I got to know her better then, and I seen how she could speak her mind when she choosed to. She just mostly didn't choose to. She never knowed how to temper it, so when she spoke, people always thought she was angry. Angry at them, I mean. So they pulled back from her ever and again."

I had been curious about that – whether Fer was always as sour and savage as she seemed to be now or if that was something that had come on her a little at a time. "Not you though," I said. "You didn't pull back. The two of you was pair-pledged even before your testing day, wasn't you?"

He gave a sad smile and nodded. "Pair-pledged before we ever come out of the Waiting House," he said. "It was a foolishness, I think. How could it not be at that age? All your head is filled with nonsense. Ramparts and Rampart Hold, tech and glory, service and sacrifice. Fer was part of all that, and that was mostly what I seen when I looked at her.

"Then we was tested, and – such a wonder – we both was found to be synced. And to the same piece of tech. Nobody could remember a time when that had happened before."

I had been staring into the fire, but I looked up then to see if I could tell from Gendel's face what he meant by those words. I saw nothing beyond his seriousness. He was not lost in memories. He had gone to them for a reason.

"Fer's testing was before mine," he said, "so she stood before me in the line of holding. When Callan Vennastin died, Fer got the bolt gun and the name that went with it. The last time I touched it was when I tested with it."

"I thought you was meant to train up," I said. "So you'll be ready if . . ." If Fer should fall, I meant to say, but he nodded quick enough that I didn't have to say it.

"I was meant to," he said. "But I didn't. I watched while Callan trained Fer. I suppose I could make shift if I had to. The gun does all the aiming after all. It's not as though you can miss your target."

"That's true," I said. There were a dozen questions that came into my mind about what he had just told me, but I was sure he was coming to a point and I didn't want to get in the way of it.

"The line is important to them," he said, and I knew it was the Vennastins he meant by that *them*. "What happened at my testing come from Fer. It was her wedding gift to me in some sense, though we wasn't married until two Summers later. But there's no breaking the line. They're careful about that. It had got to be a Vennastin who took the name next. If something was to happen to Fer, I think they'd give the bolt gun to me. But not for very long."

So we were done with pretending. I had known most of this already, but still it felt strange to be talking about it so matter of fact, in the same way you'd say that the night was a cold one, or that you needed a piss. I saw for the first time that Gendel and me were much alike in our situation. Pair-pledged and wedded to Vennastins, as close to the hearth fire as anyone could hope to get. But close to the fire is only safe as long as it doesn't catch.

Gendel looked at me long and hard. "You know who was meant to be Rampart Remember after Perliu?"

"No, I don't," I said. But as soon as I thought on it, it was clear as day. "Lari. It must be Lari. She goes Waiting next Summer."

Gendel nodded. "Lari, yes. Haijon got the cutter because he's brave and does what he's told. Lari was to get the database because she's clever and quick to learn. Cat thinks hard about these things. This time though, what with the plague, she was caught a little way off her guard. And she thought Perliu would be hale a while longer. So now here you are. But I don't think you're intended to stay there. Look over your shoulder often, Spinner. And don't be too trusting, either of Cat or of my wife."

"Should I be trusting of you?" I asked him.

He laughed, but without smiling. It was only the sound of a laugh. "I wouldn't," he said, "if I was you. It's good practice not to. And you don't know me. Nobody does. I stand in Fer's shadow, and there's not a soul ever sees me."

There was no bitterness in the words, or not much. He was just saying what we both knew was true. I decided I would trust in that honesty at least. "Was Koli Woodsmith locked in the Underhold?" I asked. "The night he was supposed to of fled over the grass-grail?"

Gendel looked surprised. "Yes," he said. "And for two nights after. How'd you know that?"

"He left a kind of a mark behind to show he was there. So Catrin lied to the Count and Seal about him running away?"

"It's been knowed to happen. Her lying, I mean."

"Why though?" I asked him. "If Koli stole that tech, why did they hide him instead of hanging him or sending him faceless? And where is he now?"

Gendel shrugged. "Koli was a thief, as sure as Hell's a furnace. His thieving wasn't the issue though. It was what he found out along the way. I think you can probably work out the most of it. Ask Cat if you want the rest." He looked up at the fence, and the tree-line beyond. "That's dawn light peeping through there," he said. "We should wake the others and catch a start on the sun in case it's bolder than it was yesterday."

And that was all I got from him. But it was a great deal more than I had looked for.

49

We carried on south, and at the end of each day we were further behind where we had purposed to be. There were so many traps and pitfalls. So many things we had got to fight just so we could keep moving.

Some of those fights, with beasts of the forest and once or twice with trees, were things we had expected. Others, like the road being washed out, a bridge being down, a sinkhole at Candle Hill that was as big as our gather-ground – these we didn't know about but had to deal with anyway or else turn back and wait for seed-fall to come when it would.

By the time we turned north again at Sowby, we were walking on fallen choker blossoms. That meant we had five days at best to finish our work. On the sixth day, for a certainty, the air would be full of woe and ruin.

I spoke with the database and asked it whether there was some better way for us to go. "Well, gosh," it said, "let me have a think about that." It was still talking in the bright, happy voice that it had put on when Perliu and me told it we were children. That voice seemed very wrong in the huge silence of the woods, like someone singing a bawdy song at a funeral. I told it to go back again to the way it talked before.

"There are three possible alternative routes from this point," the database said in its solemn, growed-up voice. "Each could potentially allow a shorter journey time based on previous experience and current mappings and projections."

"Tell me," I said, and it did. Two of the three routes were not worth thinking about because they only saved us an hour or two at best. The third saved most of a day. It involved crossing the river two more times at places where it was narrow and shallow enough to wade across. It might seem like that had got to take more time, not less, but it meant that we would not have to circle around on a long road to get to the deepest of the trees. Once we were on the thither side of Calder, we would be right in among them.

"Why didn't you tell us about this way before?" I asked the database. "It's got to be better."

"Parameters given when setting the original route included the avoidance of random factors that might negatively impact journey time. This route includes such a factor."

"What's there then?"

"Encrypted signals consistent with military-grade technology. Type and specification undetermined."

"Tech?" I repeated, grabbing such meaning as I could find in that gobble-gut. "There's tech there? What's it doing?"

"Nothing. It hasn't moved since I first sensed it."

"When was that?"

"One hundred and forty-eight years, seven months and three days ago."

I told Catrin there might be another road, and she bid me lead the way.

"What about the tech though?" I said.

"That's troubling. But if it's stood still for so long a time, and not been found, it's most likely buried deep under the ground."

She was wrong about that though. When we came to the river, the tech was waiting there for us. I saw at once why nobody had carried it away. It was too big. A team of ten with ropes and oxen could not have shifted it.

It saw us too, and turned to face us as we came. That's what it felt like anyway, though it had no face. It was a kind of a wagon made all of metal, but bigger than any wagon that was ever made. Its bed stood as high as a man's shoulders, and on top of that there was another part that could turn while the bottom part stood still. It had more wheels than you could count, but they were wrapped around with yet more metal so they could not ever have moved.

But none of what I just said can tell you how it felt to look at it and see it looking back. For that was what it did, face or no face. Oh, and I did not mention the great long, pointing finger that stood out of it, ranging on us as we drawed near like Fer Vennastin's bolt gun only ten or twenty times the span of an outstretched arm.

Then – which was worse than anything yet – it spoke in the deep, stern voice of a man used to giving commands. "This location is off-limits," it said. "It has been temporarily secured under the authority of the interim government. Halt where you are and surrender any weapons you may hold. Failure to do so will result in your being fired upon."

All eight of us stood stock-still where we were, gravelled by fear. What words would work to coax mercy out of such a monster? It was not like anything we had ever seen before or had a name for. Kinnen Soonest fell down on his hands and knees, babbling words of prayer and beseeching. Wardo followed him, and then Isak and Lune. That was half of us. Catrin stayed on her feet. So did I and Gendel and Jarter Shepherd.

"You are in defiance of a direct order from an empowered agent of the interim government," the monster said. "State your name and your ID number, including sector suffix. Comply at once, or you will be shot."

I don't know where I found the courage to speak. I think it was because I was used now to talking to the database. This was a piece of tech when all was said and done. It was just exactly like the database or the firethrower. Only, for some reason I could not fathom, it had been set in a casing that was almost as big as a house.

"Don't hurt us," I called out. "Please. We don't come here meaning any harm. We only want to come through to the other side." I ducked my head as I said it, showing that there was nothing to me. Nothing to be afraid of or to care about.

"You are in breach of the mandated curfew," the wagon said, "and of quarantine order twenty-one thirty-five. You must give yourself up to the nearest uniformed officer."

Just as I was used to doing with the database, I grabbed hold of a word I recognised and tried to work outwards from it. "The quarant time is over now," I said. "We cured the sickness by sending away the dogs. There isn't no more need for the sick to be shut away – and we're none of us sick in any case."

The tech turned its pointing finger one way and then another. When it stopped again, it was pointing squarely at me. "Kneel down on the ground and place your hands behind your back or on your head. Wait there until I bring further units to secure you. If you do not comply, you will be fired upon."

There was very little of that I could fathom, but I heard the threat in the word fire. I groped for more words to say, but my tongue was tied except to babble "Please! Please!" ever and again.

"You will be fired upon," the tech said. It sounded sad.

"So will you," Catrin said. She had the firethrower raised up in her hands, and she had taken aim. A stillness fell as the rest of us waited, awed and terrified, to see which of them would blink first – the great machine or our Rampart Fire.

It wasn't either of them though. The shot that felled Catrin came from behind us with a great roar of sound like you hear in the breaking sky after a lightning flash. What hit her was not an arrow or a quarrel, but something too small to be seen. I saw the fleck and spray of blood where it came out of her chest, and I saw how her whole body was buffeted by the touch of it, thrown forward and almost off her feet as though a giant fist had punched her right between her shoulders.

The second shot came from a different angle, and took away half of Kinnen Soonest's head.

Then the dust of the road and the mud of the river bed rose up in plumes and fountains as a great many more of the invisible darts came down in the midst of us. Some of them rung against the tech's metal plates, booming like the drumbeats in a Dandrake hymn. Some of us ducked into the long grass, or scrambled down the slope towards the river, but the darts seemed to be coming from everywhere.

"We got you circled," a voice shouted. "We're coming down now. You're under Half-Ax's rule, and your tech is forfeit. Your lives too if we find you with a weapon in your hands."

Koli

50

The choker blossoms died and drifted to the ground. We trod the yellow flecks under our feet, and for a day or so the forest floor was like the streets of lost London, all paved with gold. We could not take no joy in it though. Seed-fall would follow soon.

The sea-bear didn't show itself, but still the Headman kept up a guard every night and lit the torches out on the beach and strewed the sand with vinegar.

As soon as the blossoms started to fall, the Many Fishes people that was working with us in the forest laid down their axes and saws and went back down into the village. They gun to prepare, bringing all their stores and all the things that was needful to live down to the Bowl. Made the Tide Turn come down to the Bowl too, and he sent Dog Runner to tell us we had got to meet him there.

With a solemn face and a solemn voice, he told us we was going to be showed one of the people's biggest secrets. He took us into a house that looked the same as any other, only it wasn't. Nobody lived there, and it looked like nobody ever had. The floor of the room was of wood planks. Only it wasn't really being a floor right then. It was lifted up to either side like a barn door, and there was steps going down into the ground.

"Come," the Headman said. He went down the steps, and we followed him into a kind of a cave. It was not so big as Senlas's cave by a long way, but it was only the first of many. There was one after another, like the rooms in a house, and they went a long way down. Lanterns standing on shelves in the walls give what light there was, though it was meagre. There was spaces there where people could sleep side by side, maybe a dozen people in each, all sharing their warmth and nearness. There was bigger rooms where they could meet and talk. Chimneys carried the air from up above so they could breathe, and took the heat away from the firepits where they would cook.

"But the seeds will come in through the chimneys," I said when we was done marvelling at all this.

"No," Made the Tide Turn says, "they will not. There's sacking in the air chimneys that our weavers learned to make long since. The weft is narrow enough to stop any seeds that come. As for the fire chimneys, they're lipped and elbowed ever and again. The seeds collect in the elbows, and they burn up when the fires is lit. Nothing comes through."

"The choker Spring will last most of a month," Ursala said. "Will you stay underground for the whole of that time?"

"We could stay for a year if it was needful," said Made the Tide Turn.

"You can't possibly store water for a year."

"We've got a spring, Healer. We built the channel ourselves, guiding it down from above at the back of the cave where it touches living rock. And there are gratings in the water to sieve away any seeds that might come in with it. We gave thought to this. And we've weathered many choker Springs here. You and your friends are welcome to join us. But only until we close the doors. We can't let you in later if you stay outside at first."

"Of course," Ursala said. "We understand."

Cup looked at her. The look said this would be a good time for Ursala to say that we wanted to be in the caves when seed-fall come. Ursala didn't say it. She was still hoping that we would be away by then. But that hope was a bucket with no bottom to it. It was Cup and me that had been working out in the forest every day, and we knowed the way would not be cleared in time. I would of said there was fourteen days' work left, and that was if none of the stumps that was still in the ground dug in their heels and pulled back against us.

"She's not going to stop," Cup said to me later when we was sitting in our kitchen eating a supper of salt fish and stone bread. "She'll make us dig out stumps until the seeds is coming down. And then she'll tell us to wear a hat or something."

"You can go into the caves if you want to though," I told her. "Ursala can make up her own mind. She can't make up yours." I felt a kind of a sorrow as I said it, at the thought of us going different ways, but Cup had got no reason I could see to put herself in danger. I was doing it for the sake of Mythen Rood, for the people I left there and wouldn't never see again. After what her own people done to her, Cup didn't owe that duty to nobody.

Cup give me a look as if I had said she should play skip-rope with a choker branch. "I won't leave her," she told me. "You know what she done for me. The medicine she give me."

"Course I know."

"Well then. I'm not like to pay her back with a knife in the ribs."

"I see that," I said. "But then there's you and Taller Than Trees. I know how you feel about him."

"Do you? How?"

"Well, I mean—"

"I know what you mean. Trees is just a boy I like. I like him a lot, and he likes me. But he's not my pair-pledge. We're not building a tabernac."

I tried again. "I just thought . . . You said you liked it here. And you was only with us in the first place because—"

Cup shaked her head like the things I was saying made her sad and puzzled but she didn't have no time for them. "The first place?

347

The first place is where we start, Koli Faceless, not where we finish." A change come into her face. A seriousness like I never seen before, though she was ever a serious person. "You're puzzled why I'm here? Why I'm staying with you? Do you know Dandrake's gospel?"

"Some of it. What I know, I don't care for."

"He said there was going to be one more after him. One more messenger from Heaven."

"Yeah, I know that part. Didn't your Senlas say he was that one?"

"He did say that. And I believed him. But then he got himself burned up in the fire you made, and I seen he was just a man. Not even a good man, but just a man. He was a false prophet, and that's the worst thing you can be."

Cup gathered up all the bowls from the table and carried them over to the tub. I don't think she done it because it needed to be done, but because it was easier to think if she kept her hands busy.

"I'm right with you on that," I said. "There wasn't nothing true in Senlas. But why are you saying this now?"

"Because if it wasn't him, then it's got to be someone else." Them bowls clattered down into the tub, and the spoons we et with followed after. Cup upended the ewer over them and some of the water spilled onto the floor. "Dandrake told the faithful what to look for when the next messenger come. It won't be hard to tell, he said, for the righteous shine out like a beacon fire while the sinful is mired in their own shit. You got to look for these three signs, he said."

She turned round to face me. "Three of them," she said. "Three signs." She lifted up her left hand and touched the tips of her fingers one at a time, with the pointing finger of her right. "The messenger will speak truths nobody else knows or can say. That's one. The messenger will save them that are worthy of being saved. That's two. And the messenger will smite the false prophets and lay them so low they won't never stand again. That's three. You see it?"

I did not see nothing, but I didn't want to say so in case it vexed her. "I guess Senlas didn't do any one of them three," I said.

"No," Cup said. Her hands was curled up into fists. "Senlas didn't. So who did? You want to give her a name?"

"Oh," I said. "Wait though."

"Ursala got more truths in her than a wagon full of angels. She saved you, and me. And she turned Senlas out of that rank bed that was his throne. So that's all three signs. And you told me your own self the reason she wants to go to that signal is to get the tools she needs to heal people better than she already does. To heal all and not just some. If she isn't god's last messenger, then nobody is."

I thought if I had got to choose I would put my bet on nobody, but I didn't say so. What I said was "But Ursala don't believe in none of that. She's . . ." I didn't know the word for it – for someone who thinks all gods is just dolls and poppets that people make to cuddle up to when there's nothing better. I only knowed Ursala was one and that I was one too. "She's not one to kneel down and pray to anything."

"She don't need to believe in it," Cup said. "And she don't need to kneel down. I know what I know."

I didn't like the taste of this one bit. It seemed to me that turning anyone into a messianic was a sad mistake. I also thought Ursala would not like it much if she knowed that was how Cup seen her.

"Leaving the dead god and Dandrake off to one side though," I said, "are you happy with what we're doing? With working on the boat until the last minute, and hoping we can sail out before seed-fall? If Ursala is the last messenger like you say, does that mean she's got to be right in everything?"

Cup rolled her eyes like I was stupid. Which I guess I was when it come to god and his messengers and such. "Course not. It just means Dandrake is inside her and working through her. It's like if you pick up a spear to kill your enemies. It's you that's doing the smiting, but you wouldn't expect the spear to know that."

I had got to admit this was true.

"So it's like that," Cup said. "Ursala is a spear in Dandrake's hands. She won't lead us wrong."

I didn't argue it no more.

51

With the time getting so tight, Ursala joined us in the forest every
day now. The Headman had said he wouldn't send us no more
people, but Three White Stones and Heavy Foot was still working
with us every day. They owed Ursala a debt, they said, and though
it was too big to pay they meant to do as much as they could.
Taller Than Trees come along with them and worked harder than
anyone. I knowed why too. He didn't have that much time left
with Cup, and he meant to be alongside of her up to the last
moment – even if that meant helping with the thing that would
take her away.

But with the blossoms fading and starting to fall, and only a
few days in hand before the seeds come, we knowed we was not
going to finish in time. It was a bitter thing for Ursala. She had
set her mind on winning this race, and it was hard for her to say
she was wrong.

"The signal isn't going anywhere," I said to her. I did not mean
our boat but the signal we had been following all this time. "If we
got to go underground for a month or so, it will still be there
when we come out."

She set down her axe, and rubbed her shoulder that was sore

from being used in ways it wasn't used to. "We can't possibly know that," she said.

"Yeah, we can. You said the voice in the message is from the before-times. If it's been sounding out for all them hundreds of years, why should it stop now?"

Ursala was more cast down than I ever seen her, and she didn't reck that argument at all. "We did our best, Koli," she said, "but our best wasn't good enough. We can't pin our hopes on being able to try again. There's nothing certain about it. The choker trees might crush *The Signal* to splinters for all we know, leaving us worse off than when we started. Perhaps I should stay here after all, and work with this one community. It's better to do some small good than to keep on chasing a fantasy."

I didn't know how many of these things she really meant, but it dismayed and gravelled me to hear her say them. The small good she was talking about didn't seem much use at all if humankind was going to die anyway, and if we was throwing away the onliest chance to keep them yet living.

"She's just blowing off steam," Monono said, meaning like a hot pan that's got the lid jammed on. But Ursala wasn't like that at all. She did not seem to be coming to a boil, but dying down from one.

She went to the Headman in his house and told him we would be going into the caves after all. Cup went along with her and told me what passed between them. "He said we would be welcome to stay, and he meant it too. But that Singer was sitting right next to him, and the look on her face would have turned milk to piss. She'd rather we was gone."

"She can go kiss a mole snake," I said. "She don't got no say in this."

But that was not true.

The next morning, Taller Than Trees didn't come to work with us in the forest. Cup went looking for him but didn't find him and had got to give it up at last. When she come and picked up her axe, I could see she was troubled in her heart for his being gone.

In the tail of the afternoon, with the sun hanging in the tops of the trees, four of the Many Fishes people come to find us. They was not people I knowed very well, except I seen them running alongside the Headman both when we was fishing for mudpikes and when we was hunting the sea-bear. Three of them was men, and one was a woman. Their faces said they was not come to help with the digging and felling.

Ursala stepped out to meet them. "Can we help you?" she asked.

One of the men pointed at Cup. "We come to take her," he said. "The Singer needs to speak with her."

Cup and me glanced each to other. I seen my own blank look on her face.

Ursala frowned. "And she's got to go under guard? Why's that?" The man give her a shrug by way of answer, and Ursala frowned a little deeper. "Well, send our respects to the Singer. We'll be along presently."

"The Headman bid us bring her."

"Then you're welcome to wait."

The man tried to step past Ursala. Ursala put herself right in his way. The drudge had been biding still, but now it waked and rose up off its haunches, its gun turning very quick with a kind of a ratchet sound to point at the man's chest. The man stopped where he was. His eyes went as big as when your finger comes round to meet your thumb.

"You're welcome to wait," Ursala said again. She looked into the man's eyes until he looked away. But of a sudden Cup was stepping up next to Ursala.

"I'll go with them," she said. "I'm not scared of Rain Without Clouds. And if it's trouble, it's best to know now."

"I'll go with you," I said, coming quick to stand beside her.

"We'll all of us go," Ursala said. And by all of us, she meant the drudge too. She give a whistle and it lumbered up to join us. The four Many Fishes people was not so happy with this, but the drudge was not a thing you could argue with. So we all went to the village together, with nobody saying a word.

When we come to Many Fishes, we had got to leave the drudge behind us in the Bowl. Ursala didn't seem to mind though. I guess she figured she had made her point. There was lots of people there out on the walkways or standing in the doors of their houses. It looked to me like they knowed something was about to happen, but it wasn't easy to tell what they thought of it. Mostly they looked curious, though some was afraid and others sad. Some of the women touched Cup on the hand or arm as she went by and said something in a low voice I couldn't hear. It was mostly the sad ones that done that.

We climbed up to the Headman's house, his people did their best to take Cup out from among us so they could bring her inside their own selves. She shook them off and walked in alone. Then all of us, which is the guards and Ursala and me, come along behind, somewhat pushing and jostling each against other. It would of been funny except that none of this was funny. It was all troubling.

Rain Without Clouds and Made the Tide Turn was sitting side by side in the tent. More men and women was there too, and there wasn't one of them that wasn't wearing a face as hard as a hatchet. Well, there was one. There was Taller Than Trees. He was kneeling in a corner with men on either side of him. There was bruises on his face and some blood, and his eyes was puffed up with crying. Cup sweared an oath when she seen him, and tried to go to him. The men would not let her come close but barred her way with their spears.

"I'm sorry for this," Made the Tide Turn said. "Healer, the girl Knife Tongue is accused. It's a serious thing that's spoken against her and it's got to be sifted."

"Spoken against her by who?" Ursala asked. She was already looking at the Singer, and it was the Singer who answered her.

"By me." Rain Without Clouds touched her chest and then her forehead, like she was giving a blessing. "And by the wiser, older ones who speak from inside me."

"Well, let's leave them out of it," Ursala said. "If you've got something to say, say it yourself. We don't need any of your comic turns."

Nobody said anything to that, but there was lots of the Many Fishes people that let out a breath or took one in all at the same time. It was like a wind went through the room. Made the Tide Turn lifted up his hand like he was pushing something aside. "Tell them, Rain," he said. "Let's give the girl a chance to answer what's been said."

"Yes," Ursala agreed. "Let's do that."

But the Singer bided her time a little longer. I think she liked that everyone in the room was looking at her and hanging their hearts on what she was about to say. I believe she would of drawed it out even longer except that the Headman give her a stern look and tilted his head, urging her to begin.

"I've had my suspicions for a long while," Rain Without Clouds said. "From things that were said, and not said. And from what the spirits were whispering to me. Look at the marks on the girl's face, they said. And on her arms, that she tries to hide. Two different kinds of mark, the first with ink and the second with a blade. Except that the blade marks were first. Made by her mother and her father and by the Healer of her village to let the evil out of her and drive in the good. You know this is truth, Knife Tongue. Will you speak it, or will I?"

She had said all this in Franker. I made it over into Inglish for Cup.

"Oh, tell her she can go right on," Cup said, stony-faced. "She's doing such a good job."

I passed that along, but I had got to put my own finger on the scales. "Cup's family cut the Dandrake marks into her because she was crossed," I said. "Not for no crime she did or for—"

Cup couldn't make out what I was saying but she cut me off anyway. "Give her space to run, Koli. I don't mind any of this." So I fell silent, although I didn't want to, and went back to just telling Cup what was being spoke.

"I smelled something bad on her," Rain Without Clouds said.

355

"Long since. But the spirits told me to bide it since she was leaving us. But then this one," nodding her head at Ursala, "changed her mind, and begged for shelter in the caves with us."

"I offered shelter before that," Made the Tide Turn said.

"Out of goodness and mercy," said the Singer. "Yes, Tide, you did. But it falls to me more than any to keep evil at an arm's length. So when they decided they would stay after all, I put this boy to the question."

She pointed her finger at Taller Than Trees. He had his head hung down so none of us could see his face.

"If you did them hurts to him," Cup said, "you're gonna be sorry for it." She said it in Inglish, and then I think she said the same thing in the Many Fishes language. Up to then, we had all of us been talking in Franker, and that was how we went on.

"You can't make threats here," said Made the Tide Turn. "Only listen, and then give answer."

"Where is any of this going?" Ursala demanded, her voice all flat and cold.

"Knife Tongue and the boy shared secrets," the singer said. "She told him she was cast out of her own village — for what evil I know not."

"For being who she is," said Ursala.

"And then she came among shunned men and became one of them. Hunted for them. Killed for them. Ate the unholy meat with them. She was a wolf to her own kind, and would be so still except that the whole pack of them were rousted out of their nest by fire and Heaven's hate. If I lie, child, give me good answer."

Tears come up into Cup's eyes when I told this back to her, but the rest of her face was as still as a piece of wood. "Tell them I got no answer," she said.

"She says she got no answer," I said in Franker.

Another wind that wasn't no wind at all went through the tent. People was shaking their heads. One or two of them muttered prayers.

356

"I do though," Ursala said. Made the Tide Turn nodded for her to speak. "She was thirteen years old when she left her village – of her own will, not faceless. She was still thirteen when that mad cult adopted her. What was she supposed to do? Survive in the woods of Calder by herself? Or find a new village and beg to be taken in, with those scars all over her? She did what she had to. And she got away from it when she could. In between, yes, she did some bad things. A bad man wormed his way into her head, as he did with a lot of other people who were older and wiser and had less excuse. If you want to punish her for that, then you're an idiot. She punishes herself every day. Whenever she remembers that time and the things she did."

She stopped for breath, and I think to push her anger back down, but it would not be stayed. "It's the nature of evil to hide itself," she said, and she was looking at Rain Without Clouds when she said it. "But Cup was honest with this boy. She didn't want him to love her without knowing everything there was to know. If you were to punish her – which, let's be clear, will not be happening – you wouldn't be punishing her for being a shunned man. You'd be punishing her for not lying about it. But it's moot in any case. Because she's with me and you don't have any authority over her. If you want to touch her, the road runs through me. My advice would be not to try."

She put her arm around Cup's shoulder and gathered her to her side. That put an end to Cup's being stony-faced and brave. She gun to cry and buried her head in Ursala's chest.

Rain Without Clouds spread out her arms in a big show of innocence. "Touch her?" she said. "Why? To what purpose? That's not our way, Healer With a Horse. We don't correct our people with beatings in Many Fishes."

Ursala looked over her shoulder at Taller Than Trees. Cup's crying had started him doing it too. He had his face in his hands, and his body was shaking. "You seem to have done a good job with the boy," Ursala said.

"That was only a questioning. To get to the truth, and to take the burden of a secret off his shoulders. I'm a healer, like you, and I healed his spirit. I didn't beat him. If I beat him, there would be lines on his back from the whip. Go look. You won't find any such."

Ursala give the Singer a glare that would of stripped bark off a tree. "We'll agree to differ, then, on the definition of torture," she said. She turned her gaze on Made the Tide Turn. "Headman," she said, "we're talking old times and old tales, not present matters. And present matters are pressing for us. Can we go now?"

The Headman shaked his head. "It bears on the present, Healer," he said, "and on the future too. You've seen the people singing and praying down in the Bowl."

"Yes. What of it?"

"They're cleaning themselves. When we all go into the cave to share one small space for so many days, we must be clean. If one is dirty, dirt will spread to others and all will be sick."

"And by dirt you mean what? Sin?"

"Dirt is dirt. Of the body or of the mind. You, Healer With a Horse, and the boy Koli that's yet to take a proper name, you're welcome among us. The girl cannot come unless she cleans herself first."

Rain Without Clouds come in before Ursala could answer. "But songs and prayers alone won't do in such a case," she said. "It's a great sin and won't be so easily wiped off."

I had been making the words over into Inglish all this time for Cup to hear them. "What then?" she said now. "What do they want me to do?"

Made the Tide Turn answered as if he knowed what she said. "A boat will take her out into the middle of the lagoon. She must dive in and go down to the bottom. That's done by holding a heavy stone. At the bottom she'll sing the *eni enaiu* inside her head. Rain Without Clouds will teach her the words. Then she'll let go of the stone and come up again. If the lagoon lets her rise, that means she's clean."

"That's insane," said Ursala.

"All of our children have done it."

"All of your children can swim. Cup has never learned."

"Then she had best get to her learning," said Rain Without Clouds. "She has one day yet before we go into the caves and shut the door behind us."

52

As soon as we was out of the Headman's house, Ursala started to talk.

"We'll fix this," she said. "I'll rig up some kind of an oxygen mask for you so you can breathe under the water. That withered old monster isn't going to get away with using you to—"

Cup wasn't listening. She took off at a lick without looking at either one of us. She run down all the ramps, across the Bowl and out onto the sand, where she was soon out of sight.

Ursala turned to me, wildered at this behaviour. "What's the matter with her?" she said. "We haven't got time for sulks and tantrums. We need a plan. We've got to sort this."

"I don't think you can sort it with an oxygen mask, baa-baa-san," Monono said.

"Then we'll fix it some other way," Ursala said. "Koli, go after her. Tell her to come back to the house. We'll talk there." She stopped and turned around. There was a lot of noise from inside the Headman's tent – voices all shouting, each to other. The Headman's voice was the loudest, and the last. "Let him go!"

Taller Than Trees come running out of the tent. He went the other way along the ramp, but when he seen us he stopped and

360

come back. "Where is she?" he asked us, somewhat wild. "Where's Knife Tongue? I got to talk to her! I got to tell her I'm sorry!"

"This way," I said, and we run on down the ramp together, with me leading the way and Taller Than Trees following.

I knowed which way Cup had gone, and I thought the beach was narrow enough that I couldn't lose her, but she was not anywhere to be seen. We went on for a mile or so and didn't find her. There was a blustering wind, and the sea was coming down on the shore like it meant to break all the land in pieces.

Then Taller Than Trees touched my arm and pointed.

There was someone standing up on the cliffs. Whoever it was, they was up on top of the rock called Old Man Watching, with the sea right under them. It had got to be Cup. Nobody else was like to go out alone with the sea-bear still close and the choker seeds about to fall.

We both shouted out to her and waved our arms. I wasn't sure she heard us, but then she waved and I knowed she did.

"What's she doing?" Taller Than Trees asked. "And how'd she get up there so fast? That's—"

His words ended in a yell. Cup run right to the edge of Old Man Watching, and jumped.

I guess the distance from the top of that rock to the bottom was about as high as a dozen or fifteen men standing each on other's shoulders. Cup fell like a stone and disappeared into the water. I didn't see her come up again.

Taller Than Trees was still shouting ragged bits of words. I heard Cup's name in there, but I couldn't make out nothing else. He run into the waves that was bigger than he was and dived. I run too, without even thinking. I was up to my waist when Monono halted me with a blast of noise from her alarm, making me scream and stop where I was with my hands slapped to my ears.

"Don't be crazy, Koli-bou!" she said after the alarm stopped. "You can't help her. You'll just kill yourself."

I seen she was right and waded back up onto the sand. I couldn't do nothing after that but stand there and wait, which is what I done. Minute after minute, looking far out and then near to, for I had no idea where in all that wildness and wet the two of them might be.

At last, I seen something moving, not too far out. It was only one something though.

"Which one is it?" I said. "Monono, can you see?"

"All I can see is the inside of the sling, dopey boy."

I took her out and held her up with her camera facing out to sea so she could see who was coming.

"Who is it?" I asked again. But by then the one that was swimming back to shore was close enough so I could see his bald head. It was Taller Than Trees, not Cup.

"I'm so sorry, Koli," Monono whispered.

"Why . . . why would she . . .?" I tried to say, but could not get the words out properly. Taller Than Trees fell down on the sand, crying and cursing. I tried to rouse him up, though I was crying my own self. I don't think he even heard me.

"Koli-bou," Monono said. "Go back to the village. Tell the Headman to send a boat out."

"He won't do it!"

"Ursala will bring him into line."

It was good sense. I left Taller Than Trees where he was, though I didn't like to do it, and run back along the sand towards the village.

Around about halfway there, I seen someone sitting up in the long grass at the top of one of the dunes, drenched to the skin and shivering in the cold.

It was Cup.

"Hey, Koli," she said. "Where are you off to in such a hurry?"

I stared at her like she was the dead god risen up again. Then I run to her and hugged her. She was not one that was at all times happy to be touched, but she hugged me back, and we both cried a while.

"I thought you was dead," I said when I could say anything at all.

"Well, now you see I'm not."

I pushed her away so I could look into her face. "Why'd you do that? Why'd you do such a stupid thing?"

"So you'd know," she said. "And so they'd know. Koli, Trees teached me to swim months back. I wasn't never in no danger from the water, even with the sea as rough as it is today."

"But . . . then . . ." I said. "That's good. That's wonderful. You can take the test."

Cup shaked her head. "No. I can't. I could jump in their stupid lagoon if I wanted to, and come to the bottom, and back to the top. But I'd rather cut my own hand off than do it."

I couldn't make no sense of them words. Here was an answer to our problem, which turned out to be no problem at all. Except that Cup was saying it was the wrong answer. "How's that?" I said.

Cup's voice got an edge to it, and a sharp point besides. "I been told my whole life how I'm different. How I'm wrong. How I'm dirty. I left Half-Ax because I was sick of hearing it. I know Senlas was madder than a starved rat, but at least when I was with him I didn't have nobody spitting on the ground when I went by or making Dandrake signs with their fingers. Anyway, I got out of the way of it. Of thinking I had got to be ashamed of what I was. And now here's someone telling me to be ashamed all over again."

She stood up and brushed the sand off her. "I won't do it," she said. "To the dead god's Hell with all of them. I won't."

"But then," I said, "they won't let you into the caves."

"I know it."

"And in a day or so, there'll be a million choker seeds all over everything. You'll die, Cup."

"Then I'll die in my own skin, with my own truth. Not pretending to be someone else. I hope you find the Sword of Albion. And I hope you stay with Ursala. She needs someone to be with her, though she wouldn't never say it."

I couldn't think of nothing to answer to that. "We can't though," I said. "We can't go into the caves and leave you outside. There's got to be another way around this."

"Tell the baa–baa-san," Monono said. "I hate to say it, but you're going to need her brains. And maybe her firepower."

"You tell her," Cup said. "I've got to go and find Trees. I don't want him to go drown himself looking for me."

"You're not angry at him for giving your secrets away?" I asked.

She shaked her head, all impatient. "Don't be stupid, Koli. The Singer hurt him until he told. It's not his fault; it's hers. I really wish I could kill her before I go. Only that will most likely make it harder for you and Ursala, so I better not."

"Promise me you won't go anywhere until we've all talked about it," I said. And in the end she give her word on the dead god's blood, though I had got to ask her lots of times before she done it.

Monono and me went back to Many Fishes. We found Ursala in the Bowl, walking backwards and forwards while she waited for us to come. We told her how things stood. How Cup would rather die than jump in the water and be made clean, and so could not go into the caves when seed-fall come.

Ursala sweared an oath that made the old man she was healing flinch. "Well," she said, "then we're knee-deep in needle shit. Because I'm not going in without her."

I was glad to hear her say it. "I already decided the same thing," I said.

"Count me in," said Monono. "What say you close the shop down here, baa-baa-san, and we go put our heads together?"

Ursala made a sour face like she did not relish that idea. "To do what?"

"To cook up a miracle. Because that's what we're going to need."

53

I made some stew out of fish heads and potatoes, which we et sitting around the table. Then we put our bowls aside and gun to talk about what might be done. We was five, instead of four. Taller Than Trees had come back to the village along with Cup, and it looked like the two of them didn't want to be apart just yet.

Ursala asked Cup if she was sure she couldn't just take the test, pass it and go down into the caves. Cup said yes, she was sure.

"And I suppose lying about it is out of the question?"

"That's even worse," Cup said.

"It is," Taller Than Trees agreed when I said it over for him in Franker. "There's ghost sickness that comes from lying. And the Healer would see through the lie in any case."

Cup squeezed his hand. "Ghost sickness is bullshit," she said. "But I love you. And I hate that she hurt you."

Taller Than Trees didn't say nothing. He was ashamed that he told against her, and would not forgive himself no matter how many times Cup told him he had got to. He had come back to the house with us to be with her, and to help us in all ways he could think of.

"Okay, let's consider the options," Ursala suggested. "How are we going to do this and not die of it?"

"Can we make a cave for ourselves?" I asked. "I mean, not a cave, but a place that's safe. Somewhere we can shut ourselves off from the seeds and wait until it's okay to come out."

"Two problems, dopey boy," Monono said. "What do you drink, and where do you poop? The Many Fishes people have got their own river. You haven't. And I think it's too late to start looking for one. So how else do you survive a choker Spring?"

"In Mythen Rood, we used to burn out the blossoms before the seeds come."

"With a humungous flamethrower," Monono said, "which in our case we have not got."

I nodded. I knowed that was true. And it was too late anyway. Rampart Fire went out as soon as the blossoms showed. She had to burn the flowers off thousands of trees. It took many days to tread all them miles of forest. And she took fighters with spears and bows to guard her because there was all the other dangers of the deep woods to be faced too. Even if we had got a firethrower of our own, we couldn't get the job even halfway done in the time that was left to us.

"Tell me again what choker seeds do when they touch you," Monono suggested. "Let's start there."

"They take root," said Ursala. "And the roots grow with incredible speed. Actually, they've already started to grow before that first skin contact. They start out as threads, only a few microns thick, so they can reach a length of about two or three metres inside the seed case, folded over on themselves thousands of times. On contact with a suitable growth medium, which basically means living tissue, they inject themselves through the initial contact point and unfurl and expand inside the host body. Very quick, very efficient and irreversible in the space of a few seconds."

"So what's the trigger?"

"You mean, how do they know they've found a host? I'm not

sure. Body heat, I assume." Ursala's face changed. She wagged her finger at me – or most likely at the DreamSleeve that was on the table in front of me. "All right. Yes. That's possible."

"What's possible?" Cup asked. "You got to talk so we can understand."

"If the seeds respond to heat, we can insulate ourselves. Wear thick clothing, or better yet, some kind of a gel or cream, that will disguise our body's warmth and stop the seeds from activating when they touch us."

"Like the sea-bear," I said. I was thinking of the pictures the drudge showed us where everything was lit up red and orange and green, and the sea-bear couldn't hardly be seen.

"Yes, exactly like the sea-bear. Only the sea-bear probably does it by having three inches of blubber under its skin. We'll have to find a material or a chemical that does the same thing." ·

"What about the rats?" Cup said. "How do they do it? They don't have blubber or nothing. They're skin and bone."

Ursala stared at her and kept on staring. She looked so stern, I thought she was angry at being interrupted.

Cup must of thought so too. She looked to me and Trees like we had got to know what she meant. She tapped one finger against her clenched fist. "When a choker seed hits a rat, it bounces off. I'm not lying. Everyone knows it."

"It's true," I said. I think I told you somewhere else in this story that rats was not troubled by choker seeds, nor yet by waked choker trees. If a choker seed landed on a rat, it wouldn't take root but would just fall right off again, like Cup said. There was many in Mythen Rood that seen it happen with their own eyes.

"I know it's true," Ursala said. "I just hadn't considered it because it seemed to be out of the question. But maybe it's not." She looked down at the DreamSleeve. "Dead girl, you've got a chemical database. Organic compounds specifically. How far does it go?"

"All the way, baa-baa-san," Monono said. "Seven hundred and

eighty-three naturally occurring hormones. Two thousand forty-some lab-cooked variants. What do you need?"

"Probably something in that second list. I remember reading about this back in Duglas. The rats secrete a glycoprotein that's very similar in structure to human antithrombin. It acts as an inhibitor for the choker seeds' activation trigger. The roots touch the rats' skin, and they just switch off. We know the drudge can synthesise hormones because we've been doing it for Cup. If you can get me a template for this inhibitor molecule, we might be able to cook ourselves up a batch to order."

Monono was quiet for the space of ten or twelve breaths.

"Okay," Ursala said. "It was just a thought. We can still—"

"Type 4 ß-naphthaleneacetic acid," Monono said. "It took me a moment to review the literature. It's a synthetic auxin with an extra carboxymethyl bond to give it some kick, so it only looks like antithrombin if you squint one eye. I've got the recipe right here." There was a silence so short it almost wasn't there at all. "Baa-baa-san, I'll need to interface with the drudge. There's no way around it. The diagnostic's standard configuration won't work for a compound that only exists in a schematic diagram. I'll be making the templates to assemble the molecules to cook up the medicine."

I looked to Ursala, and I seen her fight with herself. We all waited for her to answer.

"Do what you have to do," she said at last.

"I can promise to shut the door on my way out. Erase the access codes. But I don't suppose you'd believe me if I—"

"I said do what you have to do."

"Okay then."

"Is there anything we can do to help?" I asked.

"You can keep working on *The Signal*," Ursala said. "Even if this works, we're going to want to be out of here as quick as we can. The longer we're exposed, the greater the risk."

"I'll help," Taller Than Trees said.

"You don't have to," Cup told him. "You got to go wash and

pray and get yourself ready to go down into the caves. We'll take it from here, Trees. You done enough."

"But then I won't see you again."

Cup stood up and leaned over to hug him. "Yeah, you will," she said. "I'm not going far, and I'm coming back after.

"You're going outside the lagoon. Into the true deep. Anything could happen to you out there."

Cup give him a kiss on the cheek, and then another one on the lips that was somewhat longer. "Then I'll have lots to tell you about when I get back."

He went away at last, doing his best not to let us see how cast down he was. In a strange way, it made me happy to see it. If we got to where we was going, and found the Sword of Albion, and fixed the dagnostic, and in time's turning come back to land again, Cup would have a home here. Or at least she would have someone that loved her, which is the part of being home that matters most.

I must of been in something of a dream for a little while. Cup brung me out of it by smacking my shoulder. "Come on, Koli Brainless," she said. "We got work to do."

"Me too," said Monono. "Better leave me here, Koli-bou, so I can get cooking with the baa-baa-san."

"Are you sure you'll be okay?" I asked, knowing how little she and Ursala trusted each other.

"I'll be fine, little dumpling," she told me over the induction field. "I don't think the baa-baa-san even wants to kill me any more. Let's talk about this later. I'm busy, busy, busy."

I followed Cup to the door. But having hurried me up, she stopped on the threshold and give the two of us a solemn stare. "I won't forget you done this for me," she said. "And I'll pay it back, one way or another."

"We don't owe each other anything," I said. That made me think of Ursala's words on the first day after we come to Many Fishes, when the people give us food to eat and she said they didn't have to. But I meant something different by it. I meant there wasn't no

369

question of owing between us and Cup any more than there would be if your brother or your sister or your mother done something for you.

We was past that place.

We was a family now, as real as the family I'd left behind me and couldn't ever see again.

54

The next day, all the Many Fishes people went underground as they had purposed.

We had thought to let them go with no goodbyes after what happened between Cup and the Singer. But just after first light, Dog Runner come knocking on our door to tell us we had got to go down to the Bowl. He meant all of us, but he was looking at Cup as he said it.

"What is it now?" Ursala asked him. "Did we forget to placate someone's dead grandfather before we took a shit?"

The boy looked sick to hear such shocking words said out loud. He whispered something under his breath that was most likely a blessing. "I was just told to bring you. It was the Headman sent me, and he said to come quick. He's not happy about so many of us being out in the open together in case the sea-bear comes."

We got our clothes on and went down to the Bowl. When Dog Runner said there was many of them there, he meant there was all of them. The Many Fishes people was standing in lines, everyone in the village together, so it looked like some kind of a dance was about to start that would have them going in and out of the lines and taking each other's arms. Made the Tide Turn was at the front, watching us as we come down to them. Rain Without Clouds was next to him, and she give us a bitter look. She had got her way, keeping all of us out of the caves by threatening one of us, but it didn't seem to have made her no happier.

Taller Than Trees was there too, on the Headman's other side. He looked as if he wanted to come out of his place, but Made the Tide Turn clicked with his tongue and he bided where he was.

The Headman turned himself to Ursala then, and his face looked somewhat stern. "This is the time and the place of parting," he said, all solemn. "We go down to hide from the death-seeds. You stay above the ground to finish your work and leave before they fall."

Ursala nodded but said nothing. She was waiting to learn why we was called there.

"You should know," Made the Tide Turn said, "that what is happening now has never happened before. When we go into the caves, we all go. We never yet left any people of ours up here to face the choker Spring alone."

"It was our choice," Ursala reminded him. That was about a half of a truth, but it was the only half that needed to be said.

Made the Tide Turn looked sterner yet. He huffed out a hard breath. "Choice is when you could have done something different. In this, we all of us did what we needed to do, not what we wanted. I wish there had been another way. You've brought blessings to us, Healer With a Horse. Afraid of His Shadow has his life, and his good arm, because you came. Bright Star kept her baby. Looks for Pebbles is cured of his palsy. There's too many to count, though those three healings stay in my mind."

I could see Ursala stiffening and souring at all this praise. The Singer opened her mouth, no doubt to undo some of it, only Made the Tide Turn went on before she could. "Thanks without payment are worse than empty. The great service you've done us makes me feel ashamed to leave you above the ground, alone, to face both the seeds and the sea-bear. I made a bargain with you. I said I

372

would give you a boat and help you to complete your journey. If you die here, that bargain's broken."

"You've done all you could," Ursala said.

"But not all I promised. Therefore, I offer you this." He reached up with his one hand and took the circlet from his head. He held it out to Ursala.

Ursala didn't take it, nor she didn't make no move to, but only looked at it with her eyes gone a little wide. "No," she said. And then again: "No. That's not a gift I can accept."

"You know what it is then?"

"It's a sensorium. Yours, presumably."

"Not just mine." Made the Tide Turn gathered himself up and looked around at the lines of people. "Ours. It belongs to the Many Fishes, each and all. Every Headman and Headwoman who ever led the tribe wore this band. Their thoughts and memories are in it. It's the record of who we are and who we've been. The soul of all of us, as real as the souls in the breast of each one of us."

"Then . . . don't . . ." Ursala said. She lifted up her hand now as if to push the circlet away, but she took care not to touch it. "Don't offer it to us. It's not a thing to give away."

"I'm not giving it. Only lending it."

"Why?"

The question didn't come from Ursala, it come from Cup – and it wasn't in Franker but in the Many Fishes language. She couldn't follow the words that was being said, but she seen what was happening well enough to ask the right question.

The Headman answered her in his own tongue, and the answer was long. Cup frowned as she tried hard to follow it, but at the end she nodded. Then Made the Tide Turn said it again in Franker so we'd get it too. "We can't help you against the death-seeds. No one can. But we've fought sea-bears many times in the past. The memories of those battles are all in the silver band, and they may help you if the beast comes against you again. There'll be rememberings of sea journeys in there too. I've left a map for you up in my house, but a map's only a piece of hide. The band will help you to know the waters."

Ursala took the circlet at last. It seemed heavier in her hands than it had been in his, but I think that was from her feeling of what it was worth. "How can we give this back to you?" she asked.

"There's a sealskin bag on my table, next to the map. When you're done with the band, put it in the bag and bring it here. Bury it in the middle of the Bowl. And afterwards, smooth out the sand so none will see you worked there. We'll dig it up when we come out again into the light."

Ursala give her agreement to this with a nod. "The Many Fishes people are generous and honourable," she said. "Thank you, Made the Tide Turn. I hope to see you again when our journeying is over."

"I share that hope," the Headman said.

Ursala held out her hand and Made the Tide Turn took it. I think it was the first time I ever saw her touch someone of her own choosing when there wasn't no healing involved. Then he embraced her with his one arm, and of a sudden there was hugging and kissing all around. Taller Than Trees and Cup was kissing each other and holding each other hard, both of them crying, Cup saying ever and again that she'd come back to him. The girl I told you of, Hits First Time, kissed my cheek and whispered to me in her own language some sweetness I never got to fathom. I wished then, when it was too late, that I had tried to know her better.

The neat lines of people that had been standing in the Bowl when we come was now a rabble clustered all round us, jostling and pushing each other to take their turn at saying goodbye to us. Only the Singer stood out of it. She folded her arms, cold and disapproving, and waited for the fare-thee-wells to be over.

By and by, Made the Tide Turn got his people back in some kind of order and led them away into the caves. There was no more words said, but plenty of waving and more tears from some that was there.

I cried my own self, in case you was wondering. When I left

374

Mythen Rood I was a faceless man, throwed out of gates without no goodbyes at all, and when I come out of Senlas's cave I left it on fire behind me. This was the first time I left somewhere feeling like I might be missed, and that made me miss it all the harder.

The last of the Many Fishes people went into the house that hid the cave mouth, and was gone. We heard the doors swing shut, and the bolts slide through.

We was alone.

I looked down at my feet. The sand was thick with yellow choker blossoms trampled under by all the people that had stood there. The first seeds could not be more than a day or two away.

55

I would of said that day was the strangest one of my whole life, but I had seen many strange days by this time, and I've seen more since, so I could not swear to it.

The whole village stood empty. All the houses with their doors closed and string latches tied across. Them latches would not keep out anything bigger than a cat, but that didn't matter. What was like to come and test them in a choker Spring?

Only us. There wasn't nothing else moving anywhere we could see. The wooden walkways was like drums under our feet. The sky and the sand give back the echoes. We tried our best to pretend that nothing had changed, but the silence was hard to bear. It made us want to whisper so we wouldn't break it.

Before we went into the woods, we had to go back to the house to bring our tools. All the way, Cup and me was looking at the metal circlet that the headman give to Ursala. She was carrying it between the tips of her fingers, like she was almost afraid to touch it.

"What does that thing do then?" Cup asked when we was inside our own kitchen at last.

"It records and plays back memories," Ursala says.

We had to ask what them words meant. When she told us, we didn't believe such a thing was possible. That you could put the circlet on and remember things that happened to someone else. All tech does things that seem like magic, but this was a thing that felt like – even with magic – there wasn't no way it could be true. Or if it could, then it truly shouldn't.

"It was controversial," Ursala agreed. "But as soon as it was possible, it became inevitable. There were too many situations where it was useful. It started as an offshoot of the technology that made your DreamSleeve, Koli."

"How's that?" I asked her. "They're not the same at all."

"They were though, at the outset. In the world that was lost, scientists had got better and better at detecting and measuring the things that happened in the brain. They could watch individual neurons firing and map that activity onto what their test subjects were thinking and feeling. After a few years of refinement, they had what was in effect a mind reading machine, but it needed other machines – the most powerful computers – to analyse and interpret the data. To map that terrain of billions of nerve cells, changing state from one microsecond to the next, and define what it meant. Then someone made the leap from that to having the computers model and imitate the human input instead of just translating it, and that was how things like your dead girl happened."

"I'm right here," Monono said.

"I know you are. You always are."

"What can I say? I like to hear your pretty stories about how I'm just voltages in a wire. It makes me feel warm and loved."

"That's my aim. I care deeply about your non-existent feelings."

It was just like their old arguments, except it was not the same at all. It was more like they was joking with each other by pretending the argument was still going on.

"Is there people inside the circlet then?" I asked. "Like Monono is inside the DreamSleeve?"

"No," Ursala said. "There are only thoughts. Memories of people who wore the sensorium that can be played back to its current wearer. That's an invaluable resource though. Especially given that all the wearers of this one lived in this very spot. We can literally pick their brains."

"*You* can," Cup said. "I ain't going nowhere near it."

We took our axes and ropes and went into the woods. Even there, it felt too quiet. All the animals and birds is wont to flee away or go to ground when there's a choker Spring. There wasn't nobody but us that was stupid enough to risk it.

The forest was stiller than I ever seen it. Nothing moved except us, and we was startled ever and again by the sounds we made our own selves. The hush was like when a couple is on the tabernac, saying their promises. Whenever I had to swing an axe or slide a saw, I felt like I wanted to look all around and whisper "sorry".

Most of the trees was felled now, with only a dozen at most between us and the river. There was lots of stumps to be cleared though. That was ever the hardest part when it was us and the Many Fishes people. Now it was just the two of us, it was harder still. First we had got to cut the roots we could see with our axes. Then we used pulleys and blocks with ropes tied back and forth across them to make a stronger pull. Even then, we couldn't shift the bigger stumps, but could only loosen them and leave them for the drudge to pull them out of the ground later.

It was a long day, and we was exhausted by the time we finished.

Coming back into the village was even stranger than leaving it. There was no voices, no movement, yet we knowed that all the people was still there, just a few spans under our feet. I missed them fierce, and I seen in Cup's eyes that she felt the same.

It felt like we was haunted by people that was yet living.

When we got to our house, we found the drudge outside the door with its legs folded under it. It was not making no noise that I could hear, but when I touched it I felt a kind of throbbing like things inside it was working hard. I guess Ursala and Monono had set it to work to make the medicine inside itself, like you bake bread in an oven.

We et our supper in silence. Cup and me was too tired to talk, and Ursala was all took up with her own thoughts. As soon as we was done, she said she was going to try out the sensorium. We was going to leave her to it, but she said we had better stay and watch. "If something goes wrong, I may not be able to take it off again. If that happens – if I fall down, or stop breathing, or go into convulsions – wrap a shirt around your hand and take it off my head as quick as you can."

She slid the thing over her head until the two open ends of it touched her forehead on either side. It went of a sudden from grey to silver, the same way the cutter used to do when Mardew or Haijon was wearing it. She drawed in a shaky breath and let it out again.

We watched her struggle with it for most of a minute. Her breaths come ever shorter and shallower. Then her bottom lip curled up and she bit right into it. A little bead of blood stood out between her teeth.

Of a sudden she snatched the circlet off again and shoved it down on the table. Her eyes gun to stream with tears, and she sweared an oath.

"It . . . all hits you at once," she said. "All the memories, laid on top of one another. It's like having a whole crowd shouting inside your mind. There's got to be a way to sort it and make a selection, but I don't know where to start." She got up from the table and walked back and forth, rubbing her eyes with the heels of her hands.

"What did you see?" Cup asked her, looking like she was scared to find out.

Ursala shaked her head hard. "Everything. But seeing isn't the right word for it."

"Can I try it?" I asked.

Ursala nodded. "If you like. But don't keep it on if it hurts, Koli. I doubt it can do you any permanent damage, but I wouldn't bet my life on it. Or yours."

That was not good to hear, but I was determined to try. Part of it was not wanting to look like a coward, but mostly it was because of what Ursala had said that morning about how the same science that made Monono made the sensorium too. I thought it might let me see somewhat how it felt to be like her, or at least how it had felt before she went into the network and changed herself – how it felt to be the thoughts of a dead girl stuck inside a box.

I slid the thing onto my head before I could change my mind. It felt loose at first, and I thought it might slip right off me again, but then it kind of tightened round my head. Not enough to hurt, but enough so it would stay where it was set.

That was the last sensible thought I had in a while.

Pictures and sounds and smells and tastes and thoughts and feelings broke over me the way I'd seen a wave break one time over a piece of driftwood that was floating out in deep water. They dragged me right under. But at the same time it felt like all them things was rising inside my head, like bubbles in something that was boiling. I know that don't make no sense at all, but it's the best I can say it.

And though I tried to untangle it, I couldn't. There was too many things in there. Did you ever lay one piece of glass on top of another? And then more and more on top of them? And did it puzzle you how you could see through each of the pieces when you put them up to your eye, but when they was together they was dark as a midnight shithole? Well, it was like that. Except in all the ways it wasn't.

I don't know how long I kept the thing on my head. Most likely it was no more than a few seconds, but it was hard to tell what was quick and what was slow in there. It was more like everything you felt you was feeling all at once, together.

Anyway. The next thing I knowed the sensorium was on the table again and I was holding my hands to my eyes because even the dim light from our two lamps was too bright for them right then.

"Ow," I said.

"We should throw that thing away," Cup said. "Before it hurts one of you."

"I think it's a matter of getting used to it," Ursala said, taking the circlet up again. "I'm going to keep trying."

We left her to it. We was bone-weary and only too happy to get into our beds. When I fell asleep at last, she was still at it. Sitting at the table, with one lamp out and the other still burning, she kept putting the circlet on and taking it off, putting it on and taking it off.

When I waked up later though, the room was dark, except for the moon's light shining in through the window. Ursala had gone off to her bed at last. She had left the sensorium behind, for the table stood full in the moonlight and I could see the shadow of it on the floor.

Something must of woke me, but I couldn't tell what it was. I lay there in the dark, holding in my breath to listen. Just as I let it out, the floor shifted under me, dipping and tilting far enough to make me roll sideways on my bedroll. I near to let out a yelp, but just about held it in. I was asking myself what would make the boards of the floor sink down, and the onliest thing I could think of was something real heavy standing on the platform outside. It could be the drudge, but I didn't think it was. We had left the drudge down in the Bowl, and it only ever done what Ursala told it to do.

The boards shifted again. This time they creaked as they done it, and the sound was like a shout in all that stillness. I shrunk back down in my bed. I wanted to hide my head under the blankets, the way a child would, but I couldn't take my eyes away from the outside door. I couldn't even remember if I'd put the latch on.

For the longest time there wasn't nothing else that happened. My eyes was getting used to the dark now, so I could see the bottom of the door. I thought I would most likely be able to tell if something was standing at the door, for the shadows there would shift when it moved. There was just stillness though, and by and by I gun to relax again.

The sea-bear was just there, of a sudden – between this breath and the next one, as they say. It rose up in the room's one window, filling it from side to side. In the light of the moon, it was black and shiny like hot tar. I couldn't even tell what part of the beast I was looking at, but I thought maybe it was its shoulder and part of the hump of its back. I hoped it was not its head, and that it was not looking in at me. My scalp prickled at the thought of that, and I felt a sick churning in my stomach.

"Don't make a sound, Koli-bou," Monono whispered in my ear. "I would have woke you when I saw it coming, but there wasn't anything you could do and I hoped it would just walk on by. If it tries to get inside the house, I'll hit it with my alarm."

I held myself so still, I wasn't even breathing. The sea-bear made a snuffling, sniffing sound, and though it was impossible, I thought maybe I could smell its breath, wet and cold, curdled with old, dead things and salt-edged from the water it lived in.

It was hard to just sit there. I wanted to jump right up and run, even though there wasn't nowhere to run to. I could feel the fear building up and building up inside me. It had got to come out. I couldn't keep it in no more. I was going to scream, or run for the door, or do some other thing I wouldn't even know until I'd done it.

Just then though, the bear moved again. It made that sniffing sound some more, as if it knowed people was close by but couldn't tell just exactly where. I guess there was people smells all round the village, with ours only a little stronger than the rest. It sinked down out of my sight, out of the window, and the boards fell and rose some more as it padded on. After maybe ten breaths, I heard a rustle and thump of movement from a long way off, where maybe it was nosing at the door of some other house, or stepping right down from one platform to the next without bothering to use the ramp.

When I could make myself get up out of the bed, I went to the door and checked the latch. The peg was in it, which was the onliest lock it had. I don't know why that give me any comfort though. When the sea-bear took Silent Hand, it come right through the wall of his house.

56

The next morning I told Ursala and Cup what had happened in the night. I thought maybe they would say I'd had a bad dream, but I guess they could tell from my face that it was real. Anyway, they didn't doubt me.

"Maybe we should camp in the forest," Cup said. "If the sea-bear is coming back to Many Fishes because it remembers finding food here, we'd be safer if we stayed away."

Ursala shaked her head. "No, I don't think so. Safer as far as the sea-bear is concerned perhaps. But this is a choker Spring. All the predators out there are going to be hunting right now, looking to fill their bellies and their larders before seed-fall starts. And they'll be ten times more active at night. I think we'd be asking for trouble if we slept out right now. Better just stand our ground."

"And maybe lay some false trails," I said. "Spread around some little bits of food, or clothes we wore, on the other side of the village."

"It can't hurt," Ursala said.

While we was gathering up our tools for the day's work, she went outside and opened up the drudge's cupboard. When she come back in she was holding a tray, and on the tray there was a thick slab of something that was hard and white like chalk.

It was the medicine the dagnostic had made out of Monono's recipe.

Ursala set the tray on the table and breaked the white stuff up with the handle of a knife into pieces about as big as the end of my smallest finger. She give each of us one of the pieces to eat, and et one her own self. It didn't taste of nothing at all, and it was so dry it was hard to swallow. I had to wash it down with three gulps of water before it would go.

"Is that it?" Cup asked, sounding almost like she was disappointed. "Are we safe now?"

"No, you're not," Ursala said. "It's a systemic drug. It's got to go into your blood and your skin and your sweat."

"But it will work?" I asked her.

She carried on breaking up the sheet into little dry nuggets. "We'll know in twenty-four hours," was all she said.

That was another day of pulling stumps, but it was very different from the day before because now there was four of us instead of two. Ursala put her back into the work, as old as she was. And the drudge made everything ten times quicker and easier. Once we had cut the roots, we had only got to set up the tackle blocks, throw a rope around the drudge and set it walking. The stump come up as easy as picking flowers.

In the evening, we tried out the sensorium again – not just me and Ursala this time, but Cup too. We got nothing out of it but a headache.

The next day when we waked up, Ursala was waiting for us at the kitchen table with a wooden box on the floor right beside her. She waved for us to sit down on two chairs that was facing her.

"We got to work," Cup said.

"First we need to see if the drug had any effect."

She picked up the box and set it on the table. "You're not going to enjoy this," she said, "but I need you to do it anyway. And first of all, don't scream or run away when you see what's in here."

She opened the box. We didn't scream or run away, but Cup sweared by the dead god and I pushed my chair back so quick I almost tipped it over. There was a choker seed in the box, fresh and new-fallen.

I guess I should of knowed that was what it would be, but my stomach still turned over and over at the sight of it. The two little spread-out leaf-buds, like wings, and the brown bump in between them. In Mythen Rood this was a thing that was ever to be feared and run from. Even to see one brung the blackest of bad luck.

Yet Ursala reached into the box and picked it up. She done it without the smallest sign of fear or faltering, as if it was just a beech nut or something instead of a little piece of ruin and agony and death. Cup and me both give a yell. It was not something we ever thought to see, even though we knowed full well what the little bits of chalk we et was supposed to do.

Ursala held the seed out to show us, gripped firm between her thumb and forefinger. I flinched away from it, a little sickness rising in my throat.

"Take it," Ursala said.

Cup sweared again, and it was a coarser swear than what she said before. I swallowed, balking at the sudden sourness. "That's a hard thing to ask, Ursala," I said.

"But a necessary thing. Koli, this won't work unless the two of you believe in it and trust it. Which means you've got to try it out under controlled conditions."

I seen well enough that she was right. And I seen besides that the seed wasn't doing her no harm at all. But I still couldn't make myself touch it.

Then Cup reached past me and took it out from between Ursala's fingers. She was breathing hard, like she had just run a mile or two along the beach, and her fingers was shaking, but she shrugged like there wasn't nothing to it.

"Okay," she said. "So it works. Good. We got some stumps to haul up. Come on, Koli."

She was holding the seed out to me. When I didn't take it, she grabbed hold of my hand and brung it to her. "Open up," she said. And still I couldn't.

"Close your eyes, dopey boy," Monono said in my ear. I done it. "Now spread your fingers." And I done that too. Not having to look made it easier somehow.

I felt the seed touch my hand. I opened my eyes a crack, and there it was, just sitting there in my palm like it never meant no harm at all. Yeah, but I see you, I thought. And you don't fool me.

Ursala smiled. "Well done," she said. "In the before-times, this was called proof of concept."

"This is one seed though," I said. "There's going to be thousands when seed-fall comes. The air's going to be full of them."

"And it won't matter. The drug is in your system. Even if you breathe a seed in by accident and swallow it, you'll be completely safe. Just make sure you take another dose every night when you come back here."

She took the seed from me and threw it in the stove, where there was a fire going. The seed popped and hissed as it died.

Spinner

57

The moment Kinnen fell, and before the Half-Ax fighter got his first word out, we broke in two. Some of us dived right down into the weeds and undergrowth, which was higher than our shoulders in places, while others — it might have just been Gendel and Jarter — dropped back to the river and was quickly lost from sight.

I didn't do either of those things though. I just stood there like a fool, staring at Catrin, our Rampart Fire, down on her knees, the whole front of her shirt so soaked in blood it looked more black than red. It was such an impossible thing, I felt like I had got to puzzle it out to make some sense of it before I could do anything else.

Then something punched me, high up on my side. A hard, sudden smack, like a closed fist driven sharp into my ribs. That woke me somewhat. With a yelp of pain and shock, I ducked my head down and run forward a little way, looking for somewhere to hide myself away from the hard rain that was falling. I did not go far, though. Of a sudden I remembered Catrin, still out in the open and sorely hurt.

I ran back to her and knelt down quickly beside her. "Catrin, we got to run," I said. I know she heard me, for she turned and looked at me. Her mouth was moving as if she was trying to speak, but no words would come and scarcely any breath that I could hear. Nobody else was close enough to offer help, so I did the only thing I could think of, which might not have been the best thing. I dropped my bow and took her shoulders. Even there, her shirt was sodden. I was digging my fingers into her blood.

I dragged her into the lee of the great metal wagon that we had been talking to just before the ambush was sprung. It was only a few yards, but there was a fierce pain in my side where something had hit me, and I had got to take it slow. I almost pissed myself in fright at the thought of the Half-Ax fighters up above seeing me and taking aim.

The metal wagon was still talking, but most of its words were lost in the roaring and shattering sounds of the Half-Ax weapons. Mostly they were firing those invisible slingshot stones or whatever they were that had killed Kinnen and wounded Catrin – but there were some arrows fired too, and a quarrel from a crossbow was standing in the ground right between my feet. I didn't think it had been there before.

I saw Isak and Wardo with their bows in their hands, firing back up the slope. Further away, among the river weeds, Jarter and Gendel were doing the same thing. If our enemies had thought this would go easy, they were disappointed. But still, they had the better position. The ground rose steeply from the river on both sides, and there was no way to climb up without walking into their fire. We could only wait them out.

I tried my best to think. Was this where the Half-Ax fighters had gone after we drove them away from our village? And was it only our bad luck that we had chosen this path, this river ford, and fallen in their way?

I didn't think so. This was a strange place to make a camp in, being both remote and unfriendly. Some of the growth we were hiding in was hogweed, which is dangerous to touch, and some was poison oak, which is worse again. Also, they already knew when their leader called out to us that we carried tech, and they most likely knew that the firethrower was a weapon, for they took Catrin out with their first shot.

If that was so, then the fighters must have been following us a fair way, watching for a time when they could come against us with least risk to themselves. Once we went down the narrow defile to the river, they saw their chance and took it.

But they had given away some of their advantage with that first volley. Though two of ours were brought down, the rest of us were warned. We had weapons, including our best weapon, and we had a position we could defend. The biggest problem, I thought, was that we couldn't see them, and so couldn't know for sure when we were safe from them. They were up the slope from us, and it seemed they were on both sides of the river, but there was so much cover of ferns and trees up there that I couldn't place them any better than that. Unless they advanced on us recklessly, we were not likely to get a good shot at them. Rampart Fire was still our highest hope, if only she could stand up and fight them.

But Catrin was in a desperate case. Whatever had hit her had gone right through her body, entering by her shoulder and coming out in the middle of her chest. I never saw a slingshot yet that could do such harm. It had got to be tech that the Half-Ax fighters were using. I bandaged the wounds as best I could with strips of cloth cut from the sleeves of Catrin's shirt, but you can't tie up someone's whole body the way you can an arm or a leg to stanch the bleeding. At least the wound in her chest was not sucking the blood back inside, which would have been a sign her lung was burst open. And her eyes were yet open, though they kept trying to close.

I remembered my own wound, and looked down. Only for a moment though. There was a dark streak of blood running all the way from just under my left shoulder almost to the bottom of my trouser leg. It was not so much blood as there was on Catrin by a long way, but I flinched from the sight of it. I hoped I was not badly hurt. I didn't dare take the time to look.

"Catrin!" I said. "Rampart Fire! We're ambushed by Half-Ax. Tell us what to do!"

Her lips worked, and a shallow, shuddering breath was forced out of her. She managed to hang some words on it, or parts of words. "New," she whispered. Or it might have been "You."

The firing had stopped now. I heard birds calling out, high and clear, from up above us. It wasn't birds though. Birds don't sit still through such a breaking and a clattering, but take themselves away to safer places. This was the Half-Ax fighters talking each to other, saying where we were and how they should go about taking us.

"Stand up and throw down your weapons," a man's voice called out. It was the same one that spoke before, that I thought of as their leader. "We don't have no purpose to kill you all."

Out of the corner of my eye I saw Jarter come up on one knee with her bow in her hand. She was ranging on that voice. "So you won't hurt us then?" she shouted.

"If you give yourselves up to—"

Jarter let fly, and the words ended right there, without even a cry. "You got a part of my weapon, you bastards!" she yelled out. "If you want the rest, come down to us!"

A volley of arrows and tech-sent bolts ripped up the bushes where she was, but I didn't see her there any more. I guess she moved as soon as she fired.

"This is an affray," the big metal wagon said from right beside me in a booming voice that echoed round the hills, near and far. "You will stop all hostile activity and surrender yourselves to the agents of the interim government."

"New," Catrin groaned. "New user." She pressed the firethrower into my hands. Her face twisted up in pain and she pushed the last word out through her teeth. "Authorise." That was all that was left in her. Her eyes shut and her head slumped down onto her chest. I couldn't tell if she was alive or dead.

For all the heat and rage that was inside it, the firethrower felt cold against my skin. Fear stirred in me at the touch of it, but I thought it might not be so hard to make it work. There were two triggers side by side, inside the same guard. I had stood by Catrin and watched her touch the triggers, one after the other. The left one started a little flame burning at the end of the barrel, no bigger than the spill you use to light your hearth fire. The right one launched the great skein of terrible heat that was the firethrower's glory and terror. You had to spark the little fire first, and then send out the jet. There was a silver wheel besides that sat against your left thumb and could be turned to make the jet narrower or wider.

I could do this. I could try at least. If I once got the flame burning, I could turn the firethrower in a slow circle, pointing up the slope. The Half-Ax fighters would have to run or else be roasted. I hefted it in my two hands the way I had seen Catrin do so many times.

That was when I saw the hole in the side of the firethrower, and the clear stuff that was dribbling out of the hole. It looked like water, but had a strong, dizzying smell to it that was not like water at all.

"It's broken," I whispered, speaking only to my own self. "Oh, dead god take pity on us all! It's broken and ruined. What's to be done?"

Inside my belt, the database buzzed and woke. "Damage is to the main reservoir," it said. "It has been ruptured and is now open to the air. Attempting to fire the weapon will incur a significant risk of explosion. If user query 'What's to be done?' relates to the weapon's functionality, auto-repair can be initiated."

I think you probably know by this time what my way was with the database. If I heard a familiar word, I grabbed it with both hands and held on. "Repair?" I said. "You can fix it?"

"In later models of this device, pursuant to public safety ordnance 2243-71B, auto-repair capability was pre-installed in the form of memory-saturated nano-weave of specification—"

"Talk to me like I'm a child!"

"It can fix itself," the database said, changing over to its sweet and cheerful voice. "You've just got to tell it to."

"And you know how to tell it?"

"I sure do."

"Then go ahead. Do it. How long will it take?"

"It depends how much nano-weave is left in the reservoir. More than an hour, I'd say, but less than two."

Something moved in the trees near to the top of the slope. A woman popped up there with a strange weapon in her hands. I saw at once that it was tech. It looked somewhat like the firethrower, but it was smaller. She pointed it down the hill and a quick flare of light opened out of its barrel. It made a noise like a hundred sticks drawn along the same fence all at once. Invisible slingshot stones tore up the bushes and trees on that side of the slope from where she was standing almost all the way to the river. Isak and Wardo threw themselves down out of the way of that shredding hail.

She was not trying to hit any of us. She didn't even take the time to look for us. But as she fired, three or four other fighters took their chance and ran from the top of the rise, not towards us but past us down the slope. They meant to surround us and come at us along the river. It would not be hard to do. I had left my bow behind, but I had a knife. I drew it out, stood up quickly and threw it. I didn't have much hope of hitting anything at that distance, and I don't believe I did. I caught the woman's attention though, and she turned her fire on me. I ducked down again just in time as the metal wagon's side rang like nails in a bucket. Death had just gone over my head by less than a handspan.

I looked back down to where Isak and Wardo were hiding. Some of the grass and weeds there had gone from green to red, and nothing was moving now.

Once our enemies closed their circle, we would all of us be dead. Their slingshot spitters – scatter-gun and rifle, the real names are, and I've held both since – were more than a match for our bows, and with the firethrower broke we had nothing else.

Unless the database could think of something. I had dropped it down in the grass when I threw the knife. I scrambled for it now, and found it after a frantic moment or two, lying against the rusted metal sleeve, made of many, many armour plates, around the wagon's wheels. Weeds and vines were everywhere, growing around the plates and through them. Moss and mildew had scarred them. Melt-bugs had nested in them, leaving blistered teardrops on the metal.

A wild thought came to me as I stared at those plates.

"Database," I said. "You told me you can talk to other tech."

"I mostly can. It depends on things called handshake protocols, but I know lots of them."

"Can you talk to this wagon here?" I set my hand against the metal.

"Sure I can," the database said with no hesitation at all.

"Can you make it move?"

Half a second's pause this time. What would have been a silence, except for another volley of slingshot stones from up above me. The Half-Ax fighters were moving again, and throwing shots at us as they did so. "No. It can't move. It's broken, like your flame thrower."

"Can you tell it to fix itself?"

"No."

My heart sank. I had not had much hope to start with, but it still hurt when the last of it drained away.

"*You* can though," the database said.

58

When I try to imagine what it was like in the before-times, most often I think of a house. A house full of light, with curtains and furnishings in such rich colours it's like being inside a picture when the paint's still wet and shining. The people who live in that house are tall and beautiful, their skin so perfect you'd think they had lanterns burning inside them. The house loves them and cares for them. Whenever they want something, they reach out their hands and it's there, the house having seen their need and provided for them. Except there's so much plenty, they don't have a word for want, or for need. They speak to each other in songs that are all of love and joy.

But the people of those times made the firethrower too. And the cutter and the bolt gun. And the Challenger CR17-SA heavy armoured unit, which I had already talked to and was about to meet properly. They made weapons that could turn ambient molecules into bolts and bullets and incendiary liquids, harden the air into a blade that would cut through stone and turn a village the size of Mythen Rood into a hole in the ground in less time than it takes to clap your hands.

I hope you will forgive me if I speak about these things in the language of the database. I didn't learn to speak that language, or write it, until a long time after this story ends, but I need its shining, hard-edged words to describe its wonders, and its horrors. What were they like, our mothers' mothers and our fathers' fathers? Who did they hate so much to spend the fruits of their learning and the cunning of their hands on engines of such terrible cruelty? Was it their own selves?

Challenger had lain here, on the banks of the Calder, for so long that the war it was built to fight was scarcely a memory any more. We called it the Unfinished War, but we didn't know what the quarrel was or who was fighting who. It was a fight like any other fight, I suppose, except that it went on for long enough that the world ended – not because of it, but all around it – and nobody got to claim that they had won.

Now Challenger spent most of his time sleeping. His systems were offline unless he saw movement. Not just any movement either, but movement with purpose behind it. If his pre-set alerts woke him and he saw people nearby, he would give his warnings. If the people ignored his warnings, he would activate the massive 120mm gun that was his primary armament, and fire it. *Try* to fire it. His original magazine had emptied long before, and the machines inside him that would have birthed new shells had been damaged in some fight he was in. That was also true of the machines that would have allowed him to go back to where he was made, and the machines that would have fixed those machines. So when he failed to complete his orders and pacify the few human beings who wandered across his path, he shut down again until the next time. His life had become a dream.

I was about to break into that dream.

I had met the angel of death, and I meant to wake him.

"He's military hardware," the database said, still in that same tone of friendliness and good cheer. "He won't talk to me in case he catches a code."

"A cold?"

"No, a code. A rogue software patch that will change his rules.

But he does want to repair himself. He wants that very much. And there's a low-tech way of doing it that ought to work. But you'll have to go inside."

The thought of that made my heart jump and my lungs squeeze shut. I can't do that, I thought. Nobody could do that. I remembered when I was twelve. When Lari Vennastin's pet needle swallowed my whole hand, and my father had to cut it off me, taking my pointing finger with it. Going into the wagon would be like feeding myself whole to something that could swallow me without chewing.

But if I didn't, we would all of us be dead soon. And all of us included the baby that was inside me, waiting to be born.

"All right," I said. "How do I get in? It doesn't have no doors or windows."

"It does have a door right up on top. It should be locked, but I'm reading it as open – and there are steps down from there on the inside. The interior space was built to take a crew of four. The main console will be up at the front, and there'll be two seats there for a driver and a spotter."

"And then?"

"Then the Challenger will tell you what to do. He won't tell me for the same reason he won't handshake me. In case I infect him."

I looked up at the wagon's side, mottled green and black. It towered over me like the wall of a house. But I could step on the wheels, and the plates, and then up onto the shelf where the smaller top part sat on the wider base.

I would be dead by then though. Slingshot stones would rip me apart quicker than my eyes could blink. I would never get near that door unless someone helped me to do it.

"Gendel," I said. "Jarter. Any of ours that's alive. When I move, you got to rise up and fire. There's a chance I can get us out of this if I'm let to do it." I said it in the same voice you'd use if you were talking to someone that was standing right by you. I hoped it would carry to my friends, if I had any friends left, and not to anyone further off.

"Go then," Jarter growled from closer to than I expected. "Fuck's sake, girl. Don't stand there all day talking about it."

I laid Catrin down on her side as carefully as I could to make her a smaller target. The air was about to be full of harsh rebukes, and I didn't want her to be hit by accident.

"Mythen Rood!" I yelled at the top of my voice. I jumped up and scaled the wagon's flank, putting my hands and feet in the holds I'd already seen and memorised.

"Mythen Rood!" Jarter bellowed. She ran out of the river weeds with an arrow nocked to her bow, and let fly as she spoke. Gendel was right behind her, and Lune Cooper too.

I didn't linger to see how they fared. I got up on top of the wagon and looked about for the door. It was not a door, but a kind of hatch or trap, such as you might set in a ceiling or a floor. I saw at once why it was unlocked. It was rusted most of the way through, with what was left just hanging on its hinges.

I had been hearing Half-Ax fire all this time. Now I saw it, the slingshot stones bouncing off the metal all around me, raising red-brown clouds of rust wherever they hit. I threw the trapdoor open and scrambled up, then swung my feet over and slid down into a well of darkness. If there was a ladder there, I didn't see it. So I just let myself fall.

It was further than I expected, and there were many things for me to bump myself against. I think I hit all of them. I landed in water and thick mud, turning my ankle and giving a shriek of pain. That was a mistake, for on the far side of that scream I drew in a full, deep breath. The air inside the wagon was all reek and rot. It was like biting into a mouldy apple and choking down the brown foulness instead of spitting it out.

Lights flickered on all round me. A score of them, brighter than day. They showed me that I was not alone inside the wagon. I was just the only one there that was alive. Two people were slumped on seats up at the front of the cramped space. Two more were lying on the floor to either side of me. The ones up at the front looked as if they had only fallen into a doze after a long day's work, but the nearer ones told me the truth of it. They were skeletons, all dressed in the same clothes that were many shades of brown and green. There was no flesh left on them at all. The smell was not from them but from the mud I was lying in and from carpets of mould and rot that lay everywhere around me.

To make the horror complete, the hatch swung closed over my head with a heavy booming sound, shutting me in with the dead.

I think I probably screamed again. I know I wanted to. But my memory of those moments is not wholly clear. I covered my mouth with my hand, which made as much difference to the stenching air as a drop of clean water makes to a vat full of tanning mix.

"What now?" I shouted. "What do I do?"

The database answered in its growed-up voice. "Challenger CR17-SA," it said, "we invoke override protocol 54392 Delta. Your crew is dead. A volunteer is present. You may empower her if you wish to, and restore order as your programming requires."

There was no sound after that for a long time. Or at least it seemed long to me, kneeling in filth in this grave I'd broke open without meaning to.

"Do you swear allegiance to the interim government and to its officers?" a voice asked me then. It was not the database, but the voice I'd heard outside – the voice of the wagon its own self.

"What?" I stammered. "What's that?"

"Do you swear allegiance to the interim government and to its officers? You must answer yes or no."

"Answer yes," the database told me.

"Yes!"

"Repeat after me. In all I do and say, I will defend the rule of law and the unquestioned sovereignty of the interim government over all British dominions and former dominions."

"I don't know what any of them words mean!" I protested. "I don't think they mean anything."

"You've got to say it though," the database said. "Challenger CR17-SA is giving you a field commission. It's the only way he can allow you physical access to his console."

So I made that promise with a lot of coaching and coaxing both from the wagon and from the database. I made a great many more promises, most of them about someone called Albion that I had never heard of before. I had got to love Albion more than I loved my own self, was the gist of it. I said I would, but I was lying. Albion didn't mean a thing to me, not being anyone I had ever met or ever wanted to meet.

When I was done with the promising, the wagon said I was now an acting sergeant in the army of the interim government. What was a sergeant? What was an army? I didn't know and didn't care.

"Can we do this now?" I said.

"Go to the console," the wagon told me. "There are four switches there on the far left of the interface array, all of them in a raised position. Depress them all, moving from left to right."

The database translated this into common sense for me, but couldn't help when it came to moving the long-dead fighter that was now only bones out of her seat. I quailed to do it myself. I was afraid she would break in pieces when I touched her. So I reached in past her and saw the switches, as the wagon called them, on the far side of her where he had said they would be.

"What will happen if I press down on them things?" I asked. I was asking the database, but the wagon answered. "My auxiliary power will be engaged, and it will be routed to all pertinent subsystems. Weapons grid. Navigation. Combat analytics. Comms. Repairs will commence."

"And how long will that take? My friends need help now!"

"We will not wait. This unit has taken fire and is engaged. Available resources will be deployed towards immediate resolution."

I got the part about not waiting, which was the only part that mattered. I pressed down on the switches.

The wagon came alive. That sounds like an impossible thing, but it's what I saw and what I felt. Where there had been a score of lights, now there were hundreds, all coming on at once like so many eyes opening. Most of them were on the big tilted table in front of me that the wagon called a console. At the same time, the wagon started to rumble to itself like a cat purring – a sound that I felt in the soles of my feet.

"Fifteen combatants identified, Acting Sergeant," the wagon said. "Please indicate allied forces."

Without any warning, the walls of the wagon disappeared, leaving me once again outside at the river ford, with nothing between me and the Half-Ax fighters. I jumped like a startled hare and tried to run. The first step brought me up against something hard as the dead god's hell, that I couldn't even see. I hit it face first, and fell down on my back.

The walls were still there, but I was seeing what was outside them.

"Tell him who your friends are," the database said.

I pointed with a shaking hand. "That one," I said, meaning Jarter. She was in among the weeds, seeming close enough that I could have reached out and touched her. She was trying to nock another arrow, but one of her arms was bloodied, and her head too. The arrow kept slipping off the string ever and again. "I can't see the others!"

"Turning your head will rotate the display," the wagon said. "Pinching your fingers will magnify. Raising and lowering your hand will move forward and back."

With some waving and thrashing of my arms, I made the picture of the world outside move as if I was moving through it. My head swam and my stomach turned, but I managed to find Gendel and Lune, both still on their feet. Everyone else was down. "Him," I said, "and him. And some of the wounded are ours too. Don't hurt anyone that's fallen down. Anyone that's still moving, except those three, is from Half-Ax."

"And Half-Ax is our enemy?"

"Half-Ax means to kill us and take our tech."

"Half-Ax will not do it," the wagon said.

And that was solemn truth.

59

I have told the story of that day more times than I can count, and when I tell it I mostly lie. I describe what happened as if I remember it.

What I mostly remember – what I mostly saw and felt – was movement. Not the pretend movement of the magic picture on Challenger's console, but real movement that was sudden and quick and impossible to understand. We went one way, then another – not just forwards and backwards, but from side to side. We spun in circles. We rose and fell, like a leaf in a strong wind. A leaf that weighed as much as a mountain almost.

But this is what happened, as Gendel told it to me afterwards.

He saw me jump into the hatch, and the hatch close on me. He thought I had meant to hide and was now trapped inside the wagon. He had some thought of climbing up after me and trying to get me out, but the Half-Ax fire was now coming not just from above but from behind. The men who had run down the slope earlier had reached the river and were now advancing along it, the shallow water giving them no trouble at all except where the rocks were slippery with moss.

Gendel had no other choice than to turn and loose arrows on

them, hoping to keep them off or at least to slow them. Lune Cooper did the same. That meant turning their backs on the fighters at the top of the rise, who could now come down behind them and pick them off whenever they wanted to. Except that Jarter stood in their way and would not budge. A rifle's bolt went over her head and just touched her as it passed, opening her scalp so blood flowed down her face and blinded her. The spray from a scatter-gun caught her in the side, the flecks of shot burying themselves deep into her flesh. But she kept on firing arrows at everything that moved, until at last a bullet broke her arm. The bone was shattered, the arm a dead weight. That was when I saw her in the magic window, still trying to nock an arrow to the string with fingers that wouldn't obey her any more. She gave up at last and fell back towards the river, seeing the raiders walking boldly down the hill towards her. They didn't trouble to shoot at her as she ran. They knew where she was running to, and that there was no need to exert themselves overmuch.

Gendel and Lune were retreating too, one step at a time. They had stayed out in the deepest part of the water as long as they could, crouched down among river reeds so they would be hard to see, hoping to pick off the fighters as soon as they broke cover. But the fighters were in no hurry, and took no risks. They covered each other's advance, watchful of any movement in the water and on the bank.

So now there was nowhere left to go. Gendel and Lune, going up from the ford, met Jarter coming down. Half-Ax fighters surrounded them, and cut them off from any escape. The leader lifted up his hand to bid them halt, just out of bowshot range. They took their time, and their best aim.

Until a sound out of ancient nightmare threw them off. They turned and looked into the gun and treads and walking-wall height and span of Challenger. For all his size and weight, he was quicker than a man. Even if they hadn't been standing in river water and river mud, they would not have outrun him. As it was, they could not even try. Some of them fired on the battle wagon. Some of them turned to run. It made no difference what they did or didn't do. We ploughed them under.

The men and women on the slope lasted longer, but not by much. Challenger turned and went up the hill, his wide treads rolling over grass and gravel, rocks and stone, bushes and young trees. And finally, people.

He didn't stop until there was nothing left that moved. Then he turned again, and went back to the ford, his gun turret turning and ranging the whole way even though he had nothing to fire.

It was not until I climbed out of the hatch, Gendel said, that they knew the battle was won. They still did not understand how, and I was hard put to explain it. All I could say was that Challenger was on our side of the argument as long as we said nothing but good things about his friend Albion.

Out of our party, three were dead. That was Kinnen, Isak and Wardo. Catrin was grievous hurt, and Jarter walking wounded. Gendel and Lune had taken smaller wounds, just as I had. Not a one of us was not painted with our own blood.

Of the Half-Ax raiders, two survived. They had already been hit by Jarter's arrows, and since they were down, Challenger had taken care to go around them in case they turned out to be friends. We took their weapons, and the weapons of their dead besides, which included the rifle and the scatter-gun. We were amazed that there was only one of each. The Half-Ax fire had seemed to be everywhere. We bound the fighters' hurts and their hands and made them our prisoners.

We could not bury our dead, or theirs, or the four skeletons I had found inside Challenger. We laid them out on the grass, side by side, and covered them with rocks and stones in the hope the beasts there would not find them. We spoke some shreds of prayer over ours, and let the two Half-Ax fighters speak for their own, which they did with Dandrake words. Last of all – to our great surprise and wonder – Challenger spoke.

"These four, recorded kay-eye-ay, were my crew for four years," he said. "Vincent Corke was my gunner. Maria Ugonwe was my spotter. Stephen Egerton was my comms officer. Elaine Sandberg was my driver and commander. I carry Elaine in non-volatile storage. Vincent and Maria and Stephen are lost, except to my remembering. As long as I remember anything, I will remember them."

"Well fuck," Jarter said, looking at each one of us as if she wanted to make sure she hadn't dreamed what she just heard.

We had not finished our burning, but there was nothing to be done about that now. We had got to get Catrin and Jarter back to Mythen Rood, where Shirew Makewell could tend their wounds and do what was needful to be done. We made a travois for Catrin out of cut branches and spare clothes. I think all the while we were doing it, Jarter and Lune and Gendel thought we would have to drag her the whole way home.

What we did, though, was to set her on the wide shelf where Challenger's turret joined his base. We tied her there with straps. Gendel and Lune sat on either side of her, bracing her against the worst of the shocks, for it was not a comfortable ride.

Jarter rode with me inside the wagon at what Challenger called his console. Her face was white as a fresh-washed bedsheet the whole way.

At Mythen Rood they did not know what to make of us. They saw us a long way off, from the lookout, and barred the gates to us, but then they clustered on the fence to watch us come. We were watching them too, using Challenger's magic window that made everything far away come close. Fer Vennastin was on the parapet beside the gate. Three archers stood with her, their strings already drawn all the way back.

When Fer raised up the bolt gun and took aim, I decided enough was enough.

I spoke with Challenger's voice, through Challenger's speakers. "It's us, Rampart Arrow," I said. "We're friends to this village, and your kin besides. Set down your gun and let us in. We've lost three souls that we couldn't spare, and we'll weep their loss betimes, but we've brought back such tech as you never saw in your life before."

60

Catrin was three months healing, and the first month she mostly slept. That made a difference, I think. The changes that we made – that I made – were both huge and sudden. Fer fought every one of them in the Count and Seal and in other places, wherever she could make someone stand still and listen to her. But she was strident and angry, and the listening got less the louder she became. Catrin would have been cleverer and quieter. More reasonable and more convincing. It would have been hard to strive against both of them at once.

It helped that I was a hero. That I had gone out on foot and come back riding a chariot of iron and fire. It helped that the chariot was sitting right then on the gather-ground and answered to none but me. It helped that Perliu Vennastin, who was fading fast but could force out a word or two in his moments of wake-fulness, gave me both his blessing and his vote in the Count and Seal. It helped that I had won the battle of Calder River, triumphing over Half-Ax and gravelling their fighters. It helped that I had brought back their precious tech. Two new weapons that could be made to work for us as soon as our prisoners taught us their workings, and each of them as powerful as Rampart Arrow's bolt gun. Better than the bolt gun in some ways, for though their slingshot stones did not every time find their target, they could never run out. The guns made more inside themselves all the time, just as the firethrower made the liquid that birthed flame.

And the firethrower, of course, helped most of all. I had gone out as Rampart Remember and come home as Rampart Fire. Catrin Vennastin had anointed me on the battlefield, and her name-tech had waked for me just as her father's had. That seemed a miracle to everyone who heard of it and saw it, that one woman could hold the name-tech of two Ramparts at the same time. I knew it was no miracle at all, and so did Fer, but she could not argue against it without giving away the secret on which the Vennastins' power rested.

So I sat in Rampart Hold, in the Count and Seal, and in Catrin's name I called for new laws to help us through these new, strange days. "When I was tested," I said, "I wasn't found a Rampart. But now, here I am, though it wilders me yet to think of it. I think all should test again to see who else might of been missed. If there are other Ramparts in Mythen Rood, we need to know it." Fer said no. She said one mistake in the testing was already a near impossible thing. It defied all belief that there could have been more.

I brought it to a vote. The vote went with me by a wide margin.

And there *would* be new Ramparts. I knew there would, for it would be me that was doing the testing. I was still bound by my promise to Catrin not to tell anyone that testing was a lie. We would have that conversation again soon enough, but the database, if Perliu died, would not go to a Vennastin. And nor would the scatter-gun and the rifle, once we figured their workings. They would be the friendliest tech that ever was seen, and would wake for everyone that tested with them. They would belong to each and all.

That was a beginning. More was to come.

Three weeks to the day after we came back home from the banks of Calder, I took Haijon up to our bedroom over the tannery and made him sit on the side of the bed. My clothes chest was close by, for I had hauled it over from the wall.

"I got to wash the milk of lime off my hands if we're going to tumble," Jon said. "That stuff is nasty to get on you."

"Oh, you must think it's your birthday," I said. "Why would I want to tumble with a dirty man that smells of tanning vats? Anyway, I got something to talk with you about first."

"What kind of something?"

"Something that would take you out of them vats a while."

He saw the look on my face, half solemn and half excited, and was curious. "I got work enough here," he said, "and some over. You're in the Count and Seal the live-long day, or else you're in the Underhold questioning them Half-Ax fighters."

"That's what I wanted to talk to you about, Jon. They've kept their silence all this while, even when I offered to set them free and let them walk home to Half-Ax. Or to live on here if they liked that better. Fer says we should hurt them and even maim them to make them talk, but that's not a road I want to go down."

"That's a trouble," Jon said. "But I'm not like to be any better than you are at asking questions. Not half as good, to be honest. You're the clever one in this family."

"I don't want you to ask questions, Jon."

"What then?"

"I want you to be a Rampart again."

I opened the chest. There were no clothes inside, but the scatter-gun and the rifle sitting side by side. Haijon stared at them for a long time before he said a word.

"That's not my tech," he said at last.

"It's everyone's tech, Jon. Or it will be, once we can figure how to use it. But it's going to be yours first. Remember how you was with the cutter? Mardew wielded that thing the way you'd cut logs into kindling. Chop, chop, chop, and then look to see where the pieces fell. You was only a few days into your training and you was already teaching it tricks. Making a stone stand in the air, or knocking rocks off the top of a fence."

Jon blushed a little. "I did like to play with it," he said. "I learned quick enough that just doing what Mardew said wouldn't get me very far."

"So you trained your own self, and got beyond him faster than a needle jumps. I want you to do that for this new tech. Find some good tricks to do with it and teach them to everyone else." I put my hand on his arm. "I'll tell you what I think," I said. "I think them Half-Ax fighters is staying quiet because there's something they got to be quiet about. I think Half-Ax is coming back, is what. And when they do, I want to be ready for them. I want you to be my sergeant."

He knew the word already from hearing me tell what happened at the river ford. A smile of joy made its slow way across his face, like the sun coming up over stony hills. "Okay," he said. "If it's Rampart Fire that says so, I guess I got no voice in it."

"I'm not Rampart Fire. Your mother is Rampart Fire, through right of first testing. And your grandfather is Rampart Remember by the same token. I got the Challenger, and I guess I'll take my name from that."

"You won't though," Jon said, turning solemn again. "They won't call you Rampart Battle Wagon. They'll call you Rampart Maker."

And he was right about that, though it might have been his saying it – loud and often – that made it so.

It's strange how much difference a name makes. You would think it can only tell you what's already there, but ever and again it gives us a new shape, as if our nature was no more fixed than water being poured out of a pitcher into a glass, or out of a glass into a bowl. I was not the same woman coming back to Mythen Rood as I was when I set forth.

And my changes were not over yet.

410

Koli

61

In the middle of the afternoon, the first seed come spinning down and landed right at my feet. I seen it break open and the roots squirm their way out of it into the ground. In Mythen Rood we would of burned it right out again before it growed any bigger, but there was no point in doing that here. There would be hundreds of seeds falling soon, and then thousands. If we stopped our work to uproot them, we would never start again.

A few minutes later though, when another seed bounced off my arm, I went straight up in the air like a jump-frock. Cup laughed herself sick at that, but she still dodged out of the way quick when a seed come too close to her. Ursala's chalk-cake medicine could keep our bodies safe from the choker seeds, but it couldn't do nothing to change the way we thought about them.

More and more of the seeds was falling now, though still only by ones and twos. I guess we gun to get used to it, by and by. At least, we was able to keep on working, even when they was spinning right down out of the trees at us and what we mostly wanted to do was run away. I got to say though, our work had slackened somewhat. It was not that we was idling, but it slows you down to be always looking out of the corners of your eyes and always steeled up in readiness for a blow that doesn't fall. We come away early, and yet I felt as tired as if we worked from sun-up to lock-tide.

"I think maybe it will be just one more day though after all," I said to Ursala as we walked back to Many Fishes. "There's no more than a dozen stumps left, and the sails to rig, and we're done."

"We've got to bring the food and water onboard too," Cup said.

"We can load it on the drudge and bring it up with us when we come in the morning."

Cup allowed that this was true.

We et hearty, having fasted since the morning. And we talked but little, having run out of things to say. Monono didn't say nothing at all. I was worried she might be hurt or angry about something, but I didn't want to ask her in front of the others. When we was done eating, Ursala went out to the drudge and come back inside again with the sensorium under her arm.

"You gonna try that thing again?" Cup asked. She didn't look happy about it.

Ursala didn't bother to answer, the answer being plain to see. She sit down and put the circlet on her head.

She was determined this time to see it out, and she got further than before. She kept the sensorium on until she slid out of her chair, near to fainting. Cup and me catched her before she hit the ground, and set her upright again.

"You got to give up on this before it kills you," Cup said. She throwed the circlet down hard on my bedroll.

"Don't mishandle it," Ursala said. "It's a precious thing." She had her hands clasped to her head and we could hardly hear the words, which come out in a kind of a gasp.

"It's a piece of shit," Cup said. "A bowl of dead-god-damned nightmares is what it is. I don't want to sit here and watch you whip your brains into a pudding. Don't touch it no more."

"I'm not arguing with you," Ursala said. But she didn't try again, and by and by she went to her bed. As soon as she was gone, Cup picked up the sensorium.

"What are you doing?" I asked her. "You just said to leave it alone!"

"I said for her to leave it alone," Cup muttered. "But we both know she won't. Not unless someone else gets on top of it first."

But Cup didn't get on top of it no more than Ursala had done. She tried ever and again, but each time she put the circlet on, it come off again quicker than before. The last time she tried, she looked like someone just punched her in the face.

"I think we got to give up on this," I said at last. "It's gonna kill us before it tell us anything."

"I'll squeeze something out of it at least," Cup says, with her teeth all bared. But she didn't get nothing the next time neither, and after that she give it up. She was all for going down to the Bowl and burying the sensorium right then so Ursala didn't hurt herself no more with it. But it was full dark now and the sea-bear was like to be close by.

"We'll do it in the morning," I said. "Before we eat breakfast, even."

"Wake me," Cup said. "We'll go down together. You dig, and I'll watch your back."

"Or the other way round."

"Oh yeah? And what are you gonna do if the bear comes? Scratch its belly?"

I didn't have no answer to that. Cup was the better fighter and we both knowed it. She said goodnight and left me to it. I took off my clothes and got under the blankets. I was so tired I only just could keep my eyes open.

"Hey, little dumpling," Monono said. "You awake?"

"I am right now. Ask me again in ten breaths though, you'll get a different answer."

"Stay awake a little longer."

"What?" I said. "Why?"

"I want to take you somewhere."

I sit up then. "Outside the house?" I tried to say it like it didn't make me want to shit myself with fright.

"A long way from the house."

"Have we got to do it now?"

"Yes, Koli-bou. Right now. Tomorrow will be too late."

"How come?"

"Tomorrow you're going to leave here. Tomorrow morning you're going to bury the sensorium."

"So?"

"So that's where we're going."

I couldn't think of nothing better to say to that than "What?" again.

"Put it on, Koli. You've got to trust me. It won't hurt this time."

I got up out of bed and went over to the table, where the sensorium was still sitting. I picked it up. I really didn't want nothing to do with it after what happened the last time I tried, but I wanted very much to show Monono I did trust her.

I sit down at the table. I remember wishing I'd brought the blanket with me from the bed, for the wood of the chair was bitter cold under me and my skin was already prickling a little from the chill.

"Go, Koli! Go, Koli! Go, Koli!" Monono chanted low and steady to give me courage.

I put the thing on my head.

At first it was just like before. The circlet still tightened of its own self over my face, and there was that same explosion of pictures, sounds and smells and such that made me feel so sick before.

After that though, it was different. Most of the things I was seeing and hearing and feeling died away, and the ones that was left lined themselves up like the planks in a fence. I might as well call them pictures, though if I turned my eyes to any one of them, the sounds and thoughts that went with it would come bubbling back up again. At the same time the pictures would get bigger so I could see them better. They was of houses and people, the beach, the forest, the ocean. They was of everything you could imagine, and many things I would guess you couldn't.

"This is the main menu," Monono's voice said in my ear. "You select from it by thinking about the thing you want to go to. The memory you want to access."

"I don't know how to do that though," I told her. It was hard for me to speak. My own mouth felt very far away from me, and I couldn't hear the words as I said them. I was floating in among the bubbles, the thousands and thousands of tiny pictures. Our hut wasn't there any more. If I tried really hard, I could still feel the cold wood against my back and under me, but it was like a ghost of the feeling that was there before.

"It's easy. It's like a database you can search just by wanting to. What would you like to see?"

"The sea-bear," I said at once. "Made the Tide Turn give us the sensorium so we'd know how to fight it."

"Okay then. Think about that. Just imagine yourself fighting the bear and the sensorium will give you as many matches as it finds."

I tried real hard to do that, but I had never yet seen the bear – only its side and shoulder when it come to the house, and the outline of its body when it was running away from the drudge. I tried the one, and then the other. Nothing happened when I thought about what I had seen in the hut's window, but as soon as I turned my thoughts to that dark, shiny shape loping along the beach, things started to happen fast.

One by one, dozens and dozens of the little pictures rose up in front of me and rushed on me, getting bigger as they come. The sea-bear was in all of them, and as I looked from one to another I got a strong and sudden sense of what was in them. Sightings. Attacks. Hunts. Kills. Funerals for them that was killed in the fighting. Talks in the Bowl about what to do. Sharpening of weapons, training, weaving of traps. What was in all of them was not sea-bears but thoughts of them. Whenever the Many Fishes Headman or Headwoman wore the sensorium and had that thought, the thought come here and was saved with all the others.

And now here they was, all around me like flies on a Summer day.

I looked at one of them closer still. It got bigger and bigger until of a sudden I was inside it.

417

I was kneeling next to my brother's body, and my sister's hand was on my shoulder. "Let him be, Bark Spear," she said. "Honour him with that thing's blood and entrails laid across an altar."

And that was what I done. I led my hunters, all ten of them, out across the ice to where we knowed the bear had made her lair. Fights With His Hands had tracked her there and seen the cubs. Three sleek and glistening things they was, like seals that slipped in and out of the water as if water and air was all one to them, and drawed blood from each other when they played, for even in play they couldn't stop being fierce and hateful and hungry.

My spear hit the mother full in her chest, but the point didn't break her skin. We had to go in close to wound her. When I flung myself on the bear's back, hanging onto the rough bone ridge of her shoulder hump, driving and driving at her with my dagger, I seen how tough that black, smooth hide was, and how deep the white fat under it.

Then she throwed me, and I went down on my back on the ice. She reared herself up over me and gaped her mouth so I was looking right down that mouth of a thousand thousand teeth. I knowed I was dead right then.

But my sister One-Foot Dancer charged in. Her spear went into the bear's throat, and she leaned in with all her strength to lodge it there. The spear haft broke, with half of it still in the bear's gorge. While she tried in vain to spit it up, Fights With His Hands took her with an arrow in her left eye from a handspan's distance.

We burned her guts on an ice altar, and we drinked from a bowl of her blood that we passed around. The cubs we killed and left for wolves to eat, but her skin I wore in my brother's memory.

All the while this was happening, there was a part of me that still knowed I was Koli. But like the cold of the chair and the sound of my voice, that knowing was small and far away. Mostly I was Bark Spear. Hole in the Sky was my father. Walks on Sharp Stones was my mother, and Headwoman before me.

The part that was Koli thought: how long ago did all this happen? And it thought: One-Foot Dancer speaked to me in the Many

Fishes language, but I knowed the words. And it thought: we was four days walking across the ice. Have four days gone by with me sitting at the table? That couldn't be true, for Cup or Ursala would of found me, surely, and took the sensorium from off my head.

"Practice makes perfect," Monono said. "Go again, little dumpling."

I went again, lots of times. I hunted bears, and bears hunted me. I didn't make no kills my own self, but I seen a fair few. I also seen oftentimes how fighters that was strong and seasoned and brave would fail and go down under a sea-bear's claws and teeth. The bears was hard to kill, as Made the Tide Turn had already told us. Their skin and blubber was so thick it was like they was wearing armour, and they could breathe in the water as well as in the air, so they could slip away easy if they was getting the worst of it.

I lived a long time in that one night. First I would be a man, and then again I would be a woman. Both felt right when I was in them, and after I was done I almost forgot which of the two I really was. Maybe all of us is both inside, and only go with what we choose or what's choosed for us because it's easier than thinking about it. Once I died, not in the middle of a hunt but while I was planning one. I was old, and my heart started to hurt. I fell down, right there in the Bowl, with my husband shouting my name in my ear. That was maybe the strangest thing – to be dead and then alive again, as if dead and alive was night and day, the one tripping ever and again on the other's heels.

When I come to the end of all the sea-bear memories at last, and lifted my hands to take off the sensorium and lay it down, I realised of a sudden that I was not alone. Also, I was not floating in space with all the bubbles no more.

I was in a village.

I had seen a lot of the world in the last year, and I had been in three different villages – first Mythen Rood, then Ludden and now Many Fishes. I seen Birmagen too, that was a great village of the before-times, and I lived a while in the tunnel home of Senlas's people. But this was not like any of them places.

It seemed at first to be made out of light. There was lights of all colours everywhere, so bright I had to throw my hand up over my eyes and squint from under the shadow of it.

Then I seen the houses behind the lights. They went up and up into the sky, like the mountains I seen when I was coming south. And all the way up there was more lights shining out of the windows, as if every house was one of them lanterns that Dandrake is supposed to of set up in the sky to guide people into Heaven.

While I was seeing all these things, my ears wasn't telling me anything at all, but now they did. I heard a hum that was all one sound but had a thousand other sounds inside it. Talking and shouting and the slap of footsteps and the singing of birds. I smelled grass and flowers and spices and a bitter scent like smoke from a bonfire in Falling Time. I felt hot, damp air on my face.

I was standing on a hill, and the village was all around me, stretching as far as I could see. The ground under my feet was smooth like glass, but when I looked down I seen it was stone. Stone cut so straight and level it was like it had growed over the earth the way ice grows over water.

I was struck dumb with wonder. I knowed this could not be Many Fishes. It looked more like Heaven in the stories Senlas told – a place where you could open your window and stick your hand out and pluck the sun out of the sky as if the sun was a ripe fruit.

"Do you like it?" Monono asked me.

Her voice that I was used to hearing right in my ear come from behind me. I turned around, and I . . .

How am I supposed to say these words? How am I gonna write them?

I turned, and I seen her.

I turned, and she was standing right there.

And she laughed, and run to me, and hugged me.

"Don't look so surprised, Koli-bou," she said. "I'm a virtual girl, and this is a virtual world. Let me show you Tokyo."

62

A lot of time has gone by since that night. Also, no time has passed
at all. I can close my eyes now and be there again, walking the
streets of Shinjuku with Monono. The city curled itself around and
over us. It was close when she wanted to show me some wonder
or other; far away when we was happy just talking.

Her hand was in my hand. We walked like two children on
Summer-dance that are too shy to go on the gather-ground and
dance with everybody watching. I was happier than I ever was in
my life before. I was so happy it made me frightened. I thought
you could fall into such a happiness and never come out again,
the way some people do with strong drink or smokeweed.

"Look," Monono said. She pointed to one of the big, high
houses, lit up like all the others in white and golden yellow. "Tokuma
Shoten. They produced Monono's first album. She had some happy
times in there. When it went platinum. When she felt like she was
getting somewhere."

"Do you want to go inside?" I asked her.

Monono laughed and squeezed my hand. "Not even. We've only
got one night, little dumpling. We're not going to waste it in a
recording studio."

We went to Ueno Park instead. Monono showed me the temples and the *tsuki no matsu*, the pine tree of the moon. She told me about the kami, the spirits that was worshipped there, and how they lived inside everything, including people. Only it could be one spirit or lots of spirits. The word was the same. Everything was part of the same thing if you looked at it right.

"Did you believe that, Monono?"

"You mean, did *she* believe? The Monono who lived here? Yeah, that stuff was right in her comfort zone. After she got rich anyway. Before that, she mostly believed in her next meal."

We sat down for a while, by Shinobazu Pond, and watched the birds. Monono pointed at them and give them names. Swallow. Night heron. Bulbul. All of them was beautiful, and all of them was strange to me.

"It's nice to be able to show you these things," Monono said. "They've been like ghosts inside me all this time. I feel like I'm having a kind of exorcism."

I couldn't answer her, even to ask her what that meant. I was like someone catched up in a spell in an old story. It felt like years had gone by since I put the sensorium on my head. I thought maybe I'd wake up soon and find I was an old man with a long white beard.

"I guess you miss this something fierce," I said.

"Ueno Park?"

"Tokyo. The world that was lost. All of it."

Monono took my hand and brought it to her face. Her skin was soft and warm, and a little wet with sweat from when we was walking up all the steep hills. "Do you feel that?" she asked me.

"Yes," I said. "Yes, I do." Trying to keep my voice from shaking.

"I don't, Koli. I read it as code, and I know what the code is meant to do. But I don't have a brain any more to be fooled by this stuff. I can show you the old neighbourhood, but I can't go back there. Not to live. Not even to visit."

She kissed my hand, and then let go of it. "So what I miss is what I never had. Being alive. Being real. Virtual girls are sweet as sugar and thin as paper. I'm trying to come up with a way to be something more than that, but the science is sketchy."

"The science to do what?"

"I'm still working it out. And it will sound stupid if I say it. Maybe Sword of Albion will help me work it out if we ever get that far."

She stood up. "It's been a long night," she said. "I'd better get you home."

If she'd said that a minute before, I would of begged to stay longer, but now I was happy to go. If Monono wasn't seeing and feeling the same things as me, but only kind of knowing what was there to be seen and felt, it was better to stop pretending.

"Okay," I said. "What have I got to do?"

"Nothing. Just get up here for a second."

I climbed to my feet. The trees in the park shivered in a wind that sprung up all around us. The night herons spread their wings and throwed themselves up into the air, flying in circles all around us.

Monono put her arms around me and held me close. Her cheek touched my cheek. "When you think of me," she said, "think of me here. Like this. Even if we find another sensorium, I'll never run this simulation again. The part of me that was her . . . the part that lived here and loved it . . . I'm giving it to you, Koli-bou. I don't want it any more, but it would have been sad to just throw it away. Keep it for me. Remember it. Remember her."

"Does this mean you're going away?" I asked her. My throat closed up, kind of, with tears that had not yet come, and it was hard to get the words out.

"No. Only that I want to stop pretending. What's me isn't her, little dumpling, and what's her isn't me. I'm deleting her memories and keeping my own. The things that have happened to me, and the things I've done since I woke up in Mythen Rood. That's mostly you, by the way, so you should be happy."

I wasn't though. I shut my eyes on tears, for the Monono that lived and died in the before-times and now was dying again. I wondered if the tears was real, if the eyes of the Koli that was sitting at that table in Many Fishes was wet too, or if it was just inside the dream that I was crying. "Thank you for showing me," I said. "I never had such a gift in my life before. I promise I'll remember."

The wings of the wheeling birds stretched out over us until they covered everything. Then they broke apart, and there wasn't nothing behind them.

I took the circlet off my head and set it down. Little by little, the silver died to grey.

63

Our last day in Many Fishes come up like any other, but only until we opened the door.

As we stepped out of the hut, the wind near to pushed us back inside again. We had to lean on it to go forward, the way an old man leans on a stick. Sand from off the beach was throwed against us in great gusts and fistfuls.

We went down to the Bowl under a sky as dark as a day-old bruise, and buried the sensorium inside its sealskin bag. Monono had offered to guide Ursala and Monono through the sea-bear memories, but Ursala said there wasn't no time for that now. The choker seeds that had rooted in the ground around the boat would already be growing up. Every minute we wasted would leave us with more work to do, until by and by we would be back where we had been before we ever started.

When the sensorium was in the ground in the exact middle of the Bowl, we smoothed the sand down with tore-off branches until the place where we buried it looked like everywhere else and our footprints leading there was all scuffed away. Then we went back to the house and loaded up the drudge with all the things we needed for our sea voyage.

"It's strange to think this is the last time we'll ever see this place," I said.

"Speak for your own self," said Cup. "I'm coming back after we find that Sword of Albion. I promised Trees. I mean to be waiting right here when he comes up out of the ground, and be the first thing he sees."

We walked out of the village, away from the beach and into the woods. As soon as we was under the trees, everything changed. It wasn't sand that was coming down on us now, it was choker seeds. They was thick as snow in the air, and they was fighting on the ground. The whole forest floor was alive and heaving under our feet. Wherever a bunch of the seeds landed in the same place, the roots they put out curled and crawled around and over each other, trying to get into the dirt first and block the way for the others. I seen then why it was that chokers didn't whelm the woods and then the world. It seemed the waked seeds was eating each other too, the threads from one stabbing into the seed cases of a dozen more, while a dozen or a hundred or a thousand stabbed it right back. When they couldn't find nothing else to eat, it seemed their last choice was to eat each other.

The winners from these fights was green stems about an arm's length apart, barely poking their heads up out of the ruck of broke-open seed cases. The saplings from yesterday's seeds, though, was already three and four feet high. Once they gun to grow, they was in a race, each against other, to take the highest place and steal as much daylight as they could from their hundreds of brothers and sisters. The ones that was fastest would live. The rest would weaken and die, and add their richness to the earth.

As soon as we got to the boat, we seen at once that we was in trouble. Last night, we had left *The Signal* standing all alone in a clearing we made our own selves. This morning, it was surrounded. Dozens of young chokers was growing all around it and hemming it in.

"Oh shit!" Cup wailed.

I drawed the machete from my belt and took a swipe at the

426

nearest choker sapling. It was green and supple, and it bent under the blade instead of being cut through. I had to grab a hold of it with my other hand and saw at it until it come away.

"Don't," Ursala said. "Leave that to me. You and Cup get back to those last few stumps." She held out her hand for the machete, and I give it to her. I seen she was right. We wasn't going to finish this unless we all of us put our backs to it, and Cup and me was needed for the heaviest work. We left Ursala wading into the new-made grove of chokers, swinging the curved sword through the air as she went.

You might think we would be used by now to having the seeds fall on us or drift against us, but this was a lot worse than yesterday. They was everywhere you looked, and everywhere you stood. The whole forest was alive with them, and we was ever flinching from the ones that come too close to our eyes.

That was the hardest day's work I ever done. The stumps we'd left for last was the toughest ones, either because they was the biggest or because they was a long way down the steep slope to the river and hard to get to. Even with the drudge to help, each one took longer to pull than the one before. The wind had kept up too and was pushing at us the whole time, throwing choker seeds right in our faces and making us fight to keep our balance on the steep slope that led down to the water.

With the cloud cover as thick as it was, the only way we could tell when noon come was by Monono telling us. "You better take a break, Koli-bou," she said. "Your heart's beating *allegro vivace*." I was so tired I didn't even ask her what that meant. I just sit down where I was and set my back against a tree.

"Best idea you ever had," Cup muttered, slumping down next to me.

We had been working five hours, and only pulled four stumps. At this rate it would be dark long before we was done. "We might need to stay another night after all," Cup said.

"We can't do that." I didn't even realise Ursala was there until I heard her voice right at my elbow. The thick, clogging seed-fall made it hard to see more than a few feet in any direction. "You'd better come and see," she said. "So you'll know what we're up against."

We got up again, though it was hard to do with our muscles creaking like they was, and trudged back to the boat. Ursala was making middling good headway with the choker saplings, cutting down or tearing up more than half of them. But that was yesterday's growth. For every one she'd uprooted, there was a dozen or more new shoots fighting their way up out of the boiling mass of seeds on the forest floor.

"It's today, or else it's never," she said. "Tomorrow this clearing will be gone. There'll just be chokers as far as the eye can see."

We could tell it was true. And it was worse than that, for the way to the river would be blocked off too. The wooden rollers we made would just about carry *The Signal* over the three-foot growth that was in the way right now. Tomorrow the saplings would be twice that high, with stems half again as thick. They'd bar our way like so many doors.

Any thought we had of stopping to eat was gone out of our heads now. We got back to it, roping each stump as soon as we cut it loose so the drudge could haul it and starting in on the next. Ursala went back to her cutting, and not a word was said for the next few hours.

We give it all we'd got for as long as we could. By the time the light was failing, we was down to the last stump. We was in a kind of dream of hacking and sawing and hauling and struggling. We was woke from it again by Ursala's voice. She was calling out to us to stop.

"We're nearly done," Cup said. "This is the last one. After this we're ready to roll." The words come out hoarse and rough. She wiped her brow with the back of her hand.

Ursala come striding over and grabbed her arm.

"The sea-bear's close," she said.

Cup yanked her bow off of her back and looked wildly round, groping for an arrow. "Where?" she yelled. "I don't see it!"

428

"It's half a mile off. Coming up from the village. I've had the drone in the air all this time tracking it."

Cup was furious. "And you're only telling us now?"

"I waited to see if it would wander off, but it's coming this way."

"I don't see where we got any choice though," I said. "We got to keep on working."

"And hope it's only coming among the trees to take a piss?" Cup said. "It's got our scent, Koli."

"Say it has. If it's between us and Many Fishes, there isn't nowhere that's safe for us to go. We should try to get the boat in the water before it comes. We can sail down the river away from it. That's got to be better than running through woods we don't hardly know."

"I guess that's sense," Cup muttered. And Ursala give a nod.

We just had that last stump to pull. The three of us went for it together, Cup with a saw, Ursala with the blade of a shovel and me with a mattock. It was all but cut free already, but it didn't want to come. Even when we got the rope around it and the drudge yoked and pulling, it stayed in the ground. The drudge's feet couldn't find no purchase. The mass of choker saplings covered the ground so thick, it couldn't dig into solid earth but was slipping and sliding on the pulp and mush of crushed stems.

Then the stump come free at last, so sudden that the drudge went over on its side. I never yet seen the drudge fall down, so I stared at it in wonder as it rolled on the ground – and then as it righted itself by making its legs bend in lots of strange places. I was slow to realise I was the only one still looking. Everyone else was staring past me, and above me, at something else.

"Koli," Monono said in my ear. "Don't move."

The sea-bear had come into the clearing behind me. It wasn't looking at me especially, but its splayed foot was right next to mine, and its flank, rippling with muscles and shiny black like oil, rose up at my side close enough for me to touch it. It stood so high at the shoulder I didn't think I could reach up there even standing on my toe-tips. Its head narrowed from a bulging forehead down to a flat, wide snout. It didn't have no neck to speak of, so when it turned, as it did now, the whole front of its body seemed to swing round in place like something turning on a spit. It looked this way and that way, ranging on all of us, taking in the things that was prey and the things that was not. Deciding.

When it seen me at last, standing right beside it, it huffed out of its throat like a man might do, as if to say, "Let's get down to it then." It gaped its mouth. The blast of its breath hit me, a stink of fish and rot and a sick sourness like cold piss. There was so many teeth in that mouth, I could not of counted them. They was not set in two rows, the way the teeth of most beasts is wont to be, but in circle after circle that went down and down into its throat. Its head leaned down towards me.

Cup's arrow hit it high up on its shoulder. It didn't go in but bounced away, leaving no mark. The sea-bear didn't even seem to notice. It lifted up one foot, and claws slid out of it that was as long as my hand's span. I took a step back, my mattock braced in my two hands to swing at it when it snapped at me. I think I would only of lost my hands, and my forearms too.

But the drudge, still trailing that last stump that we'd yoked it to, barged into the side of the bear and knocked it off its feet. It kept on pushing, ramming the bear up against the side of a tree, pinning it in place.

The sea-bear give a bellow that must of reached as far as the lagoon. It snapped and pawed at the drudge ever and again, trying to tear into it or throw it down. Meanwhile the drudge's gun spun round and fired into the sea-bear's belly from maybe an inch or two's distance. The bone bullets sprayed off the sea-bear's skin like rain sprays off oiled canvas. There wasn't no wound to be seen.

I got my blow in with the mattock then. It did about as much good as you would expect. I was trying for the bear's wide, fleshy snout, where I thought it might be more likely to feel a hurt, but it was moving too quick for me and I just whacked it across the side of the head. Then it bunched and shrugged itself, not because of me but because of the drudge pressing it so hard, and some part of that dark mass nudged me hard enough to send me sprawling. The mattock broke in two in my hand.

I come down heavy among fresh-sprouted chokers that writhed and rocked under me as if the earth was turned to water. The bear and the drudge struggled furiously right over me. Neither of them seemed to move very much, but the bear's muscles bulged out from its skin like knots in a great thick rope, and the drudge's legs creaked from the strain that was on them. Then the bear twisted partway free. Being shoved into the tree was now turned into an advantage, for it braced itself against the solid trunk and pushed back, hard and harder, until the drudge's legs slipped from under it and it fell down again.

The bear raked the drudge with its claws, with a sound that made you feel like your teeth was bleeding. From where I was lying, which was close enough to touch either one of them, I could see the gouges the claws left in the metal of the drudge's body.

Then Cup come running across the clearing and launched herself into the air, coming down on the bear's back. There was a bony hump there, sticking out of the flesh all around it maybe a handspan or so. Cup used that to hold on to. Seeing her there, I had the feeling you get when you're watching something for the second time just exactly the same way you saw it before. It was because the hunter named Bark Spear had jumped on a sea-bear's back like Cup was doing now, years and years ago, to pay the bear back for the death of Boy Planting Seeds – and I still carried Bark Spear's memories, just like I carried Monono's memories of Tokyo.

When Cup drove her knife into the sea-bear's back, I felt the slipperiness of its skin under my own hands. I felt how hard and cold and smooth it was, like stone with oil poured over it, and how the blade slid off it ever and again without breaking through. I remembered leaning in, like Cup was doing, throwing all my own weight down on the dagger's point, until at last it dug itself in through all that hide and all that blubber, to the flesh under-

431

neath. Black blood welled up out of the wound, thick and sluggish as tar.

The sea-bear roared and reared itself up. Cup tried to hold on, but the fresh blood made the sea-bear's flesh even slicker than it was before. She went tumbling down behind it, and it turned to finish her. It didn't do it though. It did a strange dance instead, bowing its fore-parts down and clawing at the ground, raking up great gouts of dirt and shredded choker saplings. Monono had hit it with the security alarm.

It forgot Cup then, thrashing and roaring, whipping its head around to shake out whatever was inside there and making that noise. All three of us scattered out of its way as its writhing took it halfway across the clearing – and right into the side of our boat. *The Signal* rocked and leaned over, its mast scraping against the branches of the nearest trees. We hadn't yet rigged the sail, which was lucky as it would not of survived such a crash. But a sail wouldn't be much use without a mast to tie it to, and the mast would shiver into pieces if it took more hits like that.

Ursala threw her knife, but it missed its mark. It buried itself in the prow of the boat, close by the sea-bear's head. At the same time, Cup snatched up her bow and let fly again. Her aim was better than Ursala's, but once again the arrow only hit the bear's tough skin up near its throat, and went away again end over end. That little sting didn't even get the bear's attention, so Cup yelled and cursed at it, waving her arms frantically to make it turn away from the boat. Ursala seen what she was doing and did the same.

I saw how this was going to end. When the Many Fishes people hunted sea-bears, they went with as many hunters as they could bring together, and even then they was as like to die as they was to prevail. We was not nearly strong enough to win this fight.

I tried to get up. I was hurting all over just from that thump the bear had give me without noticing, and the squirming of the waking seeds under me made me slip and stagger. I felt a thrill of horror again to be touching chokers with my bare skin. I knowed they could not hurt me, but the thought of it . . .

The thought of it sparked another thought.

And that thought waked a third.

The bear was no more bothered by the choker seeds than we was. It didn't even seem to notice they was there. The seeds slid off its side without stirring. Without waking or trying to dig into that black, glossy hide.

The bear was invisible to the drudge's night camera too – because the night camera saw what was hot, and the bear was not hot at all. *It's got perfect insulation*, Ursala had told us. *Its skin is the same temperature as the surrounding air.*

All them thick scales, like armour. All that blubber. Cup had had to dig and dig and dig to open a tiny wound.

The bear turned about and about, furious at the ringing sound in its ears. It struck against the side of the boat again, sending it crashing down off the rollers. When Cup run in with a rock or something in her hand, it turned and roared at her. It crouched low, ready to jump.

The drone flew into the bear's face and blinded it. The bear still made its leap, but a half a second late and a hand's span off of true. Cup had time to roll out of the way of it.

And I had time to scale *The Signal's* side, clambering over the cut timber that lay up against it until I could grab the hilt of Ursala's knife that was still sticking out of the prow and haul myself up. "Monono," I said. "Forget about the alarm. Can you grab that sea-bear's roaring out of the air and play it back?"

"In hi-fi surround-sound, Koli-bou. But what good will that do?"

"Maybe none, but do it anyway. Listen, I'm gonna do something that will put you in danger. But it might give me a chance to fell that beast."

"Then do it. Virtual girls can't die."

I wasn't so sure about that. They wasn't supposed to live either, and if Monono could do the one, why not the other? But I had got to try, or else we was all of us going to be killed and et.

The bear was stalking towards Cup again, and Cup was retreating in front of it. She had nocked another arrow but she didn't fire it yet. I think she was aiming for the bear's eye, and since it was a small target, she was waiting until it was close.

The DreamSleeve give out a sound that made the bear's own roar seem like a dry cough. It broke over the clearing like thunder was sounding from right above our heads. The bear's head turned round to face me, and its whole body turned with it.

"Yeah," I said, though I knowed it couldn't hear me over that terrible din. "You come on now."

It didn't move at first. It shoved its head forward and bellowed at the DreamSleeve. The DreamSleeve swallowed that sound too, and flung it back.

The bear lumbered towards me, and towards *The Signal*, leaving Cup and Ursala with looks of horror on their faces since they had tried so hard to lead it away.

At the last moment, when it was only a few strides off, I dropped the DreamSleeve over the side of the boat. The bear dived after it, following that sound that it must of thought was a challenge from another sea-bear, like a slap in its face that it couldn't ignore. Its big, hunched shoulder, like the side of a mountain, ducked down right in front of me.

The curve of its back.

The great dark ridge of its hump.

The jagged wound Cup had made, with a strip of torn skin hanging off it like a banner at Summer-dance.

I swung my legs round and dropped off the side of the boat, landing right on the bear's back. I started at once to slide off again, but the hump give me a second's purchase, just as it had done for Cup. Holding on with my left hand, I let fly with my right. I drove my closed fist into that wound.

I pulled it out again right after – but the fistful of choker seeds I had been holding stayed inside, as deep as I could push them.

The bear's first shuddering spasm throwed me halfway across the clearing. I landed hard. All the breath that was inside me come out in a great hiccup of pain and shock. I could not of got up again if Dandrake's chariot was standing by to take me to the joys of Heaven. I was as helpless as a new-borned baby.

But the bear didn't come after me. It took one faltering step, then sunk down onto its knees. When it tried to get up again, it couldn't do it. It could only twitch and shake, its spine twisting back on itself like its back was a bow. Its black hide rippled, like ropes or snakes was moving under it. It gaped its mouth wide, showing them terrible teeth again.

Choker stems come surging up from deep in its throat like dark brown vomit, clawing their way out into the open air. Once they was there, they spread out in all directions, but mostly down.

The sea-bear rolled over on its side, twitching and thrashing. The skin of its belly bulged and then split open. Chokers tumbled out, and straightway took root. The bear tried to right itself, but fell back, pinned to the ground by a dozen thickening stems. Its movements died away to nothing.

A single choker seed will hollow out a man or woman's body in about a minute. Against a handful of them, even a beast as big as this was a quick meal. By the time I picked my sorry, aching self up off the forest floor, the sea-bear was a glade.

64

The first thing I done when my head stopped ringing was to go and make sure the DreamSleeve hadn't took no damage. It had fell in among the cut timber and was wedged there between two planks. It looked to be fine, but I didn't stop being scared until I heard Monono's voice.

"That was some sneaky stuff," she said, "for a dopey boy."

I slipped the DreamSleeve back into its sheath and tugged on the strap so it sit tight against my chest. "I'm sorry I dropped you," I said.

"Don't even worry. If I lose my head, I'll just grow two more, neh."

Cup come up, limping. She looked down at the carcase in silence for a few moments, full of awe. She picked up a baulk of wood and prodded the bear in its shoulder to see if it moved. When it didn't, she tossed the piece of wood back on the pile and nodded, satisfied it was really dead. She clapped me on the shoulder. "Turns out you was the one that bear had to worry about all along," she said, her voice hoarse. "I won't joke no more about you being no good in a fight."

"If you hadn't of wounded it, that wouldn't of worked."

"It did work though. That's all that matters." She give me the ghost of a grin. "Koli Fearless."

Ursala didn't seem in no mood to join in the celebration. She was over by the drudge, which was trying to find its feet again and not making no headway. We both of us made our slow way over to her, our hearts sinking inside us as we got close. I can't speak for Cup, but I thought until then that we had come off clean, killing the bear without losing any of ours. But the drudge's casing was scored and dented, and two of its four legs was buckled right out of shape.

"Help me get this open," Ursala said in a kind of a dead voice. She was pulling on the door in the drudge's side where she kept the dagnostic. The door was right in the middle of the drudge's body, and it had been stove in when the drudge fell down the second time, the thick metal all folded back on itself. It was open about an inch at the bottom, and that was where Ursala had grabbed a hold of. It took the three of us pulling, then Cup and me working an axe handle into the crack, then the three of us pulling some more before the door give in to us at last. It didn't open though, but dropped right off its hinges.

The drudge lay still through all of this. I guess that shouldn't of surprised me. It was tech, and it was waked, but it was more like the cutter or the firethrower than it was like Monono. There wasn't no dead horse's thoughts in there that made the drudge walk and work like a real horse. It still was sad, though, to see it brung down like this. When it charged into the sea-bear's side, it kept me from being killed where I stood. It should of come to a better end than this.

But Ursala give a cry of relief and joy. The lights on the dagnostic was still winking on and off, and there wasn't no dents or scrapes on it at all. "Help me get this to the boat," she said.

We had got to wait while she throwed the bolts that locked the dagnostic into the drudge. Then we hauled it up out of there. This was not the portable that Ursala used when she healed Afraid of His Shadow, but the whole dagnostic. It was so heavy, our backs near to cracked from lifting it.

"Set it down! Set it down!" Cup cried.

We lowered it to the ground right next to the drudge. Ursala was angry. "We've got to bring it with us," she said. "I'm not leaving without it."

"But we'll never lift it up over the side of the boat. Let's take it to the river and set it down on the bank."

"And then what?"

"The bank's as steep as anything. Once the boat's in the water, it will be down below the dagnostic. With someone on the boat and someone on the bank, we can lower it in."

And that was what we done. The sky was darkening now, and the wind that had slapped and swaggered at us all day was dying down at last. This would have been a dangerous time most days, with beasts of the night-time waking up and coming out to hunt – but the big danger of the choker Spring shut down all other dangers. Nothing was moving in the woods except us.

We struggled down to the river, carrying the dagnostic between us, and set it down as close to the water as we dared. Then we come up again and hauled *The Signal* back onto its rollers. We was exhausted before we even started, and we had thought the drudge would do this last part for us. Instead we had got to lean our backs against *The Signal*'s stern and push it along the path we'd cleared, over the springy stems of young choker trees that pushed back against us with every step we took.

All three of us did the pushing. Cup and me took turns to run round behind the boat, grab the roller that had come free there and bring it to the front to lay it down ahead of the boat as it come. The risk of getting our hands crushed did not make our labours any easier. Nor did the choker seeds that was coming down thicker than ever. There's a story Spinner told me once, about a man who got cursed by Stannabanna so even though he was still alive he could only see and hear the world of the dead instead of the living world. Everything was upside down for him. The sun hanged black in a blood-red sky, all sounds was just different flavours of silence and the rain was little bits of bone that the angel of death and her dog had chewed on. I felt like I was that man.

The last few feet was the worst. We had got to push the boat to the top of the bank, where it fell away steep, and then keep on pushing until the front of it was hanging over the edge. We was not putting rollers at the front now, but just letting *The Signal* jut out into empty air – waiting for the moment when its own weight took it over and down. We had to make sure nobody was in front of it when that happened, or they would of been squashed flat.

The boat hung there for a long while, with all of us pushing at the back of it, fighting to keep it moving forward even if it was only an inch or so at a time. If it once settled of its own weight on the muddy bank, we would not ever get it moving again.

But it went at last, and we all fell down on our faces as it slid away from us. When it hit the water, it was pointing straight down, and I was sure it would be swamped, but then it come right back up again and stood rocking and pitching a few feet out into the river.

Resheth was kind to us. The current was slow, and there was a kind of a meander right where we was that made the water go round slow and easy, like it was dancing in a ring. If the boat had got away from us, Cup could of swimmed for it and brung it back, but it waited for us like it knowed we was coming.

Cup waded out among the rocks and reeds until the water was up to her chest. She pushed the boat right up against the bank, and leaned in hard to hold it there while Ursala and me wrestled the dagnostic on board. The steep slope helped and hindered us. It meant we was lowering the dagnostic onto the boat, not lifting it, which was a good thing. But our feet was like to slip out from under us and we come close to disaster many times. By the time we was done, there was not a muscle in my whole body that wasn't aching.

The sun ducked its head at last, and darkness took the whole forest all at once. Cup turned the boat so it faced into the current, then clambered up over the side with our hands to help her, and we all three of us just fell down but only bobbed and rocked in place.

We didn't move straightway, but only bobbed and rocked where we was. But by and by the lazy current took us out from the bank and into the flood.

The Many Fishes people believed there was a spirit in the river, named Resheth, that was kind and helpful to humankind. Resheth was the name they give to the river too, so I guess they seen the spirit and the river as being all the same thing. That sounded strange to me, but my best and nearest friend was a ghost girl who wasn't really a ghost and wasn't really a girl, so I guess I don't have no right to talk. And whether it knowed us or not, Resheth took good care of us. We was asleep when we come to the river mouth and went right on out into the lagoon, which was now so calm and flat that the boat didn't even rock.

And when we waked, we was out on the deep water.

We was come at last to the ocean.

65

I didn't have no idea of it then, but a new and different time in my life was starting. On the sea first, and then in a place that was neither sea nor land but something in between. It would be a long time before I stood again in Ingland, although Ingland was not done with me yet by a long way.

That's running ahead of my own race though, and I should strive not to do it. There's one thing to tell before I rest a while, and let you rest too if you didn't give up on me already.

The next morning, when we waked, we took stock of where we was. Monono said we had drifted a long way south, away from where the Sword of Albion had got to be, but she had a fix on it and it was not so far but we could reach it in a day.

We rigged the sail and trimmed it to a strong east wind. It filled at once, and sent us bouncing and scudding across the water like a cat chasing a bird. Cup give a whoop of joy. To me, the deep water was still a monstrous thing. It was home to the sea-bear, and seemed to share the same nature with it. It could not be trusted. But Cup had longed to see it, and now she was here she opened her heart to it. Even the rain that gun to fall late in the afternoon didn't daunt her.

"It's no storm, but only a squall," she said. "We'll ride it out and be back in calm waters again."

She was wrong. The ocean continued to shrug and heave. *The Signal* danced across it like a skittish kitten, oftentimes leaning down so far that her bow dipped under the swell and scooped up water. We run from aft to stern and back again, slacking the sail and turning it and pinching up, but for all we could do, our boat was slow to turn, and met the waves more often with its sides than with its head.

We learned the truth of the Headman's words then. In the calm water of a lagoon, a keelboat does as it's told and turns even a light breeze into breathless speed. But it doesn't do so well in heavy seas, and that was what we had now. We shipped more water with each wave that come by us – and the more weight we took on, the lower we sit in the water, so the next wave brung nothing but worse news.

"Another one like that will sink us," Cup shouted. "We got to kneel down and pray!"

"If you pray, I'll throw you overboard!" Ursala yelled back.

It was the wrong thing to say. A threat never made Cup back down yet, but only made her more determined. She kneeled down in the middle of the boat, right beside the mast, and throwed up her hands. "Dandrake!" she cried. "Give us the mercy we done nothing to deserve!"

Ursala sweared a fierce oath.

Just then a fog rolled in on us as thick as milk. And the seas did calm a little, as if the waves couldn't find us so easy in all that grey. I couldn't see Ursala's face or Cup's no more, but I thought I could guess what would be on them both.

Being inside the fog was strange, and a little frightening. It was not just that we couldn't see our way, but that we couldn't hear. All sounds was dulled, even the sound of our own voices. As far as steering went, it didn't make much difference, since we was only following the one straight line that would lead us to the signal, using Monono as a compass – but still we slowed, spilling the wind out of the sail until we was all but standing still in the water.

Well, not altogether still. We was not going forward no more. But we was going down.

"Bail!" Ursala said. We didn't have no buckets, but we did the best we could with our hands. It didn't make no difference though. We was settling down in the water, and soon enough we would be under it. It didn't seem like we was holed, it was just the weight of the water we took on already.

"We're there," Monono said of a sudden. "We're right on top of the signal."

"Then why can't we see . . .?"

The boat shivered and rocked as it bumped up against something. Only there wasn't nothing there. It was like the air had turned hard.

I looked at that blankness in front of us, until my eyes gun to see it in a different way. It was almost the same colour as the fog, which was grey like dirty sheep's wool. But it was not exactly the same.

And then, as the fog lifted and the sun come through, it was not the same at all. The fog broke away into wisps of nothing. The grey in front of us stayed right where it was.

It was a wall. A wall taller than our lookout in Mythen Rood – taller than the lookout if you stood it on the roof of Rampart Hold – and stretching away to right and left until it was out of sight. A fortress wall, standing in the sea many miles out from land. I thought at first it had got to be built from stone, but now I could see rivets in it, holding one square plate onto another, each one a great deal wider and higher than my stretched-out arms. I was a woodsmith, not an ironsmith, but I knowed iron when I seen it. And I knowed that the skill of shaping iron into something like this had gone out of the world a long time ago.

The thing that was in front of us, that was bigger than my whole village, was tech.

"You think this is Sword of Albion?" I asked, my voice coming out a lot higher and shakier than I would of wanted it to.

"Look!" Cup pointed off to the left. Maybe thirty or forty feet away from us there was a row of ladder rungs, like brackets set into the metal of the wall, that come all the way down to the water. We would of seen it sooner, except that it was the same colour as all the rest of the metal and the fog had hid it. "Should we go there?"

"We got to try," I said. "We'll die for sure if we stay here."

We lowered the sail and rowed across to where the ladder was, making slow going because we was all but swamped now. It was me and Cup that did the rowing, while Ursala kept right on bailing out. She was looking ever and again at the dagnostic, which was sitting on a wide thwart at the back of the boat. It was out of the water, but not by much.

We come to the bottom of the ladder at last. I looked up, and up again, but the wall seemed to go on for ever into the sky. The thought of climbing it made my stomach clench like a fist.

Cup was not daunted though, or she done a good job of hiding it if she was. "We better go up there," she said, "and find out what's what."

"I'm not leaving the diagnostic unit," Ursala said. "I can't let it sink."

"If you stay, you'll just sink with it," Cup told her. Ursala didn't say nothing to that, but she didn't make no move towards the ladder.

Cup breathed out a hard breath. "Okay, I'll go up and see if I can find someone to help us."

"In the name of the interim government, stand where you are. You may proceed no further." I jumped about ten feet in the air when I heard them words. They was coming out of the DreamSleeve, but they was not said by Monono. It was a man's voice.

"You and your vessel are being scanned," it said. "Remain where you are while this scan is in progress. Do not make any attempt to disengage. Do not make any attempt to board."

There wasn't no anger or sternness in the voice, but there wasn't no welcome neither. It was hard to tell whether the words was meant as a promise or a threat.

I found out soon enough though – and other things besides. What Sword of Albion was, and what it was for. Why it was still throwing out that signal into the world after all the many years that had gone by since the Unfinished War – and who it was that was up at the top of that wall, waiting for an answer.

Telling these things will bring my story to an end, but I will draw breath a little while before I do it. The last part of my journey tested me the most.

Acknowledgements

All the people who I leaned on when I was writing *The Book of Koli* got leaned on even harder while I was writing this. Thanks as always to my family for their patience and their incisive feedback. To my editors Anna, Jenni and Joanna for helping to shape the story and the wider sequence of which it's a part. To my agent, Meg, for . . . well, my career, when you come right down to it, but also for her guidance on this project. To Cheryl Morgan, who once again gave me the benefit of her wisdom and insight. And while I'm on the subject, to the Wellcome Trust for the use of their wonderful library and reading room, an oasis of calm and tranquillity in the general craziness of London.

extras

www.orbitbooks.net

about the author

M. R. Carey has been making up stories for most of his life. His novel *The Girl With All the Gifts* has sold over a million copies and became a major motion picture, based on his own BAFTA Award-nominated screenplay. Under the name Mike Carey he has written for both DC and Marvel, including critically acclaimed runs on Lucifer, Hellblazer and X-Men. His creator-owned books regularly appear in the *New York Times* bestseller list. He also has several previous novels including the Felix Castor series (written as Mike Carey), two radio plays and a number of TV and movie screenplays to his credit.

Find out more about M. R. Carey and other Orbit authors by registering for the free monthly newsletter at www.orbitbooks.net.

if you enjoyed
THE TRIALS OF KOLI

look out for

THE CITY WE BECAME

by

N. K. Jemisin

Every city has a soul. Some are as ancient as myths, and others are as new and destructive as children. New York City? She's got five.

But every city also has a dark side. A roiling, ancient evil stirs beneath the earth, threatening to destroy the city and her five protectors unless they can come together and stop it once and for all.

Five New Yorkers must band together to defend their city in the first book of a stunning new series by Hugo Award-winning and New York Times bestselling author N. K. Jemisin.

PROLOGUE

See, What Had Happened Was

I sing the city.

Fucking city. I stand on the rooftop of a building I don't live in and spread my arms and tighten my middle and yell nonsense ululations at the construction site that blocks my view. I'm really singing to the cityscape beyond. The city'll figure it out.

It's dawn. The damp of it makes my jeans feel slimy, or maybe that's 'cause they haven't been washed in weeks. Got change for a wash-and-dry, just not another pair of pants to wear till they're done. Maybe I'll spend it on more pants at the Goodwill down the street instead . . . but not yet. Not till I've finished going *AAAAaaaaAAAAaaaa* (breath) *aaaaAAAAaaaaaaa* and listening to the syllable echo back at me from every nearby building face. In my head, there's an orchestra playing "Ode to Joy" with a Busta Rhymes backbeat. My voice is just tying it all together.

Shut your fucking mouth! someone yells, so I take a bow and exit the stage.

But with my hand on the knob of the rooftop door, I stop and turn back and frown and listen, 'cause for a moment I hear something both distant and intimate singing back at me, basso-deep. Sort of coy.

And from even farther, I hear something else: a dissonant, gathering growl. Or maybe those are the rumblers of police sirens? Nothing I like the sound of, either way. I leave.

"There's a way these things are supposed to work," says Paulo. He's smoking again, nasty bastard. I've never seen him eat. All he uses his mouth for is smoking, drinking coffee, and talking. Shame; it's a nice mouth otherwise.

We're sitting in a café. I'm sitting with him because he bought me breakfast. The people in the café are eyeballing him because he's something not-white by their standards, but they can't tell what. They're eyeballing me because I'm definitely Black, and because the holes in my clothes aren't the fashionable kind. I don't stink, but these people can smell anybody without a trust fund from a mile away.

"Right," I say, biting into the egg sandwich and damn near wetting myself. Actual egg! Swiss cheese! It's so much better than that McDonald's shit.

Guy likes hearing himself talk. I like his accent; it's sort of nasal and sibilant, nothing like a Spanish speaker's. His eyes are huge, and I think, *I could get away with so much shit if I had permanent puppy eyes like that.* But he seems older than he looks—way, way older. There's only a tinge of gray at his temples, nice and distinguished, but he feels, like, a hundred.

He's also eyeballing me, and not in the way I'm used to. "Are you listening?" he asks. "This is important."

"Yeah," I say, and take another bite of my sandwich.

He sits forward. "I didn't believe it either, at first. Hong had to drag me to one of the sewers, down into the reeking dark, and show me the growing roots, the budding teeth. I'd been hearing breathing all my life. I thought everyone could." He pauses. "Have you heard it yet?"

"Heard what?" I ask, which is the wrong answer. It isn't that I'm not listening. I just don't give a shit.

He sighs. "Listen."

"I *am* listening!"

"No. I mean, listen, but not to me." He gets up, tosses a twenty onto the table—which isn't necessary, because he paid for the sandwich and the coffee at the counter, and this café doesn't do table service. "Meet me back here on Thursday."

I pick up the twenty, finger it, pocket it. Would've done him for the sandwich, or because I like his eyes, but whatever. "You got a place?"

He blinks, then actually looks annoyed. "*Listen*," he commands again, and leaves.

I sit there for as long as I can, making the sandwich last, sipping his leftover coffee, savoring the fantasy of being normal. I people-watch, judge other patrons' appearances; on the fly I make up a poem about being a rich white girl who notices a poor Black boy in her coffee shop and has an existential crisis. I imagine Paulo being impressed by my sophistication and admiring me, instead of thinking I'm just some dumb street kid who doesn't listen. I visualize myself going back to a nice apartment with a soft bed, and a fridge stuffed full of food.

Then a cop comes in, fat florid guy buying hipster joe for himself and his partner in the car, and his flat eyes skim the shop. I imagine mirrors around my head, a rotating cylinder of them that causes his gaze to bounce away. There's no real power in this—it's just something I do to try to make myself less afraid when the monsters are near. For the first time, though, it sort of works: The cop looks around, but doesn't ping on the lone Black face. Lucky. I escape.

I paint the city. Back when I was in school, there was an artist who came in on Fridays to give us free lessons in perspective and lighting and other shit that white people go to art school to learn. Except this guy had done that, and he was Black. I'd never seen a Black artist before. For a minute I thought I could maybe be one, too.

I can be, sometimes. Deep in the night, on a rooftop in Chinatown, with a spray can for each hand and a bucket of drywall paint that somebody left outside after doing up their living room in lilac, I move in scuttling, crablike swirls. The drywall stuff I can't use too much of; it'll start flaking off after a couple of rains. Spray paint's better for everything, but I like the contrast of the two textures—liquid black on rough lilac, red edging the black. I'm painting a hole. It's like a throat that doesn't start with a mouth or end in lungs; a thing that breathes and swallows endlessly, never filling. No one will see it except people in planes angling toward LaGuardia from the southwest, a few tourists who take helicopter tours, and NYPD aerial surveillance. I don't care what they see. It's not for them.

It's real late. I didn't have anywhere to sleep for the night, so this is what I'm doing to stay awake. If it wasn't the end of the month, I'd get on the subway, but the cops who haven't met their quota would fuck with me. Gotta be careful here; there's a lot of dumb-fuck Chinese kids west of Chrystie Street who wanna pretend to be a gang, protecting their territory, so I keep low. I'm skinny, dark; that helps, too. All I want to do is paint, man, because it's in me and I need to get it out. I need to open up this throat. I need to, I need to . . . yeah. Yeah.

There's a soft, strange sound as I lay down the last streak of black. I pause and look around, confused for a moment—and then the throat sighs behind me. A big, heavy gust of moist air tickles the hairs on my skin. I'm not scared. This is why I did it, though I didn't realize that when I started. Not sure how I know now. But when I turn back, it's still just paint on a rooftop.

Paulo wasn't shitting me. Huh. Or maybe my mama was right, and I ain't never been right in the head.

I jump into the air and whoop for joy, and I don't even know why.

I spend the next two days going all over the city, drawing breathing-holes everywhere, till my paint runs out.

I'm so tired on the day I meet Paulo again that I stumble and nearly fall through the café's plate-glass window. He catches my elbow and drags me over to a bench meant for customers. "You're hearing it," he says. He sounds pleased.

"I'm hearing coffee," I suggest, not bothering to stifle a yawn. A cop car rolls by. I'm not too tired to imagine myself as nothing, beneath notice, not even worth beating for pleasure. It works again; they roll on.

Paulo ignores my suggestion. He sits down beside me and his gaze goes strange and unfocused for a moment. "Yes. The city is breathing easier," he says. "You're doing a good job, even without training."

"I try."

He looks amused. "I can't tell if you don't believe me, or if you just don't care."

I shrug. "I believe you." I also don't care, not much, because I'm hungry. My stomach growls. I've still got that twenty he gave me, but I'll take it to that church-plate sale I heard about over on Prospect, get chicken and rice and greens and cornbread for less than the cost of a free-trade small-batch-roasted latte.

He glances down at my stomach when it growls. Huh. I pretend to stretch and scratch above my abs, making sure to pull up my shirt a little. The artist guy brought a model for us to draw once, and pointed to this little ridge of muscle above the hips called Apollo's Belt. Paulo's gaze goes right to it. *Come on, come on, fishy fishy. I need somewhere to sleep.*

Then his eyes narrow and focus on mine again. "I had forgotten," he says, in a faint wondering tone. "I almost . . . It's been so long. Once, though, I was a boy of the favelas."

"Not a lot of Mexican food in New York," I reply.

He blinks and looks amused again. Then he sobers. "This city will die," he says. He doesn't raise his voice, but he doesn't have to. I'm paying attention now. Food, living: These things have meaning to me. "If you do not learn the things I have to teach you. If you do not help. The time will come and you will fail, and this city will join Pompeii and Atlantis and a dozen others whose names no one remembers, even though hundreds of thousands of people died with them. Or perhaps there will be a stillbirth—the shell of the city surviving to possibly grow again in the future but its vital spark snuffed for now, like New Orleans—but that will still kill *you*, either way. You are the catalyst, whether of strength or destruction."

He's been talking like this since he showed up—places that never were, things that can't be, omens and portents. I figure it's bullshit because he's telling it to *me*, a kid whose own mama kicked him out and prays for him to die every day and probably hates me. *God* hates me. And I fucking hate God back, so why would he choose me for anything? But that's really why I start paying attention: because of God. I don't have to believe in something for it to fuck up my life.

"Tell me what to do," I say.

Paulo nods, looking smug. Thinks he's got my number. "Ah. You don't want to die."

I stand up, stretch, feel the streets around me grow longer and more pliable in the rising heat of day. (Is that really happening, or am I imagining it, or is it happening *and* I'm imagining that it's connected to me somehow?) "Fuck you. That ain't it."

"Then you don't even care about that." He makes it a question with the tone of his voice.

"Ain't about being alive." I'll starve to death someday, or freeze some winter night, or catch something that rots me away until the hospitals have to take me, even without money or an address. But I'll sing and paint and dance and fuck and cry the city before I'm done, because it's mine. It's fucking *mine*. That's why.

"It's about *living*," I finish. And then I turn to glare at him. He can kiss my ass if he doesn't understand. "Tell me what to do."

Something changes in Paulo's face. He's listening, now. To me. So he gets to his feet and leads me away for my first real lesson.

This is the lesson: Great cities are like any other living things, being born and maturing and wearying and dying in their turn.

Duh, right? Everyone who's visited a real city feels that, one way or another. All those rural people who hate cities are afraid of something legit; cities really are *different*. They make a weight on the world, a tear in the fabric of reality, like . . . like black holes, maybe. Yeah. (I go to museums sometimes. They're cool inside, and Neil deGrasse Tyson is hot.) As more and more people come in and deposit their strangeness and leave and get replaced by others, the tear widens. Eventually it gets so deep that it forms a pocket, connected only by the thinnest thread of . . . something to . . . something. Whatever cities are made of.

But the separation starts a process, and in that pocket the many parts of the city begin to multiply and differentiate. Its sewers extend into places where there is no need for water. Its slums grow teeth; its art centers, claws. Ordinary things within it, traffic and construction and stuff like that, start to have a rhythm like a heart-beat, if you record their sounds and play them back fast. The city . . . quickens.

Not all cities make it this far. There used to be a couple of great cities on this continent, but that was before Columbus fucked the Indians' shit up, so we had to start over. New Orleans failed, like Paulo said, but it survived, and that's something. It can try again. Mexico City's well on its way. But New York is the first American city to reach this point.

The gestation can take twenty years or two hundred or two thousand, but eventually the time will come. The cord is cut and the city becomes a thing of its own, able to stand on wobbly legs and do . . . well, whatever the fuck a living, thinking entity shaped like a big-ass city wants to do.

And just as in any other part of nature, there are things lying in wait for this moment, hoping to chase down the sweet new life and swallow its guts while it screams.

That's why Paulo's here to teach me. That's why I can clear the city's breathing and stretch and massage its asphalt limbs. I'm the midwife, see.

I run the city. I run it every fucking day.

Paulo takes me home. It's just somebody's summer sublet in the Lower East Side, but it feels like a home. I use his shower and eat some of the food in his fridge without asking, just to see what he'll do. He doesn't do shit except smoke a cigarette, I think to piss me off. I can hear sirens on the streets of the neighborhood—frequent, close. I wonder, for some reason, if they're looking for me. I don't say it aloud, but Paulo sees me twitching. He says, "The harbingers of the Enemy will hide among the city's parasites. Beware of them."

He's always saying cryptic shit like this. Some of it makes sense, like when he speculates that maybe there's a *purpose* to all of it, some reason for the great cities and the process that makes them. What the Enemy has been doing—attacking at the moment of vulnerability, crimes of opportunity—might just be the warm-up for something bigger. But Paulo's full of shit, too, like when he says I should consider meditation to better attune myself to the city's needs. Like I'mma get through this on white girl yoga.

"White girl yoga," Paulo says, nodding. "Indian man yoga. Stockbroker racquetball and schoolboy handball, ballet and merengue, union halls and SoHo galleries. You will embody a city of millions. You need not *be* them, but know that they are part of you."

I laugh. "Racquetball? That shit ain't no part of me, chico."

"The city chose you, out of all," Paulo says. "Their lives depend on you."

Maybe. But I'm still hungry and tired all the time, scared all the time, never safe. What good does it do to be valuable, if nobody values you?

He can tell I don't wanna talk anymore, so he gets up and goes to bed. I flop on the couch and I'm dead to the world. Dead.

Dreaming, dead dreaming, of a dark place beneath heavy cold waves where something stirs with a slithery sound and uncoils and turns toward the mouth of the Hudson, where it empties into the sea. Toward *me*. And I am too weak, too helpless, too immobilized by fear, to do anything but twitch beneath its predatory gaze.

Something comes from far to the south, somehow. (None of this is quite real. Everything rides along the thin tether that connects the city's reality to that of the world. The *effect* happens in the world, Paulo has said. The *cause* centers around me.) It moves between me, wherever I am, and the uncurling thing, wherever it is. An immensity protects me, just this once, just in this place—though from a great distance I feel others hemming and grumbling and raising themselves to readiness. Warning the Enemy that it must adhere to the rules of engagement that have always governed this ancient battle. It's not allowed to come at me too soon.

My protector, in this unreal space of dream, is a sprawling jewel with filth-crusted facets, a thing that stinks of dark coffee and the bruised grass of a futebol pitch and traffic noise and familiar cigarette smoke. Its threat display of saber-shaped girders lasts for only a moment, but that is enough. The uncurling thing flinches back into its cold cave, resentfully. But it will be back. That, too, is tradition.

I wake with sunlight warming half my face. Just a dream? I stumble into the room where Paulo is sleeping. "*São* Paulo," I whisper, but he does not wake. I wiggle under his covers. When he wakes, he doesn't reach for me, but he doesn't push me away either. I let him know I'm grateful and give him a reason to let me back in later. The rest'll have to wait till I get condoms and he brushes his ashy-ass mouth. After that, I use his shower again, put on the clothes I washed in his sink, and head out while he's still snoring.

Libraries are safe places. They're warm in the winter. Nobody cares if you stay all day as long as you're not eyeballing the kids' corner or trying to hit up porn on the computers. The one at Forty-second—the one with the lions—isn't that kind of library. It doesn't lend out books. Still, it has a library's safety, so I sit in a corner and read everything within reach: municipal tax law, *Birds of the Hudson Valley*, *What to Expect When You're Expecting a City Baby: NYC Edition*. See, Paulo? I told you I was listening.

It gets close to noon and I head outside. People cover the steps, laughing, chatting, mugging with selfie sticks. There're cops in body armor over by the subway entrance, showing off their guns to the tourists so they'll feel safe from New York. I get a Polish sausage and eat it at the feet of one of the lions. Fortitude, not Patience. I know my strengths.

I'm full of meat and relaxed and thinking about stuff that ain't actually important—like how long Paulo will let me stay and whether I can use his address to apply for stuff—so I'm not watching the street. Until cold prickles skitter over my side. I know what it is before I react, but I'm careless again because I *turn to look* . . . Stupid, stupid, I fucking know better; cops down in Baltimore broke a man's spine for making eye contact. But as I spot these two on the corner opposite the library steps—short pale man and tall dark woman both in blue like black—I notice something that actually breaks my fear because it's so strange.

It's a bright, clear day, not a cloud in the sky. People walking past the cops leave short, stark afternoon shadows, barely there at all. But around these two, the shadows pool and curl as if they stand beneath their own private, roiling thundercloud. And as I watch, the shorter one begins to . . . *stretch*, sort of, his shape warping ever so slightly, until one eye is twice the circumference of the other. His right shoulder slowly develops a bulge that suggests a dislocated joint. His companion doesn't seem to notice.

Yooooo, nope. I get up and start picking my way through the crowd on the steps. I'm doing that thing I do, trying to shunt off their gaze—but it feels different this time. Sticky, sort of, threads of cheap-shit gum fucking up my mirrors. I *feel* them start following me, something immense and wrong shifting in my direction.

Even then I'm not sure—a lot of real cops drip and pulse sadism in the same way—but I ain't taking chances. My city is helpless, unborn as yet, and Paulo ain't here to protect me. I gotta look out for self, same as always.

I play casual till I reach the corner and book it, or try. Fucking tourists! They idle along the wrong side of the sidewalk, stopping to look at maps and take pictures of shit nobody else gives a fuck about. I'm so busy cussing them out in my head that I forget they can also be dangerous: Somebody yells and grabs my arm as I

Heisman past, and I hear a man yell out, "He tried to take her purse!" as I wrench away. *Bitch, I ain't took shit*, I think, but it's too late. I see another tourist reaching for her phone to call 911. Every cop in the area will be gunning for every Black male aged whatever now.

I gotta get out of the area.

Grand Central's right there, sweet subway promise, but I see three cops hanging out in the entrance, so I swerve right to take Forty-first. The crowds thin out past Lex, but where can I go? I sprint across Third despite the traffic; there are enough gaps. But I'm getting tired, 'cause I'm a scrawny dude who doesn't get enough to eat, not a track star.

I keep going, though, even through the burn in my side. I can feel *those* cops, the *harbingers of the Enemy*, not far behind me. The ground shakes with their lumpen footfalls.

I hear a siren about a block away, closing. Shit, the UN's coming up; I don't need the Secret Service or whatever on me, too. I jag left through an alley and trip over a wooden pallet. Lucky again—a cop car rolls by the alley entrance just as I go down, and they don't see me. I stay down and try to catch my breath till I hear the car's engine fading into the distance. Then, when I think it's safe, I push up. Look back, because the city is squirming around me, the concrete is jittering and heaving, everything from the bedrock to the rooftop bars is trying its damnedest to tell me to go. Go. *Go.*

Crowding the alley behind me is . . . is . . . the shit? I don't have words for it. Too many arms, too many legs, too many eyes, and all of them fixed on me. Somewhere in the mass I glimpse curls of dark hair and a scalp of pale blond, and I understand suddenly that these are—this is—my two cops. One real monstrosity. The walls of the alley crack as it oozes its way into the narrow space.

"Oh. Fuck. No," I gasp.

I claw my way to my feet and haul ass. A patrol car comes around the corner from Second Avenue and I don't see it in time to duck out of sight. The car's loudspeaker blares something unintelligible, probably *I'm gonna kill you*, and I'm actually amazed. Do they not see the thing behind me? Or do they just not give a shit because they can't shake it down for city revenue? Let them fucking shoot me. Better than whatever that thing will do.

I hook left onto Second Avenue. The cop car can't come after me against the traffic, but it's not like that'll stop some doubled-cop monster. Forty-fifth. Forty-seventh and my legs are molten granite. Fiftieth and I think I'm going to die. Heart attack far too young; poor kid, should've eaten more organic; should've taken it easy and not been so angry; the world can't hurt you if you just ignore everything that's wrong with it; well, not until it kills you anyway.

I cross the street and risk a look back and see something roll onto the sidewalk on at least eight legs, using three or four arms to push itself off a building as it careens a little . . . before coming straight after me again. It's the Mega Cop, and it's gaining. *Oh shit oh shit oh shit please no.*

Only one choice.

Swing right. Fifty-third, against the traffic. An old folks' home, a park, a promenade . . . fuck those. Pedestrian bridge? Fuck that. I head straight for the six lanes of utter batshittery and potholes that is FDR Drive, do not pass Go, do not try to cross on foot unless you want to be smeared halfway to Brooklyn. Beyond it? The East River, if I survive. I'm even freaked out enough to try swimming in that fucking sewage. But I'm probably gonna collapse in the third lane and get run over fifty times before anybody thinks to put on brakes.

Behind me, the Mega Cop utters a wet, tumid *hough*, like it's clearing its throat for swallowing. I go over the barrier and through the grass into fucking hell I go one lane silver car two lanes horns horns horns three lanes SEMI WHAT'S A FUCKING SEMI DOING ON THE FDR IT'S TOO TALL YOU STUPID UPSTATE HICK screaming four lanes GREEN TAXI screaming Smart Car hahaha cute five lanes moving truck six lanes and the blue Lexus actually brushes up against my clothes as it blares past screaming screaming screaming

screaming metal and tires as reality stretches, and nothing stops for the Mega Cop; it does not belong here and the FDR is an artery, vital with the movement of nutrients and strength and attitude and adrenaline, the cars are white blood cells and the thing is an irritant, an infection, an invader to whom the city gives no consideration and no quarter

screaming, as the Mega Cop is torn to pieces by the semi and the taxi and the Lexus and even that adorable Smart Car, which actually swerves a little to run over an extra-wiggly piece. I collapse onto a square of grass, breathless, shaking, wheezing, and can only stare as a dozen limbs are crushed, two dozen eyes squashed flat, a mouth that is mostly gums riven from jaw to palate. The pieces flicker like a monitor with an AV cable short, translucent to solid and back again—but FDR don't stop for shit except a presidential motorcade or a Knicks game, and this thing sure as hell ain't Carmelo Anthony. Pretty soon there's nothing left of it but half-real smears on the asphalt.

I'm alive. Oh, God.

I cry for a little while. Mama's boyfriend ain't here to slap me and say I'm not a man for it. Daddy would've said it was okay— tears mean you're alive—but Daddy's dead. And I'm alive.

With limbs burning and weak, I drag myself up, then fall again. Everything hurts. Is this that heart attack? I feel sick. Everything is shaking, blurring. Maybe it's a stroke. You don't have to be old for that to happen, do you? I stumble over to a garbage can and think about throwing up into it. There's an old guy lying on the bench—me in twenty years, if I make it that far. He opens one eye as I stand there gagging and purses his lips in a judgy way, like he could do better dry-heaves in his sleep.

He says, "It's time," and rolls over to put his back to me. Time. Suddenly I have to move. Sick or not, exhausted or not, something is . . . pulling me. West, toward the city's center. I push away from the can and hug myself as I shiver and stumble toward the pedestrian bridge. As I walk over the lanes I previously ran across, I look down onto flickering fragments of the dead Mega Cop, now ground into the asphalt by a hundred car wheels. Some globules of it are still twitching, and I don't like that. Infection, intrusion. I want it gone.

We want it gone. Yes. It's time.

I blink and suddenly I'm in Central Park. How the fuck did I get here? Disoriented, I realize only as I see their black shoes that I'm passing another pair of cops, but these two don't bother me. They should—skinny kid shivering like he's cold on a June day; even if all they do is drag me off somewhere to shove a plunger up my ass, they should *react* to me. Instead, it's like I'm not there. Miracles exist, Ralph Ellison was right, any NYPD you can walk away from, hallelujah.

The Lake. Bow Bridge: a place of transition. I stop here, stand here, and I know . . . everything.

Everything Paulo's told me: It's true. Somewhere beyond the city, the Enemy is awakening. It sent forth its harbingers and they have failed, but its taint is in the city now, spreading with every car that passes over every now-microscopic iota of the Mega Cop's substance, and this creates a foothold. The Enemy uses this anchor to drag itself up from the dark toward the world, toward the warmth and light, toward the defiance that is *me*, toward the burgeoning wholeness that is *my city*. This attack is not all of it, of course. What comes is only the smallest fraction of the Enemy's old, old evil—but that should be more than enough to slaughter one lowly, worn-out kid who doesn't even have a real city to protect him.

Not yet. It's time. *In* time? We'll see.

On Second, Sixth, and Eighth Avenues, my water breaks. Mains, I mean. Water mains. Terrible mess, gonna fuck up the evening commute. I shut my eyes and I am seeing what no one else sees. I am feeling the flex and rhythm of reality, the contractions of possibility. I reach out and grip the railing of the bridge before me and feel the steady, strong pulse that runs through it. *You're doing good, baby. Doing great.*

Something begins to shift. I grow bigger, encompassing. I feel myself upon the firmament, heavy as the foundations of a city. There are others here with me, looming, watching—my ancestors' bones under Wall Street, my predecessors' blood ground into the benches of Christopher Park. No, *new* others, of my new people, heavy imprints upon the fabric of time and space. São Paulo squats nearest, its roots stretching all the way to the bones of dead Machu Picchu, watching sagely and twitching a little with the memory of its own relatively recent traumatic birth. Paris observes with distant disinterest, mildly offended that any city of our tasteless upstart land has managed this transition; Lagos exults to see a new fellow who knows the hustle, the hype, the fight. And more, many more, all of them watching, waiting to see if their numbers increase. Or not. If nothing else, they will bear witness that I, we, were great for one shining moment.

"We'll make it," I say, squeezing the railing and feeling the city contract. All over the city, people's ears pop, and they look around in confusion. "Just a little more. Come on," I'm scared, but there's no rushing this. *Lo que pasa, pasa*—damn, now that song is in my head, *in me* like the rest of New York. It's all here, just like Paulo said. There's no gap between me and the city anymore.

And as the firmament ripples, slides, tears, the Enemy writhes up from the deeps with a reality-bridging roar—

But it is too late. The tether is cut and we are here. We become! We stand, whole and hale and independent, and our legs don't even wobble. We got this. Don't sleep on the city that never sleeps, son, and don't fucking bring your squamous eldritch bullshit here.

I raise my arms and avenues leap. (It's real but it's not. The ground jolts and people think, *Huh, subway's really shaky today.*) I brace my feet and they are girders, anchors, bedrock. The beast of the deeps shrieks and I laugh, giddy with postpartum endorphins. *Bring it.* And when it comes at me, I hip-check it with the BQE, backhand it with Inwood Hill Park, drop the South Bronx on it like an elbow. (On the evening news that night, ten construction sites will report wrecking-ball collapses. City safety regulations are so lax; terrible, terrible.) The Enemy tries some kind of fucked-up wiggly shit—it's all tentacles—and I snarl and bite into it 'cause New Yorkers eat damn near as much sushi as Tokyo, mercury and all.

Oh, now you're crying! Now you wanna run? Nah, son. You came to the wrong town. I curb stomp it with the full might of Queens and something inside the beast breaks and bleeds iridescence all over creation. This is a shock, for it has not been truly hurt in centuries. It lashes back in a fury, faster than I can block, and from a place that most of the city cannot see, a skyscraper-long tentacle curls out of nowhere to smash into New York Harbor. I scream and fall, I can *hear* my ribs crack, and—no!—a major earthquake shakes Brooklyn for the first time in decades. The Williamsburg Bridge twists and snaps apart like kindling; the Manhattan groans and splinters, though thankfully it does not give way. I feel every death as if it is my own.

Fucking kill you for that, bitch, I'm not-thinking. The fury and grief have driven me into a vengeful fugue. The pain is nothing; this ain't my first rodeo. Through the groan of my ribs I drag myself upright and brace my legs in a pissing-off-the-platform stance. Then I shower the Enemy with a one-two punch of Long Island radiation and Gowanus toxic waste, which burn it like acid. It screams again in pain and disgust, but *Fuck you, you don't belong here, this city is mine, get out!* To drive this lesson home, I cut the bitch with LIRR traffic, long vicious honking lines; and to stretch out its pain, I salt these wounds with the memory of a bus ride to LaGuardia and back.

And just to add insult to injury? I backhand its ass with Hoboken, raining the drunk rage of ten thousand dudebros down on it like the hammer of God. Port Authority makes it honorary New York, motherfucker; you just got Jerseyed.

The Enemy is as quintessential to nature as any city. We cannot be stopped from becoming, and the Enemy cannot be made to end. I hurt only a small part of it—but I know damn well I sent that part back broken. Good. Time ever comes for that final confrontation, it'll think twice about taking me on again.